The Hive Child

Silent Skies
Book 2

Rebecca L. Fearnley

LIGHTNING HYENA PRESS

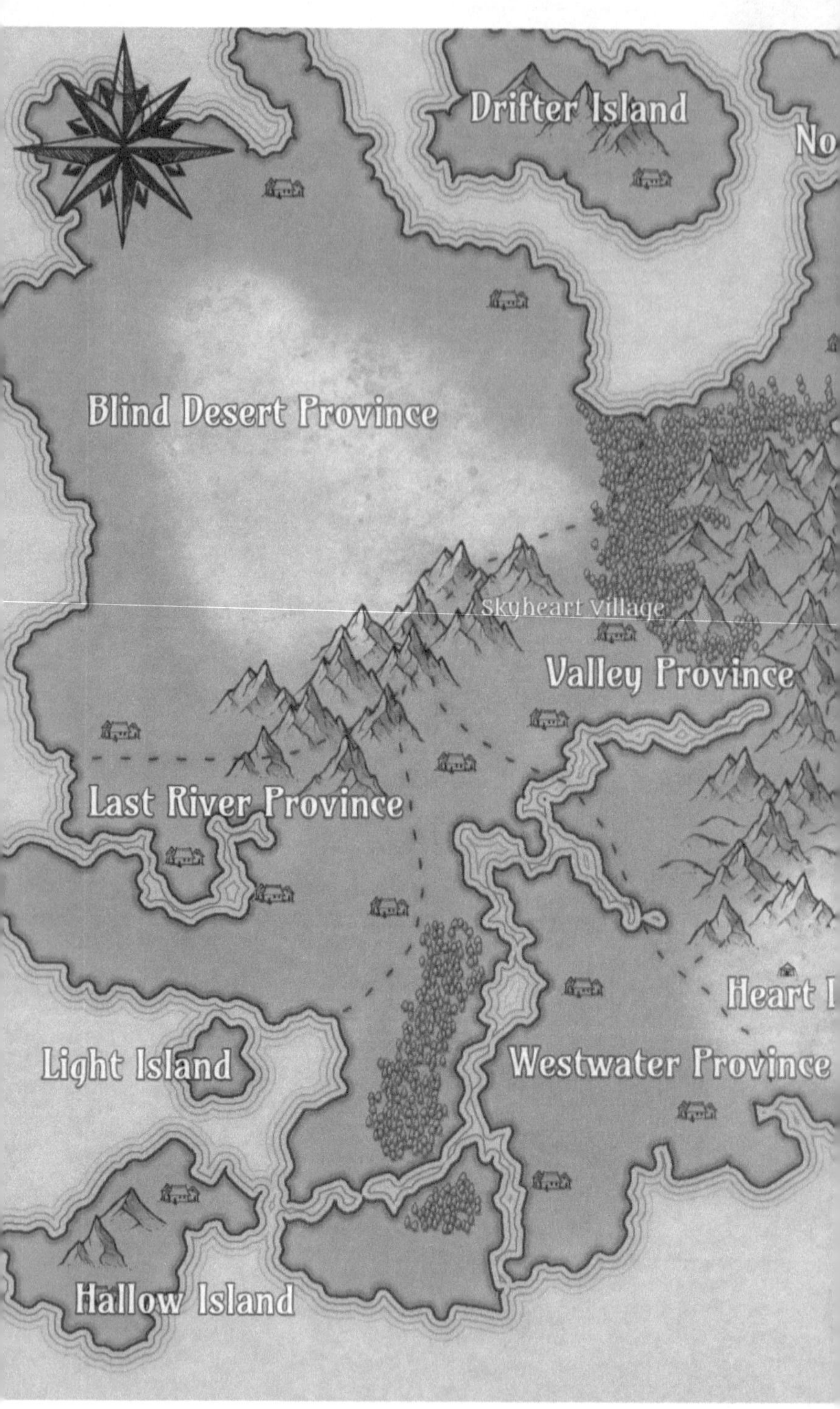

Drifter Island
No
Blind Desert Province
Skyheart Village
Valley Province
Last River Province
Light Island
Heart
Westwater Province
Hallow Island

Alphor
tip Province
East Delta Province
Whisperer Council
Landlock Province
Black Earth Province
High Savannah Province
ert Province
Southtip Province
Last Coast Province
Sand's End Village

Contents

One

Solma curses as her brother's hand slips out of hers and he smacks into the dirt with a cry.

"Up, Warren!" she shouts. "Come on!"

Warren's stricken face lifts, covered with mud, and he scrambles to his feet. She grabs his hand and they run again. The grass is tough and clinging underfoot, but they're used to this terrain now. They shove aside the coarse undergrowth and charge for the foothills. Up ahead, the scattered trees begin to thicken into a forest. Beyond, the Earthroot mountains rise like a set of vicious teeth in the distance.

Behind them, spiteful cries drift on the still, morning air and the clanging of makeshift weaponry makes Solma wince.

"Cowards!" one of the voices cries, louder and harsher than the others. "Tricksters!"

Solma clenches her jaw and resists the urge to turn and shout curses back at them. It's *not* the Whisperers' fault the land has been so poorly managed that growing anything is nearly impossible. But the villagers don't see it like that. They never do.

She risks a glance behind her and swears. Practically the whole village is after them. Even some of the Yuen—the youngsters—have scurried after their parents, waving trowels and sticks as if it's all a great game. But from the adults' faces, Solma knows this is no game. If the villagers catch up to them, they'll be beaten bloody. She grips Warren's hand tighter and lengthens her stride.

Up ahead, six of the seven Earth Whisperers in their group have reached the top of the nearest hillock. Mamba and Cobra, the two lead Whisperers, pause and turn. Solma sees Cobra's gaze drift past her and Warren to what chases them and her eyes widen. Solma clenches her jaw and powers on. No way is she looking back again.

"Faster, Sol!" comes Olive's voice from somewhere behind her. "C'mon!"

She darts by, carrying the orange-eyed Whisperer child—Taipan—on her hip. Taipan whimpers and clings to Olive's neck.

The prosthetic blade that is Solma's left foot slips in the mud. She swears, fighting for balance. Her dark hair flies into her face and she shoves it aside. She scans the horizon, fixing on the rolling shape of low-lying hills that mark the border to the mountains, and the thick, wild forest-land that covers them. They need to get to those trees.

A sharp cry rises from behind and Solma smells smoke. Fronds of it curl in the cold air and turn the clear sky a strange color. Solma grips Warren's hand tighter. His breath wheezes and he keeps rubbing tears from his eyes. Olive's reached the top of the hillock now and handed Taipan to Cobra. She barely acknowledges Cobra's thanks before she turns and tears back down the hill, looking as fierce and wild as only Olive can. Her red braid bounces on her back, catching the sunlight like flame.

From the tree-line, Aunt Bell and Dr. Roseann appear. Roseann is armed with one of their two pistols and Bell lowers her eye to the sight of a rifle, aiming unsteadily. Solma's heart lurches. She'd hoped they wouldn't have to use those in this village. She'd hoped leaving them behind at their camp would be a sign of faith while they went in to ask for supplies and offer the Whisperers' mysterious magic to help nurture the land. Foolish. She should've known. This isn't the first village they've been chased out of because the Whisperers couldn't coax growth from the soil. Solma bets it won't be the last either.

She pushes on, her blade-foot squelching in the sucking mud. Warren cries out.

"No, Sol! I can't—"

But whatever he's saying drowns in the roar of voices from behind them.

"Thieves!" yells a gruff voice. Then, "Get 'em!"

A shot shatters the morning air and Solma ducks. She shoves Warren in front of her, shielding his body with hers. But now she can't pull him along and their pace slows. The footfalls of pursuing villagers thunder against the ground, growing louder with each passing second. Up ahead, Solma glances at Olive just in time to see her make a rude gesture at their pursuers.

On top of the hillock, Bell drops to one knee and aims the rifle, which makes Solma's stomach tighten. Back in Sand's End, Bell was Fei-caste—field worker—not Gatra, like Solma was. She's never fired a rifle in her life. She's just as likely to hit Solma and Warren as she is to strike one of their attackers.

Beside her, Cobra and Mamba are kneeling on the hilltop, thrusting their fingers into the sodden earth in search of something—anything—that might act as a defense.

Solma's seen those two Whisperers raise a whole, impenetrable wall of brambles from the ground before. She knows their power. She just hopes there's something down there that can save them. But the concentration on their faces tells her they're having to search deep to waken dormant seeds.

Olive is suddenly at her side, skidding in the mud. "Dammit, Sol!" she yells. But, despite the snarl on her face, her eyes are wide with fear. She grabs Warren round the waist, ignoring his surprised cries of protest, and throws him over her shoulder.

Olive grabs Solma's hand and that familiar spark jumps between their skin, waking up the last shred of energy Solma has left. Together, they barrel up the hillside to where Bell, Roseann and the Whisperers wait.

At the top, Olive lets Warren slide to the ground. She turns to the Whisperers, all of whom now kneel with their hands in the earth. "Now!" she shouts.

The seven Whisperers close their eyes. Solma can't see it, but she knows each of them is sending waves of growth magic into the earth, searching for anything that they can bring to life. Krait, one of the young Whisperer boys, chews his lower lip desperately. Taipan has sweat beading on her forehead. The ground rumbles. Warren collapses in the coarse grass, gasping for breath. Solma drops to his side and rubs his back, his shoulders, instinctively searching for wounds. Miraculously, there are none.

"Got it!" Mamba exclaims, and Solma glances up in time to see a line of saplings burst from the earth in front of them. Beyond, the ragged mob of twenty or thirty outraged villagers skid to a halt, their makeshift weapons falling from their hands and their faces slackening with shock. They watch, frozen, as the saplings rise to sturdy trees, creating a tangled wall between them and their quarry. The village Steward, who Solma was surprised to discover was only a few years older than she is, stumbles back and the torch he carries drops into the mud and goes out. Solma curses him under her breath and finds herself thinking of Maxen. Not for the first time in the last five months, she wonders how he is, what he's doing, whether or not he's become his father.

"Sol?"

Solma jumps as Olive's fingertips brush her shoulder.

"You ok?"

Olive's fierce green eyes soften as they meet Solma's. Solma tries to smile and squeezes Olive's fingers before she brushes them off. "Yeah," she says. "Sorry. Just—"

Olive nods. "Just how many more villages we gonna be evicted from?" she wonders aloud. "I know this ain't gonna be the last."

Solma nods agreement, but can't bring herself to relax. It's undoubtedly the terrible management of the villagers causing the poor growth, but they don't see it that way, do they? Easier to blame the Whisperers than admit that they're taking shortcuts, not letting their fields lie fallow, or going back to using the old chemicals from before. The ones that so decimated the Earth in the first place. Solma's seen, in some villages, Fei-caste workers out with cans of old-world herbicides, drowning their crop in poison. She feels Olive's hand squeeze her shoulder.

"It's ok," Olive says. "We're safe."

She wraps her arm round Solma's shoulder and kisses her gently on the cheek. Solma stiffens and wonders why she does. Olive's touch isn't unpleasant. The opposite, in fact. Solma finds herself yearning whenever she and Olive are apart, electrified whenever Olive returns. So why is it so hard to accept her affection?

Olive, for her part, only frowns for a moment before she withdraws and goes to Taipan. After helping to raise a powerful wall of oaks, the little Whisperer girl is woozy with exhaustion. The three Whisperer boys are tired, too, but Taipan seems to lose more energy when she does this. Her sensitivity is deeper. She leans into Olive when the older girl wraps an arm around her, and blinks blearily. Aunt Bell scurries off to help Roseann persuade the group's two tan ponies from within the forest where they've been hiding. The three older Whisperers gather round the youngsters, Mamba and Cobra exchanging glances, their relief evident.

Solma focuses on Warren, but worry pangs through her for the little Whisperer girl who's become one of her brother's closest friends. The youngster will likely feel unwell for a few days after this. They need to find safety. And soon.

Mamba turns back towards where the villagers still stand staring, now barely visible beyond the great oak wall.

"Go home!" he calls. A wind picks up and carries his voice beyond the trees and out to the muddy plains. "We mean you no harm. Now let us go in peace!"

Solma squeezes her eyes closed, sweat pouring into her eyelashes. Behind her eyelids, Maxen's face bursts into view as she'd last seen it; twisted with rage, puckered with bee-sting scars. Any love he might have felt for her now calcified into a burning hate. When the young Steward beyond the trees finally replies, Solma can almost imagine it's Maxen.

"Fine!" he yells, petulant. "But don't come back!"

And with that unceremonious farewell, the villagers retrieve their fallen weapons and trudge home through the mud.

Solma opens her eyes and finds her brother staring at her, his meadow-green eyes still wide with shock. "That was close," he says, wiping his hand across his face and frowning at the mud left on his palms. "And there weren't no bees there, either."

Two

No, there were no bees in that village. Or any-where else. They need to find some, and soon. Solma's gut tightens at the thought that another selfish Steward might find a nest before the Whisperers do, that they might not be there to prevent a Hive War next time.

Five months they've searched and Solma's never experienced a winter like it. The memories flood her as she and Warren follow the footfalls of their Whisperer friends, navigating the strange forest that weaves between the foothills. Often, they find the ground hardens into rubble, with strange shapes looming through the tangled trees. It takes Solma a day or two to realize they're walking through the remains of one of the old towns. Most of the buildings have crumbled into nothing. The forest has had a century to reclaim it. Still, there are the tell-tale signs of the old-world here. They stop in the ruins of an old forecourt one night. The roof is thick with growth and vines climb over what Mamba explains used to be old pumps, once filled with petrol. The old-worlders, he said, used to drive vehicles that ran on oil pumped deep from underground. The roads were so full of these vehicles that the air was thick with their fumes. Not for the first time, Solma looks around her at the shadows of her ancestors' world and feels sick.

Roots criss-cross the forecourt, the boughs of great trees rest so heavily on the roof that it buckled years ago, if Solma didn't known what this place was, she would be unable to distinguish it from the natural forests of Alphor. It isn't the first such place they've travelled through. Solma remembers the old cities—now no more than debris, reclaimed by the wild—that they'd travelled through in Landlock Province. The skeletons of towering buildings reaching so high it made Solma dizzy to look at them. But now, they were just climbing frames for eager plants. Solma had heard of such places before she left Sand's End. Gerta, one of the Aldren-caste elders from her village, found Solma's prosthesis in such a ruin. But seeing them with her own eyes still sparks a deep sadness that she can't explain. It seems strange to her that trees and grasses thrive but the flowers are all gone. Solma remembers how hard it had been to grow anything back in Sand's End and wonders at the contradiction.

Mamba explained, once, that it was to do with pollination. Trees and grasses can still use the wind but, with the insects gone, other plants struggle. Solma stares at the vast trees, the thick grasses, the gripping vines, and still can't get her head around it.

Days and nights blur into one and the forest stretches on. The evidence of the ruined town falls away and now the forest is thick and natural, coating the foothills as they rise. The group settles into single file and hike in silence. The ground becomes too steep for conversation and the little ones struggle.

By the fourth or fifth day since the disastrous visit to the village, Solma has taken up position near the back, one of the pistols clutched tightly in her hand. She scans the ragged forest for signs of predators. Spring warms the air. New growth unfolds from the earth and the animals will be searching wider than their usual territories, both for mates and food to fatten them after hibernation. Redbears and wildwolves aren't day hunters but hungry animals aren't always predictable, either.

The forest canopy is too thick to allow in much light, but Solma reckons the sun will reach its peak, soon. Warren stumbles along beside her, his eyes dull with tiredness and his red-gold hair sticking to his forehead. Sweat drips off the tip of his nose. He wipes it off but doesn't complain. Solma's heart clenches. He looks so tired.

Behind her, Burdock, one of the tan ponies that pulls the supply cart, nickers softly and nudges her arm. She reaches back to stroke his velvety nose. At least the canopy of leaves keeps the sun off their backs and shelters them from passing showers. Solma finds the changeability of the weather here, in Northtip province, unsettling.

Her old village, Sand's End, was mostly cold and dry in the winter. Little grew and, if they were lucky, there was enough rain to sustain the earth for the following spring. But it turns out there are much harsher places in Alphor. Solma remembers sweltering in a burning heat she'd never experienced before in the High Savannah Province sun, as the Alphorian summer faded to Autumn. She waited out her first blizzard in Black Earth province, huddled in a tent with Warren and Olive as the snow crept higher outside. In East Delta Province, in the northwest tip of Alphor, the winter storms sent winds that flattened plant, tree and dwelling alike, soaking the little group of wanderers to the skin. And it only grew worse as they got deeper into the winter months. Days where the sun barely lit the world; thick, rumbling clouds that dumped months of rain in a single hour; frosts so harsh that Solma woke with it on her eyelashes, her teeth chattering, and her brother huddled tightly against her.

And wherever they searched, no bees.

Blume, the incredible queen bee Warren found last summer, had laid daughter-queens to repopulate Alphor. Not many, but enough. They'd flown free of the nest before Blaiz and Maxen could claim it and dispersed to find mates and wait out the winter. Solma missed the soft song of their wing muscles, the harmonious vibrato of a hundred bees humming together as they searched flowers for the precious treasure within.

And everywhere they went, they'd hoped. Perhaps there was a bee queen under the earth here? Perhaps one of Blume's daughters found a nest there?

But no matter where they went, Warren reported silence. Despite discovering a remarkable ability to communicate with insects last year, he couldn't hear them. Still can't. Alphor's days began to lengthen. The sun creeping higher. The snow and hurricanes waning. But still no bees. The skies of Alphor are as silent as they've always been, and Solma is plagued by dreams of the Hive Wars that, Bell had told them, killed the flying insects in the first place. She wakes, drenched in sweat, from visions of villagers turning on each other, bee colonies burning, the ground carpeted with the bodies of insects and everyone too angry and desperate to realize they'd destroyed their own future. She'd hoped—believed—at the end of last summer, that they might be able to reverse all that. They might have found a way to help nurture the bees back to health.

They hadn't figured on the greed of selfish men. Her old village Steward, Blaiz, and his son, Maxen, haunt her dreams too. In her worst nightmares, she doesn't manage to save Blume's daughters before Blaiz seizes control of them, ready to use them to gain as much power as he can muster, not caring that he'll destroy the bees all over again.

Solma doesn't sleep much, and takes more watches than her fair share. Olive objects, but Solma doesn't care. During the day, she walks in an exhausted daze. But, Earth! It's better than those terrible dreams.

Finally, the forest thins and gives way to the Earthroot mountains. The sun is high and distorted behind a haze of spring cloud. There's not a village in sight. Burdock snorts and plants his front hooves firmly in the earth, refusing to move. He nudges Poppy, the mare beside him, and she turns her head to eye Solma. Solma gets the message. They'll go no further today.

The three young Whisperer boys all huddle together. Krait, the youngest, flops down as soon as they stop and complains of a headache. His blue eyes are full of tears. Habu, the eldest, sways on the spot, still holding hands with King, the third Whisperer boy. King rubs his freckled face, his eyelids drooping. They're exhausted and, Solma thinks, their eyes have this strange, faraway look in them.

Come to think of it, all seven of the Whisperers look concerned and distracted. Cobra keeps touching the side of her head as if to relieve some discomfort, and Mamba's fists are clenched at his side.

Beside Olive, Taipan whimpers and rubs her streaming eyes. She's been hobbling along for the whole week without complaint, but her breathing is labored and her head lolls. She hasn't quite recovered from their escape from the village. Her brown skin, usually bright with life, is dull and ashen with exhaustion.

"Liv, my tummy feels weird," she mumbles.

Olive scoops her up and casts Solma a worried glance.

The other Whisperer girl, Ana, rushes over to lift Taipan out of Olive's arms. She nods at Olive as she does so, and holds Taipan close, soothing her. A frown bridges her brows and her eyes dart from tree to tree, searching for something. She seems unsettled, too, which unsettles Solma in turn. Ana isn't easily spooked.

Solma decided months ago that she wasn't ever messing with Ana. She's a thin, wiry thing with little flesh on her bones, her skin a light brown and mottled from the sun. Her head, like all Whisperers, is shaved, but her hazel eyes are sharp and watchful. She's a year or two younger than Cobra's fifteen summers, but with the manner of someone much older. Last autumn, Mamba explained to Solma that Whisperers take the name of the first snake that ever bit them as they rescued it from ignorant villagers. Solma wondered at that and, when she finally plucked up the courage to ask Ana about her name, she swiftly gained serious respect for the girl.

Ana is short for Anaconda, the largest, most brutal snake in Alphor. It isn't poisonous, Ana had explained, but it can grow to nearly thirty feet long, weigh upwards of five hundred pounds and its sinuous body can be as wide around as Solma's torso. Its suffocating coils can exert enough force to break ribs, spines and collarbones, and it can dislocate its jaw to swallow prey of any size.

Solma had stared, open-mouthed, at the diminutive thing in front of her, and wondered *how on Earth* she had once rescued—and survived—a snake like that. She hopes she never has reason to find out.

Ana catches Solma's eye as she hugs Taipan close. The frown drops from her face and she smiles.

Between Mamba and Cobra, the three Whisperer boys squabble and bicker. Mamba tries and fails to mediate a disagreement born entirely out of tiredness and fails miserably. Solma would find his efforts amusing if she wasn't so tired herself, so worried for her brother, who now flops down at her side and stares morosely at ground. She crouches beside him.

"Warren?"

He doesn't answer, but a tear rolls silently down his cheek. Her heart hurts at the sight.

A hand on her shoulder makes her jump and she glances up into Cobra's gentle face. The Whisperer girl's green eyes shine with concern as she absently rubs at the sun-blush in her pale, freckled cheeks. "Everything ok?"

Solma nods and tries to smile, then wonders why she's lying.

"Actually, no," she says, indicating Warren. "He's tired and scared."

"I ain't *scared*," Warren mumbles. Solma ignores him. Cobra's hand on Solma's shoulder squeezes.

"We all are," she says. "It's ok. We're far enough away now that I don't think they'll bother coming after us again. I'll persuade Mamba to stop here for a bit."

She winks at Warren, who manages a small smile in return. "Want to come help me cheer Taipan up?" Cobra asks.

"Why's she sad?" Warren asks, immediately alert. He gets to his feet, a little frown tugging at his brows. "I wanna see her."

He marches off with such purpose that Solma suppresses a laugh. She meets Cobra's gaze. "Thanks," she says. Cobra shrugs.

"Any time," she says. "Now come get some water. You need rest, too."

Solma stands, easing the pain in her right knee as she watches Cobra wander back to her charges. She's all

Whisperer now, and has been for years and years. But there was a time, a decade ago, when she and Solma were friends. When Cobra was not Cobra the Whisperer, but Kobi, the little lost girl of Sand's End who everyone thought was a boy. They'd been so close, and then little Kobi decided to go with the Whisperers and Solma, heartbroken, had betrayed her to a man she now knows was a tyrant. Ashamed, she'd forced out all memories of her dearest friend, until Cobra returned last spring. But Cobra never forgot Solma.

That old guilt festers in her gut and she rubs it away, testing her weight on her right knee. It holds. Just. Running like that is always hard on her and the week's hike hasn't helped. She catches Warren looking at her worriedly and gives him what she hopes is a reassuring smile. His eyes narrow, unconvinced, but he returns his attention to Taipan and continues offering her small sips of water from a bamboo cup.

Solma tries a few experimental steps and then wanders over to where Olive, Aunt Bell and Roseann have sat to build a fire.

"Just grab that pack over there, girl," Bell says as Solma approaches. She doesn't even look up. Solma catches Olive's gaze and the pair of them suppress knowing smiles. Solma grabs the pack.

"Here."

Bell grunts acknowledgement and begins rummaging while Solma sits and helps scoop earth out of the makeshift fire pit. Five months wandering through Alphor has changed her aunt in unexpected ways. She's leaner than she once was, with frown-lines between her brows and callouses on her hands. Her pale, freckled skin—the same as everyone in their old village except Solma, whose white skin is freckle-free and tans easily—is mottled with sun-damage and much darker than it once was. Her clothes hang off her, now. But she still wears that apron, and she still fusses relentlessly.

"Damn these matches!" she curses, popping open the box to find only two remaining. "You never got any at the village?"

Solma fixes her with a withering glare. "You mean, the one we just got chased out of?" she asks. "No, must've slipped my mind."

Bell's eyes flash. "Don't you get cheeky with me, girl!"

Solma sighs. "We need tinder, right?"

Olive leaps to her feet. "I'll come with you."

Beside her, Dr. Roseann, Olive's mother, rolls her eyes. "She ain't made of porcelain, Liv. Let her go."

Olive starts to protest, but her mother grabs her wrist and pulls her back down. Solma smiles. "It's alright," she says. "I won't be long. I wanna check on Warren, anyway."

Olive frowns and Solma feels exposed under that glare. She knows why Olive's so worried, though they've not spoken of the two violet-eyed Fire Makers from last summer. Solma shudders as she remembers their strange, new power, how, under Blaiz's instruction, they'd summoned fire from their hands and burned the remains of the bumblebee nest Solma and Warren had protected all year. As quickly as they'd appeared, the father and son had vanished, back into Alphor's wilderness. Solma has no idea where they went, but she remembers the delight on their faces as they'd burned their way through the hope of Alphor. They've haunted her nightmares all winter.

Olive watches her with concern and Solma flushes.

For a person to read her as thoroughly as Olive does, know her needs before she knows them herself … Solma doesn't remember a time when she's had that before, when she's been able to be vulnerable with someone, instead of the protector, the soldier, the Gatra.

Suddenly, she wants nothing more than for Olive to come with her, so they can hold hands as they wander beneath the forest canopy, kiss, maybe, in the dappled shadows and share each other's warmth.

But then an image flashes in Solma's head and she shudders. It's Maxen. Maxen as he was at the beginning, the pale-eyed Steward's son who kissed her so tenderly while they lay in the grass. And Maxen as he was at the end, twisted and scarred, his eyes full of hate. The truth was he'd never really loved her at all. And Solma wonders, after all her mistakes, if anyone truly can. If anyone *should*.

"Back in a minute," Solma says. She turns and hurries off before anyone can protest.

She leaves her little family bustling in the clearing and heads for the forest. They need tinder. And Solma needs to be alone, despite the danger of redbears and wildwolves ... and Fire Makers. She needs that more often these days, even though she can't explain why. The yearning for her own company, to be out from under the gaze of those she's hurt and betrayed, is almost constant. Solma knows what she's done. And the guilt buzzes like a bee-song-in-negative: angry, aggressive, discordant.

Three

By the time Solma gets back with an armful of tinder, Mamba has seen sense and relinquished control of the camp to Cobra. Four tents have been erected (it's obvious which one Krait and Habu put up) and Cobra is helping Mamba untack the ponies. Ana's got a meagre fire going. She now sits, cross-legged, with the boys either side, watching Aunt Bell stirring a sweet-smelling pot while Roseann adds ingredients. Solma frowns as she watches the Whisperers. They're fidgety and distracted and Krait is complaining of a headache.

Solma trudges over and leaves the tinder next to Bell, who glances at it and nods approvingly.

"Good," is all she says. Solma sighs.

"Where's Warren?"

Bell nods towards one of the tents and Solma glances up to see Olive emerging from it, frowning.

Solma hurries to her, hands held out in question. Olive loops an arm around her waist.

"He's in a mood," she explains. "I tried, Sol, but he won't come out. He's in there sulking. No idea why."

Solma sighs and leans her head against Olive's shoulder. The other girl's earthy scent soothes her lungs and she nuzzles closer. Olive kisses her eyebrow.

"There'll be time for that later," she whispers. "Go see your brother. I'll bring you food."

She gives Solma one more squeeze and heads towards the fire. Solma touches her eyebrow where Olive kissed it and doesn't know what to feel. Guilt buzzes inside her.

Warren is huddled at the far end of the tent with his back to the entrance when Solma dips inside. He hasn't lit the lanterns or laid out his bedroll. Instead, he hugs his knees and mutters something that Solma can't hear.

"Warren?"

He jumps and whips round. Solma sees tears in his eyes.

"Go away," he mumbles. "I don't wanna talk to anyone."

Solma rolls her eyes and closes the tent flap behind her. "Oh that's grown up," she says. "Come on, War, it's so gloomy in here."

She opens a lantern, pumps the wind-up handle and flicks the switch. The bulb blinks once, then slowly hisses to life. Solma brings it over to Warren and sits beside him, ignoring the fact he shuffles away from her and scowls at the canvas wall.

"I wanna be on my own," he grumps.

Solma suppresses another sigh. "Why, so you can feel sorry for yourself?"

"Yes."

Solma pulls her knees up under her chin, mirroring Warren's stance. "Is it helping?"

"No," Warren admits. He lets his legs slide out straight in front of him and leans back on his hands, still frowning. "Nothing's helping."

Solma waits. She's never been much good at this bit of sistering. Defending Warren from feral villagers is easy compared to helping him sort through his feelings. She remembers how she'd dismissed his fears about Blaiz last year and winces. It's not surprising he doesn't find her a comfort anymore.

Warren chews his lip. Finally, he says, "What if there ain't no more bees, Sol?" He pauses for a moment.

Then, "Or what if there *are* bees but I can't hear them no more?"

Ah. There it is. The thing he really fears. Solma's seen him watching the skies, his little face full of hope and anguish. She's sure the tremolo of bee song hums in his dreams, and that he misses that strange, chemical language he'd learned to speak last summer when Blume, the first bumblebee anyone had seen in a century, clambered from the spring soil and into his heart.

Blume died at the turn of Autumn last year. The Fire Makers—Vulkan and his son, hired by Blaiz—set her nest aflame, but she was old anyway. Warren knew she wouldn't last beyond the autumn. But Solma knows her death still hurts him, nonetheless.

And what if he's right? What if there are no more bees?

Solma leans towards him and pulls him close. "You'll hear them again, War," she says, though she's got no idea if that's true.

Warren wriggles free and wipes his eyes with the back of one hand. "You don't know," he mutters. "You're just trying to make me feel better."

Solma sighs. There used to be a time when he trusted her implicitly. But that version of him burned up in the fire that destroyed Blume's nest. He's eight now and he's seen more of Alphor in these last five months than Solma ever did in her whole life before that. Her sisterly tricks don't work anymore.

"Look, Warren," she says, trying a different tactic. "I don't know what's gonna happen any more than you, but moping and refusing to eat ain't helping your bees. Whatever happens, happens. So you might as well come get some food."

Warren scowls, folds his arms, and scoots round until his back is to her. He harrumphs at the canvas wall of the tent. Solma pinches the bridge of her nose. That went well.

"Just leave me alone, Sol," Warren grumbles. He's going for anger but his little voice wobbles and Solma knows he's on the verge of tears again. She touches his back. He flinches away. Great.

Solma emerges from the tent to find Olive holding two wooden bowls of a rich-smelling broth. Solma frowns. It's always broth when they're running low on supplies.

Olive holds a bowl out for Solma just as Cobra hurries over to meet them. "How's he doing?" she asks. Solma shrugs, stirring the broth with her spoon.

"He's worried there ain't no more bees."

Cobra makes a sympathetic face. "Aren't we all," she says, touching Solma's arm. "Want me to try? You've had a tough day. And sometimes it helps to … you know … talk to another Whisperer."

Solma's gut kicks but she bites down on whatever snappish retort threatens to make itself known. She'd tried so hard to keep Warren close all last summer and it still feels like he's drifting away.

"Yeah," she says, her throat dry. "Sure. Go ahead."

Cobra smiles. "You're a good sister," she says. "And he knows that. Don't worry."

Solma's not sure she is. Or that Warren does. But she nods her thanks anyway. Cobra ducks inside the tent. Olive folds her arms and nudges Solma with her elbow.

"You gonna eat that?"

Solma dutifully scoops up a spoonful of broth and gulps it down. It's warming and flavorful, but her stomach churns.

"Yeah," she says, dropping the spoon into it. "I'll eat it while I patrol. Bell still got my rifle?"

Olive loops her arm through Solma's and begins to pull her towards the campfire. "Not now, Sol," she says, fluttering her eyelashes in a way Solma hadn't realized she was capable of until the first night they shared a tent. "You gotta rest. It ain't even dark yet. There won't be any redbears or wildwolves out for at least an hour, so you can relax with us for a bit."

Solma squirms free of Olive's grip. "No, I can't, I—"

But *why* can't she?

She gazes at the group gathered around the fire. Mamba bounces Krait, the youngest of the three boys, on his knee as the pair of them sing an old Whisperer rhyme. Ana wears a very polite face as Bell talks her through a list of specific ingredients for the broth and Roseann has Taipan, King and Habu enthralled in some over-embellished story. Behind them, Poppy and Burdock graze peacefully, occasionally turning to watch their humans. Solma feels a tug somewhere behind her heart, pulling in two directions. One, towards the warmth of the fire and the safety of the people she's come to see as her own. The other, away as far as she can. Out into the forest. Into the dark, where she can't hurt anyone.

She shoves the bowl back at Olive, harder than she intended, feeling suddenly sick. "I can't, Liv, I'm sorry," she says. "It's my job. I gotta protect them. I promised."

Olive raises an eyebrow. "And you kept that promise. What's with you, Sol?"

But Solma's already heading in the opposite direction, over to the heap of supplies where she now sees Bell has propped her rifle, and then out beyond the firelight, ignoring the way Olive calls her name.

Four

A HAZE LAYS OVER the grass this morning, and the pale sun sets it aglow. Solma stands outside the tent, watching it swirl and flutter around her blade-foot. She clenches and unclenches her fists. Time to get going.

Bell's already up, (no surprise there) and has something delicious bubbling over a fire. She waves Solma over.

"Hungry?"

Solma shakes her head. She looks past Bell, to where all seven Whisperers are huddled together around the cart, talking in hushed tones. The three young boys sit cross-legged and wide-eyed, staring in silence between their elders. Taipan's clutching her belly, complaining loudly while Ana tries to hush her to no avail. Solma frowns as she turns back to Bell.

"What's with them?"

Bell shrugs, ladling porridge into a bowl and handing it to Solma, despite her refusal. "You didn't eat your dinner last night," she points out. "You gone off my cooking?"

Solma smiles before she can help herself. "As if," she says. She spoons some of the steaming oats into her mouth. Her stomach growls its gratitude, and suddenly she's starving. She wolfs down the porridge and hands the bowl to Bell, before turning back towards the Whisperers. Their voices are now raised enough that she can hear their words drift on the still morning air.

"I'm telling you, Mamba," Ana says. "I've been sensing it for days, and it's only getting stronger."

"My belly!" Taipan complains, and Cobra kneels beside her.

"It's alright, sweetie," she says, rubbing Taipan's back. Taipan only cries harder.

"No," she whines. "It's all buzzy!"

Ana seems to take this as evidence of something. "See?" she says, folding her arms triumphantly. Mamba shakes his head.

"Whatever it is," he says. "It's not Whispering. It doesn't feel like Whispering. It's like—"

He grapples for the right word and fails, shrugging helplessly.

"It feels familiar," Cobra says, standing and holding Taipan's hand. "And ... not, at the same time. I agree with Ana. I think we should go look."

Krait scowls. "Feels weird," he comments gruffly.

"Yeah," Cobra agrees. "It does."

Solma's got no idea what they're talking about. She's ready to go over and ask when Bell grabs her arm.

"You go tell Mamba those kids need more'n one night's rest," she says. "You hear? They're exhausted and they'll get sick traipsing about like this!"

Solma raises an eyebrow. Bell might be right, but—

"What about food?" she points out. "We're running out, ain't we? We got to get moving or we'll starve."

Bell squares her shoulders and tuts but worry gleams in her eyes and Solma knows she's hit a nerve. She touches her Aunt's shoulder.

"You can't be a mother to the whole world, Bell," she says quietly. Bell's cheeks flush.

"I'm not trying to," she mutters. "Just these seven, and you and Warren. That's hardly the whole world, is it? Now mind out while I serve breakfast."

Solma rolls her eyes and steps back as the Whisperers' discussion ends and the youngsters traipse towards the scent of food.

Solma jogs to catch up with Ana as the Whisperer girl heads towards the ponies. Ana stops at Poppy's head and offers the stocky little mare oats from her open palm. Poppy munches gratefully and the Whisperer strokes the pony's soft muzzle, murmuring. She smiles and nods when she sees Solma approaching, but there's a weariness to her and the shadow of a frown still mars her brow.

"Sleep well?" she asks. Solma rolls her shoulders experimentally. The ache of a heavy pack and nights on rough ground have tightened her muscles for the last five months, but she thinks she might finally be getting used to this life

"Better than the night before," she says. As soon as he hears her voice, Burdock pricks up his ears and trots over from the edge of the forest. He nudges Solma's hand for affection and snuffles at her pockets for food. Ana laughs.

"He really does love you, doesn't he?" she says, scooping more oats from the pocket of her green robe and pouring them into Solma's palm. "We had such trouble with him before you came with us, and now he'll only do what you say."

Solma shakes her head and scratches Burdock's cheek as he gobbles down the proffered oats. "I got no idea why," she admits. "I had nothing to do with the horses in Sand's End. And they were both huge. I was a bit scared of them, actually."

Ana winks at her. "I'm more scared of these two than I ever am of any village heavy horse. These guys have twice the attitude."

She takes a deep breath and Solma realizes the young Whisperer's been opening and closing her left fist, like she's trying to grab something. Solma almost reaches out to grasp Ana's shoulder, but then thinks better of it. She's not sure how to ask Ana about the strange conversation she overheard and they stand in awkward silence for a bit.

"You ok?" Solma manages finally.

Ana jumps and stares straight at her, copper eyes wide and shining. "What? Oh. Yes. Sorry. Just—I don't know." She bites her lip and shakes her head. "We're all uneasy. There's been a ... I don't know. We can sense something in the Earth. Something ... hard to explain. It feels kind of familiar but also like nothing I've ever sensed before and it's ... *ancient*." She stops, chewing her lip as she forages in her pocket for more oats. She offers them to Poppy and shakes her head. "Maybe we're all just tired."

Solma frowns.

"I don't understand," she says. "You mean, like the sense of a Whisperer?"

It's no secret that trained Earth Whisperers can sense the signals of those with dormant power. It's how they always know which village children have that secret ability, whisking them away despite the parents' efforts to hide them. Solma used to resent them for it, as she knows many village folk do. It still doesn't sit right with her that kids are taken from their parents so young. But gifts like that must be shared. People not sharing was what caused the Hive War that wiped out the insects a century ago. She shudders at the memory of those pictures in Bell's books, how they've haunted her since last summer. Since Maxen's betrayal.

Ana shrugs and shakes her head. "It doesn't feel like a Whisperer," she says. "It feels ..." she grapples for the word, but can't seem to come up with anything better than Taipan's earlier description. "Buzzy," she finishes.

Solma blinks, nonplussed. She's about to ask more but Poppy finishes her oats and tosses her head. Ana soothes her with a gentle touch. "They need water," she says, nodding over to where Roseann has just trudged out of the forest carrying two metal buckets. She puts them down by the fireplace and heads straight for Bell's porridge.

"Sol, can you help with the pack down?" Ana asks. "Looks like we're heading out."

She points over to where Mamba and Cobra are already dismantling their tents and Olive is ushering Warren out towards Aunt Bell. Ana grins wryly.

"I knew Mamba'd never be able to resist," she says. Solma raises an eyebrow.

"Resist what?"

"Following the signal," she says. "We're going to find out what's calling us."

Solma rubs Burdock's velvety nose with the back of one hand and tries to quell the uneasiness in her gut. "Know where we're going?" she asks. Ana shrugs.

"Beats me," she admits. "But the signal's calling us through the mountains. It'll be better if we move off early and get as far as we can before midday." She shields her eyes and squints at the sky. "I think it's going to be warm. Spring's here."

Solma's heart bucks. Spring's here but the bees aren't. Instinctively, she glances over to the fire, where Warren sits with Olive, eating porridge.

Buzzy.

Could it be? She almost doesn't want to hope it's bees that the Whisperers sense, but hope is too tenacious to be so easily uprooted. It's flowering despite her best efforts.

Olive catches Solma's eye and turns away from the fire, heading over.

"Thanks, Ana," Solma says. "I'll get the others going as soon as we've had breakfast."

Ana smiles and heads off to get water for the horses. Poppy watches her go and nickers softly. Burdock nudges Solma again, snuffling at her pockets.

"I don't have any more, buddy," Solma tells him, but he's insistent.

"Got yourself an admirer there, eh?" says Olive as she approaches. Her hands are shoved in her pockets and she's unsmiling. Solma nods.

"Yeah, seem to. Hey, Ana says we'll be moving out soon." She points to the activity of the Whisperers. Olive raises an eyebrow.

"Yeah," she says. "I'll start the pack down. You can help Bell with the little ones this time."

She turns to go but panic flares through Solma. "Actually!"

Olive freezes. Solma sees her shoulders twitch with tension as she turns back. "Problem?"

Solma feels her hackles raise. This is the Olive from before. The prickly, stubborn Olive whose frustration gets the better of her. Solma's known that that Olive still exists, of course, she just hasn't seen her for a while. Solma folds her arms.

"Yeah," she says. "It makes more sense if I pack down. I've been doing it all winter and I can do it quicker."

Olive folds her arms too, mirroring Solma. "You *have* been doing it all winter," she points out. "For five months. All that time you refused to get to know the kids. You barely talk to Cobra, who was your best friend, once. D'you know she's a really mean dancer? Or that Mamba has a wicked sense of humor? D'you know Ana's an amazing archer? She can hit a bullseye at five hundred yards. D'you even know she's got a bow?"

Solma throws up her hands. "What's your point? How's this important?"

Olive growls her frustration loud enough that Bell glances over, frowning. "These people took us in, Sol.

You understand that we're alive 'cos'a them, right? Like it or not, they're our village now. They're our family. I know you ain't a fan of Whisperers, but you got to make an effort with them—"

"I got nothing against Whisperers," Solma retorts. She might have done once, but those days are long gone. It was Blaiz who convinced her never to trust the Earth Whisperers. Before he used and then exiled her. She's disregarded everything he taught her.

"Well why then?" Olive demands.

Solma blinks. Where has all this come from? "Why what?"

"Why won't you *talk* to us?" Olive says, loud enough that everyone in the camp turns to look. Warren frowns at his sister. "Why won't you talk to me? How long you gonna hang about on the edges like this, separating yourself from everything?"

"I ain't!" Solma insists, but there's a flicker of recognition in the back of her mind. She is. She knows it. "Not on purpose!"

Olive's frown melts into something sympathetic. She reaches out. Solma steps back before she can help herself and Olive's demeanor changes again. Hurt. Angry.

"Whatever, Sol," she says. "Look, you know I'm here. I been here all this time. I was here even when you thought I weren't. But one thing I won't do is let you act like an idiot. And you're acting like an idiot."

That old anger blossoms in Solma's chest. She'd thought they were over this, Olive always sniping at her. She'd thought they really had something. Flashes of those quiet moments alone flicker in her mind, kisses stolen at twilight, fingers intertwined. She can't have made that up, surely?

"Sol?"

Warren's little voice snaps her back to the present and she glances down to find he's wandered over, clutching his bowl of porridge. He slips his free hand into hers. "Can you come sit with me?"

He gazes hopefully over to the fire. Habu's bouncing about on all fours, pretending to be a redbear cub, and King roars with amusement. Bell brandishes her ladle, admonishing them for their lack of manners, but her eyes twinkle and a smile tugs her lips.

There's nothing about that scene that Solma dislikes. But her heart hurts all the same. "Go on then, Warren," she says, ushering him over. "I'll be there in a minute."

Olive puts her hands on her hips. "Don't want to go over, do you?" she says.

Warren tugs at Solma's hand, whining. "No, Sol. Come now."

Solma glances from Warren to the busy fireside and back to Olive, whose eyebrow is raised in that infuriating *I-told-you-so* way. She offers her hand to Warren, never taking her eyes from Solma's.

"Come on, War," she says. "I'll come with you. Solma has to pack down the tents."

Warren gazes between them, his lower lip pushed out. He takes Olive's hand and gives Solma a look of such disappointment that Solma feels her world quaking. She watches as the girl she adores walks the brother she would die for over to the family she can't be part of and wonders when it was, exactly, that she became so distant.

She turns, eyes stinging, and heads to dismantle the remaining tents.

Five

THROUGH THE MOUNTAINS. IF Solma had known better, that phrase would have filled her with dread. As it is, the dread only comes two days in, when she's trying to coax a stubborn Burdock to plod along a path so narrow that one of the cart's wheels keeps catching on the edge. To her left, a mountain bolts into the sky like a great tooth. To her right, the ground plunges away in a sheer wall of jutting rock splinters. Wind buffets them, like the breath of some laughing god, and Solma thinks she's beginning to understand the pull of the old-world religions. In the face of such hugeness, even she's tempted to believe.

Although they stick to the lower passes, where the paths are less steep and there are trees and shrubs to shield them from the elements, the way is harsh. Warren spends most of his time on all fours with tears streaming down his face, trying not to look over whatever precipice he's crawling past. Bell coaxes and scolds him, but Solma sees her aunt's eyes darting fearfully, too, the color drained from her face.

A week into the mountains, Solma loses the feeling in her fingers from the cold and can't sleep for the tingling pain. With no flat ground to pitch tents, the group rely on crevices in the rock to shelter them at night, huddling together under furs for warmth. The ponies stand watchfully as the rest of them sleep, pawing the ground with unease.

The Whisperers all seem well practiced with the mountains and the younger ones are less afraid than Warren is, but they still pick their footsteps carefully and complain of tummy aches, head pain and *buzziness*. Whatever signal they're following isn't getting any weaker.

Sometimes, the path evens out and they descend into deep valleys with winding streams, trees and foliage. Solma clutches the hilt of her hunting knife and keeps her rifle ready. There are creatures here, she knows, that she's never faced before. Darkcats, with night-black coats that move in silence. Huge stormdogs that hunt in vicious packs and will chase prey for miles. They find tracks near a stream one day, and the bloody, stinking remains of a kill. The children cry when they see it, and Warren's face is ashen. They stare at the awful carcass for longer than Solma's comfortable with.

"What was it, d'you think?" Olive asks quietly. "A deer?"

Solma shrugs. "Maybe."

A phantom itch starts in Solma's missing leg and persists for the rest of the day. She fancies she sees a long tail disappearing behind every tree, yellow eyes peering from every shadow.

At least the valleys shelter them from the worst of the wind. When they ascend again, it bites like a thousand fangs. Solma's hands ache and she has to stop several times to retie the cloth around the end of her left leg. Her lucky leg, as Warren calls it. It doesn't feel so lucky right now, though. Her prosthesis keeps slipping and begins to feel cumbersome. She's never found it a bother before but this hike is taking its toll.

They walk all day and the food dwindles. Solma's belly grumbles so loudly she worries every predator within a mile is going to hear it. The kids are too exhausted to complain. Even the older Whisperers struggle. Cobra stumbles one day and Mamba only just catches her before she goes tumbling back down the slope. The Whisperer girl's eyes are glassy and un-focused. Mamba keeps a tight hold of her hand from then on.

"Maybe we should stop for a few days," he suggests. "We can't keep going like this."

But an inventory of their food reveals there isn't time to stop. They need to pass the mountains and find a village. Fast. Bell rummages in the food bags one evening and returns, looking desperate.

"We need to forage," she says. No-one replies. Forage what? There are no wild fruits, no edible flowers. They might find some tubers if they're lucky, but they'll have to dig and that wastes precious energy.

"Can't you help?" Bell asks the Whisperers. "Ain't there no fruit trees waiting underground?"

The Whisperers exchange glances and shake their heads.

"Mushrooms?" Bell suggests, the pitch of her voice rising. Mamba gives her a dark look.

"Those aren't plants," he says. "They're fungi. It's different."

Bell glares at him. "Can't you try?"

Mamba shakes his head firmly. "Only the most powerful Whisperers connect with fungi," he says. "It's forbidden for us to talk with them until we're Elders. For our own protection. There are stories.

Younger Whisperers that try tend to go … weird. It's hard to explain."

Bell throws up her hands. "Great," she snaps. "So we'll all starve 'cos you're scared to go a bit weird?"

But Mamba is adamant.

"I knew a Whisperer once," he says darkly, "who tried what you just asked."

The other Whisperers shift uncomfortably. They've obviously heard this story before. Krait whimpers.

"I was there," Mamba says. "I watched as this strange sheen covered his eyes and his jaw went slack. He wasn't the same after. His power was so huge and unpredictable he couldn't control it. He rotted a whole field in seconds with one fingertip in the soil. The Council locked him away in the end."

Bell stares at him. Solma stares, too, not knowing what to say. She had no idea Whisperers had a council. Or locked each other up. That they might have laws of their own.

"I'm not risking my troupe," Mamba says.

There's tension between everyone after that, and Bell doesn't bring it up again.

As they push on, the Whisperers get weaker and sicker. Solma hears Roseann grumbling behind her.

"Whatever this damn signal is," the doctor mutters, "it better be worth it."

They're trudging in single file up a narrow animal track when Olive, trudging behind the cart, slips. Although it's mid-morning, mist clings to the mountainside and it's impossible to see more than half a meter ahead. Olive's foot comes down awkwardly. Her ankle twists and she swears as her knees buckle. The grass is too slick with dew to hold her and she falls heavily, sliding back down the hill through a snarl of brambles. Krait screams, sending Poppy into a frenzy as Olive tumbles back down the trail, clawing at the ground, trying to grip onto anything to slow her fall. Roseann yells. Bell grabs Habu and King and pulls them off the trail to avoid being knocked over. Taipan, brave beyond her years, tries to grab for Olive, but Olive snatches her hand away so as not to bring Taipan crashing after her.

At the end of the procession, Solma drops to her belly and throws out her rifle strap as Olive slides past.

"Grab it!" she yells and Olive does. The pair of them keep slipping for a short while until the rifle wedges behind a rock and brings them to a jarring halt. They lay in the scrub, gasping for breath, before shakily getting to their feet.

"Thanks," Olive says. She brushes dirt from Solma's arm and squeezes her shoulder. "Stupid. Need to pay attention."

There's a cut on her cheek, she's bumped her eyebrow and she's favoring her left leg, but what Solma finds scariest is how shaken Olive is. She's gone pale and her hands tremble as she beats dirt from her pants. Solma tries to draw her into a hug but Olive bats her away.

"No time for that," she mutters, limping up the hill. "Let's keep moving."

Solma's insides curdle. Olive's been distant since their argument. She might sleep huddled close to Solma, but there's little tenderness in her touch and, though Solma catches Olive gazing at her sometimes, the other girl looks away quickly. It hurts.

At last, the dramatic rise and fall of the land begins to soften. The animal tracks widen and the tough scrub gives way to ferns and then trees as the forest takes over where the mountains give way. The land undulates in rolling foothills but after two weeks of scrambling up sheer rock faces, it's almost a relief.

The Whisperer children are suffering. At camp one night, Bell calls Taipan's name four times before the girl looks up from under a heap of furs.

"Didn't you hear me, girl?" Bell scolds, beckoning her over to a meagre fire. Taipan blinks and shakes her head. She points at her ears.

"Too loud," she says. "It buzzes."

Bell's mashed the remaining vegetables they have with some boiled river water and some herbs. Krait throws his up almost as soon as he's eaten complaining his tummy feels funny.

Cobra and Mamba talk in hushed, urgent tones while Ana tries to persuade the kids to sleep. Olive and Solma pitch the tents in silence while Warren sits with his arm round Taipan, coaxing her to sip some water.

Solma flops on her furs that night and wonders whether her body has ever felt so battered. She turns on her side and drapes her arm over Olive, who lays next to her. Warren snores softly on her other side. Olive tenses, then sighs and laces her fingers through Solma's.

"Hey," she says sleepily.

"Hey," Solma replies and snuggles closer. They're quiet for a bit.

"Think the Whisperers will be ok?" Olive asks.

"Dunno," she admits, worry tightening her gut. "It's weird though. I don't like seeing them all in such a state."

"Me neither," Olive says. They fall silent again and some animal mating call drifts on the night air.

"I think we've run out of food," Olive says.

They drift into a fitful sleep.

A day later, dazed and exhausted, they're trudging down a shallow incline, following a gurgling river, when Cobra stops so suddenly that Solma walks straight into the back of her. Burdock nickers and uses the distraction to graze.

Solma rubs her forehead where it clashed with Cobra's shoulder.

"Ow!" she complains. "What you do that for?"

Cobra isn't listening. She points through a gap in the canopy, her eyes full of relief. "Thank Earth!" she breathes.

Warren and Taipan, holding hands, rush over.

"Sol! Sol!" Warren says, breathlessly. "Sol, there's—!"

Solma hushes him.

"But—!"

"Not now, Warren," Solma mutters.

The procession stops. Olive comes to stand beside her and they peer up, following the line of Cobra's finger. Against the sky, a line of smoke drifts on the still air. It's not the gushing frenzy of a forest fire but the steady, gentle stream that can only mean there's a settlement nearby.

Olive swears and punches the air. Solma feels her face break into an enormous grin as Bell claps her on the shoulder. Even Roseann looks more relaxed. Warren glances between Solma and Bell, a frown forming on his face.

"Ain't you listening?" he demands. Solma cups his chin.

"Food, Warren!" she says. "And rest."

Warren gazes at her. "But my bees—"

"We'll sort that later," Solma interrupts, waving a dismissive hand. The thought of safety and food fills her with a sense of peace. Warren searches her face but can't seem to find what he hopes might be there.

His shoulders sag as he turns and trudges off towards the ponies. Solma watches him go and her gut kicks with a discomfort she can't explain. She turns back to look at the smoke and thinks Warren will likely feel better after a hot meal and a good night's sleep.

Six

Olive presses her fingers to her temples and sighs.

"This," she says through gritted teeth, "is non-sense."

Mamba and Cobra, at least, have the good grace to look embarrassed. Ana just folds her arms and glares.

"Then *you* carry four tantruming little Whisperers the half-mile to the village!" she snaps. "We'll stand here and watch while they chase you back again."

Olive glares but a smile twitches the corner of her mouth. Cobra mumbles something and shuffles over to where the four Whisperer children, now exhausted and spent from crying, are curled up in silence. Amongst them, Warren sits cross-legged with one hand on Taipan's shoulder watching Cobra warily.

The sight of the smoke two hours previously was enough to send the little ones into a panic, traumatized after fleeing from village after hostile village.

Krait had taken one look at the distant smoke and hid under the cart. Taipan burst into tears and both King and Habu went white faced and silent with shock. Even Ana was shaking as she coaxed Krait from under the cart.

The horses, sensing their humans' fear, tossed their heads, whinnied, pawed the ground and generally made everything more difficult. Warren refused to leave Taipan's side, complaining that there were *bees* nearby and *why wasn't anyone listening?*

Solma and Olive had stood there, utterly at a loss for what to do. Luckily, they had Bell and Roseann, both of whom had brought up difficult children (Solma and Olive, for example). Bell's voice rang over the melee, calling everyone to *stand still* and *be quiet*. Roseann collared King and Habu and shoved them onto the back of the cart, followed swiftly by Krait, whom Ana had finally persuaded out. Even Cobra and Mamba had reverted to children in the face of Bell's authority.

"Nobody speak," she'd barked. "Everyone in a straight line, we'll go to the tree-line. Not a *word* 'til I say so, clear?"

They'd marched in silence to the designated spot and hunkered down behind a gathering of aspen trees that marked the border to a vast plain. From there, the smudgy silhouette of what can only be a village was just visible on the horizon, close to the snaking tree-line of the forest as it winds away to the west.

Crouched between the trees with the horses finally calm and the little ones whimpering, no one knows what to say.

Bell huffs. "We should ask for help," she grumbles. "We need food, don't we?" She thrusts a finger in the direction of the distant village. "There's food. Right there!"

Mamba scowls at her and finally manages to recover some semblance of his leadership. "Look," he says, "We've all ... had a rough run of things."

Bell raises an eyebrow.

"It's natural we'd be a bit cautious," Mamba continues, "but we've no food left and the weird signal in the Earth has exhausted all of us—"

Warren leaps to his feet. "It's—"

Solma grabs his wrist and pulls him down beside her. She tries to look sympathetic when she tells him to hush, but she hears impatience creeping into her voice.

"We don't know what it is, War," she says, "and we need to sort out food before we start looking for bees." Warren growl-screams in frustration and Burdock, affronted by the noise, tosses his head. Cobra frowns.

"It's something more than bees," she says. "I can't feel the bees like Warren can, but something's nagging at me. It's ... I don't know. I can't explain it. It's like I've felt it before but it's also something totally new."

Solma frowns. That makes absolutely no sense. "Is it coming from the village?" she asks. Cobra and Mamba glance at each other, then shrug.

"Sort of," Cobra says.

"Not entirely," says Mamba at the same time.

Solma throws up her hands in frustration. Olive's also losing patience with all this mystery. She rolls her eyes.

"How d'you know you ain't all just dizzy and tired from hunger?" she asks. "It could just be *that*. Not some weird signal in the dirt. Just hunger."

All the Whisperers except Mamba glare at her. Mamba holds his hands up, placatingly.

"Look, the children are tired," he points out. "This winter's been tough on them."

Roseann snorts. "Been tough on everyone," she says. "There's only so much running away you can do before it gets boring."

Everyone looks at her. Roseann shrugs.

Ana continues to glare. For a minute—or perhaps forever—no one says anything.

"Ok," Olive says eventually, "this is getting us nowhere."

Solma scowls. No kidding. "What d'you suggest, then?" she snaps. Olive's responding glare could thaw the peaks of the distant mountains and Solma flushes with shame. None of this is Olive's fault.

Even through that infernal glower, Solma sees a flicker of hurt in Olive's eyes. She looks away quickly. Why does she always do this to people?

Warren appears at Solma's side. "Can we talk about my bees now?" he demands.

Solma and Bell hush him at the same time, but he shakes his head. "No!" he says, little fists clenched, a determined look on his face. "It's important! You're all arguing over nothing but the bees are here!"

Solma tries to wrap an arm around his shoulder but he shies away, glaring at her.

"You said you'd trust me," he says, hurt in his voice. "After last year. You promised."

Solma's heart constricts. He's not wrong. She *did* promise that. But there's no proof of bees beyond his hope and Solma wishes she could believe him. But …

"Warren," she tries again. He folds his arms and refuses to look at her.

"Don't," he says, his quiet voice full of hurt. "You always treat me like a kid."

Solma sighs and bites back the urge to snap at him. This is ludicrous. They need food, supplies, water to wash and beds to rest in.

"We should go to the village," Roseann suggests quietly. "We can send a small group to check they're friendly. The kids can wait here in safety 'til it's done."

Cobra nods approval, but the younger Whisperers squirm. Solma can't tell whether it's tiredness or fear or both, but the idea of being left alone unsettles them. Krait starts to cry, which sets King and Habu off.

"I don't want anyone to go," Taipan whimpers. Cobra tries to hug her but is pushed away. Warren rushes to his friends defense, insisting she shouldn't *have* to go if she doesn't want to, and that sets all the children off again, wailing and sobbing.

Solma reels at the chaos. The noise and fear feels volcanic inside her head. It builds and builds until she wants to scream, too.

She reaches for Olive's hand, for the warmth of the person she knows will comfort her no matter what, but Olive's hand isn't there. The other girl gets to her feet without looking at Solma and stalks over to the sobbing boys. She hitches King onto her hip.

Solma stares at her for a moment, then wanders over to the horses to calm Burdock down. She's no use with the kids anyway. She just gets cross and annoys everyone. She stands with Burdock and Poppy, a tightness in her chest, while Bell, Roseann and Olive try to sort things out. Gradually, the children calm down and Cobra comes to put a hand on Solma's shoulder.

"You ok?" she asks. Solma turns and searches the Whisperer's face. A long time ago, this girl had been her best friend. They'd taken care of each other. Solma still sees traces of that bright-eyed little girl—Kobi—in Cobra's face. But years of a nomadic life and the deep magic of Whispering have changed her, too. Solma barely knows her now, even after six months together. Yet Cobra always seems to sense when Solma's out of sorts.

Solma nods, then changes her mind and shakes her head.

"Tired and hungry," she says. "Like everyone. I agree with Roseann. I'll head to the village and see what's what. If they're gonna chase us away, it makes sense that only one of us puts ourselves in danger."

Cobra smiles, then looks past her shoulder and her eyebrows raise in surprise.

"I don't think you'll have to, Sol," she says, pointing. Solma whirls round, then grabs for her rifle.

"Get everyone outta sight," she growls. They all blinks at her in astonishment, but Olive has her pistol ready, and is barking orders, ushering the little ones into hiding.

Because on the horizon is a lone figure, head bowed, leaning against a long staff as he trudges towards them.

Seven

THE STRANGER HAS NO visible weapons on him, and doesn't seem threatening, but Solma doesn't trust him. She stands between the children she's responsible for and the man who approaches them, rifle in her hands and a deep scowl aimed at him.

"Can we help you?" she asks, in a voice she hopes suggests that they have no intention of helping.

Warren and the youngsters huddle behind the bramble bushes and now only the older Whisperers, Olive, Bell and Roseann remain in sight. The stranger holds up a hand. He stops a few meters away and lays his staff down. It's a gesture of peace, Solma knows, but she's not buying it yet. She watches as he steps over the abandoned staff and comes towards them. He smiles and the way his face creases suggests he does this often, but the smile doesn't quite reach his eyes and there's the agitated tick of a vein in his temple. Solma's eyes narrow.

He's balding at the back of his head and what little grey hair he has left is cropped short at the sides. His tanned, white skin is lined with deep grooves and there's a sparkle to his grey eyes. He's not an old man, but he's not young either. He's dressed in loose green slacks and a white linen tunic, the wrists and elbows of which are frayed with wear. It's not the grey uniform of a Fei field worker, or the blue of the Oritch-caste orchard tenders. He's not wearing Gatra-black or the brown of Aldren-elders, which can mean only one thing.

This man is Steward-caste. The thought makes Solma grip her rifle tighter.

"I'm going to reach into my pocket now," he says. "I have no weapons, only food for the little ones. May I?"

Olive draws her pistol but holds it at her side and nods at him once. Solma widens her stance, in case of a fight.

The man rummages slowly in his pocket and pulls out a pouch. Opening it, he produces hard-baked biscuits and holds them out.

Solma glances at them, then scowls at the stranger. "You eat one first," she says. He inclines his head, as if he'd expect nothing less, and lifts one of the biscuits to his mouth. He chews slowly and swallows, opening his mouth to prove the biscuit is gone.

"I mean no harm," he says, holding the biscuits out again. "My scout saw your party a while ago and he said you had children with you. He said they looked hungry."

"We are, sir," Bell says, bustling forward. "We ran out of food and been travelling through them mountains for weeks." She gestures behind her to the Whisperers, the youngest of whom are peeking out from behind their foliage hiding place. "We're hoping for shelter and rest for a few days. The Whisperers can help with the land and my niece ..."

Her words die as she sees the stranger's brows draw into a frown. He shakes his head.

"I'm sorry," he says. "We're ... things are complicated at my village. We cannot allow strangers. I'll have some of my Guard bring you some supplies and we will give you more ammunition if you need, but we can't help you any further."

Bell stares at him, aghast. Roseann grunts disapproval and even Olive's eyebrows raise high enough to disappear into her hairline. Other villages might have chased them out when the Whisperers couldn't raise crops. But what village won't even let Whisperers through *in the first place?* No one can afford to do that. No village has land fertile enough that it will yield on its own. Not for a hundred years.

"Seriously?" Olive says. The air fizzes and Solma stiffens, half-lifting her rifle. The stranger clasps his hands together and gazes at Olive.

"I'm sorry," he says again.

Solma shifts her weight, uncertain. He seems genuine. But something about him gets her back up. Solma's not got a lot of trust for village Stewards these days. Or their sons. Maxen's face flashes behind her eyelids again when she blinks.

Blink. There he is, those white-blue eyes glowing with affection, a smile playing on his lips.

Blink. He's snarling, half his face swollen with bee stings, eyes gleaming with hate.

Solma shudders and shakes the image away. It's been nearly six months since he betrayed her, cast her out and took his father's place in the village while Blaiz, stung so badly by Warren's bees that he slipped into a coma, was hidden away in that huge house.

Stewards are greedy. Stewards are liars. They can't be trusted. She juts her chin and squares her shoulders.

"We don't need help," she says. Olive elbows her hard in the ribs.

"Ow!"

"Yeah? Well stop lying then," Olive snaps. "We *do* need help. The little ones *are* hungry and I'm bloody exhausted." She turns to glare at the Steward again. "You gonna leave us out here to die, Sir? You can live with that, can you?"

Solma glares at her and Olive turns, glaring back with equal force. It hurts, Olive looking at her like that, like the last few months together have all been erased. She hopes they haven't. But she sure as hell isn't backing down. She opens her mouth to retort.

"Can I have a biscuit?" comes Taipan's small voice from between them, making them both jump. Olive and Solma glance down as the little orange-eyed Whisperer squeezes between them and scurries to the stranger. She stares at him. "I'm really hungry."

"Yeah, me too," says Warren, clambering from behind the bushes and hurrying after her.

"Yeah," say Krait and Habu, one after the other. King says nothing, only crawls wearily from his hiding place and trudges after the others, hand out for sustenance.

The stranger kneels in front of them, smiling. "Take turns, then," he says, and the kids get into a line the way Bell taught them. "One each. Don't eat them too fast."

The children each take a biscuit and stare at the stranger while they chew. Olive puts her pistol away and nudges Solma to shoulder her rifle. "I don't reckon he's a threat," she says. Solma chews her lip, trying to swallow down the nagging feeling in her throat.

She hangs back as Olive goes to shake the man's hand. Bell and Roseann head to greet him, too, and Ana, Mamba and Cobra lead the ponies over. They talk quietly, answering his questions. The children seem calm for the first time in days. Taipan even tugs at the stranger's pant leg and asks to hold his hand. He obliges, smiling.

"What's your name?" Taipan asks, still licking biscuit crumbs from around her mouth.

"Norsen," he answers. "What's yours?"

The kids clamor to tell him their names. Norsen listens patiently, then recites their names back. The children beam.

Warren steps forward, crumbs round his mouth, and taps Norsen's hand. "You ain't gonna chase us out like the others, are you?" he asks.

Norsen turns and offers a reassuring smile. Warren remains unconvinced.

"Are you?" he pushes.

Norsen crouches in front of him. "What did you say your name was?" he asks.

Solma tenses, resisting the urge to ready her rifle.

Bell puts a hand on Warren's shoulder and smiles.

"His name's Warren," she says. "My nephew."

Norsen nods a without taking his eyes off Warren, which Solma doesn't like.

"And," he says softly, "where are you from?"

"Sand's End," Bell obliges. "In Southtip Province, to the east."

Solma clenches her jaw. Why are they telling him everything? Other Whisperers must have carried news of what happened in Sand's End last summer at least this far by now. Are they just going to announce to everyone that they were involved in that?

That *Warren* was involved in that?

But it's too late to deny it now.

Norsen stares at Warren, something odd shining in his eyes. He takes a deep, shuddering breath. "Sand's End?" he murmurs. "You're a long way from home,"

He searches Warren's face and Solma doesn't like the strangeness in his expression. Her fingers twitch as she reaches instinctively for her knife. Why is he looking at her brother like that?

Warren finishes his biscuit, oblivious to the way Norsen watches him. Solma frowns but fear squeezes her throat. What is that on Norsen's face? Awe? *Reverence?* Solma likes this less with every passing second. She sweeps past the Whisperer children and stands at Warren's side, looking as fierce as she can. Norsen hardly notices. Still staring at Warren, he shakes his head ever so slightly.

"I never thought..." he murmurs. "I'd never guessed..."

Solma's done with this. She shifts her rifle and snaps the safety off, loud enough to get Norsen's attention. He glances at her and the reverence drops from his face. He eyes her rifle and then rises. He's taller than the people Solma grew up with, but he's still only an inch or so taller than she is. She's always towered over everyone and, now, she draws herself up to her full height, using it to her advantage.

"If you ain't inviting us in," she says pointedly, "we'll grab supplies and be on our way."

Norsen blinks, his gaze flicking back towards Warren, lingering there a little too long before it returns to Solma. He smiles and stands aside, gesturing towards the silhouette of his village on the horizon.

"I'm sure we can make an exception for such a small group," he says, and holds his hand out for Warren to take. "You're welcome at Skyheart Village for a few days. Who wants fresh bread?"

The Whisperer kids squeal with enthusiasm. Warren slips his hand into Norsen's with a smile and Krait races ahead.

"Well," says Olive, falling into step beside Solma, "Guess we're going to the village."

"Yeah," Solma replies, glowering at Norsen's back. This doesn't feel right. "I guess we are."

Olive bumps her shoulder against Solma's. "Quit worrying," she says. "You gotta stop seeing enemies round every corner."

Solma scowls but says nothing. She does *not* need to stop seeing enemies round every corner, especially when they *are* around every corner. She clicks the safety back on her rifle and swings the strap over her shoulder.

Ana takes charge of the ponies and the party follows Norsen towards his village. Solma's insides coil and fester, full of imagined future evils. She doesn't like that Norsen's still holding Warren's hand.

To distract herself, she stares down at Olive's hand and wishes she could hold it, but Olive sees her looking and pain flashes across the other girl's face. She tucks her hand in her pocket before Solma can reach for it and marches on ahead.

Eight

NORSEN'S VILLAGE ISN'T LIKE other villages. Nestled against the tree-line, it's surrounded by a wire fence nearing eight feet tall. Just outside the fence, the river they'd been following rushes by in an ever-strengthening torrent. The water is clear and Solma sees huge fish battling the current. The village must have done well over winter with that bounty nearby. She turns her attention away from the fish and back towards the village.

Four rickety watchtowers mark the corners of the village border and a Guard in Gatra-black, gripping tight to the leash of an enormous dog, waves them through a gate that he opens with one slap of a big, black button on the fence post beside him. Solma frowns. She can't recall any village they've been to yet that has enough power to run that sort of security. But as she passes through the gate, she thinks she hears a faint hum coming from the wire fencing and realizes the entire perimeter is electrified. She raises her eyebrows. How on Earth did this village trade for enough solar panels to manage that?

Inside, the houses are well-structured, with thick walls and glass in the windows. Almost every house has a solar panel on its roof. The dwellings are huddled together with dirt tracks winding between them and … and *flowers* growing at their edges. Solma smells lavender and chamomile, and there are red and yellow blooms she doesn't recognize. Bell gasps with delight

"Tulips!" she exclaims. "How'd they get them so healthy? I can never get any to take …"

Solma glowers at Norsen's back as the Steward chatters to her brother. None of this is making her trust him any more than she did five minutes ago. What village has time to devote to pollinating plants for nothing more than decoration? They're miles from anywhere and certainly nowhere near the richer western provinces. Even those, according to the Whisperers, rarely have more than enough solar panels to provide power for the Steward's dwelling or meagre street lighting. Certainly, no village Solma's heard of pollinates plants simply to *look pretty.* She glances at Cobra, whose frown suggests she's equally perplexed.

The main path through the village is paved—something Solma has only seen in the wealthiest places—and, as the little group trudge into the main square, there's a kind of bustle Solma hasn't experienced in any other place in the last five months. Villagers mill in twos and threes, hailing each

other with hearty waves and warm smiles. A man in Oritch blue runs a stall at the edge of the main square, fixing farming tools under an animal-skin canvas. There's a short queue of workers from all castes, chatting merrily, waiting their turn for his expertise. At the head of the square is the grand house that, Solma expects, belongs to Norsen. Though it's not so much richer than the houses of the regular folk.

But something changes as Solma and the others enter the village. Conversations pause and eyes flick in their direction. Some of the children stare openly and one man makes a rude gesture before turning his back. Solma almost begins to relax. This is more like what they're used to. Villagers are often wary of strangers and the Whisperers, struggling more and more to coax growth from the soil, are increasingly treated with disdain.

But then she realizes the dark looks aren't for her or the Whisperers. The muttered insults, the angry glares, they're being directed at *Norsen.*

Parents usher their children away, throwing glowers over their shoulders. One man, when Norsen walks past, spits on the ground behind him. Norsen pauses briefly and Solma sees his shoulders tense, but he says nothing and walks on.

Even villagers who seem less inclined to be openly disdainful of their Steward look away or become very busy as he passes them, only ever answering his greetings with monosyllables and never meeting his eye. And the Gatra are just as wary of him as everyone else, which is surprising.

Solma watches him try to strike up a conversation with the man at the repair stall, who resolutely refuses to look anywhere but at the rake he's mending and only grunts in reply. She almost feels sorry for him. Almost. But a dark voice in her head reminds her she had good reason to mistrust every Steward last summer. She remembers how many of them had greedily descended on the village, demanding they each be allowed to claim Blume's nest for their own and hoard the resulting riches. Each Steward wanted to be the power center of Alphor. None of them ever imagined that such greed would only spark another Hive War. None of them considered that Blume and her colony were beings, too, whose survival would benefit everyone.

These villagers have good reason to distrust their leader. Solma hasn't yet met a Steward who tells the truth or thinks beyond their own borders. Why would Norsen be any different?

Norsen gives up on a conversation with the man at the stall and comes back to where Solma's little group huddle in the middle of the square with their ponies and cart, being given a wide berth by any villager who walks by.

Warren appears beside her and slips his hand into hers. She glances down to see him chewing his lower lip, his meadow-green eyes wide and interested.

"There are bees here," he says quietly. "I know there are."

Solma closes her eyes. "Warren ..."

"I know you don't believe me," he says, matter-of-fact. "But it's true. Just you wait."

Solma opens her mouth to retort but thinks better of it. They're all tired. Arguing about this now would achieve nothing. She can talk to Warren when he's fed and rested. She tries to catch Olive's eye, to share a look of solidarity, but the other girl is occupied, holding Taipan's hand in one of hers and Habu's in the other as she tries to cajole them both. The kids aren't having it and stand morosely at her side. Solma watches and feels a jolt of pain through her chest. Olive's so different around the kids. That iron-hard exterior softens. When she smiles at them, she smiles with her whole body. Now, she says something and winks at Taipan, who concedes a small smile. Solma's insides squeeze.

She stares at Olive's hand and wishes it was her fingers Olive was holding, her palm Olive's thumb stroked gently. When did that all go so wrong?

Norsen reaches them, a frown bridging his brows, and is about to say something when a clipped voice interrupts him.

"Sir," says the woman dressed in Gatra black who now stands to attention beside them. Solma sees an insignia on the right breast of her uniform. The soldier salutes stiffly and shoulders her rifle, glaring at the two youngsters behind her until they, too, shoulder their weapons and present Norsen with a far less formal salute. Norsen frowns.

"Yes?" he says, and it's the first time Solma's heard a sharp, angry edge to his voice. The Gatra woman scowls. Solma stares at her. She's easily just as tall as Solma, perhaps taller, with deep brown skin and darker hair. Streaks of red weave through the braid running down her back and catch the sunlight. Her stance tells Solma she's spent most of her life in the Gathering Guard. There's a watchfulness to her that Solma recognizes. It would be very hard to take this woman by surprise.

"There's been a disagreement between the Hals and the G'mus again," the woman says. "The G'mu Yuens attacked the Hal Yuens after planting and now there's tension. They're asking for your counsel."

Norsen stares at her and Solma feels the loathing radiate off him.

Solma remembers her own experiences as a Yuen—Alphor's child-caste—and her heart squeezes. She'd been chased and attacked numerous times after her father died. Parentless, she had only Bell to protect her, and Bell was preoccupied trying to bring up Warren. Children can be cruel to each other and Solma's almost tempted to offer help, but Norsen speaks before she has a chance.

"I'll be there shortly, Reya," he growls. "First, I'll need to settle in our guests."

Reya—*Captain* Reya, Solma judges from the insignia on her uniform, and wonders why Norsen wouldn't address her by her rank—stares at the newcomers as if she's just noticed they're there. Her lips part in surprise, but then she closes her mouth and her face darkens into a frown.

"I thought, Sir," she growls, "the village wasn't admitting strangers this year?"

She says it as if she's disagreed with this policy from the start but wonders why Norsen would change his mind. Solma wonders the same and squeezes her brother's hand tighter. He wriggles and she forces her grip to soften, smiling at him. He doesn't smile back and Solma reckons the fear in her face must be obvious. Something is wrong here. It feels like a trap. The back of her neck prickles and her phantom limb itches like it always does when she feels like she's being stalked by something ugly and dangerous.

Only this time, she's not sure which direction the danger's coming from.

Norsen draws himself up, glaring.

"We'll accept these guests," he says. "I trust you can handle the Hals and G'mus until I am available?"

He says it as if trust is the last thing he feels. Captain Reya's lips curls.

"Yes," she says, darkly. *"Sir."*

She turns, beckoning her subordinates to follow, and stalks out of the square. Bell clears her throat and busies herself with something in the back of the cart while Roseann, who's never been good at hiding her feelings, simply shakes her head. Olive nudges Solma's shoulder and raises an eyebrow. Solma shrugs, but a heavy sense of foreboding settles in her gut. What is going on?

Norsen turns back to face them, his face flushed. "My apologies," he mutters. "I'd like to get you settled so you can rest. Would the Whisperers be happy to offer their services in the fields?"

Mamba steps forward to discuss this while Cobra wrangles the youngsters under control. Solma watches Norsen with narrowed eyes. He'd been ready to send them on their way earlier, even though no village can afford to refuse Whisperers' help. Now he's changed his mind.

After he learned they were from Sand's End. After he set eyes on Warren.

Solma suddenly wants to snatch her brother up and run. To fight her way out of the gate and head for the forest. She'll take the danger of wildwolves and redbears over this mystery any day. But the gate is shut firmly behind them. They can't get out. The humming of the electric fence seems to get louder and louder until it's unbearable.

She clutches Warren's hand tighter and jumps when he whimpers. "Sol, that hurts!"

"Sorry," she murmurs.

She lets go and he rubs his hand where her grip left it red. He doesn't look at her and shoves his hand in his pocket when she tries to take hold of it again.

"I ain't seven no more," he grumbles. "I don't need you holding onto me all the time."

He trudges ahead, unwilling to stay close to his sister. Yet again, Solma is left alone, an exclusion zone around her that nobody wants to enter.

Norsen directs Mamba and the Whisperers along a narrow track towards the fields and orchards. Mamba gathers his troupe and they head off. Ana leads the ponies, but Burdock takes some persuading. He pulls at his rope and turns to look back, staring at Solma. Ana steps into his line of sight and murmurs something in his velvety ear. He huffs and moves off, following the Whisperers down the path.

Taipan turns and grins at Warren, beckoning excitedly. Warren glances at Solma.

"Can I go, Sol?" he asks.

Solma strides to his side and grabs his hand again before he can run off. "No," she snaps.

"But Sol!"

"I said no, Warren!"

Warren glares. He meets Taipan's eye, points at his sister and makes a rude gesture that Solma chooses to ignore. Taipan shrugs and hares after the Whisperers while Warren sighs and stares after them. Solma looks down at him.

"It's to keep you safe, War—" she starts, but he folds his arms and turns away.

"It ain't," he protests quietly. "You just wanna control me."

Solma's gut curdles and she stares at him. "No, War, I—"

But she doesn't know what to say. How's she supposed to explain? She promised their parents before they died that she'd take care of him. Protect him. Doesn't he get how hard that is? How she lives in constant fear?

"Fine," she snaps. "Sulk if you want. But you're staying with me."

Olive glances over and beckons Solma to join her with Bell, Roseann and the ponies. Solma looks at Warren, who shrugs but follows her, dragging his feet.

Now that the Whisperers have headed for the fields, Norsen turns his attention to the rest of their little group. He clasps each of their hands in turn and asks their names.

"We were able to trade well last year and have a surplus of ammunition," he says. Solma frowns. Were they, indeed? What is going *on* in this village?

"We're happy to give you some in exchange for the Whisperers' help," Norsen continues. "But I'd ask that you leave your weapons unloaded while you're with us. You're perfectly safe within our boundaries."

Solma's scowl deepens and she clutches her rifle strap. No way is she walking through this village unarmed. Norsen pretends not to notice.

"The Whisperers have said they would prefer to make their camp on the edge of the village," Norsen says, "but I understand from Mamba that you are not Whisperers."

Solma dips her head to hide the flush in her cheeks. No, they are not Whisperers. They are exiles. A word that often sparks hate and hostility in the villages they've visited. Stripped of rank and caste, they were sent out of their village to die. Is this when Norsen chases them out?

"No," Olive says, an edge to her voice. "We ain't Whisperers, but we are their protectors."

Norsen inclines his head. "So they said. I meant no offence. I'm sorry that you had to leave your village. I mentioned it only because I expect you might be grateful for a roof over your head and proper beds."

Solma glances up sharply, searching Norsen's face. He's being serious. A proper bed. A door that closes. Windows that shut out the cold. Her heart lifts, despite her best efforts to contain it.

"We would, sir," Bell says, wiping sweat and grime from her forehead. "And a basin to wash in? The kids're filthy. We been on the road a long time."

Norsen grins. "I can imagine," he says. "Two of our Aldren villagers, sadly, succumbed to the cold this year. Their house lies empty and is to be assigned to an Oritch couple who will make their vows in the spring. But I have spoken with them and they are happy for you to use it while it is still empty. It's along that path—" he points to the track leading off the square to the north, "the final house on the left. One thing …"

The four of them pause and stare at him, eager to find the house and rest. Norsen's face turns serious.

"We are good at controlling the creatures that come out of the forest, but please don't wander into it. It's a dangerous place."

Bell and Roseann both nod their consent and head off along the northern path, Warren scuttles after them. Olive grunts agreement and makes to head off, too. Her hand brushes Solma's for a moment and their eyes meet.

"You coming?" Olive says. Solma struggles to find her voice.

"Yeah," she chokes. "You go ahead."

Olive frowns and Solma can't work out what it is she sees in the other girl's eyes. Then Olive's shoulders slump.

"Fine," she says, trudging off without another word.

Solma looks back at Norsen and finds him watching her. She scowls. "We travelled through that forest for days," she says, not sure where she's going with this. "We can handle the predators."

Norsen blinks, his demeanor unchanging.

"Please, Sergeant," he says, and Solma flinches at his use of her former title, "don't go into the forest. I want you to be welcome in my village. But if you disobey me in this, I cannot guarantee your welcome will last. Do you understand?"

And there it is. The threat she's been waiting for. He's just like all the others. Secretive. A tyrant. He's hiding something, and Solma reckons it isn't redbears and wildwolves. There's something in that forest he doesn't want them seeing.

Maxen's face bursts into Solma's mind again. Torn and scarred down one side. Twisted with rage. Hating her. She shakes the image away.

"I'll keep it in mind," she says as she turns her back on him and heads after the others.

Nine

SPRING SUNSHINE STREAMS THROUGH the bedroom window and Solma dozes in a wooden chair, her fingers loosely entwined with Olive's as Olive lays in bed. Solma smiles as she comes to, and gives Olive's hand a squeeze. Olive, still asleep, frowns and snuggles deeper under the blanket, her red hair splayed across the pillow.

When Solma had made it to the house the previous day, she'd found Roseann cleaning and wrapping Olive's leg. A livid bruise ran the length of her calf, which was swollen around a deep cut. Bell told her it was from slipping down the mountainside almost a week ago. Solma felt a growing queasiness as she looked at the wound, she hadn't realized how badly Olive had been hurt. Olive saw the look on her face and grabbed her hand.

"S'alright, Sol," she'd said, while Roseann dug around in the cut with a pair of tweezers. "Don't hurt much."

Then she'd fainted.

Solma helped Roseann and Bell carry her into the bedroom. She's never been in a house that has a separate bedroom before, but this one does, with proper beds and soft sheets and thick blankets that don't scratch.

After Roseann extracted the thorn from Olive's leg and lathered it with antiseptic, she and Bell retreated to the main room, where Bell set about making food from the supply of vegetables left by a sturdy stove, and Roseann sat at the round oak table and put her feet up on a chair. (Quickly taking them down again at the look on Bell's face.)

Solma stayed with Olive all night, furious with herself for not noticing Olive's injury. At some point, the door creaked open and Warren wandered in. He sat beside her in silence and they watched over Olive as she slept.

Now, though, Warren has disappeared from beside her chair. Probably got bored. The sound of voices rouses Solma and she blinks the sleepiness from her eyes.

It sounds like Cobra and Ana. There's urgency in their voices. That, and the smell of Bell's cooking, is enough to wake Solma fully. She glances at Olive and smiles as she re-wraps her leg and straps on her prosthesis. Olive looks so harmless when she sleeps. The opposite of how she is when she's awake. Solma strokes a flame-red lock of hair from Olive's face and plants a lingering kiss on her eyebrow.

"I'll do better," she whispers. "From now on. I will. I promise."

She doesn't add that she's got no idea how. She just knows she's got a lot of making up to do. She takes a deep, steadying breath and goes to see what all the fuss is about.

Ana and Cobra look round when she appears. Cobra smiles. They're sat at the table while Bell serves them tea and something to eat. Norsen has, so far, been true to his word and the house appears stocked with bread and hardy vegetables. There are even fresh eggs, which Bell has scrambled and served with bread to Ana, Cobra and Warren, who's also perched at the table, eager to be fed. He tucks in before Bell's even put the bowl down.

Solma stretches, feeling her spine creak, and sits beside Warren as Bell serves up another helping. The windows are large and the room is awash with morning sun. The wooden floorboards are covered with an assortment of hand-woven rugs, which are soft under Solma's bare foot. A fireplace dominates the wall opposite the stove, but it's unlit this morning. Beside it, Roseann scowls from a squashy armchair. When she sees Solma, her eyebrows raise. Solma shrugs.

"Still sleeping," she says. "Looks like the swelling's gone down, though."

Roseann grunts in reply.

Bell leans on the table, cup of tea in one hand and a frown on her face as she stares at each of the Whisperers in turn. "So," she says, "what's this about then?"

Ana glances at Cobra. Solma hadn't looked properly at Ana before, but now sees she's ashen-faced and glassy-eyed. She looks like she's about to be sick. Cobra doesn't look quite so ill, but is far paler than usual with dark circles round her eyes.

"The signal," she says, rubbing Ana's back while the other girl sits in a daze. Bell raises an eyebrow.

"What about it?"

"It's … this is the strongest we've felt it," Cobra says. "It feels like the land is vibrating. When we put our hands into the soil, it was like the Earth was screaming at us. It's … I don't know. I've felt a signal like this before. It feels so *familiar* but I can't work out why. We went over to the fields to help with planting and, on the way, Krait fainted, Taipan was sick and we couldn't get King to stop crying. It's ..." she flicks a sideways glance at Solma. "We all agree. It's pulling us into the forest behind the village."

Solma frowns. So Norsen's warned the Whisperers off entering the forest, too. The forest from which something is sending out such a strong signal it's making her friends sick. Bell swoops on Ana to comfort her, then clatters over to the stove to warm some water. She chatters at a hundred miles an hour about herbal tea and rest and gives Cobra stern instructions to bring the children to the house *right now* because the poor things have been through enough.

Cobra endures all this in silence, but she and Solma exchange dark looks, which doesn't escape Roseann's notice.

"Bell, stop your *fussing,* for a minute!" she growls. Bell glowers but complies. Roseann leans forward. "There's more to this, in't there?"

She stares intently at Solma and Solma has to persuade her jaw to unclench so she can speak. Her hands curl into fists under the table.

"There's something in the forest," she says. "Something Norsen don't want us to see. He told me we ain't welcome if we go in there."

Warren, who until this point has been occupied by his food, drops his spoon. "It's the bees," he says matter-of-factly. "I keep telling you but none of you listen."

Solma sighs. "Alright, War," she says. "We'll deal with that in a bit. But what if the thing Norsen's hiding has something to do with this signal?"

"It must do," Cobra says, shaking her head. "It's too much of a coincidence otherwise."

Bell rolls her eyes. "He don't want you going into the forest 'cos there are redbears and wildwolves in there, ridiculous girl!" she says, brandishing a serving spoon at Solma. "Didn't you notice the eight-foot fence round the whole village?"

Solma glares. "Yeah," she says. "I did. The eight-foot, *electrified* fence. Where'd they get enough solar panels to generate that kind of power? Also, the village is full of flowers. They ain't crops, either. *Decorative* flowers. Who has time to pollinate them?"

Cobra shakes her head. "When we checked through their supplies," she says quietly, "we didn't find any working pollenbots, and none of the drones looked like they'd been used in years. A mouse had made a nest in one of the headsets."

Solma throws up her hands. "So no pollinating equipment, but they're the wealthiest village we been to in six months. Norsen shares his ammo, his food, his houses. He weren't even gonna let us in... before he laid eyes on Warren." She fixes Bell with as furious a stare as she can. "Tell me that ain't weird."

"Well ..." Bell splutters. "I ..."

"It's *bees!*" Warren insists, emphasizing each word by bashing his little fists on the table. Solma looks at him and can't, in all certainty, tell him he's wrong. Could Norsen be hiding a colony of bees in those woods? Is that what he doesn't want them to find?

Cobra shakes her head. "Maybe he is hiding bees," she says, rubbing her temple. "But there's something else, too. I can't sense the insects like Warren can and, as far as I know, neither can any of the other Whisperers. So whatever this signal is, it's something different. It's bigger."

"We need to go look," Warren announces, scrambling from the table. Bell collars him.

"Sit down, boy!" she says, wrangling him back into the chair. She glares at everyone. "Now you lot listen to me. We been chased outta village after village. We trekked over mountains, survived cold and snow and rain. We need *rest*. The kids are exhausted and you, Solma, ain't exactly the picture of health! I'll not be driven outta yet another village because you can't keep your eyes in your head! *This once*, you do as you're told. No-one goes in that forest. Got it?"

Nobody answers.

"*Got it?*" Bell growls, a threat in her voice.

There are mumbles of assent round the table. Bell nods, satisfied. "Good," she says.

But when her back is turned, Cobra meets Solma's eye. There's no way they can just ignore this. And as Solma gulps down the last of her breakfast, she's already wondering how she might slip past the electric fence unnoticed.

Ten

Solma slams the door behind her. Bell is so infuriating. Four days they've been stuck in this accursed village and she's still adamant that no-one is to try to unravel Norsen's secret, whatever it is. Never mind that the Whisperer children have thrown up numerous times, that Ana fainted on the planting fields yesterday and that Cobra and Mamba have got so little sleep that they've both, on separate occasions, plopped face first into their dinner. But it doesn't matter how much Solma argues with her, Bell's word is always final.

Solma stalks along the gravel track, heading towards the village square, then changes her mind and doubles back, slipping behind a cluster of houses. She walks beyond the path where ferns sprout, unmanaged, along the line of the outer fence. She pauses a few feet from the fence itself. The warning sizzle of electricity cuts through the still morning air and Solma scowls.

She's walked the length of this bloody fence so many times and, everywhere, the same warning sizzle sounds just as loud and threatening. She's grabbed fistfuls of ferns and used them to test the electricity. Everywhere she's chucked one against the wire, it lands with a spark and a sharp snap. Not only is the fence electrified, it's *very* electrified.

There's a rustle and a kick of gravel behind her and she whirls round, hand on the hilt of her hunting knife. Her other hand reaches for her rifle strap but, of course, it isn't there. After Norsen forbade them from carrying their firearms, Bell had taken charge of all pistols and rifles and hidden them so efficiently that Solma reckons she'll have to tear up floorboards to find them. Being caught without one makes her skin prickle, but when she finally lays eyes on the source of the noise, it's just a village kid. He's half in shadow, crouched beside one of the houses. He doesn't look older than eleven or twelve, and hunger and hardship mean he's small even if he is that old. A mop of black hair falls over his face and he peers at her through a heavy squint. Solma puts on her fiercest face.

"What?" she growls.

Startled, the kid flattens his fringe over his forehead, giggles nervously and darts away. Solma shakes her head.

"Who was that?" says a little voice beside her and Solma starts so violently she almost falls into the fence and fries herself. Two pairs of little

hands shoot out to steady her and Solma glances down to find Warren and Taipan blinking up at her.

"What," Solma says through gritted teeth, "are you two doing out here? And *how* do you move so quietly?"

Taipan giggles but Warren puts his little fists on his hips. "Taipan's been teaching me," he says as if it's obvious. "The Whisperers call it wildwalking. Didn't you know that?"

Solma blinks. No, she didn't know that. How could she not know that? She's been living with these people all winter and she's not once heard them mention it.

Maybe Olive's got a point.

She shoves that thought away before it can make the old guilt fester and focuses on being angry instead. She glares at Warren.

"That don't explain why you're both out here by yourselves!"

Warren shrugs. "We been testing the dead bit of the fence," he says. Turning eight has definitely made him more defiant. He's not as scared of his sister's disappointment as he used to be.

Solma's about to keep up the scolding, but something clicks in her head before she can tell him off.

"What dead bit?" she demands.

Warren gives an exaggerated sigh and turns to point west along the fence.

"'Bout three posts that way," he says, "there's a dead bit. It's just the bottom two wires. The top ones are still zappy, but the bottom ones ain't. If you was careful, you could climb through."

Now Solma's got her hands on her hips, too. "That what you were gonna do?"

Warren has the grace to look sheepish. Taipan swings her arms.

"The boys were gonna come too," she admits without a shred of remorse, "but Krait vomited this morning and then King fainted and Habu didn't want to leave them." She adds, "wimps," under her breath and Solma suppresses a smirk.

"But you're ok?" she asks.

Taipan shrugs. "Don't feel great," she admits. Solma frowns. She does look pale. They need to find the source of this signal. And fast.

"So," Solma says, battling between being angry and deeply impressed, "you were just gonna wander into the forest by yourselves, were you? Forgotten that there's wild animals in there, eh?"

"*No!*" the kids insist in unison.

But then Taipan ruins it with, "We hadn't forgotten about the animals. That's why I was teaching Warren to wildwalk!"

Solma cups a hand to her mouth to smother a laugh. She has to hand it to them, they've been far more thorough than she has. Taipan giggles again and Warren grins.

"You ain't going out there by yourselves," Solma says. The kids start to protest again but Solma holds up a hand. "I'm coming with you."

And to hell with Bell's instructions.

Warren and Taipan exchange glances. "Okay," Taipan says slowly. "But you're not allowed to be in charge. We're going to find the signal. We've got to know what it is."

Solma frowns, but the girl is so immovable it seems pointless to argue. Let them think they're in charge.

She's got her hunting knife and she can, at least, keep them safe.

"Alright," she says. "Show me this dead bit of the fence, then."

The children grin and charge off along the fence so that Solma has to jog to keep up with them. The fence sizzles and hums and the section they stop at appears no different to any other. Solma glances left and realizes the watchtower at the northwest corner is just a little too far away to see them. She looks right and the northeast watchtower is obscured behind the boughs of an ash tree that overhangs the fence. It's almost too perfect. No one can see them. No one can stop them.

Taipan reaches towards the wire with her bare hands.

"Wait!" Solma blurts, pulling Taipan back. The fence doesn't sound any different here. The warning hum is still just as loud. "Are you sure?"

Warren casts her a withering glare, then squats in the ferns, fishing about for something. He straightens, brandishing a knobbly twig, and chucks it against the lowest wire. Solma flinches instinctively, but the stick falls to the ground without a sound and when Warren retrieves it, there's no charring or smoke. He throws it against the wire just above and the same thing happens.

"If you're careful," Warren says, "you can duck between them wires and get out into the forest without being zapped."

Solma stares. A warning prickle creeps up the back of her neck. Something about this feels off. There's a convenient gap in the electricity that just happens to be in a blind spot to both the northern watchtowers? It's almost as if it's not an accident at all.

Like it's been arranged on purpose.

Solma shakes her head. "I dunno ..." she says.

But in the time it takes her to hesitate, Warren and Taipan scramble through and are haring off on the other side. Solma curses.

Gingerly, she tests the wires with the tip of her finger and, when she doesn't fry, she lifts the safe upper wire and carefully climbs through. She's bigger than Warren and Taipan and it takes more of an effort. By the time she's managed to get free, the children have disappeared into the forest.

"Warren!" Solma hisses. "Wait!"

There's an answering giggle from the trees and Solma casts one last wary glance back at the fence before she darts after them.

Eleven

Dry leaves crackle under Solma's blade foot. She winces at the noise and casts a furtive glance back, checking to make sure they aren't being followed. Now that they're doing this, she's acutely aware of what might happen if they get caught. Bell's warnings ring in her ears and Solma grips the hilt of her hunting knife. She really wishes she had a pistol.

Warren and Taipan have no such qualms. They skip ahead, chattering. Solma tugs her knife free of its sheath. Her eyes scan the unfamiliar terrain, suspecting every shadow. Forests have never been safe places, as far as she's concerned. She remembers the giant boar from nearly four years ago, raging and screaming as he mangled her leg beyond repair ...

She shudders and shakes the image away.

"Warren," she whispers. No response. "Warren!"

The kids stop up ahead and turn back to her. Warren's eyes are huge and innocent. "What?"

"Just ... keep the noise down, yeah?"

Taipan smirks and Warren rolls his eyes. "Fine," he says. "But everything dangerous is sleeping."

Solma raises an eyebrow. "How can you know that?"

"The bees told me," Warren says, without a shred of irony in his voice. Solma's breath catches. She knows her brother's power is something new in Alphor, his ability to communicate with the insects last spring had been nothing short of astonishing. But it's been months since the last of Blume's daughters went to ground. Could he really be hearing bees? Solma wonders if his hope is turning to delusion. Still, she says nothing as the kids scurry ahead.

Because there is *something* being kept secret. Maybe it's bees. Maybe it's something else. Whatever it is, Solma will find it and expose Norsen for what he truly is.

Warren and Taipan still gabble away. Solma only half listens. Her grip on her knife is so tight it's painful but she can't make herself relax. Her eyes dart from every shadow to trembling leaf. She's never got used to the thick silence of forests, only occasionally disturbed by the rustle of an underground creature. She knows, from Bell's lessons, that the forests were once full of sound. When there were still flying birds in Alphor, they populated forest canopies and filled them with song. But that was a hundred years ago. Before the Hive Wars. Now, forests are silent, full of prowling

predators and giant herbivores with tempers to match. A phantom itch starts up in Solma's absent leg. She shakes it but the itch persists.

Ahead, the kids have fallen quiet. Taipan slumps against a tree, clutching her belly.

"It's close, now," she says, voice slurring. "Urgh! It makes me feel so sick." Warren stops chattering and turns back to her.

"Maybe it ain't bees," he says in a small voice. "Bees are a good thing. They shouldn't make you feel so ill. But ..." his eyes are huge as he stares at Solma. "I heard them. They spoke to me."

He starts to get teary but Taipan shakes her head.

"No," she says. "You don't get it. It's like ... I've got to get there. If I find the signal, I'll be ok. It's not being with it that's making us sick. It's calling to us, see."

Solma bites her lip as she draws level with the children and offers her hand to Taipan. The girl takes it.

"C'mon," Solma says. "I'll help you. Lean on me."

Taipan moans and falls against Solma's hip. Solma puts her arm around the Whisperer girl. Warren rushes to his friend's side and clasps her hand.

"I'm ok," Taipan insists, eyelids drooping. "Let's go."

Solma's not convinced, but she forces herself to relax and gives Warren a wink and a reassuring smile. He frowns at her hunting knife and she sighs, sheathing it. He's right. Nothing's jumped out at them so far. She helps Taipan over a tangle of tree roots.

And that's when she hears it.

A soft tremolo drifting through the otherwise silent forest. The sound resonates in her bones, so familiar and yet so long-missed. She freezes.

"Warren ..."

"I hear it!" Warren says, his face alight with the promise. "This way!"

He darts off, skipping over fallen branches and disappearing into the foliage. Taipan lifts her head.

"Let's go," she slurs, but stumbles at the first step. Solma catches her and looks up to see where her brother's gone. He's nowhere in sight.

"Warren!" she hisses, not quite trusting the forest enough yet to shout. Warren has no such worries. His voice carries back to her.

"Come on!"

Solma doesn't need telling twice. She lurches after him, half-carrying, half-dragging Taipan. Leaves crunch under her blade-foot. The tell-tale tremolo grows louder, separating into several songs. The trees thin and Solma sees, beyond, there's a kind of glade, large enough that it looks like it might have been cleared by human hands, but still green and ...

And are those flowers?

Spots of purple, yellow and red pucker beyond the tree-line. Solma smells lavender.

She stumbles out of the trees, catching her foot on a branch so that she enters the clearing face first and sprawls in the dirt. With a yelp, Taipan lands beside her but, when the little Whisperer girl lifts her head, she's smiling.

"That's better," she sighs, closing her eyes and taking a deep breath. "This is the place. It's coming from here."

Solma realizes color is returning to the girl's cheeks. She pushes herself onto all fours and crawls towards Taipan. The grass is so thick and green, healthy like Solma's never seen before. Distracted, she grabs a fistful and seedlings flurry from within, making her sneeze. It's so soft.

"Solma," Warren says. His voice sounds strange.

"Yeah, hang on, Warren," she mutters.

"No, Sol," he says quietly. "You need to look."

"Oh," Taipan breathes from somewhere on Solma's left. "Yes. That's what it is! That makes so much sense!"

Solma looks up. It takes her a moment to work out what she's seeing, because the figure before them is silhouetted against the bright sky. But, as Solma shields her eyes, she realizes she's looking at a little girl, about a year older than Warren. Silky hair, brown as a nut, falls to her shoulders, and her eyes, the color of oak bark with a green streak running through the left, are wide but not frightened. She's white-skinned, but with a healthy flush in her cheeks, and is chewing absently on her lower lip as she watches them. She's wearing what look like Whisperer robes, but not. They're a soft, iridescent blue-purple, trimmed with gold thread at the sleeves and neck. Her sandalled feet peep from beneath the hem.

But even that isn't the most astonishing thing about her.

"Can I help you?" she asks. Warren sniffles and Solma glances at him to see that he's crying. Silent tears roll down his reddening cheeks.

"You already did," he says, his voice thick. "I knew I heard them."

Taipan scrambles to her feet and goes to stand with Warren. They stare at the little girl in purple robes as if she's just fallen from the sky.

And then Solma sees them: the bees training a lazy orbit around the girl's head, congregating on her shoulders, her open palms, darting in and out of the sunlight like wishes on their way to be fulfilled. They're not like Warren's bees were. Solma remembers the softness of those extra-fluffy bodies against her fingers, the deep, determined vibrato of their song. These bees are different. Slender and streamlined with neat fur and a purposeful song.

But that doesn't matter.

What matters is there are bees in these woods.

And this girl, like Warren, is a Beekeeper.

Twelve

Solma gets up, staring around the glade. Something inside her lifts, like a bee taking flight, and she listens to that glorious hum.

Bee song.

It drifts around them in soft tremolo, full of industry. They watch the tiny shapes darting in and out of the light. One lands on Warren's shirt and he looks down as it cleans its antennae. It turns and stares up at him, those multi-faceted eyes gleaming with iridescence.

"I *knew*," Warren says. "You didn't believe me, but I *knew*."

Solma shakes her head. "You did," she says, still staring at the tiny, darting shapes zooming in and out of the light.

"Knew what?" asks the girl in the blue robes, making all three of them jump. Solma smiles.

"My brother ..." she says, then wonders how on Earth she's supposed to explain it. "You tell her, War."

Warren holds out a hand. "My name's Warren," he says. "I'm a Beekeeper, too."

The girl blinks, then her face breaks into a huge grin, showing crooked teeth. She grabs his hand and shakes it enthusiastically. "Great!" she says. "I'm Yennevieve. You can call me Yenn. I'm Keeper of Honeybees."

"Honey ...?" Solma murmurs, frowning. "You mean there are *more* bees?"

"Oh, yes!" Yennevieve says. "We have three hives, here. That's hundreds of thousands of bees, that is."

Hundreds of thousands ...

The number hits Solma like a punch between the eyes. This should be impossible. But Solma's encountered a lot of impossible things in the last year.

"Come meet the other Keepers," Yennevieve says, beaming at Warren. "Other kids like us."

Ok. This is too much. Solma reels. Other *Keepers*? More children like her brother? *How?*

"What's your insect?" Yennevieve asks, still holding Warren's hand. Solma glances at her brother in time to see the look of pain on his face.

"Buff-Tailed Bumblebees," he says quietly, and Solma remembers the deep, rumbling drone of their song, the black-and-gold fur of their bulbous bodies, the way they trundled happily across her brother's palm with absolute trust. "But we ain't seen any. I dunno where they are. I thought …"

He shakes his head and Solma squeezes his shoulder. He'd hoped there would some here…

Yennevieve stops and looks at him with absolute understanding. "I'm sorry," she says, stroking the back of his hand. "That must be hard. But there *will* be some. You just ain't found them yet. They'll turn up."

She turns to Taipan. "And what're *your* insects?" she asks. A faint blush blooms in Taipan's cheeks.

"I don't have insects," she says in a small voice. "I'm an Earth Whisperer."

"Oh," Yenn says, losing interest. She turns back to Warren. "Here, come and meet the others."

She pulls him towards the far end of the glade but Warren doesn't need persuading, he takes off with her, leaving little Taipan to scowl after them. Solma offers the girl her hand.

"C'mon," she says. "Let's go see."

Taipan slips her little hands into Solma's and they follow after Warren and Yennevieve.

"This is weird," Taipan mumbles. "They must be what's making the signal."

Solma frowns. "Who?"

"Yenn and the others," Taipan says. "Now I'm here, the signal feels strong but it's not making me so sick. Like it wants me to be here. Like *they* want me to be here." She casts a dark look towards where Yenn and Warren have paused at the far edge of the glade, beside a couple of weathered tents. "Even though someone clearly don't want *me* here."

Solma squeezes her hand. Poor kid. But Yennevieve's words circle her brain and she turns her attention back to the purple-robed girl. Who are these other Keepers Norsen's been hiding? Anger flashes in Solma's core. Just like Blaiz. Just like every Steward that descended on Sand's End last summer, trying to claim the bees. This man's no different, hiding children in the woods to keep their powers secret.

No wonder he didn't want them going into the forest. Selfish, greedy—

"Here we are!" Yennevieve announces as Solma and Taipan join her by the tents.

She cups her hands to her mouth and yells, "*Oi! C'mere!*"

Solma flinches. If this is supposed to be a secret, this kid isn't great at keeping it.

Almost immediately, the tent flap flies open and a squat, plump figure appears in its place, face contorted with anger. An elderly man emerges with a wide middle and a long nose, wisps of silver hair poking from between his ears and the wool hat he wears. He's swathed in so many layers it's difficult to make out his shape, but Solma sees a loose pair of pants held up with a rope belt and a grubby linen shirt under a waistcoat and several threadbare scarves. Most of his clothes are Aldren brown.

"*Yennevieve!*" he yells, waving a gnarled old cane. "What I told you! It's rude to—oh, *hell!*" the figure swears as he sees Solma, Warren and Taipan. "What you done, you foolish girl? Didn't you hear Norsen? *Tell nobody!*"

He limps towards them, leaning heavily on his cane. Solma notices one of his legs is shorter than the other and slightly twisted. The squat little man sees her staring and his face reddens.

"What?" he demands. "Ain't never seen no one who had polio before?"

Solma bites her lip. She's heard of polio, though it was never in Sand's End during her lifetime. In the old-world, it used to be preventable, but not now, and she's heard of many villages who lost children to it. Those who survived were often marked, just like this man.

He scowls. "Anyway," he croaks, "it's rich you staring, in't it?" he taps her prosthesis with the tip of his cane and Solma jerks it away furiously.

"Don't ever," she growls through gritted teeth, "do that again."

Unmoved, the man brandishes his cane again. "You'll have to leave," he says. "Now. You shouldn't be here. Nobody should. I dunno what Yenn's told you, but—"

Yennevieve grabs his hand and hushes him. "Alright, Dyl, calm down!" she begs. "I didn't bring them here, they *found* this place and look ..." she grabs Warren's hand and brings him close enough that Dyl's pale, watery eyes can focus on the boy.

"One'a them's a Keeper like us!"

Dyl blinks at Warren and the anger falls from his face. His jaw slackens so his mouth makes a perfect O.

"Well," he says. "That's different."

He jabs his cane into the ground and leans heavily against it. His scarves slip away from his hip and Solma sees there's a pistol holstered there. Her eyes narrow. Dyl catches her looking and grins.

"Yeah," he coughs. "An' I know how to use it so don't try anything." He throws back his head and calls, "Alright, then, kids! Come out! It's safe, apparently."

There's a whisper, a rustle, and two purple-robed children emerge from the tents. Another pops his head up from behind a blackberry bush and a fourth steps tentatively from the shadows of the trees. There are two boys and three girls, including Yennevieve. None of them look older than ten and one of the boys seems younger than Warren. Nervously, they flock to Dyl's side and he opens his arms so they can nestle close to him, staring at the newcomers with big, frightened eyes. Dyl gives a gappy grin.

"Skyheart's miracle children," he says, looking down at them with shining eyes. He jerks his head up suddenly and fixes Solma with a furious scowl. "And anyone threatenin' them will answer to me, hear?"

Solma lifts her hands to show she means no harm. "I'm not threatening no-one," she says, trying to keep her voice steady. "I'm just trying to keep my brother safe."

"Hmm," Dyl says, raising one prickly eyebrow. "Your brother the Keeper, eh?"

He fixes Warren with intense, tawny eyes. "Hello there, fella," he murmurs. "Welcome home."

Solma's gut twists, and she reaches for Warren's hand, but before she can grab it, a girl around Warren's age with brown skin and bouncing curls steps up to them, beaming. She pulls Warren into a hug.

"Another one!" she says, squeezing him. "I'm Leiff! Keeper of Ashy Mining Bees."

"Oh," Warren says as she releases him. "I'm—"

A boy skids over and tumbles in a heap. From the ground, he lifts his white, freckled face to stare at them with enormous brown eyes.

"Tobias!" he says. "Holly Blue Butterflies."

Solma fights to regain control of her voice. "Hi Tobias," she stutters. "Hi Leiff. We're—"

The other two scramble over, fighting each other to be first. In the commotion, one of them knocks into Taipan and she stumbles, sprawling in the grass. Solma stoops to help her up. Taipan's face is thunderous as she brushes herself down. Solma puts a protective arm round her. She's been that kid before; the one left on the outside. She's suddenly very annoyed with Warren for not noticing that his friend needs him.

A black-skinned girl with shining black hair and the tell-tale deep-brown eyes of the southern provinces hops up to Warren. She bows solemnly. "Nessa," she says. "Marmalade Hoverflies. And this is Jonah—" she points to the youngest boy, "His insects are false oil beetles."

She wrinkles her nose as if this isn't something to be proud of.

Jonah stamps his foot. "I wanted to say it!" he whines, and stalks off to sulk in the shadows.

Nessa shrugs. "I was just *telling* them!" she yells after him. "It's not *my* fault!"

Dyl gives her a stern look and she quells a little. "What you been told about pickin' on the boy?" Dyl growls. Nessa pokes her tongue out when he's no longer looking and Solma suppresses a grin.

Jonah huffs over his shoulder and Leiff hurries over to comfort him. Yennevieve scolds Nessa, who clearly doesn't feel she needs to be scolded, so the pair begin to argue. Tobias starts to cry. Dyl rolls his eyes.

"Kids," he says. "Right, everyone. Come to Dyl. We'll sit down and have something to eat."

The children stomp and trudge over to him. They flop to the grass and Dyl shuffles back into the tent, emerging a moment later with some bread, a tin tub and a knife. The children wait patiently while he sits on a shorn tree stump beside the tent, opens the tin and begins smoothing lard onto each piece of bread before handing it out. He offers one to Warren and Taipan, who both take it eagerly, but Solma shakes her head when he offers her a slice. He shrugs and stuffs it in his own mouth instead.

The glade is filled with sullen quiet and the bees gather anxiously around the children.

Now that Solma looks properly, some of the insects seem different. Some of them are fluffier, like Warren's bees, but with paler stripes and ash-grey instead of black. Some don't look like bees at all, but are long and slender, moving in dizzying, darting movements.

And, oh! That insect fluttering past her! Solma thinks back to Bell's many books but, for the life of her, can't remember what the creature is called.

"A butterfly!" Warren exclaims.

"Yes," Solma breathes. "So it is."

Dyl gives a wry smile. "Pretty, hey?" he says. Solma nods, watching it with wonder.

It's bright, brilliant blue and dancing on shimmering wings. It flutters past her face, its wings brushing her cheek. She shivers and catches Warren's gaze.

This is amazing.

But it's also a secret. And that's a problem.

Solma turns to Dyl and the Keeper kids.

"What's happening here?" she asks. "What is this place?"

The children all start talking at once, then get annoyed that no one's listening to them. Sighing, Dyl raps his cane against the tree stump and the children fall quiet. He fixes Solma with a stern stare, bushy eyebrows meeting.

"What's it to you?" he demands. Solma bristles, but Taipan puts a hand on her arm.

"We been searching for bees ever since the autumn," she says. "We saved a nest last year and the new queens flew. We had to leave the village though. The Steward was angry."

Dyl's frown deepens. "You left a village?" he asks. "What village?"

Solma's belly clenches. This seems important to Dyl, though she can't think why.

"Sand's End," she admits reluctantly. "Southtip Province."

Dyl's eyebrows disappear under his woolen hat. "Oh," he says quietly. "Yes ... Whisperers came through a few months ago with that news. Norsen sent them away, but ..." he shakes his head and turns to Warren with ... what? Awe?

Solma puts a protective hand on her brother's shoulder.

"So?" she says. "This place. What is it?"

Yennevieve stands and takes a deep breath, the other kids fall quiet and watch her, as their spokesperson.

"This," she says, "is Skyheart Insect Haven. It's where kids with insect powers come and be safe. We call the insects here to help them grow so nobody tries to take them." She frowns at Solma with sudden suspicion. "People try and take them, you know," she says. "They think it'll make them rich. Only they just end up killing the insects like before." She fixes Solma with an intense stare. "You can't take them."

Solma remembers Blaiz, remembers Maxen, and shakes her head. "No," she says. "We don't want to."

Dyl peers at Solma with a twinkling, tawny gaze.

"Hmm," he says. "I don't reckon you will. Still, Norsen ain't gonna be happy you're here."

Solma meets his gaze with defiance. "What's your job here, then?" she demands. Dyl raises an eyebrow.

"Norsen trusts me," he says. "Don't trust many people, but he trusts me. I keep these kids safe."

His hand rests on his pistol. Solma feels her skin prickle but something tells her Dyl's not a threat. Not to her, at least. She turns to the children and smiles.

"Warren's like you," Solma says, "Hears the insects. We're trying to find where his bees went but we ain't seen any."

The Keeper children huddle together and watch Warren sympathetically. Yennevieve nods, looking pained. "That's horrible," she says. "It's so hard when you can't hear them. All six of us cried all winter when ours went."

Solma stares from the little girl to Warren and back again, thinking, not for the first time, how little she understands her brother's power. But these kids, they get it. They grasp his hands or squeeze his shoulder. They want to comfort him. Solma hadn't thought, before, how badly it *hurt* Warren that he couldn't hear his bees. For bees like Warren's, loneliness means death. Not just the death of a single bee, but the death of a colony. The death of a future.

Is that what Warren's feeling now?

"Hang on," Warren says, suddenly. "Did you say six of you? There's only five."

Yennevieve looks haunted. Her eyes dart. "We ..." she says, then stops. Jonah starts crying.

"Addie!" he wails, reaching out to be scooped up. Solma realizes he's reaching for *her*. She freezes, unsure what to do, but luckily Yennevieve heaves him onto her hip. Her face is ashen.

Dyl shakes his head as Yennevieve brings Jonah over to him for comfort. He wipes tears from the boy's cheeks.

"There *were* six," Dyl says quietly. "But—"

"But one was taken," says a voice behind them. "And we don't know where or by whom."

Solma tenses and automatically reaches for her weapons, before remembering she only has her knife. The bees dart for cover, their song frantic and upset. Warren and Taipan dive behind Solma's prosthetic leg as Solma turns to face Norsen.

"Ah, *hell!*" Dyl swears.

The village Steward stands at the far end of the glade. A tendon twitches in his jaw. Beside him stands a little boy with a mop of black hair. Solma recognizes him. The boy who was watching her by the fence. He catches her looking and smirks. Little wretch must've told Norsen he saw her. Solma glares, but it's Norsen she's worried about.

"I thought," the Steward says with dangerous quietness, "I asked you *not* to step into the forest."

Thirteen

SOLMA CHURNS THE FEAR in her gut to anger. She glowers.

"You did," she says through gritted teeth. "And now we know why."

The Keeper children slink away. Tobias and Jonah crawl into the tent and the girls slope off into the flowers. Taipan and Warren hide behind Solma's legs. Dyl shakes his head.

"This ain't what it looks like, Steward—"

"Quiet," Norsen growls. Dyl scowls but obeys.

The strange old man might not have immediately drawn Solma's favor but hearing him silenced by Norsen makes her his greatest champion. She lifts her chin, staring at Norsen with defiance.

"We're from Sand's End, Steward," she says. "You heard what happened there." Norsen says nothing. "My Steward tried to take the bees," Solma continues.

"His greed nearly killed them. When he realized he was gonna lose the nest, he tried to burn it. But we fought him. And now he's unconscious and his son's got bee-sting scars across half his face."

The memory of it kicks panic inside her but she battles it down. She still sees that scene playing out in her dreams: Warren's bees converging on Blaiz and Maxen. The screams as they disappeared under a writhing carpet of insects.

Maxen's face bursts into her mind again, puckered with damage, twisted with hate. She takes a breath to calm herself, hating that familiar echo of *weakness*.

Still, Norsen is silent. His expression is thunderous but there's uncertainty in his eyes, now.

"I ain't afraid of you," Solma tells him, and then wonders if it's true.

Her heart hammers and the roar of adrenalin in her ears makes her own voice sound distant. Something nudges her hand and she glances down to see Warren appear from behind her and intertwine his fingers with hers.

The other children are frozen, their huge eyes darting from Solma to Norsen and back again. Only the soft drone of bee song keeps the silence at bay.

Finally, Dyl shuffles forward to stand between Solma and his Steward.

"This ain't necessary," he grumbles. "No need for fighting."

Norsen is as tightly wound as a spring and his furious eyes are fixed on Solma.

"A child is *missing!*" he says through clenched teeth. Solma frowns, looking at Dyl as the old man's shoulders slump.

"I know that, Norsen," he says. "But you let them into the village for a reason, eh? And I think I know what that reason were."

He puts his hand on Warren's shoulder. "Whoever took our Addie," he continues. "I don't think it were them. And you don't neither."

Taipan pokes her head out from behind Solma's leg. "We only came 'cos we felt the signal," she whimpers. "We felt it from the kids. But we didn't know. We swear!"

Her orange eyes sparkle with tears. At last, Norsen lets out a long sigh. The mop-haired boy beside him looks like he's about to speak, but Norsen quiets him with a gesture.

"No," he agrees. "I don't think that."

He pinches the bridge of his nose, a deep frown on his brow, then turns to the mop-haired boy.

"Go tell the Captain to stand down," he says. "And then you can go for your dinner."

The boy beams, his squint deepening, and darts into the forest. Norsen turns back to Solma. The Keeper children, apparently satisfied the adults have stopped arguing, wander over to greet their Steward.

Now that Norsen no longer seems angry, they aren't shy. Jonah complains of Nessa's meanness and Nessa, affecting indignation, protests her innocence. Norsen ruffles Jonah's hair, has a stern word with Nessa and settles to asking them about their insects. The children become serious, rattling off reports, talking all over each other. Norsen frowns as he listens to them.

Solma watches for a bit and then turns her attention back to Norsen. Not like Blaiz Camber. No, in many ways, he's not. Blaiz would never have stooped to settling childish disputes or given kids like this such kindness and attention. But he *would* have hidden a glade full of insects and insect-Whispering kids. Solma rests her hand on the hilt of her hunting knife, just so Norsen's aware she isn't afraid to get nasty if she needs to.

Norsen sends the children off to tend their insects and clasps his hands behind his back. "I don't intend to harm you, Sergeant," he says. "Or your friends."

Solma flinches at his use of her old title.

"I'm not Sergeant anymore," she says. Norsen ignores her.

"But now we have a problem."

Solma glares, half-baring her teeth. "Yeah," she growls. "We do."

"Yeah!" Warren adds, though the tremble in his voice somewhat diminishes the sentiment. Norsen holds up his hand.

"I can't let you leave with this knowledge," Norsen continues. "You'll have to stay here until such time as I can be sure that my village is safe."

Solma gapes, then tugs her hunting knife free of its sheath.

"We ain't prisoners," she says, tucking Warren and Taipan behind her. "And we'll leave when we damn well want to."

There's a blur of movement and the click of metal behind her, the cold barrel of a pistol presses against her temple.

Taipan screams.

"Stop it!" Warren yells, but Dyl ignores him. The man had moved faster than Solma would have thought possible.

"Drop the knife, girl," he snarls. "I ain't afraid to shoot you."

Warren clutches his sister's shirt, wailing, but Solma hushes him. She carefully re-sheathes her knife and lifts her hands in surrender. The other children are frozen, watching. No-one moves. Even Jonah's too shocked to cry.

Norsen watches with a cool, detached expression.

"This is my village," he says. "And these children are under my care."

Solma glares, her skin tingling where the pistol presses against it.

"These children," she growls, "belong to the whole of Alphor."

"And how do you think Alphor would treat them?" Dyl growls. "Think the other Stewards'll respect their power? Treat them kindly? *Share?*"

"Like you're doing now, you mean?" Solma counters.

Norsen lifts his hand for quiet. "This is getting us nowhere," he says. "Drop the gun, Dyl."

Dyl grunts and does as he's told, keeping the pistol clutched at his side.

"I don't want to harm you," Norsen says. Solma doesn't believe him. "And perhaps you and I want the same thing."

Solma folds her arms. "What's that then?"

"Somewhere safe for your brother," Norsen says. "For all children like him. And for the insects to return to Alphor."

Solma raises an eyebrow, but says nothing.

Norsen sighs. "I'm sure the children have mentioned Addie?" he says.

Solma doesn't answer, but Warren isn't so stoic. "Yeah!" he admits. "Who is she, anyway? What happened to her—"

"Warren!" Solma hisses. Warren blinks up at her.

"What?" he asks. "It's true! They did—!"

Solma nudges him in the shoulder and he grumbles but at least stops giving everything away. Solma wonders when he'll *ever* learn to think before he speaks. She risks a glance at Norsen, whose face is expressionless, though his eyes sparkle with amusement.

"Perhaps it'd be better if I told you everything," Norsen admits. Solma's lips curls.

"Yeah," she says. "It would."

Norsen flinches at her tone, but refuses to rise. Instead, he gestures for Solma to follow him. "Let me show you what we're doing, here," he says. "And then I'll explain who Addie is. Maybe there's a way you and I can help each other."

Fourteen

OLIVE'S EYEBROWS RISE so high they disappear under her green bandanna.

"So," she says, scratching at her bandaged leg. "Norsen tells us not to go into the forest. You—typical Solma—*do* go into the woods, find a bunch of insect-Whispering kids in a secret glade and now we ain't allowed to leave."

Solma bites her lip and six pairs of angry eyes glare at her.

"Yeah," she says. "That about sums it up."

Bell rounds on her.

"What'd I tell you, girl?" she snaps. "I warned you! And now look—"

Roseann puts a hand on Bell's arm and Solma's aunt huffs but quells.

"Sit down, 'Bella," Roseann mutters. Bell throws her a furious look but sits.

They're around the table at the little house Norsen has appointed them for their (now extended) stay. Mamba and Cobra sit together. Solma and Olive are next to each other in awkward silence. Beside Roseann, Ana is half-asleep on the table. Bell fixes Solma with a knife-like glare.

Mid-morning sun streams through the window above the stove, highlighting the knots in the wood of the table. A few half-drunk mugs of long-cold tea sit amongst the gathering.

Ana shifts uneasily. She still looks ill, and Mamba and Cobra don't look much better. Since their visit to the glade, though, Taipan has color back in her cheeks and her sickness has lifted. Solma hears hers and Warren's voices drifting through the open door to the bedroom, where the pair are reporting their adventure to the three Whisperer boys. Solma frowns as she listens. Warren's voice is animated, but Taipan, despite feeling less queasy, is morose and quiet.

Cobra steeples her fingers on the table and leans forward. "Right," she says. "Tell us again."

Solma sighs, but, despite her frustration, tells the story one more time.

Norsen began by leading her round the glade. It was a small clearing with long grasses and a blush of wildflowers. The dandelions and daisies were packed with hungry bees and butterflies. Hoverflies darted around the snowdrops and crocuses. While Warren played with the other children, poor Taipan tagging along behind him in sullen silence, Solma marveled at the unceasing song of the insects. Blue butterflies drew weaving flights

between flowers while bees zig-zagged across the clearing. They buzzed happily around flower heads before fluttering or buzzing home.

Home had been different for each insect. Tobias' butterflies rested on the branches of the nearby trees, their wings pressed together like the petals of flowers. Nessa's hoverflies weren't fussy, grabbing naps on any surface they could find, though they seemed to prefer tree trunks at night, Nessa explained. Leiff's ashy mining bees dug burrows in patches of bare soil the children prepared for them. Jonah's false oil beetles slept inside flowers and, it turned out, there was some tension between these two children, as Jonah's beetles fed on Leiff's bees as larvae.

Norsen smiled and shrugged when Solma expressed her horror. "That's life," he said. "Sometimes it's beautiful, sometimes it's ugly. But we need both bees *and* beetles if Alphor is to return to health. Leiff and

Jonah both understand that. They're very special children."

Clearly, Solma thought, watching as Leiff helped Jonah count his beetles, and pointed out the nests of her own bees that were failing so Jonah could direct his beetles to eat those.

Yennevieve's honeybees were extraordinary. With pride, Norsen showed Solma the three hives the children and Dyl had built. They were haphazard towers of boxes and drawers with lids of specially prepared wood to keep out rain. The bees oozed from the entrance, zooming like little comets back and forth.

Norsen led her back to the camouflage tents, where Warren knelt with Leiff and watched as Leiff explained the life cycle of her bees. Solma felt his pain properly for the first time, then. Here were these children who understood him, showing off their own power, their own link to the life around him, and his bees were nothing but last summer's memory. She tried to push that thought aside. Nothing she could do about that.

"So," she asked Norsen. "Who's Addie, then?"

Norsen's face tensed. "This way," he'd said. He led Solma over to the furthest corner of the glade, pointing to an oak tree on the perimeter. "Look there."

Solma looked and her mouth fell open. The oak's bark was covered in hundreds—*thousands*—of paper-thin, rustling wings. It took a moment to work out what she was seeing, but as the insects stirred, she realized it was another species of butterfly. This one red and brown, with what looked like bright eyes decorating its wingtips. She turned back to Norsen, confused.

"They're beautiful," she said. Norsen shook his head.

"They're dying," he countered. And that's when he'd told her about Addie.

Six-years-old and the first child in the village to come into her power. When the villagers had seen her butterflies, they'd thought she was some kind of witch, but Norsen had understood what was happening. Swiftly, he created this woodland haven for her, where she could be safe from the confusion of the villagers. He'd wanted, he claimed, to share her gift with Alphor, but the suspicion and, later, the greed of his own people had convinced him Alphor wasn't ready yet. Not until the insects had sufficient numbers to survive without their child Keepers anymore. (Solma had raised her eyebrow at this. She wondered if Blaiz justified his own greed to himself this way. But she'd said nothing.)

Other miracle children started to show themselves. Most from Skyheart, but some exiled from nearby villages for a power misunderstood by their own people. It was interesting, Solma thought, that all these children had sprung up from nearby. Something about that didn't sit right with her, but she didn't mention it. Let Norsen set his own trap. He'd slip up eventually, and Solma would be waiting to pounce.

Jonah, Norsen explained, had been carried here on the hip of his older sister, who'd collapsed as soon as she'd handed him to Norsen, and was recovering in the village. Nessa, somehow, had made it here alone and, according to Norsen, hadn't spoken a word for the first four months. Solma found that hard to believe.

For the last year, the children had been safe here, living in this haven with their insects, under Norsen's protection.

"But a month ago," Norsen admitted, "Addie disappeared. The children woke up one morning and she was gone. She'd left her shoes by the tent entrance, but her robes were missing. There was no sign of a struggle. There was no sign of *anything*. It was like she'd simply risen in the night and flown away. We've no idea where she is, or if she's even still alive." He shook his head, running one hand over his scalp in frustration. "The villagers don't know. All they know is that when a child arrives with a power like Addie's, I place them somewhere safe. The village gets the benefit of insects to pollinate our crop and flowers, but they don't know where the nests are. They know anyone entering the forest is either arrested or shot. They're angry and resentful and ... well, they *can't* know about Addie.

"The other children miss her. They're frightened. They're trying to take care of Addie's butterflies, but they can't speak with them. The butterflies miss their Keeper. Every day, more of them die."

He gestured at the ground around the oak, where the bodies of fallen butterflies lay in an ever-thickening carpet. Solma's heart lurched. Alphor had seen this before. Humans had *caused* this before.

Solma hadn't known what to say, but Norsen escorted her, Warren and Taipan to the village with the mop-haired boy.

"I don't think Addie ran away," he'd said when they reached the house in the village. "I think she was taken."

And with that, he and the mop-haired boy had left.

Solma finishes her story and falls quiet. Cobra nods, frowning. Everyone is silent except Bell, who mutters under her breath. Solma glares at her. At last, Cobra speaks again.

"How did Norsen say he plans to keep us here?" she asks.

Solma chews her lower lip. "Well, he's got this fence, ain't he?"

"But you know there's a weakness in it," Cobra points out.

"Yeah," Solma squirms under their scrutiny. How does she always manage to mess up so hugely? "Well, actually ... he don't want us to stay in the village. He wants me and Warren and the Whisperers to stay in the glade."

Five mouths fall open and Bell shakes her head firmly.

"No," she says. "The children need warm beds and good meals! He can't—"

Roseann's hand touches Bell's arm and Bell falls into a sullen silence. Solma raises her eyebrow. She's impressed.

"He can," Solma says. "But look, I got an idea. Dyl, the guardian at the glade, is quick and fierce but there's loads of us and only one of him. We could wait 'til dark and then—"

Mamba holds up a hand. "Wait," he says. "Didn't you say there was a kid missing? They've lost a ... what did he call them? A *Keeper* child, right?"

Solma frowns. "Yes," she says slowly. "But that's not—"

"I think it *is* our business, actually," Cobra pipes up before Solma can finish her sentence. Foreboding prickles in Solma's blood. This isn't what she had in mind. They need to get away from here. They need to get *Warren* away from here. Something's going on in this village, and it's not safe. It's not—

"I vote we stay and help," Ana says, lifting her head from the table. "Norsen doesn't trust us. If one of his kids is missing, then he's right not to trust us. But if we can find her and bring her back, he'll let us go freely. If we fight him and try to leave, he'll hunt us. We can't afford to make more enemies than we already have."

Solma's mouth falls open. "That," she drawls, "is a daft plan."

"Actually, it isn't," Cobra says, smiling at Ana. Solma opens her mouth to protest and then realizes that Bell and Roseann are both nodding and Mamba grabs Cobra's hand and squeezes it.

"You can't—" Solma stutters. "This is—you're all—"

She throws her hands up in frustration. This is ridiculous. Did they all lose their wits in the mountains? This is Blaiz Camber all over again! Norsen's just as bad. They're *all* just as bad. Greedy Stewards who think only of their own wealth. If they're not stopped, they'll cause another Hive War. They'll wipe the insects out all over again and half of Alphor's human population with it. What don't the Whisperers get about that? Don't they *see?*

They need to leave. They need to get Warren away from here. They need to find his bees and keep him safe—

Cobra turns her green eyes on Solma and Solma finds she can't hold her friend's gaze.

"I know what's worrying you," Cobra says.

"I bet you don't," Solma grumbles. But it doesn't surprise her when Cobra recounts Solma's thoughts as if reading them out of Solma's own head.

"We all love Warren, Sol," Cobra says. "We all want to keep him safe. But it sounds like this is bigger than him now. It sounds like we're needed here."

Solma scowls. "Norsen don't deserve our help!" she snaps.

Olive raises an eyebrow. "Maybe," she says. "And maybe not. But I reckon those Keeper kids *do.*"

And Solma can't really argue with that, can she? Although she tries.

"They ain't our problem," she says. "But Warren—"

Bell springs up suddenly, bashing her palm against the table. "Stop being so selfish, girl!" she yells, making everyone jump.

"Bell!" Roseann snaps. "Knock it off, would you?"

Bell rounds on her. "Don't you tell me to knock it off!"

Ana groans. Mamba rises to try and calm things and gets an earful from both Bell and Roseann.

Eventually, Olive stands and limps over to Bell and Roseann, standing between them. She glares at her mother and then at Bell.

"Sit down," she growls. "'fore I bash both your heads together. And don't even *think,*" she says to Bell, "about telling me off. *Sit.*"

Bell and Roseann both sit. Mamba flops back into his chair and takes Cobra's hand. He looks tired, Solma thinks. They all do. They sit in silence for a bit, lost in their own, morose thoughts.

It's Cobra who eventually speaks. "Look," she says calmly, "the answer to this is obvious. The signal came from this village and it felt, to all of us, like we *needed* to come here. It must be something to do with the Keeper children. Warren sensed bees here and now there's a missing child in the mix. We need to be here."

Olive closes her eyes and sighs through her nose. "We're trouble magnets," she laments. "The lot of us."

She qualifies this with such a vivid string of swear-words that even Roseann raises an eyebrow.

Solma's eyes dart towards the bedroom where Warren is still holding court with the other youngsters. Her heart feels like it's been driven through with splinters.

After Norsen and the mop-haired boy had left them at the door, Warren had turned to her, little fists clenched.

"We're staying," he told her. "Even if Norsen would let us go, I want to stay. We *got* to stay."

And with that, he and Taipan had turned and stalked into the house before Solma could protest.

Apparently, she's the only one that thinks this is a terrible idea.

Mamba rubs his temple and sighs.

"I think Cobra's right," he says. "The truth is, this might be bigger than all of us."

Despite her frustration, Solma's lip quirks into a smile. Mamba *always* thinks Cobra's right. He looks at her as if she's the center of his whole world and he's lucky just to be on the same planet. Cobra nudges him playfully and their eyes meet. Solma sees the electricity crackling between them and her heart kicks. Olive looks at her like that. *Looked* at her like that. But Olive hasn't met her eye in days.

"Nah," Cobra says, winking at him. "It's nothing you can't handle."

Mamba tries and fails to hide his grin and Solma can't help but smile. The boy's smitten and Cobra's totally in charge. It would be cute, if watching it didn't hurt so much. Solma's fingers itch to hold Olive's hand but she doesn't dare reach out.

"I still think we should leave," she says weakly. "Soon as we can. It ain't safe here."

"It ain't safe anywhere, Sol," says Warren, making everyone jump. He and the Whisperer children have emerged from the bedroom and he's glaring at his sister. Solma swallows the bitter lump in her throat.

"Warren," she says, but he stamps his foot.

"No!" he cries. "You didn't listen to me before and you should have! I told you there was bees here. I keep telling you but you never listen. You always think you're right and you ain't!"

His voice cracks and a sob escapes. Solma's heart squeezes as she watches him struggle to control his tears, to stay calm, to be *grown up* even though it's beyond him.

"I need my bees," he says. "And they're here somewhere. I know they are. I got to find them. And I got to help the other kids. We *all* got to."

Behind him, the Whisperer children nod solemnly.

"Warren," Solma says. she stands, ready to go to him. "Warren, listen—"

But he backs away from her. "You can't fix it with a hug, Solma!" he snaps. "Go away!"

"Warren!" Bell barks "Be nice to your sister!"

He scowls at her and pokes out his tongue.

"I'm staying!" he says. "If you don't like it, Sol, then you can *leave!*"

And with that, he and the Whisperer children scurry for the door.

"Warren!" Solma and Bell bark at the same time. He ignores them, throwing the door open and charging towards the forest, his friends in tow.

Olive throws up her hands and sighs. "Great," she says. "This is going well."

Solma glares. "Yeah, thanks for your help," she grumbles. She looks up just in time to see the flicker of hurt in Olive's eyes and tastes the bitter tang of guilt in her throat. Why does she always *do* this?

"Sorry," she mutters, reaching for Olive's hand. Olive doesn't move when Solma's fingertips brush hers, but she doesn't respond either. She stares at the floor until Solma withdraws, reddening. This isn't working out the way she'd hoped. It's all going wrong. Again. And it's because *she* can't do the right thing.

"I'd better go find them," she says, grabbing her prosthesis from under her chair and tightening it onto her leg. "Before they wander too far."

There are murmurs of agreement all round and Solma can't wait to get out of here. She's just annoying everyone. She heads to the door, hand on the hilt of her knife. She curses Bell again for hiding their firearms, but she reckons Norsen will confiscate them soon, anyway. He won't want them armed if he's trying to keep them contained.

And, as if she'd summoned him with that thought, when she pulls the door open, she finds her path blocked. Norsen stands there, one hand on the shoulder of the mop-haired boy. Solma scowls and the boy blinks through his squint and smirks.

Fifteen

AT THE SIGHT OF the Steward, Solma's hands tighten around the hilt of her knife.

"Steward," she says. She's trying not to be rude but she can hear how spectacularly she's failing. "I'm sorry, I—"

She tries to push past him but Norsen doesn't move. He smiles. Solma's scowl deepens.

"Solma?" Bell's says from inside. She descends into a fluster when she sees who's at the door. "Earth's sake, girl!" she squeals. "Invite him in!"

Solma slowly steps aside, glowering as Norsen steps past her with the mop-haired boy in tow. Solma watches with narrowed eyes as they head towards the table. The boy flops into a chair and immediately stands again at a sharp look from his Steward. Embarrassed, he smooths his fringe over his forehead and his squint deepens in embarrassment. He's pale-skinned,

Solma notices, and the contrast between his hair and his complexion is striking. Just like her own. The thought makes her breath catch for a moment.

This boy looks like she does. Like her Dja did. Could he have come from the same place as her father?

The boy glances up, catches Solma's eye and gives her a gap-toothed grin. Solma glares at him, but his squint is so severe that she wonders if he can see anything through it. She can't even make out the color of his eyes. Nonetheless, Solma can't shake the feeling that he's oddly familiar. But maybe it's just that he looks like she does, that he reminds her of her Dja. The boy turns to Norsen.

"Why we here again?" he asks.

"Because I have a job for you, Ig," Norsen replies.

He gazes around the room, reading the expressions of the assembled group. No-one has moved. Mamba and Ana watch Norsen with barely concealed suspicion. Roseann doesn't bother to look at him at all, but Olive is about as subtle as Solma has been and glares openly.

There's no time for this. Solma glances out the still open door, hoping that Warren is hiding nearby to sulk. But there's no sign of him. She needs to find him and the Whisperer kids. They can't just be left to wander off alone.

"Close the door, Solma," Bell says, bringing two mugs of steaming broth to the table, "with you on this side of it. The kids'll be fine." She offers

the food to Norsen and Ig. Norsen declines but Ig snatches his without thanks and slurps the contents.

Solma scowls. For a lingering moment, she considers disobeying. What's Bell going to do if she darts outside and hares after Warren? Bell's got a mean right hook, but she's got to catch Solma first. Curiosity stills her, though. She doesn't like the idea of Warren and the Whisperer children out there alone, but she likes the idea of leaving Norsen with the rest of her family even less.

Grumbling, she closes the door and stalks back to the table, flopping into a chair and propping her prosthetic leg up on the seat. She glares at Ig, daring him to challenge her for the chair. He shrugs again, his attention occupied by his mug of broth.

Greedy kid.

"I'd like to introduce you to Ig," Norsen says, ruffling the boy's hair. Ig endures the affection with obvious embarrassment.

"Huh?" he says, apparently by way of greeting. He puts his mug down and some loose droplets of broth spill onto the table. Bell's brows draw together in an angry line, but Ig doesn't notice. He wipes his mouth with the back of his hand.

"Hi?" he tries again.

Olive raises an eyebrow. "Hi, Ig," she smirks. "You got something on your chin."

Ig paws at his face but fails to remove the offending article. He goes back to his mug of broth.

"Ig's been with us since the beginning of winter," Norsen says, clapping the kid on his shoulder. "Lost both his parents in the northern snows and no-one else in his village could take him in. He took his chances in the wild and came to us, didn't you, Ig?"

The boy peers up at Norsen through thick lashes and nods gormlessly. "Yeah."

Solma catches Olive's eye and the two of them look away again quickly to avoid snorting with laughter. It feels good to share a moment with Olive again.

"In fact," Norsen continues, "he brought Tobias to us just before the snows came. He's a good kid, but he needs purpose and I've asked Dyl to train him. He'll stay with you in the glade and if you have messages for the village, he'll carry them for you."

Ig's smile falters. "I will?"

Norsen nods. "Yes, son, you will." He catches Solma's eye. "And he's to act with courtesy at all times. I'll want a report on how he gets on."

Solma frowns. It's clear Ig is there to keep an eye on her, not the other way round. She sighs. No point arguing until she understands more about what's going on here. Solma knows how to bide her time.

"You want him to help Dyl protect the Keeper kids, right?" she asks. She's trying to be polite but there's clearly enough of an edge to her voice that Bell fixes her with a glare. Norsen nods.

"Yes," he says. "That's the idea."

Solma gestures towards the door. "But your Gatra are well-trained," she points out. "I seen them. And your Captain Reya seems a tough type. Why don't you station them at the glade?"

It's a good enough question that every pair of eyes in the room turns to Norsen. Solma smirks as he shifts his weight uncomfortably.

"That's not your concern," he says. "This is my village and I organize it as I see fit."

It's not a good enough answer. Solma knows it isn't and feels a swell of triumph. Olive leans forward, her brows drawn together.

"Solma's right though," she says. "Seems a bit odd that you got all these precious children out in the middle of the forest with no-one but an Aldren and a Yuen to protect them?"

Ig shuffles awkwardly and flattens his fringe, blinking at the floor. Norsen, however, now looks like he's getting angry.

"I don't have to justify my decisions to a group of strangers," he growls. "You will stay in the glade with the children. You will form part of their guard and Warren will spend time with the other Keeper children, where he belongs. Dyl reinforces a chemical boundary around the glade every evening to keep predators out and the insects in. You will be safe. But you went against my word and now there are consequences."

"Like what?" Olive challenges, rising from her chair. She's still unsteady on her injured leg but it's enough of a challenge that everyone in the room stiffens. Solma's hand goes automatically to her hunting knife. Norsen glares.

"As you said," he replies smoothly, "my Gatra are well-trained. If you try to leave, it won't be a problem to hunt you down."

And there it is. The threat Solma's been waiting for. Just like Blaiz. Just like Maxen. She hopes the others see it now. She tugs her hunting knife free of its sheath, loudly enough to draw Norsen's attention.

"We don't take kindly to threats," she growls.

Norsen sighs, closing his eyes. Beside him, Ig burps.

"I'm not trying to threaten you, Sergeant," he says. "I'm just trying to keep my village and these children safe."

There's a long, complicated silence. Blood roars in Solma's ears but she can't tell if it's from anger or fear. A phantom itch prickles in her missing leg. She needs to find Warren. This village isn't safe. Norsen can't be trusted. She glares at him, hoping he can feel her mistrust and loathing. She knows what he is. He's just like the others. Greedy, selfish, thoughtless—

At last, Norsen averts his gaze.

"I gather, Sergeant," he says quietly, "that you and your squadmate are both excellent shots. I'm sure the children in the glade would sleep easier knowing you were watching over them."

Solma says nothing.

It's Olive who speaks. "You'll let us keep our firearms?" she asks, eyes narrowed. Norsen thinks, then nods slowly.

"Some of them," he says. "For now. I'm willing to believe you want to protect the children more than you want to take them." He fixes Solma with a hard stare. "You care a lot about your brother, Sergeant."

Solma glares back and wonders where this is going.

"Yeah," she says. "I do."

"Then I would ask," Norsen says, "that if anyone threatens him or the other children, whether you know them or not, that you do not hesitate to do what's necessary to protect them. Will you do that?"

Solma stares. Confused, Olive flops back into her seat. Ana lifts her head from the table and the complicated silence descends again while everyone tries to work out what's going on. Solma holds Norsen's gaze. Something weird is happening. Something she doesn't understand. Her eyes flicker towards Olive for a moment and she wishes they were alone together so they could talk about it.

Or alone so they could *not* talk about it.

Solma feels this tug under her solar plexus, pulling her towards Olive. Towards the one person with whom she doesn't feel she needs to be tough. Olive will know what to do. But right now, she's staring hard at Norsen and seems to have forgotten that Solma's there.

Olive sighs. "You could be here forever waiting for her to answer you," she says. "We'll get our stuff and head out shortly."

Solma scowls as Bell hurries into the bedroom. There comes a series of bangs and crashes and a sound very much like a floorboard being wrenched up. Bell returns with two pistols in their holsters and both Olive's and Solma's rifle. She places the firearms on the table for Olive and Solma to collect and the Whisperers rise, casting puzzled glances towards Norsen. Ig scratches his nose and sniffs loudly, peering at his Steward through his thick lashes and long fringe. Solma almost feels sorry for him. She's certain she could take this kid out with one good kick to the shin. He's no threat to them at all.

Dyl, on the other hand ...

"Norsen, I should find my brother," Solma says. "Thank you for visiting—"

"Oh, don't worry about him," Ig pipes up, grabbing his mug from the table and holding it out to Bell with the expectation of a refill. (Bell scowls and gives him no such thing,) "I saw him an' the others heading up the path towards the glade. He knows where he's going. He'll be there by now."

Solma feels a tightness loosen in her core. Just a little. Having Warren out of her sight makes her squirm with unease.

"Still," she says. "I got to check on him."

Norsen inclines his head. "Of course," he says. "Ig can take you."

Solma bristles at the smoothness in his voice. Blaiz was good at that, too: pretending to agree with people and all the while hiding his greed under that disguise.

Solma hitches up her rifle.

"I can make my own way, thanks," she says, more harshly than she'd intended.

Everyone looks at her.

"Sol," Olive tries, gently. She brings Solma's pistol and rifle to her and her hand brushes Solma's arm. Solma wants to reach back, clasp that hand and close this agonizing distance between them. But bitterness swirls in her mouth and she can't believe Olive, of all people, is agreeing with Norsen. Olive, who'd called Solma out on her own similar mistakes last year.

You're being a fool, Sol.

And oh, she *had* been a fool. But who's the fool now? Solma marches to the door before Olive can touch her. She clenches her jaw. *You're a fool, Olive.*

She doesn't say it, but she's sure Olive can tell she's thinking it.

Never again. Whatever Norsen's up to, Solma's not planning to leave it unexposed. She pulls the door closed behind her and doesn't look back.

Sixteen

WARREN DOESN'T PAUSE FOR breath as they reach the fault in the fence. He ducks through and he would keep running, except four voices call out behind him.

"Hey, Warren!"

"Where you going?"

He skids to a halt and turns. The Whisperer children stand in a line on the inside of the fence, peering at him.

"We should go back and get Solma," Krait says meekly.

"Or Olive," Habu agrees. "We shouldn't go into the forest on our own."

Warren sighs. "They're all too busy arguing," he says. "Just like always. It's got to be up to us. I know my bees are here and maybe those other kids have seen them. We got to go!"

The boys mutter and scuff their bare feet against the dirt. They're obviously scared. Warren gets it. It has been scary lately, but they can talk about that on the way. It won't take Solma long to come after them and try to stop Warren because she's got this weird thing about getting everything completely wrong before she gets it even remotely right.

"Come *on!*" Warren begs, but the boys don't budge. He looks to Taipan for support. "You're coming, right?"

Taipan scowls, her orange eyes ablaze. She doesn't look scared, actually. She just looks angry, like he's done something wrong.

"Tai?"

She folds her arms. "We should wait for Solma and Olive," she says. "Kids are going missing."

Warren gapes. "It's just one kid," he points out. "Anyway, it's Keeper kids, not Whisperer kids. You lot don't need to worry."

Taipan flinches like she's been struck. "Us lot," she echoes. "I thought you were one of *us lot.*"

"I am," Warren splutters, confused. "I mean, I was ... but now ..." he gazes towards the trees, where he feels the constant call of insects pulling him towards the glade. He knows the others feel the pull of that place, too. They've been feeling it for weeks.

And as if on cue, Habu doubles over and throws up. The others rush to comfort him.

"Urgh," he groans. "Stupid signal."

Warren brightens. "Taipan's been feeling loads better since she went to the glade!" he points out. "You need to go there and then you'll stop being sick!"

The boys don't look convinced. Taipan turns her blazing eyes on Warren. "You can't run off," she tells him. Warren frowns. That's funny because she was perfectly happy to run off into the woods before. It was *her* idea that time. What's got into her?

"I thought you wanted to help?" he says. "You were gonna help us find Addie and my bees?"

"Yeah, we will," King says, looking unsure. "But if there's someone grabbing kids then maybe we shouldn't go by ourselves—"

"Look," Warren says, imploring. "I got to go. I know it's not the same for you all because you're not Keepers—"

Taipan folds her arms. "Yeah," she says, her voice as sharp and mean as she can make it. "We're not Keepers. And you're supposed to be one of us, Warren. We took you in. We gave you our food. You're *our friend* so you should listen—"

Warren's too impatient to let her finish. "It's different now!" he bursts out. "I ain't the only one, am I?"

The Whisperer children stare at him in silence. Even Habu, his face green with nausea, looks disappointed.

"Go on then," Taipan says, turning her back on him. Warren's not certain, but he thinks he hears a tremble in her voice. "Never mind us. We're *just* Whisperers. Go back to your Keeper friends. See if we care."

Warren stares at the back of her shaved head. What's happening? This isn't how it's supposed to be. He needs them. They can't just turn their backs on him—

But that's exactly what they all do. One after the other.

"Sorry, Warren," King murmurs as he turns. They start to walk away.

"Tai?" Warren calls, his insides curdling as he watches his friend—the best friend he's ever had—heading away from him. "Taipan?"

Her shoulders tense at his voice but she doesn't turn round. She keeps walking and the boys follow, leaving Warren by himself on the other side of the fence. He stamps his foot.

"Fine!" he yells after them. "I'm not one of you anyway. I don't need you, then, do I?"

He wipes the back of his arm across his eyes as they prickle with hot, angry tears. "Stupid Whisperers," he mutters, hating the way his voice quakes. He turns and charges into the forest. Never mind them. He doesn't need them. He's not a Whisperer, he's a Keeper, like Yenn and the others.

He knows where he belongs.

But he can't make the tears stop. Every time he wipes them away, new ones are there ready to spill down his cheeks. He hates crying, but that doesn't stop it happening all the time.

Everyone's losing it. His sister's determined to mess everything up as usual, the Whisperers are all acting weird. Everyone's arguing about nothing and in the meantime, there's bees in that forest and no one is listening! He kicks at a tree and stubs his toe, which only makes him cry harder.

There's a buzz in the back of his mind. Actually, there's a lot of different buzzes. Layer after layer of insect song, floating through his thoughts. Honeybees sound so different to his buff-tails. The buff-tails were all bumble and bluster, the bulldozers of the bee world. Their strength and patience were so beautiful. Warren aches for it. Honeybees feel different, though. The timbre of their song is purposeful. There's an energy to them that Warren can't catch hold of yet. There are thousands of them, yes. Thousands of individual bees, with their own fears, their own purpose, shaped by memory. And then there's the whole. The *hive*. He feels it in his brain like a single, living entity. It's not just the queens speaking, it's *all* the bees, speaking in the harmony of a hundred thousand voices, all saying the same thing.

And they say ...

Help us.

Warren clutches his head until the voices inside dull a little. The trouble is it isn't just the honeybees. He feels the darting flight of the butterflies. Soundless but full of flashing color. He hears Leiff's ashy mining bees, zipping from flower to flower. They're loners, those bees, bickering occasionally. Jonah's beetles upset Warren. They're hungry for solitary bees, lying in wait on flowers until they can snag their prey and lay their eggs on it. Warren feels their hunger. He shivers. Nessa's hoverflies are more sweet-natured. Their song is muted in Warren's head and they're flighty, distract-ed things, darting around in zig-zag shapes.

But the honeybees ...

It's like nothing Warren's ever felt before. The vastness of that mind-that-is-not-a-mind. The intelligence. The oneness. It's both alien and wonderfully familiar in Warren's head. The buzz of every lone bee adding a single note to the whole, impossible chord. And it sings ...

Help us.

"Stop it!" Warren moans, clutching his head again. "I can't think when you're all buzzing about in there like that!"

"When who's buzzing where?" says a voice.

Warren yelps. He's no idea how Yennevieve managed to move so quietly, but she's right in front of him, staring with those intense, brown eyes. Warren blinks, then looks around, realizing he's made it to the insect glade without even noticing.

"No one," he answers quickly. "Nowhere. I'm fine."

Yennevieve cocks her head, unconvinced. She chews her lower lip and Warren notices that honeybees orbit her as if they are tiny planets and she their brilliant sun.

"Where's your friend?" she asks, looking past him. "That girl?"

"Taipan?" Warren asks in a small voice. He stares at his feet, not sure whether to be furious with Taipan or just to miss her. "She ... didn't want to come."

Yennevieve watches him, then shrugs. "Oh well," she says. "She probably just doesn't get it. Why don't you come have something to eat? Ever tried honey before?"

Warren blinks. "No," he admits. "What's honey?"

Yennevieve smiles. "It's—"

But whatever she says is drowned out by the chatter of honeybees in Warren's mind. Thousands of them talking at once.

Life and—

Sweet sustenance

Flower flower flower

Wing fuel

Is there enough?

Life and—

It's ours! It's ours!

Sugar sticky sweet

Warren shakes his head again and the buzzing fades, but the bees around Yennevieve seem agitated, their song growing harsher. Yennevieve closes her eyes, her lips forming words Warren can't quite hear. But he can ... *smell* them. She's talking bee. That strange, chemical language made of wing-buzz and scent.

It's alright, Yennevieve tells the bees. *We won't take more than we need. The boy needs to eat. The hive won't starve.*

The bees hover anxiously around Yennevieve's head. They aren't convinced. But they power off towards their hive, anyway, going about their business without complaint.

Yennevieve opens her eyes and smiles. "Sorry about that," she says. "It's hard to produce honey and they get a bit possessive about it. I was just—"

"Calming them down," Warren says. "I know. I heard."

Yennevieve's eyes widen momentarily. "You—?"

She pauses as a bee buzzes over, circles her head once, then lands on her palm. Warren steps closer, fascinated, as the bee waggles from side to side then rushes round in a half circle and performs the strange waggle again.

"Is it sick?" he asks, concerned. Yennevieve laughs.

"No, silly," she says. "She's dancing."

Warren frowns. He can't help but feel that's ridiculous, but it wouldn't be polite to say so, and Yennevieve is watching the bee with utmost concentration. When the bee has performed her strange routine several times, she powers her engine, hovering a few inches from Yennevieve's face.

"Thank you, little friend," Yennevieve says, and the bee zooms off. Warren watches it go, marveling at the noise of it all. The incessant, never-ceasing, ever-harmonizing cacophony of constant *sound*. They buzz-flutter-zoom-dart-sing. Warren's never known the sky to sound so full before.

But it's still empty of the thing most precious to him. Where's the deep, rumbling tremolo of buff-tails? He knows they're near. He feels them on the edge of his mind. The ache returns so forcefully he clutches his belly. Earth, he misses them.

"Come on," Yenn says. "We'll take some from Foxglove's hive. She's the oldest queen and her workers are strongest."

Warren has no idea what that means, but he *is* hungry, and the closer he gets to the honeybee hive, the duller the ache of missing his own bees feels. He plods after Yennevieve as she leads him towards the hives. Warren peers towards the camouflaged tents and spots Leiff kneeling by the bare earth where her bees nest. The other children wander about through the flowers, intent on their tasks. All the while, the sky is full of song. Sunlight catches on purple butterfly wings or shines off the stripy fur of the bees. Despite the ache, Warren smiles.

His bees would love it here.

"Here we are!" Yenn says, stopping outside the tallest hive. Several hundred bees rush out to greet her, coating her sleeves with a carpet of bodies. Yennevieve whispers that strange scent-language again, pulling out a drawer in the top of the beehive. Warren gets a flash of that fragrance again. The calming words Yennevieve speaks to the bees.

It's ok. It's ok.

She reaches into the drawer and, from it, lifts a tray coated in bees. She whispers again and the bees disperse, leaving the tray exposed.

Warren gasps.

The tray glistens with a deep, golden liquid, that's oozing down its surface, coating everything it touches in a thick glaze. In the sun, the liquid gleams like something ancient and precious and Warren breathes in the sugary scent.

"Honey," Yenn says. She holds her finger under the flow of liquid, then pops it in her mouth. Her eyes close and she shudders with delight.

"Mmm," she says. "Try it! It's the yummiest thing you'll ever taste."

Warren frowns. He's not sure about that. Yennevieve's never tried Aunt Bell's cooking. But he's curious, and the sugary scent is tempting. He reaches out a tentative hand and lets the golden stuff ooze onto his finger.

"Now, put it on your tongue," Yenn says. "And try not to cry with happiness."

Warren pops the fresh honey into his mouth and realizes Yennevieve was not in the least bit joking. It's so sweet it almost stings his tongue, an electrified thing in his mouth. It coats the back of his teeth, oozes down his throat, the impossible, intense sweetness lingering long enough that he wants more, more, more. There are tears in his eyes. He holds back a sob. Earth, if Solma could taste this! For the first time in a long time, he wishes his sister was with him. He wishes he hadn't snapped at her so much. She's just trying to keep him safe, even though it is suffocating him.

If she tried the honey, maybe she'd see. Maybe she'd understand.

"That's—" he says, but he doesn't know what it is.

"That's honey," Yenn says, puffing up proudly. "Before we lost the bees, ancient humans used to live on it. They used to seek out honeybee hives, climbing the tallest trees just to get a taste! They were heroes when they returned. It was more precious than the brightest jewels. Until it wasn't anymore, and we forgot how it kept us alive for thousands of years."

She looks sad and Warren wants to cheer her up. "Honey?" he suggests, holding his finger back under the endless ooze. "It really is the yummiest thing I've ever tasted." Though, somehow, that phrase doesn't do it justice. Yennevieve smiles and takes another fingerful for herself. They eat until the bees grow restless.

"Better put it back," Yenn says, gently sliding the tray back into place, and pushing the drawer closed. "They work hard making it, it's not fair to take too much."

"No," Warren says, trying and failing to keep the disappointment from his voice.

Yennevieve studies him. "You can hear my bees too, can't you?"

Warren nods. "Yeah," he says. "They're very loud. They're the loudest insects in the glade."

Yenn blinks at him, chewing her lip again. There's a little bulb of honey still gleaming on her chin. "You can hear the other insects, too, can't you?" she asks. Warren shrugs.

"Yeah," he says, casting a dark glance over his shoulder to where Tobias and Jonah play outside the tents. "I don't like the oil beetles very much."

"Hmm," Yenn says. "That's very interesting. Would you like to meet my other hives? My other two queens are called Primrose and Orchid."

Warren frowns at his hands, wondering what Yennevieve finds so interesting. The question lingers on his tongue, like the taste of honey, but he's too afraid to ask.

Instead, he just says, "Yeah, okay then."

~ Orchid ~

THERE'S SO MUCH DANCING but none of it makes sense. The workers are discordant. Their wing beats clash. It hurts to hear them. I wander through the endless combs, an entourage surrounding me. Every time I stop, they rush to my aid. Groom. Feed. Usher. But I feel their anxious song vibrate through the comb. The dancing makes no sense and I am not laying as I should be.

I'm a mother now, to several thousand larval bees, all curled in comb cells, fattening as they're fed. But most of these bees are my sisters. Our mother left with a swarm a few suns ago to make another hive. We don't know if they lived but it doesn't matter.

What matters is that our hive should be at full strength now, bursting with my own daughters. But it isn't. And the dance makes no sense. My sisters grow old and die and I know I'm still young. My daughters should be swelling our ranks. The comb should tremble with their footfalls and wingbeats. But it doesn't. Too many cells are empty. But I can't lay faster, and my sisters are lethargic from their foraging flights. Their leg baskets are only half full, their nectar stomachs carrying almost nothing.

Why isn't the dance making sense? The dance is everything ...

I am the third queen of this hive. I inherit a legacy passed to me by my mother queen and her mother queen. But now, the hive is failing and I am too young. I don't know what to do. I try to keep my fear in check. I know my sisters smell it. I know if I don't temper it, if I don't start laying soon, their loyalty will wane. I'm not important. Not really. The hive is everything. The hive must survive. And if I don't lay, if my fear infects the comb ...

They will kill me. It's only fair.

So I keep moving. Feel the tremor of ten thousand bee feet reverberate through the wax. The industry, the dance. I fold my antennae over my head so my fear-scent is held in check. And I lay. One egg. Two eggs. It isn't enough. It's exhausting.

This can't be right.

My mother laid all these sisters. Laid me and ten other queens for me to best. And I did. I killed them all. Grappled with my queen sisters, wrenching sinew and exoskeleton, a jab of my stinger into their thorax or head, their bodies curling in agony. But there could only be one queen, and I was so strong.

I'm not anymore. Something drains me. I eat but I lose condition and my attendants know it. I feel their anxious scent swirling with my own, the way they check me, shake me, bully me into laying. I smell what they're saying.

The queen is sick. She doesn't lay. Perhaps ... perhaps ...

I know what that *perhaps* means. But there are no other queens to take my place. And we are too few.

I rally myself, press my thorax to the comb and send a series of short, sharp tremors through the hive. My sisters stop to listen and I broadcast as hard as I can.

The queen is alive! She is laying! Do not be afraid. Do not stop. Dance.

The effort of that alone renders me dizzy and my attendants rush forward. Honey on my tongue, bee feet grooming my fur. I shake them off. I know what I must do. I must lay. I must ...

Three eggs. Four. Five. My attendants stuff the cells with bee bread for when my babies hatch. But there isn't enough, and their movements are lethargic. Their eyes are dull. They stumble.

What's happening to us?

The dance of foragers quakes through the hive. I feel the language of it. *Where do we forage today? Here! No, here!*

It hurts, the way the dance is an argument. It shouldn't be this way. The dance is harmony. The dance is life. But now, they don't feel each other's wing beats. They don't wait for the dance to finish before they answer. There's so much confusion and it makes. No. Sense.

Six eggs. Seven.

Suddenly, the tremble in the comb is urgent, excited. I feel the way the scent changes, the darkness stirs with warning.

Breach! Breach!

Above me, the hive splits open and daylight pours in. I press myself to the comb as my attendants swarm around me, buzzing furiously. My sisters hurry to the entrance, flooding out in a mass of bodies, ready to mount a defense. Their pheromones drift on their wingbeats and ...

It's ok, they say, calming. *It's her.*

I feel the hive quieten. It's her. The bee-that-is-not-a-bee. She came to us before I was queen. I've never known the world without her, but my sisters carry memories of a time before, when there was struggle, when we had to fly miles and miles to find life-giving nectar, when many workers would leave at dawn and less than half would return. But the not-bee-girl changed all that. Since she came, we have found flowers. Since she came, we've lived well.

Or at least, we did, once.

I smell her calming words, the softness of the scent she sends drifting through the hive.

It's ok, bees, she says. *It's ok.*

But it's not ok. I am so tired. My body cannot make eggs. My sisters are awash with confusion and the comb hums with discord. We are dying. Something is killing us and I don't know what.

There is someone new with the not-bee-girl. I catch his scent and curl my antennae back. A male. Drone. Lazy, insufferable things! I remember my brothers when I still had many of them. Sipping the honey they never made, munching the bee bread they never foraged, then flying off to court foreign princesses. I have laid no drones. Drones drain a hive.

But this one smells ... different. He does not smell of want or demand. In fact he ...

He talks bee.

I feel the scent of him mingle with the not-bee-girl's, with our own. He smells strong. Stronger than the not-bee-girl. I lift my antennae to catch the sharp tang of his language.

Hello, his scent says. *I'm no threat.*

Now the not-bee-girl and the not-bee-boy talk in that air-shaking language of theirs. I don't know what they say but the way their scents waft through the hive is enough to calm my sisters. I press my thorax to the wax, listening to the dance.

Tell them! Tell them. They can help!

Can they? This is bee business. They won't understand. How can they? But my sisters insist. For a moment, their dance is how it should be: strong and harmonious. They agree.

Tell them!

That settles it. I can't disobey. That's not the way we are. The dance is everything. So, when the not-bee-boy reaches a hand inside the hive, my attendants and I crawl aboard. They flurry around me, concerned, but I send waves of reassurance and they settle.

The not-bee-boy lifts me into the sun so he can see me better. I'm not used to the sun on my fur. I shudder at the exposure but I hold firm. I let him look. That great face of his, a landscape all its own, changes shape.

The not-bee language is a strange one. A mix of vibrating air and subtle movements. I have heard the not-bee-girl call this *a frown*. The not-bee-boy is frowning at me. I can't remember what this means. My attendants buzz and hum, rushing to my side in case of attack. But there is no attack. Instead, I smell understanding. He's learning about us by looking, by the feel of my feet against his skin. He watches my attendants buzz about his hand. He sees the way my abdomen trembles as I gasp for air. He sees the lethargy of our hive. And then he speaks in scent.

Something is wrong, he says. I press my thorax to his skin and hum a response.

Yes.

What is it? He asks.

I don't know, I admit. It's always strange, talking to the not-bees, but talking to him feels ... natural. *I don't know, but it's killing us.*

The not-bee-girl smells scared. The strength of it blasts through us and my sisters are in turmoil, flooding from the hive to take up battle stations. I try to calm them, but I'm not standing on the comb and they can't hear me. The not-bee-boy senses something is wrong. He puts a hand on the not-bee-girl's shoulder until she calms. He lowers me back into the hive and I'm relieved when my feet touch the comb and I reconnect with the dance. I stare into the not-bee-boy's face as they close the hive and the bee-heated darkness is whole again. But our not-bee-girl's fear-scent still penetrates the hive, infecting the air.

She's scared for us. She's afraid we're dying.

And she should be, because we are. And none of us know why.

Seventeen

EARTH, THIS KID WON'T give up! Solma doesn't break stride as she turns to scowl at Ig over her shoulder. He stumbles as the forest closes around them, still nattering away despite the fact it's making him gasp with the effort.

"This is ... great that your ... gonna help ... do you ... want me to ... carry your gun?"

Solma laughs. "No," she says. "I *want* you to leave me alone."

Ig trips over his feet, sprawls in the leaf litter and scrambles to get up again. Solma doesn't bother to help him.

"No can do ..." Ig pants. "Norsen's ... orders."

Yeah, Solma thinks, scowl deepening. Orders. She remembers those. Don't question, don't think. Just *follow*. Her fists clench around her rifle strap.

"I don't care about Norsen's orders," she growls. "I care about my brother. And I don't need you."

Ig chuckles and his laugh descends into a coughing fit. "Yeah," he splutters. "'Cos … you don't need … anyone, do you?"

Solma feels that like a punch in the ribs and has half a mind to deliver a similar blow to this jumped-up little kid. She rounds on him.

"You don't know nothing about me!" she snarls, thrusting her face close to his. He holds his hands up in surrender, then flattens his fringe, hurriedly.

"Alright!" he protests. "Sorry, I din't mean—"

"I don't care," Solma snaps. She's no idea what it is about Ig that gets her back up. It's as if he's got this constant smirk lurking behind his eyes, like he thinks she's a fool. She turns her back on him and picks her way through the leaf litter.

"Why you, anyway?" she asks, not even bothering to look at him. Ig scurries to keep up.

"Why me what?"

Solma rolls her eyes. "Why'd Norsen pick *you* to keep an eye on us?" she clarifies. "What are you, eight? And You're not Gatra, right? You've not even been in the village a year, so why you?"

Ig scowls. "I'm thirteen, actually," he grumbles. "And anyway, it's 'cos Norsen trusts me."

"Yeah, I get that," Solma growls. "But *why?*"

Ig shrugs. "Guess I got one of those faces," he suggests. Solma looks at him, at the way he peers through his net of eyelashes, never fully opening his eyes, at the way he flattens his thick fringe over his forehead.

"Yeah," she drawls. "I don't think it's that."

She presses on and Ig scampers after her like an eager pup.

"I mean," he says, panting, "Norsen ain't had an easy time of it with his Gatra and the villagers an' all. They don't like him right now. They think he's doing the wrong thing with the insects and the kids. They think the kids were found by the village so they belong *to* the village. Norsen don't see it that way."

Solma clenches her jaw. "Like hell, he don't."

Ig either doesn't hear or chooses not to respond. "And when I first came, I was pretty sick and almost dead. Norsen looked after me. Like, personally. In his house. He shared his food. He gave me clothes. He treated me like family. I guess I owe him, really."

Solma chews her lip. "Don't Norsen have kids?"

Ig hesitates, then nods. "A daughter," he offers quietly. "But we ain't s'posed to talk about it."

Solma casts him a sideways glance. "Whatever," she says. Like she cares about Norsen's personal life. It's whatever else he's got planned that she's concerned about. Ig falls quiet and Solma doesn't want to talk anymore. They move on in silence.

Spring is well under way and already, the sun is stronger than it's been for the past months. Sweat prickles Solma's forehead as she walks. Ig stumbles along behind her but is, mercifully, silent.

Ahead, the trees thin and Solma sees the glade, peppered with flowers. Childish laughter drifts between the trees and insects zip through the dappled sunlight. The tightness in Solma's chest eases at the sight. A smile pulls at her lips as she watches a little bee zoom past. There is hope.

There's hope as long as men like Blaiz are kept in check. And Norsen is a man like Blaiz, even if no one else sees it.

"Warren?" she calls, heading into the clearing with Ig on her heels. "Warren, are you—"

"Sol!"

In a flurry of arms and legs, he comes crashing into her. His red-gold hair sticks up at odd angles and his eyes are wide. Behind him is Yennevieve. Honeybees trace lazy orbits around them both and Warren has several crawling on his shoulders. Solma wraps her arms around him.

"Hey," she says. "You ok? You ran off—"

"Never mind that," Warren says, untangling himself. "We got to help! We can't leave."

Solma raises an eyebrow at him. "Well," she says, confused. "You said that before, but Warren, look—"

"Addie, yes, yes," Warren says. "You're worried and all that, but this is important. This is bigger than me. And also we have to save the bees."

Now both Solma's eyebrows lift. "What?" she says. "Again?"

Warren nods. Bees zoom around his head. "They're sick!" he says, pointing to the three hives at the edge of the clearing. "Orchid's sick!"

Solma blinks. "What's an orchid?"

Warren growls with frustration. "You're not listening!"

"I *am* listening!" Solma retorts, her temper rising. She snatches a glance at Ig and there's that smirk, twisting his lips. Solma reddens. Yet again, this is not going the way she'd hoped.

It's Yennevieve that steps forward, bees drawing excited halos around her. Solma watches them congregate on the seams of her robes.

Yennevieve smiles. "Hi, Solma," she says. "It's ok. Orchid is one of my three queen bees. She's named after a flower."

Solma nods, still unsure where all this is going. "Right," she says. "And this is important because ...?"

There's an edge of impatience to Solma's voice but Yennevieve doesn't seem to notice. She's trembling. Solma feels a stab of concern.

"I showed Warren the hives," Yennevieve explains. "Primrose and Foxglove, the other two queens, have healthy hives. But Orchid ..." she pauses, looking lost. She's just a kid, Solma thinks. Only a year or so older than Warren. Tears sparkle in the girl's eyes. Something's wrong. Solma's impatience drains away. She crouches in front of the children.

"Ok," she says. "Explain everything to me."

But both Warren and Yennevieve now can't speak. Warren's shaking with frustration and Yennevieve looks like she'll break if she opens her mouth. Instead, she grabs Solma's hand, leading her over to the three hives. Solma balks as bees flood from the outer hives, filling the air with song. She can't understand it the same way Warren can, but she doesn't need to. It's meaning is obvious.

Intruder! Intruder! Don't come near!

Yennevieve begins to Whisper. All Solma sees is the way her lips move, forming words too quiet to hear, communicating only through scent and vibrations. As Yenn Whispers, the bee's song calms. They congregate around Solma, hovering inches from her face or landing on her arms. There are so many, their feet prickling Solma's skin. She freezes, resisting the urge to brush them away. If she hurt one accidentally, Warren would be furious.

He's already furious, she realizes as she glances at him. The tremble in his curled fists is a barely-contained rage except ... no, not rage, fear. He's scared for the bees all over again. Scared he can't fix it this time. Solma's heart constricts. He's still so young. They all are, these children.

"See?" Yennevieve says, her voice small and frightened. Solma frowns. See what? There's nothing wrong! They wandered over to the hives and now she's covered in bees. The two hives to either side are crawling with the little things, buzzing about and—

Oh.

Solma's eyes fall on the middle hive. The hive from which no bees flood. The hive that, now that Solma is looking carefully, has fewer bees trundling from its entrance. Adjusting her prosthesis, she waves the healthy bees away and crouches in front of the middle hive, holding out her finger so a tired little bee can climb aboard. She lifts the tiny insect into a patch of sunlight so she can examine it more closely.

Ig comes to get a better look. He wrinkles his nose. "What's wrong with it?" he asks. No one answers him. Nessa and Yennevieve both throw him contemptuous looks but Ig ignores them.

Sensing the sun on her fur, the little bee falls still. Occasionally, one of her antennae lifts, as if in question, only to sag again as if she doesn't have the energy to hold it aloft. Her fur is lackluster and patchy, and—

"Are her wings supposed to look like that?" she asks. She holds the bee out to Yennevieve so the younger girl can look. Yennevieve claps her hands to her mouth. She lets out a cry of horror that brings the other children running.

"No!" she whimpers. "No, no, no!"

"What is it?" Leiff demands. "Yenn? What's wrong?"

Jonah starts to cry as Nessa wanders over to stare at the bee on Solma's finger. Her face falls. "Oh," she says. "Oh, no."

Solma frowns. "She can't fly, can she?"

Nessa meets Solma's gaze, eyes glistening. "Not with wings like that."

Solma glances at the bee again, at the way her delicate, gossamer wings look crumpled and twisted as if they've been crushed. The bee ignites her flight muscles but her wings barely flutter. Leiff has managed to calm Yennevieve, and, sniffling, Yenn holds her hands out for the bee.

"Give her to me," she says, tears pouring down her cheeks. "I ... I should be the one to do it."

"Do what?" Solma asks as the sick bee staggers onto Yenn's palm. Yennevieve Whispers softly to her until the little bee goes very still. Her hands tremble. Nothing happens.

Yennevieve shakes her head. "I ... I can't," she sobs. She holds the bee out to Warren. "Can you?"

Warren starts to cry, too. Solma doesn't understand. Warren wipes tears from his eyes and tries to look brave as he scoops the little bee from Yenn's hand. Then, with a sob, he snaps his hand closed, crushing the bee.

Solma cries out in horror and grabs for Warren's hand, revulsion bringing bitterness to her throat. "What?" she demands. "What are you doing? What's wrong with you?" She rounds on Yenn. "Why would you make him do that?"

Nessa and Leiff step in front of Yenn, glaring murder at Solma as they form a shield in front of their friend. "Leave her alone!" Nessa yells. The sound of shouting makes Jonah cry harder and Tobias kneels beside him, trying to hush him. But Solma barely hears it. Her ears are ringing. Yennevieve begins to weep openly. Warren opens his hand and Solma sees the broken body of the bee inside it. Her stomach lurches. Warren gently tips the dead bee onto Yennevieve's palm, fresh tears pouring down his face.

"I need ... to put her far away ... from the nest," Yennevieve gulps. She turns and trudges into the forest.

Solma stares at the other children, too horrified to know what to say. It's Warren who finally speaks, his voice full of grief.

"She was leaving the hive to die," he murmurs. "She was sick. Sickness is bad for the hive. She didn't want to infect the others. Only ..." he raises those big, green eyes to meet Solma's. He's trying not to cry. "Only they're already infected."

Solma stares at him and the air around her grows heavy.

Sick bees and a missing child, growing discord in their little group, too many voices speaking at once and no one willing to listen.

She wants to run. So badly, she wants to gather Warren into her arms and just take off. Leave. Head into the wild with him and hide him somewhere, keep him away from all this horror.

But the truth is, the horror and madness will always find him, won't it? Wherever he goes, danger will follow. Like it will for all these kids. The image of the Fire Makers flashes again in her mind and she shudders, remembering their glee and laughter as they'd burned the last of Blume's miracle nest. She remembers the cruelty flashing in their violet eyes, the way the flame tattoos above their eyebrows seemed to burn just as brightly as the real flames they conjured.

They're still out there, and who knows what they're up to?

They'll never be safe. Safety doesn't exist. Solma thinks of Olive and Bell and Cobra, how willing they'd been to fight. She closes her eyes.

Blink. And there's Maxen. Cruel, hateful. She didn't matter to him. She never mattered.

But Warren did. Warren always did.

She opens her eyes. There's only one thing to do, isn't there? Solma gathers her brother into a hug and squeezes him close. "Ok," she says. "It's ok."

They'll have to stay. There's no other choice. Here, at least, Warren is among others like him. And there's strength in numbers. No one takes down a tyrant on her own. Solma holds him at arm's length and meets his gaze.

"I'll help you," she says. "'Long as you promise you won't leave my sight. That you'll stay safe. That's all that matters, Warren."

Warren sniffs and wipes his nose. He nods slowly.

The other children drift away. Tobias wraps his arm around Jonah as the younger boy sobs. As the Insect Keepers disperse, Solma catches sight of Ig, standing in the center of the glade. Watching.

Eighteen

SOLMA KICKS HER BLADE foot into the tree stump she's been sitting on, making Olive jump and swear.

"This ain't getting us nowhere!" Solma hisses.

Under the shade of the oak where Addie's butterflies congregate, Tobias and Nessa both cast wary looks in Solma's direction. Solma reddens.

"No," Olive says, her gaze accusing, "Your tantrums ain't getting us nowhere. They ain't gonna tell us nothing if you keep on like that."

Solma scowls but does as she's told. She hates it when Olive's right, and she's right most of the time. The mid-morning heat draws sweat onto her brow and the glade is alive with insects, zipping back and forth. Above, the sky is a relentless blue. Solma settles on the tree stump, hitches her pants up and unstraps her prosthesis. She unwraps the cloth from around her limb to let the skin breathe. From her own tree stump seat, Olive watches, then unclips her water bottle from her belt and hands it over.

"Thanks," Solma mutters, taking a long drink.

She hands the bottle back and forces herself to take deep breaths, watching Cobra and the young Whisperers emerge from their tents. In the last four weeks, the insect glade has been a flurry of activity. The morning after Norsen's visit to the house, The Whisperers packed down their camp and moved to the glade. The youngsters complained and Taipan sulked the whole way, but now that they're here, at the heart of the signal, they're all feeling better.

Still, the Whisperer kids keep to themselves and the Keeper children eye them suspiciously. They're two distinct groups, even though they ought to be working together. Only Warren acts as the bridge between them, and he's become frazzled over the last few days trying to make sure everyone gets on. He and Taipan are distant. The orange-eyed Whisperer girl conjures flowers from the soil where she's told, counts the flowers with the others and checks the health of the land, but she does it in sullen silence. Solma doesn't blame her. She gets how the girl's feeling. Like the world is changing faster than she can cope with.

Warren, though, has found his feet. Solma softens as she watches her brother crouched in the grass with Leiff, a fluffy bee in his cupped hands. He's smiling—really smiling—for the first time in months as he talks quietly to the little creature. Solma can't work out if the tightness in her heart is joy

or terror. She's not happy that so many people know about Warren's power, even if he's not as unique as they thought he was.

Mamba appears from the shadow of the trees, muscles straining as he carries two buckets filled with water. Ana follows, leading the ponies and offering to help, but he refuses (even though he clearly needs it). She meets Solma's gaze and rolls her eyes. Solma smiles.

Mamba deposits the buckets next to where Roseann has her doctor's case open and is treating Jonah for a cut finger. Yennevieve—poor Yennevieve—hovers behind Jonah, her bees drawing lazy orbits around her. She's been quiet since the discovery about Orchid's nest, and Solma has no idea what to say to her.

The Keeper girl's eyes keep darting to the trees as if she's afraid of what might come out of them. Not that anything would. Dyl diligently resets the chemical boundaries around the glade every night. Solma's helped him do it on several occasions. He's meticulous. He takes his job seriously, and if Solma so much as twitches in a way he doesn't like, the pistol is out of its holster in seconds.

But somehow, Solma doesn't think it's redbears or wildwolves that Yenn's worried about. Puzzled, she puts it out of her mind and her eyes drift towards Dyl.

He sits in the shadows, a little way from them, one hand, clasping his pistol, resting on his knee. He hasn't taken his eyes of them for over an hour. Solma scowls just to show she's not afraid. He presents her with a rude gesture, which she returns until Olive slaps her hand down.

"Don't!" Olive scolds. "We're supposed to be making friends."

Solma lowers her hand. "Never been much good at that," she says.

"I know," Olive grumbles.

Solma ignores her and holds out on the staring match with Dyl for as long as she can manage, but the old man isn't backing down. Sighing, Solma looks away. Olive's right. No point antagonizing him.

As soon as she'd got back to the glade that day, after Warren had rushed at her, making noises about sick bees and saving the world (again), Dyl had appeared and confiscated Solma's weapons. He'd returned her rifle with a single cartridge and told her she could keep her hunting knife.

"And the pistol?" she asked. Dyl shook his head.

"Mine now," he growled. "You got enough ammo in that to see off a wildwolf if it comes through the barrier. That's all you need."

Olive had her rifle taken but has been allowed to keep her pistol. Dyl counted out the rounds for her. They both have the guns taken off them after dark. So far, Olive's handed hers over each evening without complaint. Solma can't understand it. They've been told they're not prisoners, but they clearly are. The only reason they're allowed their weapons at all is to protect the children. And because Warren's a keeper. What little trust they're afforded is all down to that.

In the meantime, Solma and Olive are tasked with finding as much information about Addie as they can, looking for leads, playing detective. Solma's not sure she's cut out for this. She sighs. "They're not telling us anything," she points out. "How're we supposed to help if they won't let us?"

Olive shrugs.

"They're scared," she points out. "You're scaring them."

"I ain't scaring them!" Solma splutters. Olive raises an eyebrow at her and nods at the tree stump where Solma's blade foot has left a splintered gash. Solma scowls. Alright, so maybe she *is* scaring the kids, but maybe they should be scared. A Keeper child has gone missing, they need to tell the truth about what they know!

But it's pointless using that argument on Olive, so Solma bites her tongue and watches as Olive strips the flesh from a chunk of sugar cane with a knife. Norsen obliged when Olive requested her favorite treat and Olive closes her eyes in appreciation as she pops the stringy flesh into her mouth.

"You'll ruin your appetite with that," Solma says. "Bell's making pie at the house, with real pastry."

Olive shrugs. Solma watches Olive's lips as her jaw rotates around the cane and has to look away before her blush gives her away.

Last night, for the first time since they left Sand's End, they slept in separate beds: Olive in the Whisperer tent, as their protector, and Solma alone in her own tent with Warren, on a thin mat, a stone digging into her left shoulder as she lay awake and tried not to wish Olive was there beside her. Even now, Olive's within touching distance, and yet Solma doesn't think they've ever felt so far apart.

Every time Solma thinks she's worked up the courage to mend the breach, Maxen's face flashes behind her eyelids.

Blink. Smiling, brushing a strand of dark hair from her face as he leans in for a kiss.

Blink. Snarling. Face puckered with bee stings, as he leans in for the kill.

And Solma loses her nerve.

She re-wraps her leg and straps her prosthesis in place.

"We need them to talk to us" she complains again, nodding at Nessa and Tobias. Nessa catches Solma looking and pokes her tongue out. Olive shrugs.

"They're afraid," she says. "And we're strangers."

"It's been four weeks!" Solma protests. "We ain't strangers no more!"

Olive makes a vague noise of agreement and offers nothing else. It's odd, how little the kids want to say. They do their best to avoid Olive's questions and run away from Solma. Once or twice, Solma's caught the five of them huddled together, whispering urgently. But whenever she approaches, they scatter.

Something's not right. Why can't Olive see that?

A shadow blocks the sun and Solma looks up to see Roseann, one hand on Jonah's shoulder.

"Brought the youngest," Roseann mutters. "His finger's fine so don't let him use that as an excuse. He's got stuff to say, ain't you, Jonah?"

Solma and Olive both snap to attention as Roseann ushers Jonah between them. He sits cross-legged in the grass, clutching his freshly bandaged finger. There's a green beetle on his shoulder and as Jonah lifts his dark eyes to Solma, the beetle raises its antennae in question.

Jonah looks hunted. He chews on his lower lip as his eyes flick between Solma and Olive. He stares pleadingly at Roseann but she's unyielding.

"You tell them what you told me," she says, then plants her hands on her hips and stands over him, blocking his escape. Jonah lowers his gaze and mutters something. Irritation prickles in Solma's throat. This is pointless. What's wrong with these kids? Don't they want their friend found?

She opens her mouth to berate him but Olive's hand is on her knee and the breath goes out of her. Olive's fingertips barely brush her skin, but Solma feels everything that touch says as if she's been electrified.

Say nothing.

Wait.

Solma closes her mouth, face full of thunder. They don't have time for waiting, but they don't have time for her to mess this up either.

Jonah glances behind him, staring at the path that leads out of the glade and back to the village. Olive kneels in front of him.

"Jonah?" she says quietly.

Jonah's little brows draw together in a frown. Then, he seems to come to a decision and lifts his head, speaking with breathless speed.

"I saw Addie that night and she was leaving with someone," he says. He casts a frightened glance towards where Nessa and Tobias have both sat up under the oak tree, glowering at him. He lowers his voice a little more. "I didn't see who it was," he admits. "But Addie went with him."

Solma frowns. "That's it?" she asks. "Earth's sake! *Ow!*"

Olive's foot collides heavily with her flesh-and-bone ankle and Solma glares. What was that for? Olive is unrepentant. She doesn't even look at Solma, focusing instead on Jonah. She leans forward and offers the kid her water bottle.

"You thirsty?" she asks. Her voice is gentle and Solma's heart twists again. Olive is so rarely gentle. The only time she's ever seen that side of her is when they're alone together, which hasn't been for a while.

Jonah blinks suspiciously, but takes the bottle and has a long, grateful drink. Water dribbles down his chin. He wipes his face with the back of his hand and returns the bottle.

"Thanks," he says, and manages to give Olive a small smile. Olive winks at him.

"S'okay," she says. "Look, kid, you're being really brave. I get this is scary, but you want your friend back, right?"

Jonah nods, his dark eyes shining with hope.

"I thought so," Olive says. "So, can you answer some questions for us? You ain't in any trouble. You know that, yeah?"

Jonah's eyes wander over to Nessa and Tobias again, then flicker towards the forest path. Just like Yennevieve. What's he looking for? Both Nessa and Tobias are sitting perfectly still, watching. Solma's heart sinks. Whatever secret they all have, Jonah's not going to tell. Not with the others glaring at him like that ...

Jonah clenches his fist. Eyes shining with determination, he meets Olive's eye and nods. "I want Addie back," he says. "So, I'll tell you."

Solma's mouth falls open. Brave boy. And, she thinks as she gazes sidelong at Olive, that was some persuasion. Under the oak, Nessa and Tobias both stand. Worry gleams in their eyes.

"Jonah!" Nessa yells. Jonah turns his back on them and speaks fast.

"Quick! Ask me!"

Nessa breaks into a run as if sheer willpower alone can keep Jonah silent. Roseann strides over to intercept the girl and Nessa slides to a halt, staring up at the doctor with guilt written all over her face.

"We're just—" she says, but Roseann's glare silences her.

Olive's gaze flicks from Nessa and Tobias to Jonah. Her eyes narrow.

"Was Addie taken?" she asks. "Did it look like she didn't want to go?"

Jonah shakes his head. "No, she wanted to go," he says. "I watched her. She left her shoes behind. She was talking with the other person. It was only quiet but that's what woke me up."

Olive nods. Solma bites the inside of her cheek to keep herself from speaking.

"And no one else woke up?" Olive asks. "No one saw?"

Jonah hesitates, then shakes his head. "I was ... having a bad dream," he says, uncertainly. "That's why I woke up."

Solma frowns. "Hang on—" she says. Olive kicks her again and, with a yelp of pain, Solma forces herself into silence. But this doesn't feel right. Was Jonah woken by his nightmare or by Addie talking? Why's he looking so guilty?

"Did you get a good look at the other person?" Olive asks. Solma lets her breath go all at once. From the look on Jonah's face, she knows exactly what he's going to say. He shakes his head.

"No," he says. "He was in the trees and I couldn't see."

Olive latches onto that a beat before Solma does. "He?" she asks roughly, her voice urgent. "You sure?"

Jonah lets out a whimper and Olive checks herself. "Sorry, kid," she says, her voice gentle again. "But this is important. You *sure* it was a he?"

Jonah blinks furiously against tears and nods.

"Jonah!" Nessa says again, dodging around Roseann. She stands over Jonah, looking furious and terrified. Jonah quails, but his eyes never leave Olive's.

"Yes," he says. "Cross my heart. Addie went away … with a man."

Nineteen

ADDIE WENT AWAY WITH a man.

The beetle on Jonah's shoulder uncouples its carapace and extends a pair of lace-like wings. It takes off and heads towards the flowers. Jonah watches it go, chewing his lip. Olive's still kneeling in front of him but he won't look at her.

There's a shout from Roseann and Solma glances round to find that Tobias has managed to dodge around the doctor and now joins Nessa next to Jonah. They take up position either side of him, like a pair of prison guards, and fold their arms, glowering. It might have been an intimidating display if they weren't both skinny, malnourished children. She raises an eyebrow.

"Can we help you?" she asks. Tobias shuffles his feet and looks to Nessa for guidance, Nessa looks murderous.

"He don't want to talk to you no more!" she snaps. "Do you, Jonah?"

Jonah frowns, scratching at the soil. Solma fixes Nessa with her most thunderous scowl. Interestingly, Olive doesn't try to stop her when she speaks this time.

"He was fine talking to us a moment ago," she says. "Anyone would think you're trying to hide something."

Uncertainty flashes across Nessa's eyes but the girl is fiercer than Solma gave her credit for. Her expression hardens and she puts a hand on Jonah's shoulder.

"He don't want to talk to you no more," Nessa insists through gritted teeth.

From the shadows, Dyl stands and leans heavily on his cane.

"Nessa," he says sharply. "You leave the boy alone, you hear?"

Nessa glares at him. She squeezes Jonah's shoulder and he flinches. Still staring at the ground, he shakes his head. "No," he whispers. "I don't, actually."

He gets up and Nessa puts an arm round him, looking for all the world like a protective big sister as she throws a bitter scowl over her shoulder at Olive and Solma. But Solma doesn't miss the way Jonah's shoulders tense at Nessa's touch, or the way he tries to lean away from her, his little hands curling into fists.

Olive and Solma watch the children scuttle off.

"Well that got us nowhere," Solma grumbles at last. Olive's still watching the kids.

"Hmm," she says. "Maybe not nowhere."

Dyl holsters his pistol and wanders over to them.

"That was odd," he growls. "He's never told me that before. None'a them have."

"Right," Solma says. Her leg itches. She pulls her prosthesis off again, swearing, and manages to get the cloth tangled up while trying to unravel it. Olive rolls her eyes.

"Just ... stop a moment, Sol," she says. "Breathe, yeah?"

She smooths the cloth out and wraps Solma's limb, making sure it's secure but not too tight. Solma feels Olive's hands brush her skin, trying not to show the jolts of yearning the touch sends through her.

I miss you, she wants to say. And I'm sorry. And I want you.

But she doesn't say any of that.

Olive hands the ends of the cloth to Solma to tie herself and sits back on her heels. "Addie went off with a man," she says as Solma secures her prosthesis over the cloth. Her leg still itches, but nothing's going to change that. She nods.

"Yeah," she says, "I heard that bit."

Dyl scratches the back of his neck and shakes his head. Solma searches his face, the grooves in his skin are deep, a map of every worry and fear he's ever felt.

"That's news to me," he admits. "But you know what happened that night. From me, anyway."

Solma doesn't say anything. Dyl told them all he could on the first day they stayed here. Solma could tell it took a lot out of him. As the only guardian of the children, he kept watch each night, sitting in the middle of the glade with his pistol on his lap, watching for predators, both animal and human.

Of course, he was always tired. Of course, he was always frightened. He'd asked Norsen for help looking after the children but Norsen stubbornly refused. Dyl—and only Dyl—was to be their protector.

So is it any wonder that, on that night, Dyl fell asleep? His chin drooped onto his chest and the pistol slipped from his grip. He'd slept so deeply that no sound of Addie's peril had roused him.

He'd been shaken awake the next morning by a stricken Yennevieve, to find that Addie was gone.

"I was so sick that morning," he says. Solma frowns. He's said that several times. "Dunno what it was. Felt like I threw up every meal I ate." He shakes his head again. "Prob'ly just guilt."

Solma catches Olive's eye and there's a moment of silent understanding between them.

This was months ago, yet Norsen hasn't stationed anyone else at the glade, hasn't relieved Dyl of duty, hasn't made any change to keep the children safer.

The children who have the most precious gift in Alphor. Olive frowns, and Solma sees she's starting to agree that this stinks.

Dyl looks on the verge of tears. "I really did try," he says. "I searched that forest all day. I yelled her name. I just ... this damn leg."

Before she knows what she's doing, Solma's reached up and squeezed his arm. "It ain't your fault," she says. "I ... none of this makes sense. But you've kept these kids pretty safe on your own for a long time."

Dyl looks up at her, his tawny eyes shining. "It's not just—" he starts to say, then checks himself. He clears his throat and puts his gnarled old hand over Solma's. "I hope we find her."

Solma can't hold his gaze. She looks away and the three of them stand in silence for a while.

"So," Solma says, getting to her feet. "We're looking for a man. Could be a stranger, could be someone right under our noses. We got no clue. And for some weird reason, the kids aren't talking."

Olive raises an eyebrow at her. "Well, then we should—"

But whatever they should do is drowned out under the sound of an excitable Ig bursting into the glade, yelling his head off.

"Sergeant!" he yells, windmilling his arms as he crashes through the grass. Whisperer and Keeper children scatter from his path but he doesn't notice. "Sergeant!" he yells again, skidding to a halt in a cloud of grass pollen and narrowly avoiding a collision with Olive. Solma splutters on the explosion of pollen and scowls.

"What?" she demands, and Ig balks at her ferocity.

"I just—" Ig hangs his head, pushing his dark hair down over his brow. Solma feels a pang of guilt but irritation wins over again and she glares.

"*What*, Ig?" she says again. Olive folds her arms, equally annoyed.

"Steward needs the Whisperers," Ig says, shuffling his feet. "I'm sorry, I didn't mean—"

Olive waves his apology away. "He needs the Whisperers so much you had to come crashing over here, terrifying everyone?" she asks. Ig sneaks a glance at her and sees her lip curling into a smile. His own twitch upwards in reply.

"Um ..." he says. "No. He just needs them."

Olive nods. "Ok, so maybe you don't got to scare everyone next time?"

Ig blinks at her and nods. "Yeah, maybe."

Olive stands, clapping Ig on the shoulder as she does so. "Which Whisperers?" she asks, heading into the center of the glade with Ig at her heels.

"All of them," he says, recovered from his embarrassment. "The Fei say the northern fields are giving 'em trouble ..."

His voice fades as a breeze stirs the grasses. Solma watches them go, wondering how she'd never noticed how good Olive is with kids. Already, Ig's skipping along beside her, gazing adoringly as she speaks. With nothing more than a gesture, Olive's gathered the Whisperer children in a clamoring crowd around her. The three boys stand to attention, Krait and King vying to be the tallest. Taipan giggles.

Within moments, Mamba has brought Cobra and Ana to the gathering and the seven Whisperers head off, following Olive and Ig. It's taken less than a minute for Olive to mobilize them. Maybe she should have been Sergeant after all. Solma frowns at that. Not that it matters anymore. They're both exiles now, neither of them are even Gatra. Villageless and casteless. But none of that felt important when Olive's fingers were laced through Solma's, when she was tucked against Olive at night, their hearts beating in unison, stolen moments when Olive stopped being the hardened soldier and became gentle, tender. Earth, Solma misses that girl.

Dyl watches her quietly.

"She's something, eh?" he says, nodding towards Olive. "Never met anyone like her before."

"No," Solma says, hating the wobble in her voice. "And you never will again."

"Hmm," Dyl says, straightening his hat. "Well, if I was fifty years younger and it was me she looked at like she looks at you ... I'd—"

Solma can't take it. She rounds on him. "You'd what?" she demands.

Unmoved, Dyl chuckles. "Nothin'," he says. "It don't matter."

He shuffles towards the tents where Nessa, Tobias and Leiff huddle together, whispering about something. Solma shakes her head. She's so tired she can barely think straight and they've got no closer to finding Addie. Guilt, her old friend, curdles in her gut again and she feels sick.

Blink. Maxen's behind her eyelids, smiling, loving.

Blink. Snarling. Ferocious.

Solma shivers and curses herself. Self-pity isn't going to help Addie. It isn't going to keep Warren safe.

"Think, Sol," she mutters.

If Jonah saw Addie going off with a man, then the other Keeper children need to be warned not to trust anyone, whether they know them or not. And one of those children, she thinks with a lurch of her gut, is Warren.

Twenty

WARREN HOLDS HIS HANDS out, smiling as honeybees dance on his palms. He giggles.

"It tickles," he says.

"Keep still!" Yennevieve scolds, but she's grinning too.

She cups Warren's hands in her own, the sun shining off her blue-purple robe. Solma watches them Whisper with their heads together, eyes closed, as Yenn's bees dance across her brother's hands. For the first time in months, Warren's cheeks glow with a sun-blush. Though his eyes are closed, Solma knows that there'll be a shine in them when they open, the kind of light she's hoped, all winter, she'd see when she looked at him.

And it's strange how broken she feels, watching him. Isn't this what she'd wanted? The way he smiles as the insects waggle and scurry across his skin, drawing goose bumps in their wake, the way he gazes at them in awe and wonder and ... *understanding.* So why this splinter of fear in her heart?

She shivers, despite the spring warmth, and steps forward, careful not to disturb the youngsters. From the nearby shade, Burdock lifts his head and nickers to her. She puts a finger to her lips and he watches, ears forward with interest.

"There!" Yenn murmurs, her smile dimpling her cheeks. "Can you hear them?"

Warren's grin is huge now. He chuckles happily. "Yeah!" he says. "I can ... they're saying ..."

He frowns with concentration, chewing his lower lip as he focuses. Solma's eyebrows lift. The dancing bees. They're *talking* to him.

"They're saying ... flowers at the wood's edge, and there's a direction ..." his frown deepens. Yenn opens one eye.

"Thirty degrees left of the sun," she says.

"And there's lots to eat. Enough for ..."

He stops, his eyes flying open as the bees lift in a black-and-gold cloud and zig-zag towards the forest. Warren tracks their flight until his eyes fall on Solma.

"Sol!" he says, throwing his hands in the air. "Did you see? Did you—?" His smile falters at the look on her face. "What's wrong?"

Solma forces herself to smile as she ruffles his hair.

"You look happy," she says. "Good to be back among bees, hey?"

Warren nods, eyes shining. "Yeah," he says. "They sound different to Blume. It's weird. Blume's bees were blustery but these ones, they got all this focus. And Leiff's bees, they sound like—"

He stops as he realizes how Yennevieve is looking at him. Solma stares between them, consternation drawing her brows together.

"What?" she asks.

Yenn shrugs. "Just ..." she says, "never come across a Keeper who can hear *all* the insects before. Most of us only got one species."

Solma stares, feeling like she's been punched.

"Wait," she says. "You mean, none of you can—?"

Yenn shakes her head. "We only get one insect each, normally," she says. "It's like a ..." she screws up her face, trying to find the word. "Like a language. We can't talk to them all, just one. Except him. He can talk to them all." She smiles. "A proper Hive Child."

Warren blinks, looking from Solma to Yennevieve and back again and Solma sighs. Great. This complicates everything. She pinches the bridge of her nose for a moment, trying to stop the swirling in her head.

"Ok," she says. "In which case, Warren, what I have to tell you is even more important."

The children's smiles disappear as Solma explains Jonah's revelation. It's not lost on Solma that, when she mentions the man Addie disappeared with, Yennevieve grabs Warren's hand, her face ashen.

"Who said?" she asks in a tiny voice. Solma frowns.

"Jonah," she says. "Did you know?"

Yenn bites her lip and says nothing. Solma closes her eyes and takes a deep breath, quelling her irritation. There's no point getting angry now.

"Look," she says, opening her eyes. "We don't know why that man took Addie. It might be nothing to do with her power, but ..."

But it probably is. Solma sees in their faces that the kids are thinking it too. It can't be coincidence: Addie is a Keeper, a child with a power that could either save Alphor, or make a specific few very rich. Solma clenches her jaw. She hates to admit it, but Norsen may have been right to hide these children away. She's still not convinced about his motives, though.

Unless ...

Unless Norsen has something to do with Addie's disappearance.

Once the thought lands in Solma's mind, it spreads deep, insidious roots. His behavior doesn't make sense. The kids are in danger and he won't even post his Gatra at the glade to keep them safe. Secrets and lies. Just like Blaiz. Just like Maxen.

Blink. He's smiling at her, brushing hair from her face.

Blink. Snarling. He wants her dead.

Solma presses the heel of her hand to her forehead and wills the images of Maxen away. She needs her mind clear.

She takes a deep breath. She's a soldier, a Gatra—at heart, if not in name. She's faced down monstrous wild boar and survived (just), she's killed raiders in defense of her town, she's protected Warren from her enraged steward. It's time to be that person again.

"Who keeps watch at night besides Dyl?" she asks. Yennevieve blinks, nonplussed.

"No-one," she says. "It's just us an' him. He resets the chemical boundaries every morning and evening. We used to go with him, help him carry the canisters while he'd spray the trees, but he don't take us since you arrived. He just goes out by himself."

Solma chews her lip. "O-kay," she says, trepidation mounting. "But Dyl keeps watch all night *every* night?"

Yenn shrugs, like she's never really thought about it before. "He sleeps in the morning," she offers, as if this makes up for it. Earth, no wonder the old man looks so tired! That's madness. Solma glances at Dyl as he stands with Nessa and Tobias, listening to them chatter. Poor man. That's a lot for one person. Now that she looks, she sees the heaviness in his frame, the way each smile looks as much effort as hoisting an iron flag. He's tired, guilt-ridden and doesn't know where to turn.

She knows how that feels.

Solma turns back to the children.

"And since Addie disappeared?" she asks. "Anything changed?"

Yennevieve shakes her head. "No," she says. "We never had no reason to worry before what happened to Addie. There are predators out there, but we never been attacked." She thinks for a moment. "Well, Addie saw a massive redbear once, and it was really scary, but it sniffed at where the barriers had been laid and then took off, sharpish." She giggles. "They hate the chemicals Dyl put down. They won't come near us. That's why we ain't allowed to leave the glade after sundown. Steward's very strict about that."

Solma scowls. "But I ain't talking about predators, Yenn," she says. "Not that kind, anyway. I'm talking about a man. Men can move through chemical barriers, can't they?"

Yenn bites her lip, eyes darting towards the forest path. She won't meet Solma's gaze. "I guess," she says quietly. Solma folds her arms, but Warren takes Yenn's small hand and smiles at her.

"It's ok," he says. Solma decides not to correct him.

It's not ok. None of it makes any sense. What kind of Steward puts kids as young as this, as precious as this, in the middle of a forest with only an old man to take care of them? Either Norsen is beyond careless, which Solma doubts, or he's set up the perfect circumstances for a kidnap.

"Well," she says without thinking, "either he's got what he wants and Addie's long gone by now, or he'll be back."

Yennevieve finally looks up. "Oh," she says in a small voice. "What do we do?"

Before Solma can reply, the sound of footsteps drifts through the undergrowth. In a flash of instinct, Solma shoves the two children behind her and unshoulders her rifle. She only has a single shot in it, courtesy of Dyl. She flicks the safety off and raises it in time to see Ig stumble into the glade and squeal when he realizes Solma's gun is aimed directly at his head.

"Holy Earth!" he swears, and Solma lowers her rifle, showering him with far more offensive language.

"What the hell is wrong with you?" she yells. Ig stiffens and smooths down his black fringe.

"I was just ... coming to ..." he falls silent, hanging his head.

Solma flicks the safety back on and shoulders the rifle. "You got to be more careful," she growls.

Ig nods and sniffs, raising his head and blinking profusely. His squint deepens when he feels bad and he hurriedly flattens his fringe again. Solma has no idea why she finds that so aggravating.

"Sorry," Ig says, quietly. Solma grunts.

"Fine," she says. "But you gotta move around more carefully from now on."

She squeezes Warren's shoulder, hoping he can feel all of her courage and none of her fear. She winks at him.

"I need to find Olive," she says. She almost grabs Warren's hand and demands he goes with her, but wandering between the glade and the village is dangerous enough with only the predators to worry about. If there is a man out there, waiting to kidnap more Keeper kids, she doesn't want to give him a chance to take Warren. Dyl's here and so is Roseann, skulking in the shade and talking to nobody, as usual.

Solma kneels in front of the children and fixes them with a hard stare.

"You two, *stay here*. You keep close to Dyl," she says, "and pass the message on to the other kids. Trust no-one, even if you recognize them. Especially if you recognize them."

Warren blinks at her. "What about you?" he asks. "If there's a man out there, you shouldn't go in the forest by yourself, Sol."

Solma smiles and chucks him under the chin.

"I'll be alright, War," she says. "I'll have Ig with me. Ig!" she barks, and the boy jumps to attention. "You any good with a knife?"

Ig frowns. "Er ..."

"Good," Solma says. She rummages in her belt and pulls out a multi-knife. She flicks it open and hands it to him. "Keep it in your hand. Anything—or anyone—comes at you, give it a quick jab. Softest bits are the throat and eyes. C'mon, we're going to find Olive."

Ig holds the knife out like it might bite him. "Er ..." he says again. Solma sighs with impatience.

"Just ... keep it in your hand and keep an eye out. Got it?"

Ig stares. "Er ..."

Solma rolls her eyes, plants a kiss on Warren's head and glares at Ig. "Come on, then," she says. She grabs Ig by the elbow and pulls him hurriedly down the forest path. Olive needs to know about Norsen. Everyone needs to know about Norsen. Solma's never been so certain in her life that whatever this is, whoever took Addie, it's coming from inside the village.

She just hopes she's doing the right thing.

Twenty-One

SOLMA CRASHES OUT OF the forest and has to cart-wheel her arms to regain balance before she collides with the electrified fence. She rights herself before her nose skims one of the wires.

"Ig?" she calls. The boy's so slow. He's dragged his feet the whole way and he tripped over something and went sprawling in the leaf litter about twenty minutes ago. "Ig? Which is the safe part, again?"

No answer.

"Ig?"

Solma glances behind her and curses when there's no sign of him. Earth, how is it possible for him to be so useless? She's half a mind to leave him. He'll probably turn up eventually. But the forest looms above her and Solma knows Ig stands no chance against a fully grown redbear.

"Dammit."

She should go back for him. She doesn't have time for this.

"When I get hold of you, Ig—" she growls.

"You'll what?" says a voice behind her, and Solma whirls round, rifle aimed in seconds.

Captain Reya doesn't even flinch. She stands on the other side of the electrified fence with one hand on the hilt of her hunting knife and her own pistol aimed at Solma. The ghost of a smile flickers across her face.

"Still got a Gatra's instinct, eh?" she says. She removes her hand from the hilt of her hunting knife. "I ain't gonna shoot you. And you ain't gonna shoot me, neither."

Solma hesitates. She's got no intention of shooting anyone but she can't seem to make herself lower the rifle.

Reya watches her for a moment, then shrugs and lowers her gun.

"Ig'll be fine," she says. "He's been running in and outta that forest since he arrived. Norsen's little lackey, he is." Her brows meet and Solma sees lightning flash in her hazel eyes. "He's tougher than he makes out. The safe bit's here, by the way."

She gestures to the section of fence in front of her. Solma lowers her own gun and shoulders it, stepping through the harmless wires. She faces Reya and folds her arms.

"Something's going on," she says. "And you know it."

Reya searches her face, then glances away with an angry growl.

"I know less than you think I do," she says. "And why should I trust you of all people? A month after one'a those special kids disappears, you and your lot show up and your brother—"

She clenches her jaw, a darkness passing across her face. Solma bristles.

"My brother *what?*" she snarls, moving closer until she's inches from Reya's face. She's surprised to find Reya's half an inch taller than her. She's rarely had to contend with that before. This close, Solma sees the grooves and lines in the Captain's face. There's a faint scar running along one jawbone. She's seen violence. Serious violence. So it's no surprise when she snorts a laugh at Solma's bravado.

"You know what," she says. "Your brother's like them other kids. Some sort'a power over the insects. The insects that are s'posed to be dead. Yet here they are, all in a glade in Skyheart under the watch of our Steward."

Well, that about sums it up. Solma sighs and steps back.

"And one of the kids is missing," she says. "Disappeared a month ago."

Reya's frown deepens but she says nothing, just stares at Solma as if she could peel every thought from Solma's head with nothing but her eyes. Solma hates that this woman scares her a bit, though she's not sure why.

"Know anything about that?" she presses. "Or why Norsen's done nothing to protect the kids that're left, even though they might be next?"

Reya shakes her head. "If I was allowed to take my Guard into that glade and set up a perimeter," she says, "don't you think I'da done that months before Addie disappeared? Don't you think I'd be there right now, combing that forest for any sign of her? Don't you think—"

She stops, a deep snarl curling her lips. A vein in her neck jumps and there's a tremble in her jaw. Solma stares and, suddenly, she gets it.

"Addie," she says. "She's your daughter?"

Reya huffs a half-hearted laugh. "My niece," she says. "My sister's kid. Zamia died two years ago. A vicious raid. Bullet shattered Zam's shoulder and we couldn't get it all out. Infection set in … it wasn't pretty."

She gazes over Solma's shoulder and into the forest, as if the ghost of her sister is out there somewhere, waiting to be called home. Solma almost reaches for Reya's arm, then thinks better of it. She clears her throat.

"I'm sorry," she mutters.

The Captain says nothing for a moment, just glares into the distance, her jaw clenched.

"Addie's other Mum got sick after that," she mutters after a while. "Din't want to be alive anymore, I don't reckon. Left poor Addie all on her own. So, I took her. Nothin' else for it, was there? It was that or—"

She snaps her mouth shut and glares. "Look, girl, we all lost people, ain't we? Everyone I know's got buckets of grief and orphan kids on their doorstep."

Solma nods. That's true. "But this is different, right?" she says. "What's Norsen up to? Where is he?"

Reya shrugs. "No idea," she says. "He's always disappearing. Mostly he's in that bloody forest. Earth knows what goes on in that head'a his."

Solma tenses. "I think *you* know," she challenges. "I think you reckon he's got something to do with your niece's disappearance. I think you know he ain't as harmless as he makes out. I think he ain't interested in protecting the kids 'cos he's the reason Addie's gone and that's why he won't let you in the forest. Am I wrong?"

Reya stares at her, a strange light in her eyes. "No," she says. "You ain't wrong."

"Ok," Solma says. They're getting somewhere now. "So why would he do that? What's he doing with them?"

Reya shrugs. "I got my suspicions," she says. "Can't prove nothing though, can I?"

Solma waves a dismissive hand. "I don't care about that now," she says. "I wanna know what you think."

Reya narrows her eyes. She's silent, fixing Solma with that same, peeling stare. Finally, she speaks. "What d'you think any other village would pay for a kid who could control the insects?" she murmurs. "They could triple their chances of a good harvest. They'd have a surplus of goods to trade. And ain't it a coincidence that the kids with that power end up here? Under Norsen's nose?"

Solma stares at her. "You think he's gonna sell them," she breathes. "You think he's trading *kids?*"

Reya shrugs. "Like I said," she mumbles, "can't prove it."

Solma chews her lip. Selling kids? That's more than she can stomach. And it only makes sense if Norsen's got a way to draw the kids with that power to him. If he can guarantee that, when they discover their power, they'll flee their village and come right here. To him.

"The signal," she says, grabbing Reya by both shoulders. Reya jerks free.

"What?" she growls. "What signal?"

Solma flaps a hand towards the forest. "Before we crossed the mountains," she says, "the Whisperers felt something. A signal that was making them sick. Cobra reckoned it was familiar but new and it didn't make no sense, and Warren was convinced it was his bees. But it's the Keeper kids, in't it? Whisperers can sense the power of other Whisperers. It's how Cobra found Warren. Put enough Keeper kids in one place and their combined signal's gonna be strong enough to draw others. That's what he's doing. As long as he's got enough in the glade to draw others, he can sell some, and Skyheart stays wealthy 'cos of the Keepers here, nurturing the insects."

Triumph and rage vie for dominance in her core and Solma can barely keep still.

"It makes sense!" she says. "The chemical barrier don't just keep the predators out, it keeps the insects *in*. He can stop them flying across Alphor like they should. He sells the kids, their insect species goes with them. It's a perfect way to profit from all this."

Reya stares at her, a frown bridging her eyebrows.

"Alright," she says. "Maybe you're on to something. What d'you need?"

"I need to find Olive," Solma says. "And I need to get Warren outta here—"

Reya grabs her arm so tight Solma's fingers tingle. She struggles, but Reya's too strong.

"Get off!" Solma growls, her other hand reaching for her knife. But the look on Reya's face gives her pause. Reya doesn't look angry or vengeful. She looks terrified.

"Please," she says. "I know he's your brother, but we need your help—"

Solma tugs her arm free, glaring. Reya holds up her hands.

"Think about it," she says. "Now that Norsen knows about Warren, you think he's gonna let him go? If you run, he'll come after you. He'll hunt you. I know you and Olive are tough but Norsen's Gatra is huge. He'll send us after you. And we won't all disagree with it. He'll bring Warren back. Ain't nothing you can do about it."

Solma glares, rubbing her arm, but a coldness settles in her gut. Everything Reya says is true. Their only chance is to expose him. To hope enough people in the village will be disgusted by what he's doing. To spark a revolution. Again. Solma closes her eyes. Does every Steward in Alphor need to be overthrown before she and her brother can live in peace?

"We need to set a trap for Norsen," she says. She darts past Reya and strides down the path, new energy driving her.

Reya falls into step beside her. "What trap?" she demands.

"I dunno yet," Solma admits. "And we might need to be patient. But if we're right, he'll be after another kid soon. If we're ready, we can catch him."

A smile spreads across Reya's face.

"For Addie," she says. Solma nods.

"And for Warren," she agrees.

Twenty-Two

WARREN WATCHES HIS SISTER disappear among the trees. He clasps his hands together and tries to focus on the whisper-breath of bee feet as one lands on his finger. It sits there quietly for a bit, then fires its engine and zooms off into the sun.

He looks at Yennevieve's stricken face and offers her a smile.

"Don't worry," he says. "Sol's a fighter. She'll figure it out."

Yenn chews her lip and nods. "Yeah, ok," she says. She doesn't sound convinced. Warren puts his arm round her but she wriggles away. He frowns but decides it would be silly to have an argument over it. She's just worried about Addie.

Warren gazes at the path his sister and Ig have just disappeared down. He closes his eyes, letting his mind fill with the busy song-scent of the glade's insects. It's still such a muddle and he has trouble discerning the bees from the butterflies and the beetles. Somewhere nearby, though, he knows his buff-tails are waiting. He can feel the tell-tale tug on his heart. But they've been in Skyheart for ages now. Spring is slowly turning into a warm, promising summer and there's still no sign of them. He opens his eyes to find Yenn watching him.

"You miss them, eh?" she says. She doesn't even have to ask what he's thinking about and this, alone, lifts Warren's spirits. "I get it," she tells him. "You'll find them."

Warren nods. "I hope so," he says. "I feel them. I reckon they're close but I don't know where."

"I'm sure they're safe," Yenn says. "Sometimes, the insects do better just having their Keeper nearby. Mebbe just you being here helps them to keep going. They'll find you if they need you."

Warren can't look at her. He so wants that to be true but he's not sure. He misses them so much it hurts.

There's a rustle in the undergrowth and both children jump, whipping round to face the disturbance.

"Dyl!" Yennevieve yells.

"Roseann!" Warren shouts at the same time.

Immediately, the glade is on alert. Roseann leaps out of the shade, a knife in hand. Dyl's a little slower but his pistol is aimed squarely at the tangle of rustling brambles. There's a snap and a tearing sound.

"Ow!" the bush says.

Dyl lowers his pistol. "Dammit, Ig!" he snarls. "What the hell you doing in there?"

The bush gives way, disgorging Ig in a ridiculous heap in the grass. There are leaves in his hair and his shirtsleeve is torn. He scrambles to his feet, flattening his hair over his forehead before he brushes himself down. He peers through his eyelashes, sees Dyl and grins.

"Hey!" he says.

Dyl glowers and says something unkind under his breath. He turns away, shaking his head, and limps back to where the other children are busy with their insects.

Roseann stays beside Warren, glaring.

"You were s'posed to go with Solma," she says. Ig shrugs.

"Got lost," he admits. "She goes way too fast. I didn't want to go chasing her through the forest, so I came back here. Safer."

He beams at Roseann, who scowls. "Fine," she says after a while. "But you stay here. I'm not having you crashing about, scaring everyone. Next time, I'll just let Dyl shoot you."

Ig's grin falters, but Roseann's already turned away.

Warren offers Ig what he hopes is a reassuring smile.

"It's ok," he says. "My sisters' strong and a good soldier. She'll be fine."

Ig blinks at him, then grins. "Yeah," he says. "You're right. Can I stay with you two, instead?"

Warren's about to nod, but Yenn grabs his hand and pulls him round to face her. She looks stricken and angry and keeps casting dark glances at Ig.

"Shall we see if we can listen to Orchid's bees?" she asks pointedly. "We need to figure out why they're sick."

"Who's sick?" Ig asks before Warren can answer. "What's sick?"

Yenn throws a scowl over her shoulder. "Ain't none of your business!" she snaps. Warren sees Ig's face fall and feels bad. It's important to include other people. He thinks briefly of Taipan and feels a pang of guilt. But that's different, he thinks. She keeps *deciding* not to be his friend. It's not his fault if she keeps walking off.

Is it?

He hears Bell's voice in his head, now.

How would you like it, young man?

And the answer is always the same. He wouldn't like it. Not at all. He decides he'll make more of an effort next time he sees Taipan. He might even try to apologize. Now, though, he offers Ig a hand. "We'll show you," he says. "But, you got to promise to be very quiet."

Yenn's scowl deepens but she doesn't argue. Warren pulls Ig away from the honeybee hives, to where he can sit in the shade with a good view. The older boy flops in the grass with a sigh and rubs his arm where the brambles scratched him. Warren offers him as big and warm a smile as he can manage.

"Just sit here," he says. "I dunno if you'll see much, but you got to keep very quiet, ok?"

Ig nods dumbly at him and settles, cross-legged, in the grass. "Are the bees sick?" he asks.

Warren feels a spike of fear as he nods.

"Yeah," he says, quietly. "One of the hives is sick."

"Can you fix it?" Ig asks, so urgently that Warren tenses. The other boy's face is so fierce and hopeful that Warren steps backwards at the force of it. He bites his lip.

"I dunno," he admits. "But me and Yenn are gonna try."

Ig looks like he might be about to say something else, but Yenn calls impatiently and Ig looks away. Unease stirs in Warren's gut as he stares at Ig, wondering why the older boy makes him feel so sad and confused. But there's no time to worry about that now. The bees need him, and that's always more important. He heads over to Yenn, ignoring the way she glares at Ig. What's she got against him, anyway?

"You ready?" she asks. Warren nods, closing his eyes as Yenn kneels next to the hive and begins to Whisper. Bees clamor from the narrow entrance, flooding the little platform just outside. But Warren feels their lethargy, the discordance of their song and the way they blunder, dizzy and uncoordinated. He kneels beside Yenn and holds out his hands. A few bees clamber aboard and Warren holds his palms flat for the bees to dance.

But their lackluster movements, their confusion, their uncertainty ...

This isn't dancing. It's like something's taken their voice away, left them mute and disconnected. Warren's heart feels tight. He watches the lost honeybees on his palm and wants to cry. They can't speak. They can't explain what's wrong.

It's up to him to listen harder. And there's one bee in the hive who might still have her voice. He squeezes his eyes closed, still feeling the gentle tap of bee feet on his hands, and casts his mind into the hive, searching for Orchid.

~ Orchid ~

THE HIVE STINKS OF sickness. My daughters hatch with twisted wings and blunt antennae and their sisters kill them. They kill them quickly because they love them. A jab into the head with a stinger. My daughters carry the bodies far away, depositing them I-don't-know-where.

The hive dwindles, and there are echoes of mutiny among the workers. They dance of regicide. I don't blame them. My eggs are few, the larvae weak. Many die before they pupate and the daughters that do hatch are malformed and sickly. If I cannot lay, the hive needs another queen.

But there are no other queens. And the workers haven't decided, yet. Only a few, angry sisters dance of death. The others are unconvinced. My life is spared. For now.

The queen cells lay empty, and we are too few. The comb barely trembles with bee feet. The hive smells of fear, burning my antennae. I press my thorax to the comb and send signals through the hive.

I'm here, I say. I'm laying. I'm trying.

But the workers aren't convinced.

A call comes from outside, whisper-scent and vibration. The not-bees are out there, asking what's wrong. My workers clamor to the entrance, buzzing with eagerness to tell. We need help.

But I hear the confusion in their dancing. They're not saying anything. They can't. The sickness has addled them. They can't dance. They can't speak. I feel their muteness like a stab in my mind and the fear is enough to freeze me. My attendants rush to my aid, grooming frantically. I feel their worry, their love, their fear. They need their queen. But their queen is so weak, now.

And then the not-bee-boy's strange scent drifts through the hive. I feel it prickle on the tips of my antennae, soft with concern.

I don't understand, he says. *They make no sense. What's happening to the hive?*

What's happening to the hive? If only we knew. I press my thorax to the comb and buzz, wafting scent and vibration back to him, trying to explain.

We are broken. We stumble and the dance makes no sense. We are full of discord. Our song is broken. Help us.

The last plea is so un-beelike I startle myself. The hive does not ask for help. The hive is life, a mind made of many minds. The hive is everything and the hive never needs help.

But we need help now. We are so sick. So, I send the plea out again, as strong as I can.

Help us.

He hears the plea. I feel the tension in his scent, the way his concern couples with determination. There's something different about this not-bee-boy, something in him that makes me feel that maybe there's hope. He smells like the dance of the Earth. When he's near, I think perhaps we are not beyond saving.

Help us, I call again, thrumming my message through the comb.

I don't care if the workers hear, or if they think I'm weak for it. Perhaps they will kill me for it. I would not blame them. But if my plea saves the hive, my death will be worth it.

Twenty-Three

WARREN GASPS AND STUMBLES back from the hive, eyes flying open. Alarmed, the bees on his hands burst into flight, buzzing in frantic circles round his head. Warren falls on his rump in the grass, but he barely feels it. Orchid's deep, despairing cry still echoes in his mind.

Help us!

That's what she'd said before. A distress call in scent and vibration. He sniffs, but that only draws the bitter scent in deeper and he splutters on it. Yenn offers him a hand and heaves him to his feet.

"You ok?" she asks. "I was trying to listen but I couldn't hear. It was all jumbled and I couldn't—" her voice fades and Warren sees her lips trembling. She feels their pain like he felt the pain of his buff-tails. He remembers the moon badger attack on Blume's hive nearly a year ago, how he'd felt those powerful claws as if they were tearing his own flesh. He knows exactly how Yenn feels. He hugs her.

"The babies aren't forming properly," he says, pulling away. "So, we got to find out what's making that happen. My Aunt Bell's got tons of books. We could ask her?"

Bell's back at the house in the village. She was clear with Norsen when he asked them all to move to the glade. She'd folded her arms and said no way was she letting all the kids sleep out in the forest unless they could get a proper breakfast each morning, and to do that, she needed this here stove. Warren grins remembering it. Norsen realized quickly he wasn't going to win that argument. So, every morning, Bell wakes early in the glade and trudges back through the forest with Ig or Roseann so she can prepare food. Warren's stomach grumbles. He's hungry, too, and there'll be food wherever Bell is. He turns to Yenn with a hopeful grin.

Yenn hesitates. "I'm not very good at reading," she admits in a small voice. Warren takes her hand.

"That's ok," he says. "I'll help you."

Yenn sniffs and gives a teary smile. Around them, bees from the two healthy hives zoom back and forth, their song confident and true. Ig clears his throat, and both the Keeper children remember he's there. Yenn scowls again, turning away from the other boy. Warren watches her, frowning, then gives Ig the warmest smile he can manage.

"Can you read, Ig?" he asks, carefully. He's learned that, in some places, that's a dangerous question. Ig's brows draw together in

embarrassment and he shakes his head. Warren shrugs. "That's ok," he says. "Maybe you could help us unpack the books."

Yenn huffs but says nothing. Ig beams. He leaps to his feet. "I can do that!" he says. "I'm strong. Look!"

He curls his pale arms either side of his head, displaying barely perceptible biceps that quiver with the strain. He puffs out his chest and Warren decides that, in this instance, kindness and the truth won't work well together.

"Great," he says, and beckons Ig over. Solma said not to leave the glade and Warren hesitates on the path. She'll be angry if she realizes he's disobeyed her. But this is important! Orchid's hive doesn't have time to waste. Warren glances back into the glade, chewing his lip.

He takes a deep breath. "C'mon," he says, with more confidence than he feels, and heads into the forest.

"Warren El-Yuen!" a sharp voice calls, making the three children freeze. They turn to see Roseann marching towards them, face full of thunder. "Where do you think you're going? You not hear your sister tell you to *stay put?*"

Warren shuffles his feet. "Yeah," he says, "but—"

"But what, young man?"

Warren scowls. This isn't fair, is it? Why do adults always get to boss him about when they always get everything wrong? They think just 'cos they're bigger and stronger, they get to be in charge. He folds his arms.

"I got to see Bell!" he says. "Please! It's important!"

Roseann folds her arms. "Young man—"

"*Please*, Roseann!" Warren begs. "Come with us. You can keep us safe. But we got to go!"

Ig and Yenn both stare at him, but Warren's not backing down. Orchid needs him. He feels her tangled scent of fear, even now. She's a good queen. He knows it. She's young and frightened, a bit like him. She doesn't know what's going on either. They could almost be one and the same, and he isn't letting her die.

Roseann glares at him. She casts a glance over her shoulder to where Dyl stands guard over the other children, then sighs and unsheathes her knife.

"Fine," she says. "Come on. I ain't lingering in them trees any longer than I have to."

She strides into the forest. Warren grins and grabs Yenn's hand. They scurry after her. Ig trots to keep up, even though he's easily four years older and a foot taller than Warren. They keep close to Roseann, walking in her footsteps. Ig's unbelievable, though. Warren's never known anyone to make such a racket in a forest full of predators. Every sound makes Warren wince.

"Does this mean," Ig asks as he trips over a tree root, "you're a honeybee Keeper, too, Warren?"

Yenn flashes a scowl at him and grumbles under her breath, but Ig doesn't seem to notice. Warren casts her a sideways glance. Her cheeks are flushed and her eyes look scared.

"Sort of," Warren admits, still watching Yenn. "It's a long story."

He feels bad saying that. He hates secrets. Secrets were a currency his old Steward used to control people. And Blaiz used them against his sister. Solma was spinning with so many secrets last summer that she had no idea who to trust and, in the end, she chose wrong. But Warren's eight now, and he's not a baby anymore. He knows it's more complicated than that. Sometimes, secrets are necessary. It's just hard to work out *when*.

Up ahead, Roseann makes a noise of disapproval, as if she can hear what Warren's thinking and she doesn't like it. Warren sighs. Ig's on their side, after all. And he's harmless, isn't he?

"Truth is," he says, "I thought my bees were buff-tailed bumblebees. I s'pose those *are* my bees, really. They're the first ones I heard. But ... I hear all the insects."

"Gosh," Ig whispers, flattening his fringe over his forehead. "That's good, isn't it?"

Warren shrugs. "I dunno," he admits. "Sometimes all their songs jumble up together. It's hard to understand."

"Ah," Ig says, nodding sagely before losing his balance and falling against a tree. He rights himself, cheeks flushing. "Well, I reckon that comes with practice."

Warren frowns. "What d'you mean?"

"You only found a bee last year, didn't you?" he points out. "And Skyheart ain't had its insects for much longer. The insects are new and so's your power. There's a reason Whisperers train right from young to call up plants from underground. They got to practice. Maybe you got to practice, too."

Warren's eyebrows lift. "Yeah," he says. Ig's making a lot of sense. "Maybe."

Ig grins. "You can do it," he says. "You *got* to. I know! I'll help you!"

Warren smiles but, in a flash, Yenn's forgotten her sulk and turned on Ig.

"You can't do nothing!" she snaps. "You ain't a Keeper. Just ... leave us alone!"

Warren stops short, gaping at Yenn. What's wrong with her? She's being mean and Warren doesn't like it. This isn't the gentle Keeper girl he first met a few days ago. She's ferocious. Warren clasps his hands to his belly as it squirms with unease.

"Yenn," he mutters, but doesn't know what to say next. Instead, he just looks at her. Yenn stares at the ground, but the frown on her face tells Warren she doesn't regret her outburst.

Roseann has stopped too, watching the children with interest. Warren looks to her for support, but

Roseann offers none. Yenn turns her glare on him, hazel eyes flashing with fire.

"*You* don't get it either," she says. "And we don't got time to talk about it. Orchid needs our help."

She picks up her pace, storming through the trees ahead of Roseann. Warren thinks he sees her lift a hand to wipe her face, but he's too shocked to call after her. Other humans are complicated beyond reason. Give him a bee over a member of his own species any day. Even a glade full of myriad insects is easier to decipher than that girl.

"C'mon, boys," Roseann says, gruffly. "Sooner we're out of the trees, the better."

Warren offers Ig an apologetic smile. Ig shrugs, pretending nonchalance, but Warren sees the tightness in his jaw.

"It's ok," Ig says. "She don't like me."

"Why not?" Warren asks, following the path Yenn took through the trees. Ig shakes his head.

"Dunno," he says. "I don't think she's happy the Steward likes me."

Warren frowns. "Norsen?" he asks. "Why'd she care?"

Ig shrugs again. "Dunno," he says, in a tone that makes Warren think he absolutely does know, he just won't tell. More secrets. Secrets that hurt people and make them argue. Warren rubs his eyes but it doesn't dispel the tiredness lurking behind them. Yenn's right about one thing, though: Orchid's hive needs them. So, for now, he puts everything else out of his mind.

Twenty-Four

SOLMA SNAPS AWAKE WITH a yelp and claws the air. The image of Vulkan, the violet-eyed Fire Maker she'd met at Sand's End last summer, fades and she's lying on her back, staring at the canvas ceiling of her tent as it shifts in the midnight wind. Just a dream.

She closes her eyes and takes a few deep breaths, waiting for the tremble in her hands to calm. She's been dreaming about those damn Fire Makers more often lately. Whenever she closes her eyes, she sees flames in their hands, the tattoos above their eyebrows gleaming in the light of their destruction. Those two could be anywhere, and here at Skyheart, Solma can barely keep her brother safe from Norsen and his greed.

So far, Norsen hasn't fallen for the trap she and Reya set for him. There's nothing to do but wait and watch. Somewhere out there, Reya and her most loyal

Gatra patrol the forest, disobeying Norsen's orders, for the sole purpose of catching their leader.

Solma sighs. Beside her, Olive snores gently, her sleeping bag slipping off her shoulders. It's the first time in ages they've shared a tent again and Solma's grateful for Olive's company. She strokes a strand of hair from Olive's face, smiling. It's warm tonight, despite the breeze, but that's not what keeps waking Solma. She tucks her hands under her head and tries to calm her whirring mind. It doesn't work. She's bone-weary, every muscle aching for rest, but there's no taming her thoughts.

She'd been so angry with Warren when he'd turned up at Bell's. Hadn't she told him to *stay in the glade?* Bell weighed in—remarkably, on Solma's side for once—and Warren got upset. Everyone was shouting and no-one was listening. In the end, Solma stalked out of the house, dragging Ig with her (that damn kid!) and left Warren and Yenn at the table, poring over Bell's books. Warren had one thing on his mind. Bees, bees, bees. Solma could barely think straight for frustration. Doesn't he *get it?* A Keeper child has been kidnapped and they've no idea who took her or where.

He and Yenn have been sleeping at the house for the last two weeks at Solma's insistence. Behind a locked door is exactly where she wants Warren, at least until she can prove Norsen's treachery. She fetches them every morning, shadowing their every step. Warren doesn't hiccup without her knowing and she can tell it's bothering him. He's yelled at her numerous times. Partly, Solma thinks, it's because he and Yenn can't work

out what's wrong with Yenn's bees. She knows it's getting to him. He spends so much time sat outside that hive with bees crawling on his hands. He's obsessed, and Solma's losing patience with it. Every day they're here is another day he's under Norsen's power. Another day she might wake up to find he's disappeared, just like Addie. The thought makes her gut curdle.

She rolls over so she can peer between the flaps of the tent entrance, checking the moon. She frowns. Almost time for her watch. She sits up, careful not to disturb Olive, and fumbles for her cloth and prosthesis. She wraps her leg, cursing the dark when she struggles to tie it properly, and fits her prosthesis over the top. No point lying here thinking awful thoughts. She might as well go relieve Roseann early.

Outside the tent, Solma's skin prickles with gooseflesh despite the warm night. The sky is clear and she hugs herself as she gazes at the swathe of stars that pepper the velvet black. Ribbons of space dust glow pink and blue between the pinpricks of light.

Solma lowers her eyes and checks her hunting knife is in her belt, then picks her way through the darkness to the tree stump in the middle of the glade. Roseann is there when she arrives, her chin slumped against her chest, eyelids fluttering. The pistol rests loosely in her hand and she's about to slip off her seat and sprawl into the grass when Solma shakes her awake.

She jumps to attention, pistol raised in an instant, but Solma calms her.

"Easy," she whispers. "It's just me."

Roseann stretches and shakes herself. "Am I late?" she mumbles. Solma shakes her head.

"No, I'm early. And you need sleep."

Roseann doesn't argue, which is a measure of how tired they all are. Solma hasn't had a full night's sleep since before she left Sand's End. Fear keeps her awake. Fear and guilt. She pushes that thought aside. Self-pity never caught a tyrant. Shame never saved anyone.

Solma takes the pistol from Roseann and watches the doctor trudge towards the tents. The night closes around her again, deep silence occasionally punctuated by the rush-and-skitter of small mammals in the undergrowth. Solma nudges the tree stump with her blade foot and decides to stay standing. Pacing will keep her alert. She checks the chamber in the pistol. Three shots this time. Dyl's been more generous than normal. Solma allows herself a small smile. Whatever she thinks of the old man—and she thinks a lot of things—she can't deny his relentless dedication to protecting these kids.

She wanders in ever-widening circles around the glade, eyes trained on the tree-line. Burdock lifts his head from sleep and nickers softly when he feels her approach. "Good boy," Solma whispers, scratching his forelock as she scans the glade for signs of movement. Nothing.

Somewhere among those trees, Reya and a few of her most trusted lieutenants are patrolling the woods. They have been since Solma and Reya met at the edge of the village two weeks ago. It's been an operation to ensure they can sneak out of the village undetected, and every uneventful night is another that they might get caught. Solma doubts Norsen will be lenient if he discovers their disobedience. She thinks of Blaiz and Maxen, of how quickly they'd exiled her when she'd outlasted her worth. She shudders. No doubt Norsen will be just as harsh. They need a reason to tear him down.

There's a rustle in the bushes to her left and Solma snaps to attention. Her pistol is up and aimed, adrenalin coursing through her as she scans the tree-line. Something scurries over her flesh-and-blood foot and she kicks it off.

A snap, a muffled curse. Solma creeps forward, testing the ground before each step, advancing with practiced silence. Taipan's a good wildwalker now and Solma's been joining Warren's lessons for the last two weeks. She's glad of her newfound stealth. It means she can get close enough to the edge of the glade to see a figure rise from the undergrowth and hurry down the forest path towards the village. A tall figure with a stride Solma recognizes.

In the dark, she can't be completely sure, but it looks like Norsen.

Despite herself, Solma grins. This is it. What else would he be doing out here in the middle of the night? Solma hesitates at the edge of the glade and glances behind her. She can only just make out the silhouettes of the tents, gently illuminated by starlight. Her friends sleep in those. Her family. Olive. If she leaves now, there'll be no one to watch over them. But she's certain that the danger is in the forest now, creeping towards the village, convinced he's got away with it again.

Solma clenches her jaw and follows.

The forest is pitch black. Shadow within shadow. Solma blinks to adjust to her eyes but even the meagre starlight barely filters through the canopy. Solma resists the urge to wind up her torch, but the darkness is making it hard to keep her footing.

She stumbles and catches herself against a tree, holding her breath while the figure up ahead freezes, glancing around. This is pointless. Madness. She ought to turn back. But then the figure hunches over and Solma hears the tell-tale whine of a torch being pumped. A pale, watery beam flickers to life and Solma ducks behind the tree as the beam swings in her direction. She covers her mouth, fighting to keep her breathing steady.

The figure gives a grunt of satisfaction and swings the torch beam back onto the path. Solma peeps round the trunk as the figure moves off, she waits a moment, then follows.

With the torchlight illuminating his feet, it's impossible to mistake Norsen. Solma recognizes his shoes, the dusty cuffs of his slacks, his stride. What's he doing out here in the middle of the night?

No one sneaks around at night for honest reasons. Well, except—

The irony of that thought pulls her up short and she frowns. It shouldn't be just her tailing Norsen. Where's Reya? The Captain promised she and her most trusted Gatra would be waiting to spring their trap. This is what they've been waiting over a fortnight for. Where are they?

She picks up her pace leaning against trees to avoid tripping. Norsen's sped up, too, as if he knows he's been caught out.

But Reya never appears. No Guards spring from the darkness. Solma's pulse quickens and panic claws at her throat. Something's wrong.

She pauses, staring after Norsen and the retreating torch beam. This isn't right. And the glade with the precious Keeper children in is now left unguarded. Was that Norsen's plan? Lure her away? She needs to go back.

She pauses, leaning against a tree, cursing under her breath. She's going to have a very serious conversation with Reya tomorrow. But, for now, she needs to head to the glade and finish her watch.

And that's when the cry drifts through the forest, and Solma's heart stutters.

"Wake up!" someone roars. "Kid missing!"

Norsen hears it, too. Up ahead, he stops and the torch beam swings towards the glade. Solma has time to register that it falls across her face—that Norsen's seen her—before she turns and tears through the darkness.

Twenty-Five

OLIVE STUMBLES FROM THE tent, just as Solma skids to a halt by the tree stump in the center. Olive pins her with a torch beam, eyes flashing. "Where the hell were you?" she demands. "You got my pistol?"

No time to argue. Solma hands Olive the pistol and tugs her hunting knife from its sheath. Other torch beams flicker to life as the Whisperers emerge. The Keeper children huddle together outside their tent, gathered around Roseann as she hunches over the prone figure of Dyl. He's sprawled in the grass, woolen hat askew and a nasty bruise blooming just above one eye.

Cobra and Mamba appear beside Solma, looking stricken.

"Who called the alarm?" Solma demands.

"It was Ana," Cobra confirms. "She was sleeping in the tent with the Keeper kids. Said she heard a scuffle.

Found Dyl unconscious outside and ...” She shakes her head.

Solma clenches her jaw. “Get all the kids in one tent,” she says. “Count them. Arm yourselves. Then stay hidden.”

They both nod and rush to gather the kids. The children whimper and protest as the Whisperers usher them within the canvas walls. Taipan puts her arm around Jonah’s shoulder and guides him gently inside. Mamba and Cobra duck in after them.

“How many?” Solma barks, aiming her pistol into the forest shadows.

“One missing!” Mamba calls back. One of the children starts crying and then the others follow.

“Who?” Solma demands. There’s a pause.

“Tobias!” Cobra cries. “He’s taken Tobias!”

A snap and a rustle by the forest path. Three torch beams swing across the glade to illuminate Norsen as he stumbles into the light. Olive raises her pistol and, to Solma’s surprise, Cobra and Ana both appear in the tent entrance, Cobra brandishing a wicked-looking sickle and Ana with a short-bow, an arrow nocked and aimed at the Steward. Solma suppresses a wry smile.

Norsen doesn’t even flinch. “What’s happened?” he demands. “Who is it?”

"It's Tobias," Olive growls without lowering her pistol. Norsen sways on the spot, puts his head in his hands. "No," he says. "Oh no."

"Stop it!" Ana hisses. "Stop feeling sorry for yourself. They can't have gone far. Go get him!"

Yes. Go get him. Save the kid, they can deal with Norsen after. Solma takes off, pushing through the foliage, muscles straining as she dodges trees. But she's got no idea what she's looking for, no trail to follow. Did Tobias go with the man like Addie did or was he snatched? Is she searching for two figures—one large, one small—or a single, burly silhouette, carrying a struggling child? How is Norsen in on this? And where the *hell* is Reya?

She doesn't even know if she's headed in the right direction, but she must keep moving, keep chasing.

"Tobias!" she screams. But there's no reply. The trees swallow the milky moonlight and there's nothing but inky darkness everywhere. The ground is treacherous, laced with undergrowth that catches Solma's blade-foot. She stumbles, cursing. She grazes her elbow, knocks her knee. But she mustn't stop.

"Tobias!" she yells again. Somewhere not far away, a wildwolf howls and Solma's gut twists. Beyond the chemical boundary, there's no protection from predators. A wildwolf, even a lone one, is not something Solma wants to face alone. In the dark, the memory of an enormous boar tearing down on her looms in her mind. It's eyes red with fury, its shoulders bunched with muscle. She relives her leg disappearing under its tusks. She shakes her head, thrusting the echoes of that day away.

She's alive, she's armed and there's a boy missing.

A rustle of movement behind her makes Solma whirl round, knife ready. Olive lurches from the dark, eyes wide at the sight of the blade, and throws up her hands.

"Easy!" she growls. "It's me!"

Solma lowers the knife, relief flooding her. She manages to muffle a sudden sob, but Olive's not fooled. She grabs Solma's shoulders, shakes her fiercely, and then kisses her. Solma feels the force of that kiss and the way it pulls the panic from her, replacing it with strength.

"Don't give up," Olive says, pulling away. In the forest shadows, her face is ferocious, but there's love shining in her eyes. She squeezes Solma's arm. "Which way?"

Solma peers helplessly through the gloom. There's no sign of Tobias. Nothing. It's too dark to spot tracks or signs of disturbance. Solma shakes her head.

"I don't know ... I ..."

It hits her. Tobias is gone. Though Solma was awake, though she and Reya had a plan, though they were armed to the teeth, they were outwitted. Someone managed to sneak into camp and snatch Tobias while Solma was distracted. Norsen must have someone helping him and, whoever this man is, he's good at this. They won't find Tobias tonight.

The same thought occurs to Olive. The other girl's face twists with frustration and she drives her boot into a nearby tree, swearing. Solma wipes sweat from her forehead and realizes her hands are trembling. She curls them into fists but it isn't enough. She still wants to chase, but chase who? Chase where? The forest has wrapped itself around Tobias and the man who took him. Solma curses. She curses again, pouring out every terrible word she can think of, but it doesn't help.

Eventually, the tears come. In an instant, Olive's arms are around her, drawing her close, and Solma breathes in the other girl's familiar smell. Gunpowder and sugar cane, fresh soil and safety. She buries her face in Olive's neck and Olive holds her tighter.

"It ain't your fault, Sol," Olive growls. "You hear?"

Solma pulls away, smearing angry tears from her eyes. "I was on watch," she mumbles. "It was my job and I got distracted. I left my post—"

And now another Keeper child is in this kidnapper's hands. What does he want with them? Solma pushes that question away before her mind can run away with it. Olive reaches for her but Solma backs away, ignoring the pain in Olive's eyes.

"Sol ..." Olive murmurs, but Solma's not having any of it. She doesn't deserve forgiveness. She failed. Again.

Just like last time.

Blink. Maxen's face, smiling.

Blink. Scarred and snarling.

She can't get him out of her head, can't dismiss his cruel sneer or the warmth of his treacherous kiss. Her lips tingle with the memory, and sting with it, too.

"Norsen was in the forest," she says. "That's why I left the glade. I saw him and I followed him, and that's when Tobias was taken."

Olive stares.

"Why?" she asks. "Why'd you follow?"

Heat flushes Solma's face. "Reya and me," she mutters, "had a plan. We think Norsen's trying to trade the kids. Reya was in the forest, waiting. We were gonna catch him."

Olive's eyebrows disappear into the tangle of her hairline. "Reya was in the forest, too?" she demands. "Where was she, then? Why ain't she come to help?"

Solma shrugs. Good question.

"We have to get back to the glade," she says, pushing past Olive.

"Sol, wait!"

Olive reaches for Solma's hand but Solma pulls away. Why does she keep messing up? She doesn't wait. She heads towards the glade, tears blurring her vision. After a moment, she hears Olive following her. They're silent until they reach the glade's perimeter. Olive doesn't reach for Solma's hand again.

Dawn is creeping over the horizon by the time Solma and Olive return. Ana and Cobra raise their weapons, then lower them when they see who it is. Ana rushes over.

"Any news?" she asks. Solma just looks at her and Ana's face crumples.

Mamba appears in the tent entrance and puts his arm round Cobra. Beside them, Dyl is now awake and sitting up, sipping from a cup Roseann holds to his lips. His hand keeps wandering up to the bruise above his eye and Roseann slaps it away.

Norsen paces the glade, ranting. Behind him, sat on the tree stump in the middle of the glade with a mighty great cut across her forehead and an expression like thunder, is Captain Reya. Solma's heart kicks. This is all wrong. All of it. Thank Earth that Warren is safe in the village tonight. It could have been him.

The thought sends a knife of anger driving through her and she makes to storm over to Norsen. She still has her knife in her fist. She raises it.

"Sol," Olive hisses. Solma ignores her. "*Solma!*"

Olive grabs her arm, tight enough to make the tips of Solma's fingers tingle. Solma struggles. "Get *off* me!"

Olive doesn't. Instead, she pulls Solma towards her so their faces are inches apart.

"Don't be an idiot," Olive says. Solma glares. Olive, of *all* people, does not get to deny her this.

"I'm not being an idiot!" she protests. "Don't you get it? It was him. It must've been—"

"I know," Olive says, her fierce green eyes holding Solma's gaze, looking straight through her. "Don't you think I know? And what d'you reckon he'll do if you confront him in front of everyone? You think he'll let us walk away? Hell, Sol, you think he'll let us *live?*"

Solma stops struggling, hating that Olive speaks sense. Earth, she wants to hurt that man! She'll find out where those kids are, what he's done with them, if she has to cut that information right out of his heartless chest. Olive loosens her grip and brushes her hand down Solma's arm, lacing their fingers together. She squeezes.

"Think about the kids," she says. "Think about Warren. We got to be clever."

Solma sheathes her knife. "Okay," she agrees, still glaring at Norsen. "Clever. But clever don't mean we do nothing. Agreed?"

Olive frowns, searching her face. She doesn't trust Solma not to do something reckless and Solma hates that she's probably right about that, too. Olive knows her so well, it's infuriating.

"Agreed," Olive says. "I'm with you, Sol. I know you don't think I am. But I am." She lets go of Solma's hand and they head towards Norsen. He stops ranting to watch them approach. Behind him, Reya glares at his back as if she'd like to stick a knife in it.

"Any sign?" Norsen asks. Solma frowns.

"None," she says.

Norsen curses.

"I thought they were after Yenn," he says. "It would make sense. The honeybees ... they'd be the most lucrative ..."

"Yenn ain't here," Solma snaps, hand on the hilt of her knife. She removes it at Olive's warning glance. Clever, they'd agreed.

"No," Norsen says, pacing again. "I know, I ... she's with Bell, isn't she? I thought because ... so I came here and ..."

He's not making sense. Solma's frown deepens as she watches him. His pacing grows frantic.

"Earth's sake, Norsen!" Reya growls. "Just tell them!"

Norsen rounds on her. "You do not get to give me orders!" he rages, loud enough that the rest of the glade falls silent and a few curious faces peep from inside the tent. Norsen doesn't notice. "You've disobeyed me!" he says. "Broken my law, went out into the forest and *now* another child is missing. What should I believe, Reya? You think you and your Gatra are above suspicion just because it's Addie that went missing first?"

Reya's glare intensifies. "How," she says through gritted teeth, "could it *possibly* be me who took Tobias? You were with me, remember? In the village. *Hitting me round the face!*"

Solma's mouth falls open. "What—?"

Everyone ignores her. Solma stares at the vivid gash across Reya's forehead.

"What did you expect me to do," Norsen demands, "when I found you halfway through the door of the house where two Keeper children were being kept safe?"

The bottom falls out of Solma's gut and she sways. Olive catches her.

"Sol? Sol, it's ok."

It's not ok. Someone tried to harm Warren, broke into the house where her family were sleeping and she wasn't there to protect them. She clutches Olive's hands, unable to catch her breath. Nobody pays her the slightest bit of attention.

"I expect my Steward to believe me," Reya says, standing. "Help me get the bastard I saw sneaking round in there, rather than arrest me and the five Guard I ordered to help!"

"I've only got your word for it that there *was* anyone else in the house!" Norsen snarls. They're inches from each other now and everyone is silent, staring. Olive steps forward.

"Right," she says, her voice ringing across the glade. "Shut up, both of you. What the hell happened in the village? *What's going on?*"

Norsen and the Captain glare at each other for a few seconds, hate sizzling in the air between them.

"Someone tried to break into the house," Reya says at last. She doesn't need to say which house. That much is obvious. "I saw them fiddle the lock. I went to follow, and got hit round the back of the head." She turns her glare back on Norsen. "By the time I'd convinced my Steward I was trying to *protect* the kids, not take them, whoever was in the house had gone." She shakes her head and says, through gritted teeth, "Arrested by my own damn subordinates. As if being concussed weren't bad enough."

Silence. Solma can't breathe. She can't even bring herself to ask. She can barely feel her hands as they grip Olive's tight enough that Olive winces. There's no air in her lungs. Olive puts an arm round her.

"And the kids?" Olive asks. "Warren? Yenn?"

Norsen gives a wry smile. "Think we underestimated Bell," he admits. "There were signs of a struggle when we got inside. A smashed window, some of the furniture knocked over, and Bell stood in the middle of it all, brandishing a rolling pin. Said she walloped someone with it and they broke out through the window to get away. The kids are safe. For now."

For now. That's not good enough. It never was. This needs to end, now, and as relief floods Solma, making her knees buckle, she stares between Reya and Norsen and wonders who the hell she's supposed to trust.

Did Norsen attack Reya to help the intruder get away? Or were Reya and her Guard sneaking into the house to help whoever was in there? It's an impossible tangle and Solma still can't catch her breath. She closes her eyes, forces herself to slow down and focus. Slowly, her knees steady, her pulse calms and she feels Olive gently stroking her knuckles. She closes her eyes and replays Olive's words in her head.

I'm with you, Sol.

She takes a deep breath, drawing strength from Olive's touch.

"Right," Norsen says, pacing. "Things need to be done. You can't disobey my orders, Reya. That can't go unpunished—"

"Can't it?" Reya snarls. They fall to arguing again.

There's a sound from the tents and someone clears their throat. Olive tenses.

"I think," she says, loud enough to stop the argument, "some'a these kids might be ready to tell us the truth now."

Norsen and Reya look at her curiously. Solma turns and stares, too, but Olive isn't watching them. She's frowning towards the tents, where everyone else stands in silence. Norsen, then Reya and Solma turn and follow her line of sight. Solma's eyebrows lift.

Nessa, Jonah and Leiff have crept from within the tent and now stand in front of the Whisperers, their hands clasped, staring guiltily at their bare feet like they've got something big to say.

Twenty-Six

SOLMA STANDS UNDER THE oak, careful not to disturb Addie's butterflies. They hang limp and lackluster, wings rustling in the mid-morning breeze. Tobias' holly blues have come to join them, settling on the trunk next to the oak and falling into a stupor, as if, without their Keeper's energy to direct them, they've forgotten how to live.

Solma throws a scowl towards the tents, where the four remaining Keeper children and Warren sit cross-legged around Bell's meagre cooking fire, quietly eating breakfast.

Bell had arrived as the sun peeked over the treetops, still gripping her rolling pin as she ushered Warren and Yennevieve into the glade and turned to berate Ig for being so slow. Uncharacteristically, she'd hugged Solma without so much as a cross word and Solma felt a tightness in her throat. Bell had a cut above one eye, a livid bruise across her collarbone and was holding one arm awkwardly.

"I'm sorry, m'girl," she'd said, a wobble in her voice that made Solma's throat constrict. "I should'a listened. I—"

Solma squeezed her tight and told her to hush. For some reason, she couldn't stand Bell apologizing to her.

Solma had left Bell by the fire. Her dress was torn at the hem and she'd demanded a needle and thread to fix it, complaining loudly when Roseann insisted she sit down and have a doctor look at her first. Her arm, it turned out, wasn't broken, but she had wrenched her shoulder badly and was warned off confronting mysterious assailants with rolling pins for the foreseeable future.

"What'm I s'posed to do then?" Bell demanded as Roseann pressed a cold cloth to her head. "Just stand aside and let the oaf take these kids? *Of course, sir, take the little'uns, my doctor's forbade me from smashing your face in.* Not on your life!"

Roseann ignored her.

Ig had rushed over to Norsen, gazing at the Steward like an adoring son at his father.

"What happened?" he'd asked, and thrown an accusing look at Reya, who scowled back. Norsen ushered him over to the other children and Solma noticed Yenn glaring.

Now, all the children—Whisperers, Keepers and Ig—eat breakfast. The older Whisperers stand back, waiting. Ana tends Burdock and Poppy,

who keep tossing their heads and wandering over to see what everyone's doing. Reya sits sullenly by the tents and Norsen paces in endless circles around the fire, like a wildwolf alpha protecting his brood. It's making Solma nervous. They need to get *on*. These kids are hiding something and Solma doesn't care how much Bell insists that children need a proper breakfast. Two children, at least, might not be getting any breakfast at all.

And it could have been Warren.

Solma marches over to the fire. She's had enough of this. No more waiting. She stops in front of Bell, hands on hips.

"Okay," she says. "They've eaten. Now, they talk."

Bell frowns but doesn't object. She looks tired, her hand wandering to her bruised face. One of the tents flies open and Olive emerges. She meets Solma's gaze and nods. The adults gather and sit among the children, waiting.

"Alright," Olive says. "We need answers."

Ig pipes up, eager to speak, but splutters on a too-big mouthful of bread. Eyes watering, he reaches for a cup of water nearby but knocks it over, spilling the contents into Nessa's lap.

"Ig!" Nessa squeals, leaping to her feet.

Roseann rolls her eyes, gives Ig a whack between the shoulder blades to dislodge the offending morsel and drags him up, shoving a refilled cup of water into his hand.

"Drink," she says. Ig drinks.

"Sorry," he says, when he can finally speak. "I just—"

"Shut it," says Roseann. "Sit."

Ig sits.

There's a brief commotion while Bell dries Nessa off. Jonah and Leiff fidget. Solma jiggles her leg against the ground and glances at Warren. He's been utterly silent all morning and won't leave Yenn's side. His face is ashen, eyelids drooping. He's barely slept, Solma can tell. Taipan tried to sit next to him earlier but Warren clung to Yenn's robe until Taipan gave up and wandered, tearily, to Cobra for comfort. They're all subdued, their expressions haunted. Children shouldn't look like that, Solma thinks. It's all wrong.

Finally, Nessa settles down, as far away from Ig as she can manage.

"Now," says Olive, staring at each Keeper child in turn. "We know you ain't told us the whole truth. No sense denying it. No point getting cross for it. But Tobias is missing as well now, and we won't find him 'less you tell us the truth. So. Speak."

She waits. The Keeper children exchange dark glances. Ig wriggles but Roseann glares him into sub-mission.

Leiff whimpers and rubs her eyes. Nessa can't meet anyone's gaze. They stink of guilt and it's getting on Solma's nerves. She opens her mouth to scold them. She's done with this secrecy.

But then Jonah speaks.

"It wasn't just a man," he says. His voice is small, trembling with shame. "I mean, it wasn't just a man that Addie went with. There were two of them."

"Two men?" Solma asks, confused. "Addie went by herself with two men?"

Jonah shakes his head, cheeks flushing. "No," he mumbles. "It was a man and a boy."

The world tilts sideways and Solma sags, her heart a herd of wild horses. Everything blurs for a moment before it becomes suddenly crystal sharp. Olive puts out a hand to steady her.

"Sol? You ok?"

"A man and a boy ..." Solma echoes. In the black behind her eyelids, their faces appear, demonic, full of fire. Their violet eyes gleam, their smiles are too wide for their faces and the flame tattoos inked above their eyebrows gleam eerily.

"The Fire Makers," she says. "Vulkan and his kid. They're here, ain't they? It's them."

No one says anything. They all just stare.

"They ..." Jonah's bottom lip trembles. "We tried to make them give her back," he says. "But then they made their hands on fire and it scared us. They told us we had to let them take her. If we didn't, they'd burn everything. The glade, our insects. Everything. They said they'd know if we'd told. They'd always know."

Leiff cries quietly. "And I couldn't wake Dyl," she sobs. "He was too asleep. Didn't matter how much I shooked him. He never came to."

She leaps up to throw her arms round Dyl, sobbing loudly. "I'm sorry," she chokes through her tears. Dyl hugs her close.

"No, wee girl," he says. "It's me should be sorry. I knew something was amiss with you all when I woke, but I was so focused on finding Addie. And I was so sick that morning. I must'a been slipped something to keep me under. They're clever, them two."

Leiff nods and hugs him tighter.

Olive touches Jonah's shoulder. "Did you see their faces?" she asks. Jonah shakes his head.

"Was dark," he says. "And they had scarves over their mouths and noses. The kid didn't speak. Just laughed and made fire with his hands. The man, he spoke. His voice was horrible."

Solma glances at Warren, who's listening in terrified silence. His face is slack with tiredness but there's a furnace in his eyes. He looks ready to fight.

"O-kay," Ig says, frowning. "But, why, though? Why they come to take Keeper kids away? Makes no sense."

Olive's face darkens. "It does," she says. "Remember last year? Half the Stewards that invaded Sand's End thought Vulkan and his lad were under their command. They'd all paid him off. They're mercenaries, ain't they? What's the chances they're working for someone?"

Solma looks up to see Reya and Norsen cast each other accusing glances and her gut curdles. It could be one of them, couldn't it? But why would it be Reya? Addie's her niece after all. Family ...

But desperate people have done terrible things before. Starving parents have abandoned their kids. Greedy Stewards have used their sons as bait for unsuspecting young women. After all, Solma hardly knows Reya. Or Norsen. She doesn't know what either of them are capable of.

Solma stands, dusting down her shirt. She looks at Bell and Roseann.

"We need to leave," she says. "Now, while we still can. While Warren is still safe."

Every pair of eyes turns to her and Solma doesn't like what she sees in them. Surprise. Disappointment. Bell looks like she's never been so insulted in her life.

"You're many things, my girl," her aunt says, quietly. "But I never had you down as a coward."

Solma stares. She's about to speak but Warren pipes up.

"I ain't going," he says. There's no meanness in his voice. He's just stating a fact. "I ain't leaving my friends. It ... what if it's our fault Addie and Tobias are gone? We can't leave. Not now. We got to stay."

Solma gapes. Nobody tells him to be quiet. Bell doesn't even tell him to be nice to his sister. They all agree.

"This is—" Solma says. "You're all—"

But two faces, above all the others, quell her into silence. Olive stares at her with dismay, a frown bridging her brows. She looks away when Solma meets her gaze.

And Cobra. Quiet, gentle Cobra watches her with an expression that makes Solma want to cry or break something or both. There's no anger there. She's looking at Solma in that way she did last summer, as if she's simply waiting for Solma to make the right choice. As if she has faith her friend will get there. Eventually.

"You can't leave," Norsen growls.

At the same time, Reya mutters, "You gotta stay."

It's the first time Solma's ever heard them agree. They glare at each other.

Cobra ducks from under Mamba's arm and takes both Solma's hands in hers. "Think about it, Sol," she says. "What happens if we go? Warren's never going to be out of danger. The world will still be broken."

She searches Solma's face. "Alphor isn't big enough for you to get as far away from Sand's End—from *him*—as you think you need to. Sometimes, we gotta stand firm and turn to face what we're running from."

Solma wrenches her hands free, hating that a piece of her broke at Cobra's words. Could she be right? Maybe this isn't about Warren after all. Maybe it's about Maxen. Maybe it's about who she thought he was, and who he turned out to be. Nausea claws at her throat and she leans forward, hands on her knees. His face swims in her mind.

Blink. I love you.

Blink. I'll kill you.

Her eyes lift to Olive, who's staring at the ground. Solma thinks she sees tears in Olive's eyes and her heart lurches. She wants to gather Olive in her arms and kiss her and hold her. And say she's sorry. And say she hates this. And yell at her for not wanting to run, too. But she can't seem to close the gap between them. Her shoulders drop.

"Fine," she says, hating herself. "But *you,*" she points at Warren, "don't leave my sight and I swear, if either of *you,*" she points at Norsen and Reya, "are responsible for this, I'll kill you myself. Got it?"

Norsen glares. Reya folds her arms. They've got it.

Solma's gaze sweeps the gathered group. So, this is happening. They're staying. At the mercy of a man and a boy who lurk in the shadows, waiting to wrench the world apart as easily as pulling wings off a bee. Solma grips the hilt of her knife.

"Ok," she says. "Then let's get to work."

Twenty-Seven

THE FOREST IS SO quiet. Solma keeps her pistol in one hand, the cannister that Dyl gave her clutched in the other. She scans the trees for redbear cubs. They often hunt from above before they get too big to climb, and their claws are sharp enough to kill. So far, the branches are empty. There's no sound but the crunch of dirt under Solma's blade foot as she trudges the boundary that Dyl's made, spraying the trees he's notched to mark the chemical barrier.

Solma stomps over tree roots, muttering to herself. It's been just over a fortnight since Tobias disappeared and everyone's still on high alert, though there's been no sign of the Fire Makers—or of Tobias—since that night. Norsen put Reya under house arrest, but Bell says the entire village hears her cursing him through the window. Solma frowns. Some part of her still wants to trust Reya, doesn't like that Norsen's locked her away. It feels like he's got rid of one of the few people brave enough to challenge him.

Solma clambers over a particularly huge root and stops, frowning. She doesn't recognize this part of the forest. Somewhere to the north, she hears the river and ahead is an enormous tree. Its branches are bare, bark black and decomposing. Right down its center is a great slash, like some god has cleaved it open. It takes Solma a while to realize it has, in fact, been struck by lightning. It must've been dead for years but, even though the tree itself is no longer living, there are living things sprouting all over it. Fungal growths of the most extraordinary colors and shapes burst from its branches and cluster round its base. Networks of silver threads lace it, coating it with a fine film. Solma wanders over to it, mouth open. It's oddly beautiful. She runs her fingers over the bark and flakes of fungus come away in her hands. She brushes them away, remembering what Mamba said all those months ago about how fungus affects the Whisperers.

Makes them go weird, he'd said. She shivers.

A humming comes from the base of the tree and Solma looks down to see several honeybees clustered around the blackened bark. She frowns. That's odd. They shouldn't be out this far. The chemical barrier shouldn't let them go beyond the village. What're they doing out here? There are no flowers nearby.

She watches as they power off among the trees, their song carrying back to her on the still, summer air. Then there's silence.

Solma shakes her head. She's not paying attention. She's wandered too far. This is way beyond the chemical barrier. She gazes at the fungus tree for a little longer, then turns and heads back towards the glade. She makes a mental note to report the bee sightings to Dyl. They'll need to strengthen the barrier if the bees are breaking through it.

Sun slants through the canopy and it feels like Solma's walked for an age. She needs to pay better attention. There's a birch tree ahead with flaking, silver bark, its trunk slightly twisted. Solma sighs with relief when she sees the little notch in its trunk and rattles the cannister. She checks the boughs for redbear cubs and, satisfied, sprays the foul-smelling aerosol up and down the trunk of the tree. She wrinkles her nose, then gazes out beyond the chemical barrier, to the forest where she knows Cobra and Ana are searching. They've been out every day since Tobias' disappearance. They've started looking sick again and, yesterday, Cobra said something about how the signal feels rent apart. Solma doesn't really understand it, but it's affecting them all. Taipan had such a headache this morning that Bell had to wrap a cloth over her eyes to stop her screaming.

Solma moves on, following the well-trodden track Dyl's made over months of trudging this path every night. Sooner she finishes this, sooner she can return to the glade. She hates being away from Warren. He's surrounded by people she trusts who have shown their quality in a fight more often than Solma likes to think about.

But still.

Her phantom leg itches and she scratches it without thinking.

The cluster of trees to her left rustles. Solma whirls to face it, pistol aimed, dropping the cannister so she can unsheathe her knife. She's half-expecting Vulkan to loom from the shadows with flames in his hands. She'd shoot him. Even though that's not what they all agreed two weeks ago.

Not that anyone's agreed on very much since then.

But it isn't Vulkan that emerges from the undergrowth. Solma drops the pistol to her side.

"What're you doing here?" she hisses as Reya moves into the light. "And how'd you get out, anyway?"

Reya smirks, holding up a key. Her brown eyes flash. "Norsen forgets that plenty of the Gatra reckon he's the one behind this," she says. "They let me out when I need. Me'n a few others been patrolling the woods at night."

Solma's eyes narrow. She's not sure if this is good news. She has no love for Norsen. Nor does she trust him. He's been secretive for the last two weeks, disappearing for hours and then reappearing when everyone least expects it.

But Reya's alerted her suspicion plenty of times, too. Solma glares at the Captain. There are new lines in her face and her eyes are wild. She looks like she's losing it.

"And Norsen has no idea?" Solma says. Reya shakes her head.

"None. Listen Sergeant," she steps forward. Solma steps back but Reya doesn't notice. "I'm convinced it's him," she goes on. "*Convinced.* He might not be the one taking the kids but I'll bet he's behind it."

"Why?" Solma asks. Her missing leg itches again. She needs to get back to Warren.

Reya's eyes dart left then right. "It's ... there's one kid he won't touch," she says. "Even though she's the most valuable."

Solma stares. "Who?" she demands. "Why?"

Reya lifts her chin, defiant. "Yennevieve," she says. "The honeybees are the most sought after, they'll make any village richer than all the other insects combined. Selling her makes sense. It makes more sense than taking the kids with the butterflies. But he won't."

"Okay," Solma says, slowly. Something about this feels wrong. Solma remembers how easily Blaiz wormed his way into her mind with clever words. She won't let that happen again. "*Why,* though?"

Reya grins. "Because," she says, "Yenn's his daughter."

Solma stares, a chill settling in her gut. Yenn is Norsen's daughter?

"That's—" Solma stutters but can't quite decide what it is. The truth is just getting even more tangled. Reya nods, eyes flashing. Solma scarches her gaze for some sign that she's lying, but there is none.

"Look," Reya says, "Those Fire Makers are gonna be back for another kid soon. Whatever Norsen's planning, he knows we're on to him. He's gotta act fast. We'll have another chance to catch him but only if we're clever." Her tongue flashes over her cracked lips. "And if he does take another kid," she adds, "we can use Yenn as a bargaining tool."

Solma watches Reya through narrowed eyes. Her skin is sallow, now, from days locked away at home. Her braid—pristine when Solma first saw her—is messy, with strands of black and red hair flying out everywhere. Her uniform is crumpled and her nails are bitten to the quick, the skin around them red and raw.

Solma sighs and bends down to retrieve the cannister she dropped. "I got to get back," she says. "Look, I don't know what the hell's going on, but I ain't letting those monsters take my brother."

Reya waits, her fists opening and clenching. Solma frowns.

"But I ain't keen on the idea of using Yenn, either," Solma admits. She thinks of the little girl with the green streak through her eye, chewing on the tips of her dark hair. How the bees orbit her like little planets around a sun. She thinks of her brother, feeling the most at home he's ever felt with these kids. Her heart gives a bit. She doesn't *want* to use Yenn. But the thought of losing Warren is such a deep wound in her mind that she can't promise herself she's not capable of it, either. "I'll keep watch," she says finally. "That's all."

Reya's shoulders slump. "Yeah," she says. "Thank you."

But Solma frowns. She's not done. "I'll keep watch of *everyone*," she says. "Not just Norsen."

Reya's expression hardens. "I guess I'd expect nothing else," she says. "I gotta get back, too."

She turns and melts back into the undergrowth. Solma blinks at the empty space where Reya stood and feels immensely tired.

She rattles the cannister again, and continues on her rounds.

The sun cuts through the canopy at a slant. The day is fading. And ahead, a little bee darts in and out of the light, it's song a single, lonely note.

Twenty-Eight

WARREN SCREWS UP HIS face, pushing his mind out until he feels the brush of butterfly scent.

It's a male, one of Tobias' holly blues. He's old now, Warren can tell, with only a few days left. He hasn't mated yet. This is really important. Warren feels the butterfly's sadness, his fear and grief. He will die soon and he hasn't mated.

It's awful. Warren's surprised something so small can feel so much pain. The butterfly has no words, of course, but Warren's mind does and all that roiling fear settles in his brain under one word.

Failure.

I've failed, the butterfly says. *I'll be erased.*

Warren's heart contracts like it's taken a punch. He gasps with sudden pain.

Everything's been so weird for the last two weeks and it feels like there's chaos around him, all this running about and everyone trying to look important. There are guns and knives and Ana's started carrying her bow around, a quiver of arrows strapped to her back. No one's thinking of the insects. It makes Warren furious and, for once, he's glad his sister's not here. He thinks he'd scream at her if she was.

Solma's been like a thing possessed since Tobias disappeared, shadowing Warren's every step, never letting him breathe without her say-so. It's suffocating. Dyl patrols the glade at all hours, and Solma and Olive have been given back their rifles.

No one sleeps.

And Taipan's still not talking to Warren. Every time he goes to speak to her, she glares and turns her back on him. Warren doesn't get it.

And now Tobias' butterflies are as bad as Addie's. And they *still* don't know what's bothering Orchid's bees.

Warren searches his ability to find the exact frequency of scents the butterfly uses to talk. He pushes color and pattern into its mind.

Go find a girl butterfly, he tells it. *There's still time.*

He feels the butterfly shift, lifting its antennae in response. But he also feels its sadness deepen. It can barely fly. It's so tired. Something makes the air heavy and the flowers taste sour. There used to be a boy who helped the butterflies find the flowers they needed, who checked their eggs

and guarded their pupae. Where is that boy, the butterfly wants to know. Is he coming back?

Warren experiences all this in flashes of sensation, scent and color dancing in his mind. He works hard to understand but the butterfly's language is swift and erratic, darting in strange directions. It's a riot of color and want, instinct and fear. But over and over, the butterfly's scent triggers a picture of Tobias in Warren's mind.

It was the same with Addie's butterflies when he tried this with them. The fear, the confusion, the lethargy. The insects aren't used to living in this harsh world, with so few flowers, such tenuous seasons and chemical boundaries keeping them in. If they could roam freely they might be ok. But confined to the glade, they need their Keepers.

Warren lets go of the butterfly's mind and snaps back to himself. He opens his eyes and the butterfly colors linger at the edge of his vision, the world ignited in blues and purples. He shakes his head until his eyes settle back to normal.

Beside him, Ig and Yenn watch anxiously.

"Well?" Ig asks, smoothing down his fringe. Yenn scowls at him.

"Not yet!" she hisses. "You got to give him a moment!"

She rushes forward just as Warren teeters with dizziness and helps him sit down.

"Deep breaths," she says, and Warren complies. The world slowly stops spinning. Jonah, Leiff and Nessa hover anxiously nearby. Jonah holds hands with the girls, chewing his lip. It's obvious how afraid he is. Warren tries to give him a reassuring smile, but his face feels strange.

Ig sits beside him, too, rubbing his back.

Olive wanders over with Taipan, who breaks into a run when she sees Warren.

"Is he ok?" she demands. She rounds on Yenn. "What did you do?"

The Keeper children all begin talking at once and it's too loud in Warren's head. He winces as he gets to his feet. "It's ok," he says. "I was just trying to talk to the butterflies and it was ... I dunno. I ain't very good at it."

Taipan glares at Yenn.

"And you *let* him?" she demands. Yenn takes a step back and shakes her head, perplexed.

Olive puts a hand on Taipan's shoulder. "S'ok, Tai," she says. "Warren's his own person, yeah?"

Taipan flushes, fists clenched at her sides. She doesn't leave, Warren notices. That's something. He smiles at her. He's been trying to smile at her more lately, to invite her to come and be with him and the Keepers.

She scowls back and Warren looks away.

Olive turns to the Keeper children and Warren can tell she's trying not to let her worry show. Olive's good like that.

"How are the bugs?" she asks, putting an arm around Taipan. Warren shrugs and shakes his head.

"Confused," he murmurs. "Dying,"

As soon as he says it, his face crumples. Yenn rushes to comfort him and Taipan's frown grows thunderous. Warren drops his face into his hands.

"I can't ..." he gulps, "I can't help them. I ain't good enough. I don't get them like I get the bees."

Olive kneels in front of Warren and holds his shoulders.

"Warren," she says. "It's ok. This ain't your fault, got it?"

Warren sniffs and nods, though it feel like it's his fault. It feels like thousands of tiny, frightened creatures are clamoring for attention in his mind, like Alphor is balanced on the point of a knife and if he steps too far in any direction, the world will tumble into nothing. He lets Olive draw him into a hug and wonders where his sister is. He's wondered where she is for a long time, really. Even when she's right beside him, she's a hundred miles away, fighting everything and everyone. He misses her.

And he's furious with her, too. He needs her to listen and she never does.

But as quickly as it came, the anger goes. He sags against Olive and cries. It feels good to cry, but eventually it exhausts him. He sits in the grass, rubbing his eyes and trying not to look at the oak tree where the butterflies congregate. They're dying and he can't save them.

Nobody says anything for a while. Leiff and Nessa lead Jonah away before he gets too upset. Cobra comes over with a mug of sweet tea and hands it to Warren with a smile. Yenn, Taipan and Olive sit with him, saying nothing, not expecting anything.

"You're doing more than enough, kiddo," Olive tells him.

Warren blinks against tears. He needs his sister. Where is she? Olive ruffles his hair.

"You know what I reckon you need?" she asks. Warren shakes his head. "A break. I think you need to go play. Run about with the others for a bit. Then a good night's sleep." She cups his face in her hands. "We'll find Addie and Tobias," she says. "Your job is to stay safe, got it?"

Warren hesitates, then nods. He's pretty certain Olive's just being nice. His job is bigger than that. Who else can keep the butterflies alive while their Keepers are missing? Who else can help Yenn heal her bees? He shivers. Olive smiles at him, but there's a frown lurking behind her eyes.

Movement in the trees and Olive's on her feet but she relaxes when she sees it's Solma. Warren watches his sister as she picks her way through the sun-dappled glade. A scowl draws her dark eyebrows together. Thunderous. She's always thunderous at the moment. Olive holsters her pistol.

"Go and play, Warren," she tells him. She's watching Solma and Warren thinks he sees pain shining in her eyes.

~ Orchid ~

THE HIVE STINKS OF decay. I press my thorax to the comb, listening. The workers sleep fitfully. But I can't sleep. I can't sleep when the larvae fail to thrive and my daughters hatch twisted.

The workers dance openly of dissent now. But what else can they do? I am failing. I should die. But we have no queens. I've tried laying daughters in the queen cells. My workers tried raising them on our royal jelly. But they die, like all the others.

I fold my antennae against my head, trying not to smell the fear of my workers. It's strong, now. It makes me sick. Beside me, an attendant stirs, hurrying to me. I feel her fur brush against mine. She is attentive, but her devotion wanes. I feel honey on my tongue and I drink. Satisfied, my attendant turns to groom me and I catch sight of something on her thorax. A lump, smooth and dark. There's no fur on it and, in the night-shadows, I think I see it *shift*.

I've seen this on other workers, on their abdomens or heads. They're on the larvae. It's those grubs with the strange lumps, that die in their cells or emerge half-formed.

I press my thorax to the comb, again, listening to the lethargy in my daughters and sisters. Perhaps these strange lumps are to blame. Perhaps *they* are the sickness.

I raise my antennae and scramble down the hive, flanked by scurrying attendants. They grab at me.

Where are you going?

I kick them off. *To speak with the not-bees.*

When I'm close enough to the entrance, I fire my flight muscles, powering my scent into the night, calling for the not-bees. Calling for help, one more time.

Twenty-Nine

Solma's never going to get any sleep at this rate. Every time Warren stirs, she snaps out of her doze and is on instant alert. And he's restless tonight, muttering in his dreams. Moonlight streams through the laced tent flaps, illuminating the frown on his face. He's whispering about twisted wings and at one point, Solma hears him ask, "what's that, in your fur? That red thing?"

Is he talking to the bees in his sleep? Probably. They're all delirious with tiredness and fear. It's no wonder.

Three weeks since Tobias disappeared and not a sign of him. The Whisperers have searched the surrounding forests. Cobra said, yesterday, that it's like she can feel something's wrong, like she can feel Tobias' signal—his power—out there somewhere, but when she gets far enough into the forest, it wanes. Something stronger and crueler takes its place and she doubles over and is sick.

Tobias is being hidden from them. Expertly hidden.

Solma sits and kicks off the blankets, tucking them up under Warren's chin. She watches as he turns over and nestles against the sleeping Olive. Solma feels a little stab of jealousy and wonders who, exactly, she's jealous of.

She hits the heel of her hand against her temple to knock the thoughts out. None of that's important right now. What's important is keeping Warren safe.

She'd threatened to throw him over her shoulder last night and carry him, kicking and cursing, back to the house. Warren refused to talk to her for the rest of the evening, breaking his sulk only to tell her it wasn't fair that he stayed safe when the others were still in danger. And anyway, it didn't stop someone breaking in, did it? He's no safer there than he is here. They'd argued, the Keeper and Whisperer children looking on with fascination, until Ana and Cobra had ushered them away. It was Olive who stepped in. Olive who suggested that Warren should sleep in their tent, where Solma could watch over him, as a compromise.

Not for the first time, Solma finds herself wishing her brother wasn't so young. Mainly, she wishes that his abilities weren't so unique. Of all the children in Alphor, why did it have to be *her* brother who called up the bees? *Her* brother whose strange talents with the insects far surpasses any

of the other Keepers? And why can't he see that his importance is greater than a single colony of honeybees?

It doesn't help that Bell, as usual, sided with him.

"We'll stick together from now on, girl," she'd said. "Leave your brother be."

Leave him be. Earth's sake! Leave him be and he'll be taken by Fire Makers for whatever purpose! Solma's never leaving him be. She's never letting him out of her sight.

She gazes at him, sweeping his hair from his forehead. His brow feels hot and his frown deepens. He mutters under his breath, then kicks limply and moans. Solma tries to hush him but he won't be stilled, so she gives up.

She hunts around for Olive's pistol and, for the sixth or seventh time since nightfall, checks the magazine and clicks the safety off, then on again. Last time she checked the perimeter, she heard what sounded like a redbear snuffling about beyond the chemical barrier. It sounded big, and she'd been poised to shoot, in case the barrier scents weren't strong enough to stop it. But the creature trundled away soon after and there's been no sign of predators since.

The chemical barrier might be working to keep the insects in and the carnivores away, but it's not stopping a shadowy man from kidnapping the Keeper children.

Warren stirs again. "Yenn?" he mumbles. "Yenn, the bees!"

He kicks out. "Yenn!"

Suddenly, he's upright, eyes wide as he flails in the dark. Solma drops the pistol and rushes to hold him still before he hurts himself.

"Warren," she whispers. "It's ok!"

Warren's eyes stare wildly. He clings to Solma and she holds him close. How long has it been since she hugged him like this?

But as soon as he wakes fully, he struggles free. "Where's Yenn?" he demands. "The bees. I need to tell Yenn."

Solma flaps at him to be quiet. How do they know Vulkan and his kid aren't out there now?

"Hush, Warren," Solma begs. "It's just a dream—"

"No!" Warren snaps. "You don't get it. The bees. There are red things on them. Growths eating them alive. I need to find Yenn!"

He kicks off the covers just as Olive stirs and, before either she or Solma can do anything, he's darted out into the night. Solma swears and fumbles for her prosthesis.

"Go after him!" she growls. Olive doesn't need telling twice. She snatches the pistol and bolts after Warren, leaving Solma to wrap her leg. Solma's hands shake with fear and it seems to take an age to secure her prosthesis. She hears Warren wailing Yenn's name, hears other tents being drawn open.

Dyl's voice raises above the others.

"Kids, back in your tents! *Now!*"

Then Solma hears Warren's cry of despair and she's on her feet and tearing out of the tent. There's no time to grab her rifle so she snatches up her hunting knife and unsheathes it. Outside, the glade is in chaos.

"Yenn!" Warren shrieks. "*Yenn, where are you?*"

Everyone's awake, now. Ana rushes over to calm the ponies who paw the ground in distress. Roseann and Mamba have lit torches and the weak beams dart across the glade. Warren's panic infects everyone. Dyl barks orders at the Keeper kids but none of them are listening. Bell appears with a kitchen knife in one hand and her rolling pin in the other. Ig emerges beside her, smoothing his fringe over his forehead.

"S'going on?" he mutters sleepily. No one answers him.

Several children cry and Solma can't see anything.

"Olive?" she yells. "Warren?"

She crashes into someone with a grunt and glances up to see Cobra's terrified face inches from her own.

"What's happening?" she demands. Cobra's eyes are wide, her face ashen and milk-pale in the moonlight.

"Yennevieve," she says. "Yennevieve's gone!"

Solma's heart kicks and doubt roils like smoke in her mind. Yenn was the one kid Norsen would never target. Maybe she and Reya got it wrong.

Or maybe Reya misdirected her on purpose.

She grips Cobra's shoulders.

"When?" she growls. "How?"

Cobra shakes her head. She can't speak. The moon's reflection swims in her eyes.

"I don't ..." she manages. "I don't know."

Solma darts round her. She finds Warren in the middle of a cluster of children, all panicking. Warren clutches the sides of his head, face screwed up.

"They're frightened," he whimpers. "They're angry!"

He's talking about the damn bees!

Olive runs over from the edge of the glade, Mamba on her heels.

"There's movement in the forest," she says. "Come on!"

Solma hesitates, glancing at the cluster of children. But Roseann and Ana are ushering the precious youngsters into a tent. If they don't go now, Yenn will disappear like Tobias. Solma sees Dyl hand Ig a pistol and tell him to stay with those kids. He charges into the forest with Roseann and Bell, heedless of predators, yelling Yenn's name.

Solma should stay with Warren. But he's looking at her now, face streaked with tears, eyes pleading. And if nothing else makes up her mind, that does. She unsheathes her knife and bolts for the forest, Olive on her heels.

They crash into the undergrowth. Tree branches rip at Solma's cheeks, lashing her bare arms. She fumbles for her torch and realizes she's left it in the tent. She swears.

Olive is more organized. She hits her own torch against the heel of her hand and a weak light gleams.

She aims the beam at the ground and they pick their way through the forest.

"Yenn!" Olive roars. "Yennevieve!"

No answer. A tree mammal shrieks in the canopy. Various night creatures skitter from their path, disturbed by the noise, but there's no reply from Yenn.

Solma's breath quickens, anger turning to fear. How does this man keep eluding them?

She stumbles over a tree root and grazes her shoulder against a tree, wincing. Olive comes to a halt beside her, scanning the forest with the torch beam.

"How the—" she begins, and then a distant voice drifts on the night air.

"Get *off* me!" Yenn protests. "Dja, stop it!"

Solma's mouth falls open as Olive's torch beam swings towards the noise. Up ahead is Norsen, marching towards the village, with Yenn's wrist gripped in his hand.

Thirty

Norsen freezes. He turns, meeting Solma's gaze. Shock sparkles in his eyes. Yenn fights with everything she has.

"Sol!" she cries. "Olive! Tell him to get *off!*"

For a time, no-one says anything. Norsen looks between Olive and Solma, guilt replacing the shock in his face. Olive aims her pistol. Solma just stares, fighting to understand.

This makes no sense. She's missed something important and it feels as if It's right in front of her.

"Let her go," Olive growls. "Everyone's looking for her. Let her go."

Norsen's expression hardens. "You don't get to tell me what to do with my own daughter!" he snarls. Olive only looks surprised for a moment before she bares her teeth, stepping forward.

"It takes a properly twisted person," she says, her voice low and dangerous, "to kidnap their own kid. To *sell* their own kid. Let her go, or I'll shoot you and I won't feel even a little bit bad."

At that, Yenn stops struggling, her eyes wide. "No!" she says. "He ain't kidnapping me! He just—"

A figure crashes from the undergrowth, silhouetted in Olive's torchlight. Yenn squeals, Olive shoots but the figure's too quick and the bullet shrieks into a tree. Norsen pulls a pistol from his belt and aims it.

"Stand down!" he commands as the dark figure comes to a halt just out of Olive's torch beam, aiming a rifle at Norsen. Solma sees a braid slip across the figure's back. The torchlight gleams off black hair tinted with red. Norsen lets go of Yenn and shoves her behind him. She whimpers but doesn't run. "I said stand down, Captain!" Norsen says.

Olive moves the torch so the beam falls across the figure and, of course, it's Reya. Her dark eyes flash with fury. Her teeth are bared and there's a light in her eyes Solma doesn't like.

Norsen looks livid. A vein jumps in his neck.

"I knew it," he growls. "I'll not let you have my daughter, you hear? And I'll kill you myself if you go near any of those other kids."

Yenn looks at him, touching his sleeve. "Dja ..." she says.

Solma catches Olive's eye. She sees her own puzzlement reflected back in Olive's gaze. This is all wrong.

Olive beckons to Yenn. "Come here, little one," she says. "It's alright."

Yenn hesitates, casts her father a fearful glance, and then scuttles to Olive. Solma breathes a sigh of relief and turns back to the Captain. She and Norsen still have guns trained on each other, their eyes aflame with hatred. Someone is going to fire. Someone is going to die and Solma doesn't understand anything.

"Reya," Solma says. Olive makes a warning noise, swinging her pistol between Norsen and Reya. Solma reaches towards Reya. "Reya, stop," she says quietly. "Drop the gun."

Reya's breathing hard, her hands trembling against her rifle. She grits her teeth so hard Solma can see the muscles in her jaw spasming painfully. She winces.

"Reya, it's ok," she says, gripping the Captain's shoulder. "Drop the rifle. He ain't going nowhere. We got him."

"No," Reya says, lowering her gun. "We ain't got him. 'Cos it ain't him, is it?"

Solma stares at her and the torchlight illuminates moisture on her face. Tears draw tracks down the grime on her cheeks. "What?"

Reya shakes her head. "It ain't him. He's taking Yenn because he's scared for her. He wouldn't be scared if he knew what was happening. He don't know anything. He's as scared as the rest of us."

She's shaking so hard that Solma's worried she'll fire the rifle without meaning to. Slowly, Solma reaches across her and takes the gun, laying it on the ground. With nothing in her hands, Reya hugs herself and lets out a sob.

"It ain't him. He don't know where Addie is. No one does. She's gone."

She doubles over, gasping for breath. Norsen lowers his pistol, staring.

"That doesn't make sense," he says. "If it's not you, then—"

"It ain't me," Reya sobs. "And it ain't you, neither. It's someone close enough to fool us both."

Solma frowns, her gaze meeting Olive's again. Olive looks just as nonplussed. She's dropped her pistol to her side and has an arm around Yenn while the Keeper girl cries.

"I don't get it," Olive says. "Why would—"

But whatever she was going to ask is cut short by the cry that shatters the night air. Solma sees Olive's eyes widen. The base drops out of her stomach. Her pulse roars in her ears, so loud it almost drowns out the scream that echoes from the glade.

Almost.

"*Where is he?*" comes the roar. "*Who saw him? Warren!*"

She'd know that voice anywhere.

"*Warren!*" Bell shrieks and shrieks.

Solma's never known a fear like the one that grips her now. It closes her throat, squeezes her heart, numbs every part of her except instinct.

"No ..."

She takes off, leaving Norsen and Reya behind, ignoring Olive calling her name. Without Olive's torch, the darkness envelopes her. She bashes her shoulder against trees, catching her cheeks on low hanging branches. She stumbles but is on her feet again in moments. She follows the sound of Bell's terrified voice, feels the wrench in her heart that means her brother is gone. Snatched, taken. *Stolen.*

Fury swells inside her.

Whoever has him, she's going to kill them.

The trees thin and starlight winks through the canopy. Torchlight thrashes across the darkened glade. Panic grips the children and they're all wailing. Screaming. Solma lengthens her stride, not caring that sharp branches lash her face.

At the edge of the glade, she crashes into someone. The someone grips her shoulders, a torch beam illuminating their face. It's Bell. Her hair is all over the place, eyes wild. Her lip is bleeding, her dress is torn at the shoulder and—

And she's burned.

The flesh is still smoking, a livid red with flecks of char around the wound. Bell barely even seems to notice that her upper arm has been cooked.

She shakes Solma hard. "*Find him!*" She growls.

Solma snatches the torch from Bell and takes off, yelling. She follows the tunnel of light, shrieking her brother's name.

"*Warren?*"

No answer. The forest is full of shouting. In the distance, a wildwolf howls. Then another. Solma has no room in her heart for more fear. She is nothing *but* fear.

Suddenly, Olive is beside her, also yelling Warren's name. Ana joins her, an arrow nocked in her bow, and Cobra's with them, too, her sickle flashing in the moonlight.

"Which way?" Solma demands. "Who saw them go?"

Cobra's eyes are huge in the torchlight. She shakes her head. Ana peers through the canopy at the moon, then turns and points into the dark. "That way," she says. "Roseann said she saw a shadow heading east, carrying something."

Vulkan, carrying Warren. It must be. Solma clenches her jaw. They set off, spreading out. The Whisperers disappear into the forest, their torchlight flickering between the trees. Solma and Olive stick together, fighting their way through the thick growth.

"Sol," Olive says, panting. "Sol, slow down—"

Solma doesn't hear her. Can't hear anything except the drumbeat of her own fear. She left him. She drew everyone into the forest and left her brother laid out like bait.

The guilt drives her harder. Her blade foot catches on bracken but she wrenches it free, driving on.

"Solma!" Olive yells. "Stop!"

But Solma can't.

Her brother is gone. The world slips sideways, becoming arrhythmic. Solma can't see. She's blood and panic.

And then a hand grips her arm, dragging her to a halt. She turns, snarling, to find her face inches from Olive's.

"What're you—?"

But Olive isn't looking at her. She's looking past her, and as Solma watches, she sees the anger in Olive's face drain away. There's a sound behind her and Solma whirls, brandishing her knife.

A figure steps into the torchlight.

Thirty-One

IT TAKES SOLMA A moment to realize the figure standing in Olive's torch beam is Ig. He blinks, raising his hand to shield his eyes.

"Did you find anything?" Solma demands. Ig shakes his head, lowering his hand. He fixes Solma with a glare and there's something strange about his eyes.

"No," he says. "And even if I had, I ain't telling *you*."

Solma blinks, nonplussed.

"Look, kid," she says. "We ain't got time for this. Warren's missing and we need you back at camp—"

"I ain't going back to camp," Ig says. "I ain't going anywhere with you and your stupid group. I'm done, you hear?"

Something cold creeps through Solma's gut, some knowledge, nagging and urgent, tugging on her mind. There's something she knows, something obvious, that would unlock this mystery.

"What are you talking about?" she demands. "We need—"

"I don't care what you need," Ig says. His voice is different, somehow. *He's* different. He's angrier. That jovial innocence is gone and he stands rigid, glaring at Solma without a squint. With eyes she's never seen the color of before. Eyes of …

Eyes of flame.

Solma feels as if she's been punched.

She stares at this boy and finally recognizes him. She remembers him running from her, remembers him turning, triumphant, to yell at her, *We knew you had the bees!*

She remembers him stood beside his father, lifting his hands as he conjured fire from the Earth and set everything alight. She stares into his eyes and she sees it, now. That glowing violet. A cruel smile twists Ig's lips. He sweeps his dark fringe aside. Just above one eyebrow, is a tattoo of a flame. One that matches his father's.

Solma's breath deserts her.

"You …" she says.

Ig's twisted grin widens.

"Me," he agrees. "You remember now, yeah? Took you long enough."

Solma hates that he's right. How did she not see it? It was his eyes. His eyes that he disguised with that squint and which, now, shine that

bright, accursed violet she remembers so well. How did she not recognize this kid?

"What've you done with my brother?" she demands. He doesn't answer. "Ig!" she persists, stepping forward. She feels Olive's hand on her shoulder but wrenches herself free.

"*Ig! Ig!*" the boy mimics. "You're all so stupid! It's *Ignis*. Like the fire, get it?"

Olive says nothing and Solma senses the other girl's shock. Olive lifts her pistol and aims it between Ignis's eyes.

"I should kill you now," she growls. "Unless you tell us everything."

Ignis laughs. He lifts a palm and fire bursts from it, illuminating the forest around them in an eerie, orange glow. Solma steps back, her knife raised. She stares at the fire and thinks of Bell's charred arm. Did Ig do that to her? This clumsy, ridiculous kid? The flame crackles and flickers on Ignis's hand but there's no smell of cooking flesh. It doesn't harm him at all. The fire reflects in his purple eyes. His cruel smile widens.

"Think you know everything, don't you?" he snarls. "Think you're the only one who's got a plan for the future. Well you ain't. You ain't getting those kids back. They got somewhere else to be. Especially Warren." He laughs. "Never knew your brother was quite so precious. A right little Hive Child, eh? Why control just one or two insects when we got the whole lot?"

Cold spreads through Solma's gut. She's afraid to ask, but she needs to. She needs to know. "Where?" Fear pounds her ribcage. "*Where is my brother?*"

Ignis chuckles. "Going back east," he says. There's triumph in his face. "Where it started. Maxen says hello, by the way."

He turns and snaps his fingers. The fire flashes out, plunging Solma and Olive into darkness. There's a rustle as he darts away, his laughter drifting back to them on the cold, night air.

Solma curses and Olive staggers forward, aiming her torch beam between the trees. Ignis is gone. There's no trail, nothing to follow. He's gone and the Keeper children are gone with him.

"No!" Solma screams. "Where is he? Give him back!"

She's trembling as she charges forward, hacking at brambles, fighting through undergrowth.

Olive grabs her wrist and wrestles the knife from her, then pulls her into a hug. "It's ok," she says. "It's ok, Sol."

But it's not ok. Warren's gone and it's her fault. Just like last time.

Solma fights back tears of fury and despair. "I should've known," she says, pulling back. "I should've—I should've seen—"

Olive squeezes her arm but Solma nudges her off. It's too much, that electric touch against her skin. Doesn't she see that Solma's a curse? Solma turns away before she can see the look of dismay on Olive's face.

"It's all happening again," she growls, hating how her voice cracks. "Just like Blaiz. Just like Maxen."

She feels Olive stiffen behind her at the sound of those names. There's a long silence.

"It ain't your fault, Sol," Olive says. "None of us saw."

Gooseflesh prickles on Solma's arms. She's not sure if it's the cold, or a sudden need for Olive to hug her again. Earth, she needs this girl! But Olive's turned away.

"C'mon," she calls over her shoulder. "We need to tell the others."

Solma hesitates, then follows. Her empty hands tremble. Ignis has gone and so have the Keeper children. She's failed. Again.

The darkness has never felt so complete.

Thirty-Two

Olive's breathing is slow and regular. It's taken her bloody ages to fall asleep and Solma's arm has gone numb where she's been laying on it for the last hour. She pushes herself upright, careful not to make a noise. Pins and needles shoot up past her elbow. She bites back a yelp. She can't wake Olive. Olive will only try to stop her.

She throws off her blankets and rolls them, quickly. She didn't take her prosthesis off before she went to bed, and she didn't get undressed either. She had no intention of sleeping.

With all the panic and injuries, it was impossible to set out after Warren yesterday. Bell was too injured to travel and some of the Whisperers were hurt last night, too. Cobra took a blow to the head from an unseen assailant, which left her dizzy all day, and Ana's walking on a crutch, her ankle tightly bound after she was knocked to the ground. Mamba's limping, too, and Roseann took a deep cut to the arm that keeps opening. It seemed enemies were everywhere that night and Solma's started to fear it isn't just the Fire Makers they've got to contend with. But right now, all she can think about is Warren.

If no one else can travel, she'll have to go after him alone.

She grabs her pack, shoulders her rifle, and slips through the tent flap. The night is clear and the full moon casts milky light over the glade. Everything is silent.

Solma's not sure who's on watch right now, but as long as she sticks to the shadows and doesn't make noise, whoever it is shouldn't notice her. She sneaks round the edge of the glade, hugging the tree-line, until she finds where the ponies have been tethered. Burdock's ears prick up when he sees her and she calms him with a nose rub. Burdock blinks those big, liquid eyes but doesn't utter a noise. Clever boy.

Solma unties his rein, keeping an eye on Poppy. The mare's head droops in sleep and Solma hushes Burdock as she coaxes him away. He comes willingly, watching her as if he understands everything.

Solma leads him round the edge of the glade, until they're by the path heading back to the village. She'll need to ride him from here. If she can get a head start, no one will realize she's gone until it's too late to stop her.

She's never ridden a horse before, though, and even stocky little Burdock suddenly seems taller than she's happy with. He nuzzles her, snuffling at her shirt for treats.

"Not now, boy," she whispers. "Hold still, I gotta—"

"Going somewhere?" comes a voice from the darkness. Solma jumps and grabs her hunting knife.

A bulb hisses to life and Dyl's face appears in the yellow glow of a lantern. Solma's heart falls. She re-sheathes her knife.

"Yeah," she says, turning her back on him. "To find my brother."

"Hmph," Dyl says. "Going alone, are you?"

Solma turns back to him, scowling. Dyl's eyes reflect the moonlight and Solma reckons she sees something in them she'd not noticed before. What is that? Sorrow? Regret?

"Yeah," Solma says, squaring up to him. "Alone. Ain't no one else well enough to come with me but

I gotta get him back. I promised I'd keep him safe. He needs me. I—"

There's a sudden tightness in her chest and she can't talk. Panic flares in her throat. She staggers back and her shoulder bumps Burdock's flank. Dyl grabs an arm to steady her.

"Easy there, girl," he says. "Sit down a minute."

Solma throws him off. "I ain't got time—"

"You got time to listen to an old man's advice 'fore you go charging off into the wilderness," Dyl says gruffly. "If what I got to say don't change your mind, then you go. I won't stop you. But you listen first."

Solma says nothing, but a yawning pain opens in her chest. Every second she wastes here is another second's distance between her and Warren. She needs to find him. But Dyl's eyes lock with hers and she can't move.

"Think, girl," he growls. "What good's it gonna do? Planning on being eaten by redbears or dying in the mountains before you reach him, are you? What use are you to him dead?"

Solma stares. Is this all he's got? She knows this already. She doesn't plan on dying. She's a good shot and a fierce fighter. She can survive. And if she doesn't, at least she's tried—

"Your brother ain't the only one who loves you," Dyl says. "Or who needs you. And he won't want you to kill yourself for him." He's still holding her arm, but he lets go now and leans heavily on his cane.

"When you first got here," he says. "Bet you wondered why Norsen would post an old Aldren like me guarding Alphor's most precious kids, hmm?"

He raises an eyebrow. Solma sighs. She can't exactly deny it. "Yeah," she says. "So?"

Dyl scowls. "I known Norsen since he was a Yuen," Dyl says. "Since he was an infant in arms. Him and his twin brother."

Solma's breath catches. Norsen has a twin?

"What—?" she splutters. "Where—?"

"Dead," Dyl says, and the word sends cold shooting through Solma's body. Dyl doesn't wait for her to respond. "He was only tiny," he says. "No more'n four or five. Tannis, his name werc. Bright little thing. He'n Norsen were inseparable. Close as anything. I been Aldren all my life," he taps his weaker leg and gives a rueful grin. "Can't exactly be Fei or Oritch when I can't walk far or bend down. Can't be Gatra when I can't hunt. So I was always in charge'a looking after the Yuen. Norsen and Tannis were my wards."

Solma doesn't like where this is going. She puts a hand on Burdock's side to steady herself. The pony nickers softly.

"One day," Dyl says. "They disappeared. Ran off, like kids do, into the forest. It happens, sometimes. It's why we tell the Yuen horror stories about redbears and wildwolves, to keep them in the village, but them boys never knew the meaning'a fear. Off they ran, different directions. I chased after them, 'course, but with my leg, I couldn't keep up.

"Took me ages to find Norsen. He'd broken a finger tripping over a tree root and was wailing like nobody's business. I took him home, left him at the house, then went back out looking for his brother."

He shakes his head and, in the moonlight, Solma sees tears sparkling on his cheeks.

"I should'a alerted the whole village," he says. "Should'a called for help. But I never did. I wanted to fix it. They were my responsibility. If anyone was gonna face redbears and wildwolves and risk their life, it was gonna be me.

"If I'd asked for help. If I'd alerted the village, Tannis might still be alive."

He looks away for a moment. Solma wants to speak but has no idea what to say. She reaches for Dyl, then thinks better of it and watches until Dyl turns back to her.

"We found him—or most of him—a mile and from the village."

Solma swallows the taste of bile in her throat. She doesn't want to know this. Can't help picturing Warren's body, mangled by some vicious predator. She says nothing.

"If I'd admitted I didn't need to do it alone," Dyl says. "He might've lived."

He stares at Solma, searching her eyes. She can't look at him.

"I'd die for these kids, Sol," he says. "Any one'a them. But especially Yenn. I'd die for that girl a million times over to atone for her uncle. We can't none of us do this alone, Solma."

He hobbles towards her, hand outstretched. "Let me take the pony," he says. "Go back to your tent. Sleep. Or try to. The Fire Makers ain't gonna harm your brother."

Tears sting Solma's eyes. "How d'you know?" she demands, hating the tremor in her voice.

Dyl stares until she squirms. "'Cos he, and the kids like him, are the key to everything," he says. "Be smart, girl. You spent too long running on instinct. Now's the time to *think*."

Solma glares. But he's right. She's just one girl. Just a frightened teenager in the wilderness, fighting against the greed of a boy she thought loved her, once. What the hell can she do?

She wilts, feeling the tension bleed from her shoulders and a heaviness settle in her gut.

"Fine," she says. She'd meant it to sound defiant, but it just sounds petulant. She hands Dyl Burdock's rein and slips past him without looking back. Her eyes feel hot and her vision blurs.

Behind her, Dyl coaxes Burdock back to where Poppy is tethered. Solma climbs into her tent, lays her rifle by the entrance and unstraps her prosthesis with shaking fingers. Olive hasn't moved. Solma unrolls her blanket, curls up under it, hugs her knees and doesn't sleep for the rest of the night. She counts every second. Every second is another footstep Warren takes away from her.

Thirty-Three

THERE'S A CHILL IN the air this morning, and not just from the clouds drifting across the sun. Everyone's giving Solma a wide berth and she knows it. She knows her glare could shatter glass. Bell and Olive are both avoiding her and Solma hates that she's glad. She's not sure she can face them. Especially not Bell. Solma watches her aunt as she hobbles across the glade, never letting the Keeper children out of her sight. Despite the pain of her arm, which is tightly bandaged in a sling, she watches those four kids with dogged attention. And they cluster round her like frightened puppies. The color is gone from Bell's cheeks and Solma hasn't seen her smile in days. She frowns as she watches Bell struggle to kneel beside Leiff when the girl beckons her to examine a bee nest. They need to get going. They need to find Warren.

Ignis said they'd be heading east. They can't delay. But
…

She looks at everyone. At Bell wincing with every
movement. At Cobra, throwing up again while
Roseann rubs her back. At Ana, who still hasn't got
the hang of those crutches.

They're broken. It's been two days since Warren
disappeared but there's still no way they could travel.
There's no way they could fight. Solma itches all over,
hating that her brother is moving further away and
there's nothing she can do. Hating that Dyl was right.

She searches the glade for him now and spots him
sat under the shade of a tree, whittling something,
watching her. She shivers and looks away.

Norsen came to the glade early this morning, looking distressed. Solma bristles just thinking about it.
He'd given orders, posted some of his Gatra around
the chemical barrier. Reya's been pardoned and is
somewhere out in the forest now, searching. They'll
be back in an hour with a report and Solma will take
her place. She'll hack this whole forest to pieces if she
must. She'd cut down anything that stood between
her and her brother. She doesn't care anymore. Nothing matters like he does.

Solma huffs a frustrated sigh and scans the edge of the glade. The six Gatra Norsen's posted all watch her nervously. They're young, the eldest barely two years' Solma's junior. They hold their guns awkwardly, fear in their eyes. They'd be useless if Vulkan and Ignis turned up. Solma fixes each in turn with a withering glare, then turns her attention to the Whisperers.

They look sick again, their faces ashen and drawn. Krait's thrown up twice this morning already and Roseann's had to give King and Habu something for their headaches. Taipan sits quietly, tears rolling silently down her cheeks. She hasn't stopped crying since Warren disappeared.

Something nudges at Solma's elbow and she turns to see that Burdock has wandered over and is looking for attention. She scratches his forelock.

"Hello, boy," she mumbles. Burdock blinks slowly at her. Solma rests a hand on his shoulder, feeling his warmth. It's soothing. It helps her think. Dyl's right. She needs to *think*. But her thoughts are splintered things that cut her mind. She can't hold them long enough and they all seem to fight with each other. She's a hurricane.

She needs to find her brother. She can't go alone, but perhaps there is someone she can persuade to go with her.

Movement between the trees makes Solma and the six Gatra snap to attention. Their rifles lift in unison, trained on the undergrowth as Olive emerges. The rifles lower, a collective breath released.

The Gatra return their attention to the perimeter, but Solma can't take her eyes off Olive. The other girl looks thunderous. She picks her way across the glade to Solma and Solma's heart bucks.

"We need to talk," she says as Olive draws level with her. Olive nods.

"Yeah," she agrees. "We do."

"We can't wait around here," Solma says. "The Fire Makers are taking Warren east. If Bell and the Whisperers can't travel, then you and me got to go."

"Sol," Olive says quietly. Solma barely hears. The words tumble out, unchecked.

"I ain't letting Maxen get away with this. I'll kill him first."

"Sol ..."

"If we leave today, we can cover good ground. I'll bet anything—"

"*Sol!*" Olive barks, making Solma jump. Olive meets Solma's eyes. It takes Solma a while to realize Olive has been crying. Olive ... crying?

Solma feels her gut tie itself in a knot. Olive runs a hand through her flame-red hair and stares into the distance.

"I can't do this no more," she says. Solma frowns.

"What are you on about?" she demands. "We don't got a choice, Olive. We got to find those kids. We got to find Warren. You heard Ig, he's—"

"No, Sol," Olive says. "I can't do *this*. With you."

Solma stares. Olive's words don't make sense. A slow pain yawns inside her, like a monstrous mouth opening.

"No, Olive," she chokes. "No, please."

She reaches for Olive's hand but the other girl snatches it away. A single tear draws its way down her cheek.

"I'm sorry," she says. "I know you're missing Warren but I just can't, I—It's my fault. I shouldn'ta pushed you into this—"

"You didn't push me," Solma insists. "I wanted to. I wanted *you*. I still do, I—"

"No," Olive says, cutting Solma off. "You wanted him. I should'a seen how he'd hurt you and I should'a realized you'd need time. I can see how you think about him whenever stuff goes wrong. He haunts you. You know you talk to him sometimes, in your sleep?"

Solma doesn't know what to say, doesn't know how to cross this canyon between them.

"Olive, I don't want him. I—"

"It's ok, Sol," Olive says, with a small smile. "I don't blame you. I love you. You gotta know that. It ain't your fault, it's … look, I thought I was strong enough to wait for you but I ain't. It just … it hurts too much." She bites her lip and Solma aches to kiss her. But she can't. A sob escapes her before she can stop it.

"I'm sorry, Sol," Olive says. "I really am."

She turns before Solma can say anything, disappearing into the tent behind Roseann. Solma stares after her, waiting to feel the hurt she knows is coming. But she's just …

Numb.

Tears sting her eyes.

Blink. Maxen's face, smiling, bending down to kiss her.

Blink. Scarred and snarling.

Solma shakes her head until the images fade. It's all so broken. And it's her fault. Her knees buckle and she sags against a tree. The world tilts, blurring.

How has this all shattered so fast?

A sob escapes her, then another, and before she knows it, she's crying bitterly. She hoists her rifle onto her shoulder and lurches into the trees, away from the questioning eyes, away from the stares, and away from the glade, which feels heavy with her failure.

She runs until the noise of the glade fades to a murmur and slumps against a birch, crushing her eyes closed. Behind her eyelids, Maxen's face appears. He's laughing. He's laughing because she's lost and he's won. Because who the hell is she to fight against the Stewards of Alphor? Who is she to think she can run from him?

A rustle in the bracken makes Solma lift her pistol, snarling.

Bell wades through the foliage, scowling at Solma until Solma rolls her eyes and lowers her gun, flopping in the leaf litter with a soft thud.

"What?" she snaps. "Come to tell me off? Come to tell me to stop being so selfish? What d'you want, Bell? Say your bit and then leave me alone, would you?"

Bell frowns at her and says nothing. Slowly, she removes her arm from the sling, wincing as the cloth brushes against the bandaged injury. She straightens it, hissing air through her teeth. Her face tightens with pain and Solma wants her to stop it. If Bell wants to make Solma feels bad, she's doing a great job but Solma's hit the limit of her guilt.

"What're you doing?" Solma asks. "You'll just make it worse."

Bell ignores her. She raises her hand in front of her face and flexes her fingers. They don't move as they should.

"Roseann said the feeling might not come back," she says, shrugging. "It was worth it, though. Smacked that villain right round the ears with my rolling pin."

Solma feels her mouth twitch, and Bell catches her eye, winks. "It don't matter, girl," she says. "My left hook's just as strong as my right. When we face him again, I'll hit him so hard his eyes'll fall right outta his evil ol' head."

Solma can't help it, she snorts a laugh. Bell comes to sit beside her, sliding her injured arm back into the sling. She takes Solma's hand, squeezes it. Solma squeezes back.

"I'm sorry, Bell," she says, feeling tears sting her eyes again. "I'm sorry I didn't—I couldn't—"

She feels her face crumple. Bell lets go of her hand and wraps her arm around Solma's shoulder, drawing her close. "Oh, my girl," she says, kissing the top of her forehead. "I'm the one should be sorry. You had to be so brave all this time. It ain't fair."

Solma presses her hand against her eyes. The sobs wrack her and she can't speak. Bell holds her and just lets her cry, the grief and shame and hurt boiling from her in hot tears and gasping breaths.

When Solma is spent, they sit in silence. Solma lets herself be held. Bell strokes her hair softly.

"We got to leave here," Solma says after a while. "We got to go find him. *I* got to find him. This is all my fault. I messed up again, I—"

Suddenly, Bell is kneeling in front of her, eyes as fierce as Solma's ever seen them.

"Now you listen to me, girl," she says. "You ain't to blame. Not any more than I am. Than Olive. Than Dyl. Than Warren himself is, y'hear? You are one girl, Solma. One powerful, beautiful, brilliant young woman. But you ain't alone. You never was. You cannot take all this on yourself. I won't let you."

Solma stares into her aunt's eyes and sees layers and layers of grief there. She sees the death of her own mother—Bell's sister. The death of her father. She sees every loss Bell ever suffered and there are many. But there's something else in Bell's eyes, too. A fierce, unyielding love. Solma sees herself reflected there and she manages a small smile.

"I wanted you all to forgive me so much," she says, covering Bell's hand with her own. Bell laughs.

"My girl, there weren't never any question of forgiveness. There weren't never any blame at all."

Solma frowns but says nothing. Bell kisses her forehead.

"I got to find him," Solma says after a while. Bell shakes her head.

"*We* got to find him," she corrects. "Think of Warren's bees, eh? They can't make it alone, can they? But in their hundreds, their thousands, their tens of thousands, they're a force to be reckoned with."

"But we ain't bees," Solma points out. Bell chuckles.

"No," she agrees. "But we ain't islands, either."

She lets go of Solma's face, brushing a strand of hair from Solma's cheek. "We know where they're going, Sol," she says. "We'll find him. Together. You hear?" Her face darkens. "And next time I see Vulkan, I'll knock out all his teeth and play them like an old-world instrument."

Solma snorts. "Thank you," she says. Bell shrugs.

"Come on." Bell offers Solma her good hand. "We best start packing."

Thirty-Four

YENN LOWERS HER HANDS and lets the honeybee worker shuffle onto the hive platform. She's lethargic, her antennae heavy and slow. And there's a blood-red lump attached to her thorax. Solma was right. Since Orchid alerted Warren before he disappeared, Yenn's been looking out for the strange red lumps. She thought Warren's sister was hysterical at first. But she wasn't. At least, not completely. The red lumps are real.

Most of the bees in her hive have them. Once, she saw one moving and realized it was a *creature*. A creature, feeding on the bees. She went and threw up after that, then cried, and now she's spent. There's nothing to do. After she found the lumps on her bees, she ran to Warren's aunt and asked for her books. For an afternoon, she sat, racing through the pages until she found the information she needed.

She knows what these things are now: A parasite. *Varroa Destructor.* She knows that a hundred years ago, the Beekeepers of the old-world fought these pests. It was the bees' poor diet and the use of the old pesticides that made them vulnerable. Although nobody knew for sure until it was too late. But knowing what they are doesn't help her. She has none of the medicines the old-world developed to fight this pest. No idea how to fix them.

Yenn watches the bee fire her engine and zoom towards the forest. They've been doing that a lot lately, though there are no flowers in the forest. Those that fly that way rarely come back. They're losing the way home. Or perhaps they're going to die. Yenn's not sure.

She glances at the other Keeper children, huddled under Roseann's watchful eye. She should go and comfort them. She's not as old as Nessa or as clever as Leiff, but she *is* the Steward's daughter.

Only she's got no idea what to say. She wants to ask her Dja for help but he looks half-broken himself. Besides, these insects need her as much as they always have. But every time she closes her eyes, listening for the thrum of their dance, they send the same message over and over.

Where is he where is he where is he?

Yenn's little heart breaks. To hear them call for him. She's not sure she can fix this on her own. If Warren was here, they could work this out together. If he was here—

Yenn turns her back on the honeybees, shuddering as the panic of Orchid's sick hive jolts through her. Her shoulders clench. For once, she

wishes she wasn't a Keeper. She wishes that she was just an ordinary girl, oblivious to the return of the insects, and how they're probably going to die again before they even get going. She's never wished that before and it pulls her up short.

She can't do this. She can't fix it. It's all going wrong. It's all—

The world goes blurry. Her lungs feel a size too small. She can't get any breath. It feels like a huge hand has reached under her ribs, grabbed her heart and is squeezing. Her legs buckle beneath her. She's on all fours. She's dying and no-one's even noticed—

"Yenn?" says a voice above her. A voice she recognizes. A face swims into view. Brown skin. Head freshly shaved. Orange eyes, bright as a sunset. Taipan frowns. "Oh," she says. "You're frightened. You need to sit down properly, like this."

Taipan guides Yenn until she's sitting with her back against a tree. Taipan crouches in front of her, watching.

"Stop fighting it," the Whisperer girl says. "It'll happen anyway. Just let it come and it'll be over faster."

Yenn's not sure what she means. The clawing panic that's wrenching her heart and closing her lungs will kill her if she lets it. She has to fight it or she'll die. She'll die.

"You won't die," Taipan says, as if she can hear Yenn's rattling thoughts. "Let it happen."

Yenn's not sure she can hold it back. She squeezes her eyes closed, clenches her fists ...

And then the panic breaks the dam she's raised and it's a tornado. A great wave. A hole opening in the ground beneath her. Hot tears burst from her eyes, spilling down her robe. Sweat prickles all over her face. She's burning up. She's freezing cold. She can't *breathe*.

Taipan grabs her face and leans her forward just as Yenn throws up. The sticky mess lands in the grass and she avoids choking on it.

Gradually, her body settles down. She wipes her mouth with the back of her hand.

"Ugh,"

Taipan blinks. "Wait here," she says. She scurries towards the tents and returns with a filled waterskin. She hands it to Yenn. "Drink."

Yenn drinks.

She's still shaky, but she no longer feels like she's going to burst. Her vision focuses on Taipan's concerned face.

"Thanks," she croaks. Taipan shrugs.

Yenn practices breathing, relishing the cool air in her lungs. She concentrates. Taipan sees her frowning and sighs.

"I'll go if you want," she says, and stands. For the first time, Yenn notices that the other girl's voice has an edge to it. She grabs Taipan's hand before she knows what she's doing.

"No!" she says. "Don't—I mean, please stay."

Taipan's frown deepens. Yenn can practically see her weighing up this choice and she realizes how much she's hurt Taipan, even though she didn't mean to. From that first, dismissive moment they met and all the times since. All the times Warren has chosen to be with her over the friend who saw him through the hardest winter of his life. All the times she made Taipan feel ordinary and boring, made her feel that she couldn't understand because she wasn't *one of them*.

She wonders what that even means any more. She lets go of Taipan's hand.

"It's fine," she says. "I get it."

She turns away, expecting Taipan to leave. There's a rustle of robes and Taipan's kneeling beside her, the frown gone. They stare at each other for the longest time and Yenn is so ashamed of herself that tears burn her eyes.

Taipan lets her cry. She doesn't hug Yenn, but she doesn't leave either.

"You scared?" she says after a while. Yenn wipes her eyes on the back of her sleeve and nods.

"Yeah."

Taipan smiles. "Me too," she admits. "I miss Warren."

Yenn manages a watery smile. "I miss him, too. I think—I think my bees need him. I think they'll die without him."

She feels her face crumple again. Something brushes her hand and she glances down to find that Taipan's holding it. She looks into the Whisperer girl's face and thinks her eyes are *so orange*. She's never met anyone with eyes like that before. Eyes the color of sunset. The color of fresh flame, the color of never-giving-up.

"Look, Yenn," she says. "Warren's great, but he's just a kid like the rest of us. If he could save the bees, then so can we. And then we can save *him* too."

Yenn isn't sure she believes any of that. Orchid's bees are asking for Warren. They're relentless, desperate. They need him. But Warren's not here and Taipan's offering something different. Something that feels a bit like hope. Before she knows what she's doing, Yenn grabs it with both hands.

"What can we do?"

Taipan thinks. "What do you know about the bees being sick?" she asks. Yenn explains about the twisted wings, the lethargy, the way they keep flying off into the forest which doesn't make any sense. She explains about the strange red creatures living on her bees, sucking them dry. Tears burn her eyes again as she talks, but Taipan listens intently. She nods, frowns, asks questions.

"Right," she says when Yenn's finished. "What do the other queens say?"

Yenn stares. "What d'you mean?"

"The other queens," Taipan says again. "You said they were healthy. Only they're right next to Orchid's hive, so why are they healthy and Orchid isn't? You asked them, right?"

Yenn gapes. How has she not thought of this? She slaps a hand to her forehead. "I didn't!" she admits. "I don't know!"

Taipan rolls her eyes. "Honestly," she says. "I thought you Keepers were s'posed to be *smart*."

Yenn looks at her. Taipan raises an eyebrow, and then they're both grinning. The remaining tension fizzles away. "C'mon," Taipan says.

Yenn gets to her feet. This close to the Whisperer, she smells the earthy scent of flowers on Taipan's clothes. It smells so much like her bees that she thinks they're one and the same. The flowers and the creatures who feed from them. They can't exist without each other. It seems right that Taipan's at her side right now.

They head to the hives and Yenn's heart lifts as she closes her eyes and reaches out her scent.

~ Orchid ~

THEY HAVE STOPPED DANCING. The comb is almost
silent, only the slight tremors caused by bee feet re-
mind me there's any life left. Three of my attendants
have died, and there are too few healthy daughters to
replace them.

Almost every bee in the hive is now peppered with
the shifting lumps. A bee-eating mite. They clamp
onto us with fierce jaws and suck life from us. There
are two on my thorax and one clinging to my abdomen, sapping my health. I feel the way they shrivel
me, how the whole hive is suffocating under their incessant appetite. I tried grooming them off. So did my
attendants. But there are always more.

No-one dances of new flowers. The honey stores are
running dry.

And the not-bee-boy is gone. Gone where? I don't
know. I can sense him, somewhere in the distance,

almost beyond our reach. But we're too weak and tired to search, though we need him.

The not-bee-girl is trying. I feel her fear. She's sick, too, though not sick like we are. She's sick in her heart. She sees what's killing us but doesn't know how to stop it.

I shuffle across the comb, press my thorax to the wax and give three, short buzzes. They echo through the hive.

I am alive. I am laying. Don't give up.

I feel the workers pause to listen, the half-hearted buzz of their reply. I limp to an empty cell and dip my abdomen into it, ready to lay. I wait, anxious for an egg.

I wait and wait but there is no egg. I can't lay. My body shudders with effort, twitching with pain, but I can't lay. If I can't lay, we will die. All of us.

But the hive must survive.

We love our not-bee-girl. We love her like a sister. Like a daughter. Like one of our own. But our scent reaches out beyond her, seeking the boy. The boy who sings the language of every insect, who's heart is a hive of its own. We sense him. My sister-workers dance of him. It's disjointed and tangled, but they feel him. He's close by and we need him.

If they can find him, he could help. And there's nothing left to try. It's the only thing we all agree on.

So the strongest of us power their flight engines and sing out beyond the trees, following the scent of the not-bee-boy.

But we are tired. We are weak. And not one of our strongest sisters comes back.

Thirty-Five

FOR THE FIFTH TIME in as many minutes, Solma checks the position of the sun. Olive and Cobra should be back by now. It's been two days since Bell found her crying in the forest and Solma's eager to go. The cart is packed. Roseann's directing the younger ones to ready the tents. Solma shifts her weight, restless.

Beside her, Mamba keeps trying to catch her eye but she glares steadfastly at the trees. She can't deal with his concern right now. She's got enough of her own.

"They're late," Mamba says. Solma's scowl deepens.

"I know," she growls. Mamba doesn't hear the impatience in her voice.

"Where are they?" he asks.

"How should I know?"

She regrets snapping the moment the words are out of her mouth, but at least he takes the hint this time. He falls silent, hands in the pockets of his robes. Solma casts him a sideways glance. She's never seen him look so uncertain. The weight of the future lays heavily on his shoulders, too.

Bell had a point. It isn't just her.

"Try not to worry," she says, and means it. "Cobra's no pushover and if I could choose anyone to fight by my side, it'd be Olive. That girl's got the heart of a redbear."

Mamba manages a small smile. "Yeah," he says. "Thanks. How're you holding up?"

Solma feels the scratch of fear in her throat again. She glances into the center of the glade where the other Keeper children wander listlessly while Dyl sits on the tree stump, watching them with the vigilance of a mother redbear supervising her cubs. Solma thinks he looks older, if that's possible. She turns her attention to Yenn and Taipan, whispering by the beehives. She sighs.

"I'm ok," she says. "I mean, I'm not but ..."

There's a rustle as Olive and Cobra emerge from the trees. Cobra looks pale, her eyelids drooping.

"Co!" Mamba cries, rushing over. He kisses her forehead, cups her face in his hands. "Are you hurt? What happened?" He pulls her into a hug, smothering her reply. She sighs and pushes him off, but there's tenderness in her eyes.

"I'm fine," she says.

She looks towards Solma. "But you need to tell the others to stop packing."

Solma starts to protest, but Olive interrupts. "Just hear her out, Sol."

Solma frowns but obeys.

Cobra closes her eyes and leans her head against Mamba's shoulder for a moment, as if drawing strength from him. Solma watches them, then glances up and catches Olive's eye without meaning to. A jolt passes through her.

They both look away quickly, and Solma clutches her belly.

At last, Cobra opens her eyes.

"The signal," she says. "You know it's started making us ill again? I think I've worked out why."

Solma scowls. What has this got to do with anything?

"The signal must be the Keeper kids," Cobra continues. "But when Tobias disappeared, the signal split.

It's like it existed in two places and it felt wrong. The wrongness got worse when Warren disappeared, but it was more than that. You remember us saying it felt familiar and new at the same time? It felt like we'd sensed it before? That's because we *had*. Or at least, we'd sensed part of it and not realized."

A coldness creeps through Solma. "The Fire Makers," she says. "They're a kind of Whisperer, aren't they? They were here, tangled up with the Keepers."

Cobra nods.

"But that's impossible," Solma says. "It took us months to get here. How were they here long enough for their signals to mix?"

Cobra shrugs helplessly and leans into Mamba's chest. He wraps a protective arm round her and rests his cheek on her head. Solma watches them for a while, then averts her eyes again.

"The point is, though," Cobra goes on, "I can still feel it. The signal is split, but it hasn't gone. They haven't left. We can't go east, Solma, because Warren is *still here* somewhere. He's nearby. We can sense him."

Solma's breath catches. Hope hums like bee song in her chest.

"I don't get it," Mamba says. "They've got what they wanted, right? They've got three Keeper kids and we know it's them now. Why wait around? If I was them, I'd already be halfway to Sand's End. It doesn't make sense."

Cobra shrugs. Olive frowns, and Solma feels the coldness in her gut intensify. He's right. That doesn't make sense, and that unsettles her.

She lifts her gaze and catches Olive staring at her. Solma closes her eyes and …

Blink there's Maxen's face, scarred and snarling, ordering her exile.

But when she blinks again, it isn't Maxen's face she sees. It's Olive's. Olive stood beside her in defense of the village. Olive meeting her gaze as she tells her not to be such a fool. Olive beside her in the tent at night, their arms around each other. Olive's hand in hers. Olive's laugh. Olive's kiss.

She shakes her head, eyes flying open. It's all so obvious now. She wants to pull Olive into a hug, to kiss her and never stop, to say she's sorry a thousand times for the hours she wasted on a boy who never loved her when she should have been with the girl who always has.

But Olive's already trudging towards the tents, waving at Roseann to stop dismantling them.

Solma turns away from Mamba and Cobra and angrily wipes her hand across her eyes.

Earth, she needs to sleep!

Something brushes her shoulder and she turns to find Cobra smiling at her. "It's not too late, Sol," she says, drawing Solma into a hug and somehow knowing everything she's thinking. Solma buries her face in Cobra's shoulder, this friend she betrayed and then forgot and who found a way to forgive her.

"It's never too late."

Solma frowns. She's not sure that's true, but before she can respond, a shout goes up amongst the Skyheart Gatra and Solma sees them turn and salute. Norsen appears on the path from the village, looking haggard and pale. He's alone. No Gatra in attendance. He waves at the Guards to stand at ease. His eyes are distant, troubled. Yenn runs to him and he scoops her into a hug. Solma watches him and can see nothing but love. He's made mistakes. It's his fault her brother is gone.

No it isn't. She knows who's fault it is, really.

And he's not the only one who messed up, is he? He catches Solma's eye and she nods in greeting. Norsen nods back. Solma hoists her rifle and follows Mamba and Cobra over to the tents.

~ A Moment ~

OLIVE WATCHES SOLMA SETTLE by the fire with the Whisperers. Cobra holds her hand. Krait wanders over and clambers onto her lap and she folds an arm around him. Olive smiles. She knew Solma had it in her. She watches the girl she loves—and oh, she does still love her—as the tension goes out of her shoulders, as the touch and the smiles of others calm her. She's been so alone, even surrounded by all these people. Olive's heart both hurts and sings to see her shedding that loneliness. She wants to go to her, to kiss that dark-haired head and hold her closer than close.

But she can't, can she? Not now. Maybe not ever again. She sighs, watching King and Habu scurry over. The boys come to sit round the fire. Krait complains loudly of a headache. Habu clutches his tummy and groans. Roseann sits among them, patiently handing out medicine. She meets Olive's gaze and rolls her eyes.

Olive snorts a half-hearted laugh, but her eyes drift towards the honeybee hives.

Only Taipan seems less affected by this new split in the signal. She's pale, yes and she's already been sick once this morning, but determination keeps her upright. Olive is surprised to see her with Yennevieve, heads together and muttering as they kneel outside the hives. Those two have spent so long disapproving of each other, but something's changed. A little bee flashes in front of Olive's face and she blinks, lifting her hand. The bee fusses around her finger before landing on her knuckle, abdomen pumping for air. Olive doesn't speak bee but she's certain this isn't one of Orchid's. She's too healthy, her body full of strength, her fur bright and lustrous. She finishes cleaning and then takes off, powering into the forest in the direction of the river. Olive frowns. They shouldn't be able to do that. The chemical boundary should keep the bees in, but Olive's seen a lot of the bees do that lately. And the bees that head towards the river are always healthy and strong. None of them have the red growths of Orchid's hive.

Another bee lands on Olive's still-outstretched hand and Olive watches her as she pumps her abdomen, gasping for breath. This bee is definitely one of Orchid's. Her fur is lackluster and pale, her wings seem dull and discolored. Olive watches her with a growing sense of sadness.

But then the little bee fires her engine and zooms off, drawing a zig-zag path into the forest. Olive frowns. She'd expected the sick bee to follow in the path of the healthy one, towards the river. But it doesn't. This one is heading in the opposite direction. East, towards the mountains.

East.

What if …?

She stands, checking her weapons. She hopes she won't need them, but she never knows. Roseann frowns as her daughter marches past, heading towards the beehives, but she doesn't ask. Roseann learned a long time ago that Olive doesn't take well to mothering. Still, Olive's aware of her Ma's eyes on her as she crosses the glade and kneels in front of the west-most hive, smiling at Taipan and Yenn. They frown at her, confused.

"What're you doing?" Yenn asks. Olive shrugs.

"Getting to know the bees," she says. She points at the hive in front of her. "This Orchid's hive?"

Yenn and Taipan exchange glances and nod. Olive focuses on the hive. She doesn't have the children's talent, so all she feels when she places her hand against the hive walls is the gentle buzz of the bees within and the sense of awe that always comes with being so close to insects. They're so small, so insignificant, and yet without them, the ecosystems have collapsed and the human race is dwindling

This hive is quieter than the others. The sick hive. The one Warren spent so much time with, his mind entangled with theirs, trying to work out how to heal them. He knows these bees. And they know him.

She moves back from the hive and crouches, watching. Bees emerge in a steady stream and head into the glade. Most spread out and visit the flowers peppering the ground, but a few of the bigger, stronger ones zoom into the dark forest. They always head in the same direction. East. Always east. Olive's patrolled this forest, rushed through it searching for kidnapped children. She's travelled the length of Alphor before she arrived at Skyheart and she knows there are no flowers that way. No flowers have grown wild in Alphor for a century. The only ones that exist are those planted and pollinated by human hands. The river is in the opposite direction and so is the village. There is nothing out east that the bees could need or want.

So where are they going?

"Wait here," Olive tells the children.

The girls shuffle their feet but do as they're told. Olive rises and follows the bees towards the forest. They're too fast for her to track any single bee, but as soon as she loses one, she waits and another zooms by in the same direction. Hand on her knife hilt, Olive creeps after them. They never deviate. Each one's powerful engine drives it deep into the forest, following the same flight path as the one before it and the one sure to come after.

It's not lost on Olive that these bees are larger and stronger than the others, as if the hive's most powerful workers are being reserved for this mission. A few meters into the forest, one lands on Olive's wrist. She lifts her hand and watches in astonishment as the little bee trundles onto her palm, buzzes to get her attention and begins to ...

Dance?

Olive heard Warren and Yenn talk about the dancing bees before, but she'd dismissed it as the imaginings of two children. Now, she watches, open-mouthed, as the bee on her palm vibrates her wings, wiggling her abdomen. She walks up Olive's hand, then rushes round in a half circle and repeats the strange, waggling dance.

It means something. It's a communication, Olive knows it. Earth, how she wishes she had Warren's power at this moment.

But the little bee is convinced Olive can understand her, so Olive will try. She holds the creature up to the light and concentrates. The bee always waggles in the same direction, upward along Olive's hand, but not directly upward. It's a forty-five degree angle. Olive shields her eyes and peers up, through the forest canopy.

Up can't be the direction the bee wants her to go. Or can it? If it is, this is hopeless. A bee can go up but Olive can't. She has to believe there's another explanation.

Directly above her, occasionally peeping through the canopy, the sun hangs like a glorious golden eye.

The sun! Olive remembers now. In Bell's books, it said that honeybees navigate using the sun. So the forty-five degree angle of the bee's dance must be in relation to the sun.

Olive glances back at her hand to find the bee waiting, antennae raised in question.

"I'm here, little friend," Olive says. "Keep dancing."

And the bee does keep dancing. She sets off again on her strange, upward waggle, then races round in a half circle to begin again. When her dance is complete, she lifts her antennae, waiting for Olive to understand. When Olive does nothing, the bee hurries to repeat her strange instructions. It's always the same number of half circles she rushes in. Always the same number of repetitions.

Olive knows the direction she must go in, now. So what else should the bee's dance tell her?

Distance?

It's as good a guess as any. The repeated circles must tell her how far she must go, though Olive has no idea what each circle might mean. A meter? A hundred meters? Still, Olive smiles.

"Thank you, friend," she says. "I'll do my best."

The bee finishes her dance and, with a kick of her strong engine, powers into the forest gloom. Olive loses her amongst the foliage, but she heads in the direction she hopes the bee indicated, forty-five degrees from the sun. A few minutes later, another bee zooms past. She follows it for a short way until it disappears, then waits for the next. As long as the bees are heading this way, she isn't lost.

The forest thickens, roots arching from the ground in tangled structures so that it's difficult not to stumble. This deep into the forest, barely any light penetrates. Olive trips, curses, grazes her hand against rough tree bark. She can barely see the bees as they zoom past her anymore, but she hears their song. She pushes on.

She's so intent on following the bee's instructions that she doesn't notice the first little body. Or the second. But there's a cluster of them under the shade of a sapling that catches her eye and she crouches, sadness forming a lump in her throat.

Five little honeybees lay, dead, amongst the leaf litter. Their fur is dull, their legs folded beneath them. There's not a mark on any of them, but Olive sees that each has a shiny, blood-red lump on her abdomen or thorax. Orchid's bees. They never made it to where they were going. Whatever they're searching for remains hidden and the hive isn't strong enough to find it.

Gently, she scoops one of the bees into her palm and examines it. She has a horrible feeling it might be the bee who danced on her hand.

Olive lifts her gaze from the little bee and peers into the thickening gloom of the forest. Up ahead, she sees how the forest starts to thin and the foothills loom beyond. There's nothing for the bees out here. No water. No flowers. No hope.

Except ...

It's impossible, ludicrous. It can't possibly be true. But she can't shake the thought. These are the bees Warren has spent all summer with. These are the bees who flew into his dreams. These are the bees his mind linked to, whose dancing and song has so deeply entangled itself in him that perhaps ...

Carefully, Olive scoops the bee bodies onto her palm and carries them back to the glade. She has an idea.

It's a long shot. But it's all she has.

Thirty-Six

Warren's nearby. Solma's heart lifts at the prospect. He's close. There's still a chance.

But something else nags at the corner of her mind. *Why* is he still nearby? Maxen and Sand's End are miles away, months of journeying. Why are the Fire Makers waiting? They can't expect to steal more Keeper children now. And they have the most powerful one.

They have her brother.

So why wait?

The glade is full of activity. Norsen's Gatra—no longer under suspicion—are out in full force, patrolling the glade and surrounding woodland. There are a lot of them, a far greater force than Sand's End ever had. They command patrol dogs and they're armed to the teeth, magazines slung across their shoulders so the bullets catch the sun. Most of them are young, but there are some older ones, in their twenties or early thirties. Either life expectancy in Norsen's Guard is far higher than it ever was in Blaiz's, or they don't have such a shortage of bodies to hold guns. Either way, they're a sullen lot and follow orders grudgingly. Solma's glad of their presence (even though it's come too late for Warren) but that doesn't mean she has to like them.

The remaining Keeper children sit in a quiet circle under Dyl's watchful gaze. Whenever a soldier passes too close, they shuffle closer to Dyl, clinging to the legs of his pants. Dyl's hardly said a word for days, but his attention rarely leaves his Keeper charges. Solma watches as he turns down Bell's offer of food. Bell scowls and shoves the bowl into his hand anyway. The Whisperers mill about listlessly. Mamba and Cobra headed out this morning to help in Norsen's fields. It's pollinating season and some of the crop needs encouragement. Ana's stayed behind, though, to watch over the younger Whisperers, who are suffering with what they now know to be the split signal. The only person currently unaccounted for is the person Solma really wants to see. Olive disappeared into the forest an hour ago and Solma's anxious for her return. Cobra's words echo in her mind.

It's not too late. Never too late.

Solma's been thinking about what Bell said, too. Warren wouldn't want her to fight for him alone. That's not how he works. Like Yenn said, he's a Hive Child, a boy whose mind has become a colony. If they're going

to save him, she needs to become a colony, too. And that starts with apologies. It starts with forgiveness.

By the ponies, Ana spots Solma and waves at her. Solma heads over, smiling when Burdock butts his nose under her elbow for attention. She scratches his forelock.

"Everything ok?" Ana asks. She's got her bow slung across her shoulders and the quiver at her hip. She's been fletching arrows all morning and Solma's watched, fascinated. She really doesn't know her friends that well. She really hasn't tried.

She shrugs but meets Ana's gaze with a smile. Everything is not ok. But she understands it better, now. She understands that the fear she feels for the future isn't hers alone. She glances up in time to catch Norsen's eye and nods in acknowledgment. He nods back before he heads out of the glade and back towards the village.

"I mean," Ana says, reddening, "I know it's not."

"No," Solma agrees. She's remembering Cobra's words again. "But it's not hopeless, yet."

Funny how saying that makes her heart swell. It's not hopeless yet. Warren is nearby. There's a chance.

Solma peers over Burdock's long neck and scans the glade, watching Taipan and Yenn murmur in front of the beehives, Jonah plods over to Roseann in need of comfort, the Gatra tread their patrol paths. Everyone's working together. Solma closes her eyes and lets the sound of insect song wash over her, lets it buzz harmonies in her heart.

Maybe it'll be ok. Maybe it won't. But it's not hopeless yet.

Movement to the north draws the Guards' attention, but it's only Olive, returning. She announces herself and glares down the Gatra until they lower their weapons.

Solma's heart trembles like a startled animal. She can't fight for Warren alone. And there's one person she wants beside her. Someone far more worthy of her love than Maxen ever was.

Olive marches towards the gathered children. She looks like she means business. There's a determination in her face that gives Solma pause. Something's happened.

"Wait here," Solma tells Ana. She heads over to meet Olive.

"I got to talk to you," Olive says.

Solma nods. "Yeah," she says. "I got to talk to you, too."

Olive raises an eyebrow.

Solma takes a deep breath. The truth is such a prickly thing and it threatens to stick in her throat now. She mustn't let it. She cannot fight alone. She closes her eyes.

And behind them is the face of the person she's loved all this time.

Blink.

It's Olive. Always Olive. Solma's eyes fly open.

"The truth is," She says, almost breathless, "I'm a fool. I miss you. I want you. And … I think I love you, too."

Olive's mouth twitches in a half-smile. "You think?"

Solma hesitates, but there's no point in lying, is there?

"Yeah," she says. "I think I don't trust my own feelings yet. I'm not gonna pretend Maxen didn't mess me up. He did. He still does. I don't know who I can trust, who I can love. But I got to figure this out and I can't do this alone. I can't ..."

Olive smirks and a smile tugs Solma's mouth.

"I know you've been saying this to me for months," she says. "Like I said, I'm a fool. I just ... I really thought Maxen loved me and he didn't and ... I got so much wrong. I can't hardly trust myself and sometimes ..." She bites her lip, but there's no turning back now. Olive deserves honesty. "Sometimes I feel like maybe you shouldn't love me. Like maybe I don't deserve it."

Olive watches her for the longest moment, those deep, green eyes searching Solma's darkest truths. Then, she throws her arms around Solma's neck, kissing her. "I get it," she says. "But that ain't true, Sol. I love you for *you*, and that means I love you for messing up as much as I love you for getting it right. You try. That's what matters." She pulls away and smiles, and there's so much affection in that smile that Solma thinks her heart might burst. Olive snakes an arm around Solma's waist. "Let's try again," she murmurs. "Just, no more hiding from me, 'kay?"

Solma grins and hugs Olive back, breathing in the other girl's scent of musk and gunpowder. She buries her face in Olive's shoulder.

"'Kay," she agrees. "I'll do my best."

They pull apart and Olive's fingers entwine with Solma's. Solma reckons she feels their pulses align. She smiles, stroking her thumb across the back of Olive's hand. This feels like harmony. This feels … right.

"What d'you need from me?" she asks. Olive's grin disappears.

"I reckon I know how Vulkan and Ignis moved across Alphor so quickly," she says. "And … I think I know how to find Warren."

Thirty-Seven

YENN AND TAIPAN BLINK at Solma with their mouths in a perfect 'O' shape. They're holding hands. That's new. Solma remembers the depth of Taipan's scowl when she'd first met Yennevieve, realizing this girl in purple robes with a green streak in one eye understood Warren in a way she never would.

But now, Warren needs them both. No-one is an island.

Solma feels Olive's warmth beside her and she lets their arms touch. Olive's closeness electrifies her.

"What do we know?" Solma asks, addressing the younger girls. They look at each other.

"They got a parasite," Yenn says. She holds out her palm, on which sits a little bee. The creature's antennae droop. There's a dullness in her fur and her eyes are cloudy. Yenn points to the blood-red lump clinging to the bee's thorax. Solma stares at it and feels sick.

Compared to the bee, it's huge. Solma sees the way it pulses as it saps the bees life. She grips her stomach. No wonder the bees are so ill.

"D'you know how to fix it?" Olive asks. Yenn and Taipan shake their heads.

"But," Taipan says, "Foxglove's and Primrose's bees don't have it. They're ok. We been talking to them."

"Great," Solma says. "So ... what are they saying?"

Yenn frowns. "It don't make sense," she says. "They're dancing us towards the river. But there ain't flowers by the river."

Solma puts a hand on Yenn's shoulder and smiles. "Okay," she says slowly. "What does that mean?"

Yenn looks uncertain, a frown creasing her forehead. Solma gets it. She crouches in front of Yenn, searching the girl's eyes.

"It's ok," she says. "Really. This might not work, and if it don't, it ain't your fault. But we reckon Vulkan and Ignis have a passage through the mountains. Olive thinks that's how they move across Alphor so quickly. Orchid's bees are heading East, to them mountains, 'cos maybe that's where Vulkan's keeping Warren. Only, they can't find him because they're too sick. If we can heal them, they might lead us to him."

Yenn nods.

"Okay," Solma says. "So, do you know how we might heal them?"

Yenn takes a deep, worried breath. "Well," she says, "Orchid's bees ain't heading to the river. Maybe something by the river might be stopping Foxglove's and Primrose's bees from getting sick. If we can find it, maybe we can heal Orchid's hive."

Solma smiles at her. Yenn still looks concerned and Solma recognizes that shine in her eyes. She's seen it in Warren's eyes often enough. A weight no child her age should have to carry. Solma cups her hands under Yenn's so that now, they're both holding the little bee.

"It might not work," she admits. "But I reckon we got to try."

Yenn stares for a moment longer, that uncertainty still clouding her gaze. But Taipan steps up beside her, puts a hand on her back. Her orange eyes are bright with hope and belief.

"You don't have to do this alone, Yenn," she says. "And I'll help. We'll do it together."

Yenn smiles nervously at her, then turns back to Solma and Olive. She nods. "Okay," she says.

"Let's start with Foxglove," Taipan suggests. "She's the older queen, right?"

Yenn nods. "Yeah." She turns to explain to Solma. "She's calmer than Primrose. I dunno why, 'cos they're a similar age. Just different personalities, I guess. I reckon following her workers will be easier than following Primrose's."

Solma nods. A year ago, she'd have scoffed at that idea, but Warren's taught her better. It's amazed her to learn that the bees *do* have personalities. Just like Warren's little buff-tails, some are shy, some are gregarious, some are grumpy and some are patient. Even in their short lives, they experience the world differently.

Taipan leads them to the hives and stops in front of Foxglove's, giggling as a few workers zoom out to greet her.

"Hello, bees," she murmurs.

Yenn holds out her hand. Solma leans forward to get a better look but Olive holds her back. "It's alright, Sol," she says. "Let them work. Trust them."

Solma forces herself to relax. "Sorry," she says. Olive shrugs.

"It takes time."

She plants a kiss on Solma's shoulder and Solma feels the tension in her limbs evaporate. She leans into Olive, closing her eyes. For once, Maxen isn't in the darkness behind her eyelids. Olive wraps an arm around her.

"You still gotta pay attention, Sol," she says, laughing. Solma grins and opens her eyes.

Foxglove's bees rush over to the two youngsters, drawing mad circles around their heads before they land on Yenn's palm, shoulders and the sleeves of her purple robe. She crouches in front of the hive and Taipan squats a little way off, watching. Yenn cups her hands together and six or seven workers congregate on her fingertips. Solma strains to see. Yenn closes her eyes. Solma feels a stab of sadness, watching her. She's seen Warren do this so many times.

"I need your help," Yenn says. She says it out loud, so the others can hear. But Solma knows she says it in bee, too.

The workers lift their antennae, buzzing their wings anxiously. They're listening. Yenn hesitates and opens her eyes, glancing at Taipan.

"How do I explain it?" she asks. "I can't—" she bites her lip and Solma watches her sadly. It's an awful vision to give a bee. This hive is healthy. They haven't been in Orchid's hive. They don't know the pain of twisted wings or the horror of shriveled, malnourished larvae.

One little worker fires her engine and lifts into the air, hovering before Yenn's face. Solma sees the moment the girl's eyes meet the bee's strange, multi-faceted gaze. Something passes between them. Solma feels Olive's fingers brush her own. She grips them tight.

Please. Earth, she hopes this works. She hopes so hard it aches.

Movement on Yenn's palm draws Solma's attention and Yenn grins. The bees on her hand rush about in an excited frenzy. Yenn flattens her hands to give them more room. Each little bee finds her own position. And then ...

"Taipan!" she whispers. "Tai, look!"

Taipan scurries to Yenn as Solma and Olive shuffle closer, peering at the gathering of bees clambering over Yenn's fingers. The bees buzz.

And they dance. Each in time, their bodies swaying. Solma's mouth falls open. Each reaches the pinnacle of her dance at the same time and rushes round in a half circle, beginning again.

"That's ..." Taipan says. "What does it mean?"

Olive grins. "I saw this before!" she says. "They dance instructions, right? They're leading us somewhere. To flowers, or—"

"Or a cure!" Solma breathes, feeling her pulse quicken with relentless, painful hope. "There's a cure and they're telling you where it is!"

Yenn glances at Solma, grinning. Solma's heart swells until its almost painful. Maybe this is it. Maybe Orchid's bees will heal. And maybe they'll lead Solma to Warren.

"What do we do now?" Yenn asks, but Taipan's already haring off. She calls back over her shoulder.

"We follow them, obviously!"

Obviously. Solma feels a smile spreading across her face. She catches Olive's eye and Olive's grinning, too.

"C'mon, then!" Olive says as they watch Yenn charging after Taipan.

Solma takes a breath, holds Olive's hand tight, and follows.

Thirty-Eight

THE FOREST DARKNESS ENGULFS them quickly. Maybe it's the thickness of the canopy. Or maybe it's that Solma knows Vulkan and his treacherous son are somewhere nearby. Solma keeps thinking she sees the orange flash of a fire starting out of the corner of her eye, but when she turns, there's never anyone there.

Olive watches her with a frown. "It's alright, Sol," she says. "It ain't just you out here."

Solma smiles weakly and tries to calm down, but her shoulders are bunched and her fist grips her hunting knife. The kids scurry ahead, bees drawing frantic halos around their heads.

Yenn sticks close to Taipan and the bees hover around them, occasionally landing on their hands to dance again. They're insistent and always directing them west—the opposite direction to where Orchid's sick bees are flying—past the village and towards the river. Taipan keeps rushing off, only to be accosted by seven or eight little bees, buzzing around her until she turns back.

"What's wrong?" she demands after the fourth time this happens. She lifts a finger and a bee lands on it. "Why'd you keep doing that, huh?"

Solma wishes Taipan wouldn't talk so loud.

Something shuffles in a nearby bramble bush and Solma whirls round, knife drawn. There's nothing there. Bees flock around her and a couple land on her shoulder. Solma feels the whisper of their feet against her skin. She lifts her finger and a bee climbs onto it, dancing the same dance as before. This time, it's as if there's an impatience to her routine. When she's done, she turns and lifts her antennae, staring at Solma as if to say, *what is it you don't get?*

Solma looks up to see Taipan and Yenn staring at her. She fights down the scratch of fear in her throat.

"S'alright," she says. "It's nothing. Let's go."

They keep pushing west, picking their way over huge, arcing roots as wide around as Solma's whole body. The forest canopy is so thick that barely any sunlight breaks through and, when Solma peers up, the trees seem miles tall. The leaf litter here is deep enough that Yenn and Taipan disappear in it up to their knees and have to hitch up their robes to avoid tripping. Without the sun to guide them, most of the bees seem less certain, but a few of the workers insist they're going in the right direction.

Where are they going? Something about this part of the forest seems familiar. Solma frowns, wondering if the creatures have misunderstood. This makes no sense. They shouldn't even be able to come out this far. This is way beyond the—

Understanding wallops Solma between the eyes and she reels.

"Oh Earth," she murmurs, gripping Olive's hand tight. "I know where they're going."

Olive raises an eyebrow at her, but there's no time to explain. Solma takes off, haring past the children.

"This way!" she calls, heedless of the noise. The others follow, yelling questions that Solma ignores. Excited, the bees power ahead. This is the right way.

Gradually, the trees thin and Solma hears the distant gurgle of a river. The ground begins to slope down towards the rushing water and Solma notices stumps and broken branches crumbling with rot. The bees zoom to these decomposing things and clamber all over them.

Solma skids to a halt, gasping for breath, grinning all over her face.

Straight ahead, blackened, twisted and awash with color, is the fungus tree she stumbled across months ago.

It looks even weirder and more beautiful than it did back then, with huge, orange-and-pink fungal blooms festooning its scorched branches, pale yellow mushrooms sprouting from its trunk and, everywhere, those silver filaments criss-crossing it like spider's silk.

And ...

There are bees here.

Hundreds of them, scuttling all over the tree, buzzing happily.

Yenn's escort of bees rush over to join the gathering and the four, following humans creep forward. Yenn grabs Taipan's hand. Olive grabs Solma's.

"How can they be here?" Olive asks. "Ain't this miles from the chemical barrier?"

Solma nods. "I saw this before," she says. "But it makes sense now. Foxglove's and Primrose's bees must've found a gap in the barrier that leads them here."

Yenn grabs her hand. "Orchid's younger, though," she says. "She's a new queen. Maybe she don't know to look for this. Her bees found a gap that they're searching for Warren through, but they don't know where the cure is."

Her heart thuds with sudden understanding.

"Maybe they'd have found it if the barrier hadn't confused them," she says. "We cut them off. It's our fault."

This is why the insects can't survive without their Keepers. They've separated the glade from the rest of the forest, like cutting off a body from its lung. It's no wonder Orchid's bees struggled. She glances at Yenn, face full of sadness.

Yenn touches Solma's hand, eyes shining with tears. "You didn't know," she says. "Let's get a better look."

They edge closer. It's hard to tell in the gloom, but Solma thinks the bees are eating the silver threads that lace the tree. But bees don't eat fungus. They need *flowers*, not rot.

Only ...

"The fungus," Olive whispers. "The fungus is the cure."

She grins at the children. "You did it!" she says.

But Yenn is frowning, her little fists clenched.

"Yenn?" Solma asks. "What's wrong?"

Yenn looks at her, lower lip trembling. "We ain't done it," she says. "Orchid's bees won't make it this far. They're too sick to reach the cure."

The hope in Solma's heart curdles to fear. It hurts so much. They came so close, but Yenn's right. Orchid's bees will never have the strength to fly out here and, even if they somehow did, they'd never make it back.

Olive paces, chewing her lower lip. "We could carry them?" she suggests. "A few at a time, a handful each, and bring them out here."

Solma considers. It could work. But that means trip after trip into the forest, carrying handfuls of sick bees. It'd take them dozens of trips at best and every time they step into the forest, they're risking the attention of wildwolves and redbears.

Or Fire Makers.

But do they have a choice?

She turns again, peering at the dead tree where the bees feed. The idea hits her so fast she reels at the impact of it. She turns and grabs Olive by both shoulders.

"No!" she says, fiercely. "We bring the cure to the bees!"

Olive blinks at her. "What?"

Yenn's shaking her head. "We don't know what they're looking for," she says. "We could bring back the wrong bit. It'll take us ages to work it out—"

"No!" Solma says again, excitement overriding caution. "The *whole* cure! All of it!"

Olive stares at her. "You want us to carry a whole *tree* back to the insects?"

Solma feels the laugh die on her lips. Olive's right. That's a crazy idea. The weight of this task crashes down on her again and she flops heavily onto the ground.

"Get up, Sol," Taipan says. Solma looks up to find the Whisperer girl standing beside her, eyes full of determination. "We can do it. We can bring the cure to the bees. Just not in the way you think."

She holds up her hands and waggles her fingers.

Behind her, she hears Olive breathing, *"Ohhhh,"* as she understands. Yenn's eyebrows shoot up under her fringe. Solma frowns.

"You ain't allowed," she says. "Mamba ..."

Taipan huffs an impatient sigh. "Mamba's not here," she says. "And connecting with the fungus might be the only way."

Solma shakes her head, grabbing Taipan's hand. "But the stories ..." she says. She remembers Mamba's face as he'd described that weirdness Whisperers experience when they connect with the fungus. The weirdness that terrifies them all.

"Didn't Mamba say only the most powerful Whisperers can do it?" Solma protests, echoing Mamba's words.

Taipan raises an eyebrow. "You saying I'm not powerful?"

Behind her, Solma hears Olive suppress a laugh. She grips the Whisperer girl's shoulder. "Are you sure about this?"

Taipan's lower lip wobbles but she nods. Despite her fear, she holds Solma's gaze.

"I want to try," she says. Her voice cracks a little, but Solma searches the girl's orange eyes and knows she's thinking of Warren. Taipan crouches and digs her fingers into the damp earth, closing her eyes.

Solma stands beside her. No-one moves. They barely breathe. Taipan's eyes dart beneath closed lids. Her brows bridge into a deep frown as she searches, pushing her mind deep beneath the soil. Every so often, she shakes her head and says, "nope," as if dismissing something. Finally, her eyes fly open and she gasps, making Solma jump and then stare.

Taipan's eyes are wide, still that unusual orange they've always been, but now there's a strange, pearlescent sheen to them. Dark rings appear around her irises and something shifts in her gaze. She seems to see past Solma. *Through* Solma, beyond everything.

"Oh," she says, her voice distant. "Oh, wow ..."

She withdraws her hands from the soil. "That was ..." she stands, dusting off her robes. She turns shocked, amazed eyes up to Solma.

"I had no idea ..." she says. "It's ... a *network,* deep underground. Millions and millions of those silver threads all criss-crossing through the forest, linking each of the trees so the trees can ... *talk* to each other. It makes the forest work. It *is* the forest. It's everything. Every blade of grass, every flower, every sapling." She grins. "It's not weirdness. It's *life.* Everything connected. Everything joined—"

Solma turns her gaze to the canopy above. It's an impossible thing to comprehend. For seventeen years, she's walked this broken continent and never known that there'd been a silent language spoken beneath her feet. No one is an island. Everything is part of something else. Even the rot beneath the earth. She grins.

"Can you bring it to the glade?" she asks. Taipan grins back.

"No need," she says. "It's already there. We just need something to bring it up to. It needs dead wood. And damp."

Olive clicks her fingers. "The stump in the middle of the glade!" she says. "Can you grow it there?"

Taipan nods. "Yeah," she says. She seems different. As if a veil has been lifted behind her eyes.

"Right," Solma says. "Let's go."

It takes an age to get back and Solma's got this strange feeling they're being followed. But whenever she glances behind them, the forest is empty. Olive grabs her hand again and Solma feels that familiar, electric jolt as their skin touches.

"It's alright, Sol," she says. "This'll work. It's a good idea."

Foxglove's honeybees zig-zag through the forest ahead of them, circling back to make sure the humans don't get lost. Solma's grateful for their song. She watches Taipan ahead, somehow changed, gazing at the forest as if she's never truly seen it before.

The forest thins and dapples of sunlight pepper the ground. The glade is nearby. And Taipan can grow the fungus and Orchid's bees will heal and—

The buzz of their honeybee escort changes. They land on Yenn's shoulders, clambering all over her.

They land on Taipan, too, and some zoom over to Olive and Solma, drawing frantic orbits around their heads. Solma stops.

"What is it?" she asks. "What's wrong?"

Yenn shrugs. "I don't know," she says. "I—"

The bees take off again, flying in delighted circles. Solma waves them away.

"Stop it," she pleads. "We need to—"

"Hush!" Taipan breathes, eyes wide and staring into the distance. "Listen!"

They listen. The honeybees land on their clothes and still their wings so their song falls quiet.

And Solma hears it.

That deep, confidant tremolo she remembers from last summer. A bee engine that roars with strength. There must be dozens of them, and Solma would know that sound anywhere. Warren was right. He was *right*. Solma so wishes he could hear this glorious sound. Her breath catches. Tears sting her eyes.

"Can't be," she says, hoping it is.

She turns towards the sound, not daring to breathe. From among the trees, a little shape emerges, zig-zagging at eye-level, its fur deep black and gold with a buff-colored rump. It's one of Warren's bees. One of his dear buff-tailed bumblebees.

And look at her! She's big and powerful, eyes bright and gleaming. She zooms straight for Solma, landing on the hand Solma holds out for her. That familiar whisper of bee feet against her skin sends electricity roaring through her. She stares at the fuzzy creature.

"Hello, bee," she says. "My brother missed you. I missed you."

She holds the bee up into a dapple of sunlight, watching as she cleans her face and wings. The honey-bees sit quietly, sensing the humans need a moment. Taipan scurries forward to have a look. Yenn comes, too, and Olive touches Solma's arm.

"Is it one of Blume's?" she murmurs. Solma shakes her head.

"I dunno," she admits. "I can't tell. Warren would know. She's very far away from Blume's nest but … she could be one of Blume's granddaughters."

The thought fills her with lightness and sadness. It should be Warren standing here with the bee on his hand. But he's not. She doesn't know where he is and his bees were in this forest all the time. Perhaps, through this strong worker, his beloved Blume lives on. Solma cups her hands around the bee and holds it next to her heart, feeling how those feet shuffle against her skin.

And then she's off, powering back to her nest. Her song drifts through the forest long after she's out of sight. Solma watches her go, a heaviness in her heart.

She misses Warren more than it should be possible to miss anyone.

Olive's fingers lace through hers again, their hands fitting perfectly together. She smiles. Someone else takes her other hand and she looks down to find Taipan staring back at her, with that new depth to her orange eyes. Yenn takes Taipan's hand, smiling.

"We'll find him," she says. "'Cos we won't give up. 'Cos there's lots of us and we're smart and determined. We'll find him."

Solma smiles. She squeezes the two hands she holds and sees how Taipan squeezes Yenn's hand, too. No one is an island. No-*thing* is an island. Solma breathes in the earthy forest air.

"C'mon," she says, smiling. "We got bees to save."

~ Orchid ~

THEY SMELL OF HOPE as they approach and the few thousand healthy workers rush to greet them. The not-bee girl skips ahead of the flower-scent girl, and there are two others. One smells sharp and angular. (We don't like her. Scent of death on her.) The other smells of contradictions. She smells a bit like the death-scent-girl but also a lot like the not-bee-boy. The missing boy. The one we have died searching for and not found. His scent lingers on her like pollen clinging to bee fur.

The not-bee-girl is joyful. Her footfalls send tremors through the hive, and each tremor says *It's ok! It's ok!*

I don't know how it can be ok, but my workers seem to know something I don't. The hive hums with hope and my attendants hassle me closer to the entrance.

A thrill runs through the comb. The scent of the not-bee-girl fills the nest cavity, full of purpose and ideas. She's trying to communicate but she's not a bee, is she? She can't dance the way we can. Her scent-speak is clumsy. I feel my workers' confusion as they listen, trying to make sense of her. I think …

I think she's saying there's a cure. I listen intently as my workers relay the message throughout the hive. But it's puzzling. It doesn't make sense.

Something's happening outside and my bees swarm to the entrance to investigate. They stamp and buzz and scurry. The hive feels more full of energy than it has all summer and I feel the tentative fragrance of hope. I listen as my sisters and daughters describe what they see. And it seems impossible.

They tell me the flower-scent girl is in the middle of the glade. She kneels by the dead tree stump and opens her eyes wide. They tell me her scent has changed, that there's a depth to her now that wasn't there before. She smells of *life*. Connectedness. Summer rain, decay, biting winter winds and dormant seeds.

She drives her hands into the earth and her eyes are like sunsets. Around her, the ground trembles and delicate, silver filaments climb the tree stump. They move over it and through it, covering it with a silver film. They sink into the wood, warping it, eating it. Strange, fruiting bodies sprout from the stump and we realize she's growing fungus. Our antennae fold back against our heads in confusion. This makes no sense.

Why give us fungus?

I lift my antennae, tasting the air, listening for my workers' dance.

Thousands of bee feet pound the wax and the comb quakes. In a line, they follow each other, waggling, then rushing in a half circle, then waggling again. More and more join in. Even my deformed and exhausted daughters, who will soon be killed by their sisters to keep the hive healthy, join in the dance. Everyone dances.

The momentum rises. I listen hard.

It smells of health, the dance says. *It smells of hope.*

And then, in a single, mad rush, the healthy workers scurry for the entrance, streaming towards the flower-scent girl and the strange, silver-thread fungus she grows.

I wait in the dark. It feels like an age before the workers return, but when they do, there's excitement. They carry something new. Pieces of the silver, thread-like substance the flower-scent girl grew. They feed the thread to their sick and ailing sisters, and to me. It's earthy and pungent and I don't like it at first, but they are insistent.

You must! They buzz, their urgent scent stinging my antennae. I don't want to, but I must try. I take the stuff in my jaws and chew it down. When my attendants have run out, they fire their engines and fly for more.

The not-bee-girl stands by the hive, watching and waiting. The flower-scent girl is beside her and I feel the death-scent girl and the contradiction-girl waiting, too. I feel their hope and fear as it taints the air. I feel how much they want us to survive. To thrive.

But there's something else, too. Something they need from us. Something only my healthy hive can give. But we are not healthy. Not yet.

So when my workers return with more of the silver threads, I chew it down. It doesn't have the sweet, sugary energy of honey, or the thick, life-giving flavor of pollen, but I feel the way it strengthens. The parasites don't seem to be sucking me so dry. One or two start to fall off. I notice the workers begin to shed their parasites, too, and they carry the revolting bodies of the invaders out of the hive, far away, where they can do no harm.

I don't know how long it takes, how many nights pass before I wake and my body tells me to lay. I haven't laid in so long and the feeling is so urgent I barely wait for my attendants before I rush to find an empty cell. I lay egg after egg after egg. My workers buzz with joy, packing the precious, egg-filled cells with pollen for when the grubs hatch.

I don't know how long it will take to shed the parasite, or if we will ever fully recover, but the comb trembles with purpose now. With hope.

There is more to be done.

I wait for the morning when the not-bee-girl returns. She has something to ask me and I will listen. Because I already know what she wants me to do.

Thirty-Nine

THERE'S A HUSH IN the glade this morning. The children are gathered around Roseann, sat by the tree stump in the center. They sit patiently, talking in hushed tones. The Whisperer boys fidget incessantly but quell under Roseann's glare. Dyl sits with them, on a makeshift chair the Whisperers have cobbled together from branches and spare canvas, seeing as his preferred tree stump has been commandeered by fungus. He sits forward, leaning against his cane, watching the children with silent intensity.

They all keep glancing at the tree stump they're gathered around and no-one wants to get too close. Solma doesn't blame them. It's completely transformed. The silver threads are barely visible now, having woven through the dead wood, but Solma knows they're still there, under the surface. The stump itself is a riot of color, with fungus of the strangest shapes bursting from it. Solma's sure most of them are poisonous. She's warned the children never to touch them. But it's keeping Orchid's bees healthy, now. That's what matters.

Because they need the bees for what comes next.

Solma wanders through the crowd, checking everyone. Norsen hangs back in the shade, flanked by Reya and two of her Gatra. He looks tired. The circles under his eyes have darkened and his face is gaunt. Reya doesn't look much better, but there's a steely determination to her now, and a focus that reassures Solma she's up for this fight. Now that she has her Steward's backing, she's single-minded enough to get this mission done. Solma nods at them both. Reya returns the salute and Norsen gives a small smile.

Yenn and Taipan sit at the front of the gathering. They're quiet, but Solma's heart lifts to look at them. Yenn is cross-legged, her palms upturned so honeybees can wander across them. They're all Orchid's honeybees, energetic and mite-free, with a new luster to their fur. It'll take time for the hive to reach its full strength, Yenn says. But it's possible, now. Orchid's laying again. She might have time, before winter, to make the hive strong enough to survive until next spring.

Beside Yenn, Taipan sits with her eyes trained on the tree stump in front of her. She's been ... different since she connected with the fungi in the forest. There's a distance to her, as if she's distracted by a voice no-one else can hear. Her power has grown, too, and Solma's seen her footprints bloom with flowers. Mamba was furious at first. He didn't speak to Solma

for nearly a week, but, though mushrooms bloom in her footsteps, Taipan hasn't rotted anything bigger than the tree stump so far and Mamba's fear is gradually waning.

Solma has sat with Taipan over the last few days—while they've waited impatiently for Orchid's hive to heal—and pored through Bell's books, trying to find any reference to what it was she felt.

The books showed an underground network of fine filaments called *mycelia*—the silver threads. These threads, the book said, link the trees, the plants, the soil ... everything. They're the network of the earth. The system that directs energy wherever it needs to go.

Because nothing is an island. Because everything is connected.

And now, Taipan is plugged into that network, too, and that strange, dark ring around her irises has remained.

Solma smiles at her. Taipan smiles back.

A commotion by the honeybee hives draws Solma's attention and she glances up to see Olive laying into one of Reya's Guard. The poor kid doesn't look more than fourteen, but he's glaring at Olive with enough venom to lay out a horse.

"You challenge *everyone* that comes into the glade!" Olive yells, loud enough that everyone turns to look. "Got it? Any more've these kids get taken, that's on you!"

The Guard splutters a protest, but Olive's already turned away. "Don't wanna hear it," she says. "And keep your eyes on the forest."

The Guard scowls, mutters something under his breath and turns to face the forest as Olive instructed.

Solma feels her gut twist as she watches Olive storm towards her. A few days ago, Olive wouldn't have yelled at a Guard like that. She's tired and stressed, like they all are. Solma wants to gather Olive into a hug and hold her tight until all the tension melts out of her. But there's no time. There never is.

Bell comes to stand beside Solma, clutching a little hemp bundle tied at the neck with frayed ribbon. Solma recognizes it as a bundle of seeds. Bell had kept loads of them in the basement under their house back in Sand's End, hoarding them for a time they might be needed. And that time has finally come.

"Each Whisperer's got a bundle," she says. "We chose sunflowers. Hardy and noticeable. If anyone's in trouble, the Whisperers can grow them."

Solma nods. "Reya should take Krait," she says. "I'll go with Habu and King'll go with Olive. The older Whisperers are better able to defend themselves so they can each go with one of the Guards. Taipain stays here, of course."

Bell frowns and grunts agreement. "How's Taipan coping with—you know?"

Solma smiles. None of them quite know what to call it, this new strange *thing* Taipan's able to do. But it's proving useful. Already, she seems to be able to use the mycelia to sense signals from one plant to another. If someone is in distress, the Whisperer they're with can grow a sunflower. Using the mycelia, Taipan can sense when a flower's gone up and where, even if she can't lay eyes on it.

They've tested this. Solma still isn't quite able to believe it. But now, the little Whisperer girl has a key role to play. She can tell a back-up squad of Gatra exactly where to go if anyone's in trouble.

And they're expecting trouble. Whatever Vulkan and Ignis are waiting for, whatever they've got planned, Solma expects this will force their hand. There will be a fight. Solma's gut tightens at the thought. She's not happy about sending children into a firestorm. A part of her still wants to leave everyone else here and go out alone, endangering no-one but herself.

They've talked about it, though. All of them. Around a fire in the evening, while Bell served hot tea and they took turns talking about what they feared, what they wanted. The children were adamant. They want to find Warren and the others. They want to help. They don't want to be left behind.

Solma doesn't like it, but she sees the wisdom. The kids have gifts that can help.

And no-one is an island.

She shrugs in response to Bell's question, unsure how to answer. "I think she's ... I dunno," she admits. "It ain't scaring her, anyway. She's trying to teach the others to do it. I reckon Cobra'll pick it up quickly. Mamba's less sure, and I don't think the younger boys understand."

Bell snorts a laugh. "They'll come around," she says. Solma doesn't doubt it. Those kids are hardy. She needs to remember that.

"It's making me wonder what Mamba was so scared of," she admits. "Or who told him the fungus was so dangerous."

Bell shrugs. They stand in silence for a bit. Bell puts an arm round Solma's shoulder.

Movement draws Solma's eye and she turns to see Ana leading Poppy and Burdock. The ponies are tethered to the cart, on which Mamba and Cobra are arranging their supplies ready to head off. They'll be leaving soon after they retrieve Warren. (Solma refuses to think the word *if*.)

Warren isn't safe here, now. None of the Keeper children are, but Norsen's still taking some persuading that these kids might be safer living a nomadic life with the Whisperers than here, where the Fire Makers can find them.

Solma's working on it. Olive's working on it, too, though less subtly.

Ana leaves the ponies to graze behind the kids. Mamba and Cobra hop down from the cart. Their seed pouches swing on leather straps around their necks. Cobra catches Solma's eye, touches a hand to her seed pouch, and smiles. Solma smiles in return. She hopes she looks calm, in control.

She doesn't feel those things.

A whisper of movement beside her, warm skin brushes against hers and there's Olive, her hand slipping into Solma's as if it belongs there. (It does.) Solma relishes the electric pulses that passes between them.

"You ready?"

Solma takes a breath. She's not ready. Not really.

But she can't do this without them. Not this time.

She nods. "Yeah," she says. "I think so."

Olive kisses her. She draws back and stares at Solma, eyes focused and fierce. "Whatever happens," she says. "You focus on the job. Trust us. We can do this."

Solma clutches her belly as fear churns her gut. "I will," she says. She hopes she's telling the truth.

Olive watches her and Solma hopes it's not obvious what a riot is going on in her head. It probably is. Olive never misses anything.

Solma takes a breath and loosens her grip on Olive's hand, their fingers slipping apart. Olive turns towards the gathering of children. "King," she calls, beckoning the Whisperer boy over. "Yenn."

The Keeper girl jumps at the sound of her name. She stands and Taipan stands beside her. They pick their way through the little crowd of children, who watch them in silence. Yenn chews her lip nervously but Olive reaches out and takes her hand, smiling.

"You got this, kid," she says. Yenn clenches her little fist.

Solma watches as Olive leads Yenn over to Orchid's hive. Solma sees Yenn trembling and hates that they have to ask the kids to do this.

But she knows there is no holding Yenn back. Solma clears her throat and the children's eyes turn to her. The murmur of adult conversation falls silent. Even the ponies prick their ears, as if ready to hear their part in this. Solma closes her eyes.

Behind her closed lids is Warren. And Olive. And Bell. The Whisperers who guided her through winter, Dr. Roseann who has healed their wounds and soothed their hunger.

Blink.

And it's only love she sees behind her eyelids. Only safety. Only home.

She opens her eyes. "Ok," she says. It begins. "Whisperers, find your soldiers."

There's a scramble as the children leap to their feet. The Keeper kids stay close to Roseann but the Whisperers spread out until each is stood next to someone with a gun. Krait stands beside Reya, looking as fierce as a seven-year-old can. Habu slips his hand into Solma's. Ana has an arrow nocked to her bow and stands beside Bell. Mamba and Cobra each stand next to a Guard who doesn't look older than they are. Solma surveys them. This will be her team. She and these eleven other people are her hope of finding Warren.

"You know the rules," she says. "Stay with your partner. Whisperers, you're the signal if anything goes wrong. Plant sunflowers so you're always close enough to feel one when you touch the earth. Any sign of danger, you send up the sunflowers until they bloom. Fast as you can. But soldiers," she turns now to address the Guard assembled around the glade, watching her, "Protect the Whisperers. If they go down, you're on your own. So keep them safe. We need them for communication. See anything off. *Anything at all*," she pauses, staring so intently that half of Norsen's Gatra averts their eyes. "You send up a signal. Vulkan and Ignis are planning something. We don't give them a chance. Got it?"

There's a murmur of agreement. Solma's not satisfied.

"*Got it?*" she demands, hand on the hilt of her knife. The effect is immediate. The Gatra snap to attention, and "*Yes, Sergeant!*" rings out across the glade.

Solma catches sight of Bell smirking and allows herself a brief bloom of pride. This is her plan. Her rescue mission. It's her brother at the end of it. But this belongs to everyone.

She turns towards Yenn and the honeybee hives. Norsen's gone to stand beside her and she's slipped her little hand into his. On her other side is Taipan, quiet and distant, and watching as if there are a whole bunch of things only she can see.

"Ok, Yenn," Solma says. "It's time."

Yenn lets out a little noise that could be acknowledgement, or could be a half-suppressed whimper. But she turns to the hive and closes her eyes.

"Let's do it, then," Solma says. Yenn's brow creases. She spreads her arms wide.

And calls her bees.

Forty

YENN MUTTERS UNDER HER breath, but the bees will be listening to a different language.

Solma sees the Gatra shift, anxiously. Many have never been this close to the insects and these tiny, strange creatures make them nervous.

The skin on the back of Solma's neck prickles as the air thickens. She wets her lips, wondering if anyone else senses the change. The Whisperers do. Habu squirms. King clutches the side of his head. Mamba and Cobra both jump as if they've been stung. Mamba puts his arm around Cobra and meets Solma's eye with an unspoken question.

What if they can't do this?

And Solma knows there's only one answer. They have to try.

A low rumbling comes from the hive and the air trembles with anticipation. Solma forces her hand to release the hilt of her knife. The low keening of the bees intensifies until it seems like its buzzing, not just in the air around her, but deep inside her head, too.

Honeybees burst from Orchid's hive. Even in its depleted state, there are thousands. A great, black-and-gold mass that swirls in a heady vortex around Yenn, gossamer wings vibrating the air with such intensity it sounds almost monstrous. Solma can barely breathe at the sight of them. They darken the glade, landing on every blade of grass, every flower, coating the trunks of the trees. Even the Whisperers balk at the sheer number and Solma sees a few of the Gatra step back, eyes wide with alarm.

"Hold!" Solma yells. She's not sure if anyone can hear her over the rumble of the bee song, but the Gatra hold their ground, standing to attention. Solma sees Cobra's eyes widen as she leans into Mamba's side. The Whisperer children watch with nervous faces. Even Ana looks uncertain as the bees flex and shimmer in the summer air.

They land all over Yenn and Taipan until the girls are coated with a thick layer of bees. Solma has to resist running over to wave the mass of creatures away.

But the girls are both smiling, watching the swathes of bees scuttle over each other. Solma forces herself to relax. She needs to trust these kids.

No-one is an island.

Yenn stands still, hands outstretched, grinning. Bees clamber all over her, buzzing incessantly. What are they doing? It looks like chaos, the way they scuttle over each other, clamoring for space ...

And then Solma sees the shift. A few bees on Yenn start dancing, waggling their bodies from side to side. Some on nearby flowers and trees take up the dance. The glade hums with their song.

"Olive ..." Solma breathes. "Look ..."

Olive grins. "I know," she says. "It's something, eh?"

And it is. More than something. It's everything. Tens of thousands of bees on every tree, grass blade and flower dancing the same dance, their wings setting the air a-flutter, their lustrous fur catching the sun so that the world seems to be made of gold.

Yenn turns to Solma, eyes grave.

"They reckon they can find him," she says, though Solma barely hears her above the roar of the bees. "But they ain't certain. They been looking and looking, but they never been strong enough. They couldn't go far enough." She grins. "But they reckon they can, today."

She lifts one hand and a small escort of bees detaches from the main swarm.

"They got to search," Yenn says. "I'll stay here and listen to the dance. These bees can go out first. Follow them. Tai can send messages through the sunflowers if the dance changes."

Solma nods, trying to keep her face neutral. The plan had seemed bizarre when she'd suggested it a few days ago, but now, watching the bees and the Gatra with their attending Whisperers, it seems beyond ludicrous. *Follow the dancing bees and hope they lead us to the missing children.* Yeah. She's amazed no-one laughed at her.

But no-one did. And they're not laughing now, either.

Yenn Whispers to her little escort of twenty or so bees, and the insects zoom to Solma. They land on her shoulders, her sleeves, her knuckles. Yenn points to the forest.

"That way," she says. "Go."

And Solma does. Holding Habu's hand, she takes off into the forest, running to keep up, as the bees Yenn sent to her power their engines, rushing ahead.

The other Whisperers charge after her, followed closely by their soldiers. Olive unholsters her pistol, her other hand holding King's. Together, they head after the bees and the noise of the insects' dance fades as they move further from the glade.

Two of the attending honeybees detach from the main group and zoom south.

"I'm on it!" Cobra yells. She kneels and presses a sunflower seed into the soil. Closing her eyes for a moment, she Whispers and the soil moves, parting to reveal a green shoot. It pushes towards the sun, strengthening. Cobra leaves it just as a yellow bud begins to open at its head. The bees that split off circle anxiously nearby, waiting for their human charges to follow.

"Let's go!" Cobra says to her Guard and they disappear after the departing bees.

A few minutes later, another bee breaks away from the main group, followed by Bell and Ana. Mamba and his Guard go after the next small group. And then another group of three break away. Reya and Krait hurry off after a lone bee and then there's only five left. Three follow on this same path, never wavering as the forest darkens around them, heading dead west, towards the foothills. But the last two zoom in a wide circle before taking off north. Olive grabs Solma's hand, squeezes it.

"See you soon," she says as King kneels in the soil to Whisper his sunflower to life. Then Solma's watching the girl she loves vanish into the undergrowth. Her head roars with hope and fear and uncertainty.

And it's funny how all three of those things sound like bee song.

Forty-One

Solma feels Habu's hand slip from hers as she lengthens her stride. She turns to see him sprawl in the leaf litter, a flash-memory of that chase from the village beyond the Earthroot Mountains streaking across her vision.

"Warren—" she says, before catching herself. "Up you get, Habu."

Habu's already up, face full of grim determination.

"Wait!" he calls suddenly. "I need to plant a seed!"

Solma skids to a halt as Habu kneels, presses a seed into the earth and Whispers. The honeybees circle impatiently. One lands on Solma's shoulder and starts dancing.

"I know, little one," Solma says.

Habu springs up, a young sunflower now ready to bloom in the spot where he'd been kneeling.

"Let's go!"

They race off again and the bees zoom ahead, doubling back to check the humans are following. Solma wonders where the others are, whether they've found any sign of her brother.

It seems like they've been running for an age. Habu stumbles again and scrapes his knee. Solma hitches him onto her back and carries him. It slows her down, but he's tired. Earth, aren't they all? Maybe the Whisperer kids should have stayed at the glade like the Keepers. Maybe she shouldn't have let them come—

"Let me down now, Sol," Habu says after a short while. "I'm ok."

The forest thins. Light penetrates the canopy, dappling the forest floor. The ground begins to rise slowly. They've reached the foothills. A modest stream gurgles nearby, sunlight flashing off its surface. The bees follow it upstream, their song carrying through the trees.

Slowly, the landscape changes. They're no longer running through a forest but wandering along the foot of a great hill. The trees are smaller here, scrubbier, with twisted trunks and tough leaves. Here and there, the earth gives way to jutting rock, which the stream splashes over, crystalline droplets glittering in the sun.

The bees pause on a fern leaf, abdomens pumping as they gasp for air. They've come so far and they're tired, barely recovered from the mites. One buzzes her wings, trying to power herself into flight. But she's too exhausted. Her wings fall still.

Solma stares around her. It feels like they're so close and there's no time to wait. The air bristles with energy that makes the hair along Solma's arms stand on end. Somewhere near here, she knows, the Fire Keepers are hiding. She turns to Habu.

"Can you grow another flower?"

Habu glances up from where he's leaning on his knees, gasping for breath. His face is flushed and sweat shines on his shaved scalp. He nods and kneels. It only takes a moment, but Solma feels as if she's watching the sunflower grow of its own volition; taking weeks to break through the soil.

"We need it all the way open," she tells Habu as she scoops the exhausted bees onto her palm.

"But—" Habu protests. Solma hushes him.

"I know an open sunflower is the signal," she says. "But something's up that hill. We need everyone here. Warren's nearby. I know it."

Habu frowns but does as she asks. Solma barely waits for him to finish before she deposits the bees in the center of the flower. Gratefully, they dip their tongues to drink the sweet nectar. Solma waits as they sate themselves, churning her blade-foot into the soil and staring back along the foot of the hill where scattered trees mark the end of the forest. Time passes, too much time. Where's Olive? Where are Cobra and Mamba?

The bees were still searching when they broke off from the main group. Either the workers have turned back by now to dance to the hive that they've found nothing, or they should have doubled back and headed this way, leading Solma's friends with them.

Solma shields her eyes and peers at the horizon, but there's nothing. No movement. Not even the twitch of a rodent in the undergrowth. Her skin prickles with gooseflesh.

"I think the bees are done," Habu says. Solma returns her attention to the sunflower where the bees are powering up their engines.

One little bee flies in excited circles around Solma's head and then hurries northeast where the land rises towards a steep wall of rock. The other bees follow and Habu charges after them. Solma hesitates long enough to draw her hunting knife. She feels a pull beneath her solar plexus, drawing her in the same direction the bees are going.

Warren's this way. He *must* be.

Grass and soft earth give way to rock and Solma and Habu have to scramble. They clamber higher as the bees draw anxious orbits around them.

Solma pulls herself onto a narrow ledge of rock and turns to help Habu. Below them, the land falls away in a short but steep drop. They're high enough that Solma can see the forest sprawling across the land, and above them, over the peak of the hill, the first of the Earthroot Mountains looms like a threat.

The bees hurry to a fold of rock in the side of the hill, underneath a rocky overhang, and disappear into the shadows. Solma frowns. She glances down at Habu, who's examining a scrape on his knee. He looks up, distressed, and points to the cut.

"I know," Solma says. She offers him her hand. "Roseann'll have something when we get back. C'mon."

Habu mutters irritably, but takes Solma's hand. His bare feet, Solma notices, are caked in mud, criss-crossed with scratches. She winces.

The bees zoom over to them, landing on their hands to dance before taking off and powering back to the rocky shadows. Solma squints into the darkness and then her eyes widen.

A cave. The passage through the mountains.

Olive was right.

It's so well hidden, it's no wonder they missed it when they passed this way all those months ago. Even if Solma had somehow tracked Warren and Tobias back to this spot, she'd never have noticed the cave without the bees. One of the workers wanders over to her and she lifts her palm so the tired creature can land.

"Thank you," she says. She's sure the bee doesn't understand her, not like it understands Warren anyway. But the bee buzzes her wings in what might be acknowledgement, then fires her engine. She and her two sisters disappear down the hill into the forest, the sunlight catching on their golden fur. They vanish among the trees.

Solma watches them go. They'll head back to the glade to dance this to their sisters. Solma's not sure what'll happen once Orchid's hive knows where Warren is, but Yenn's promised to send as many bees as she can persuade. Solma remembers the power of the swarm. Last year, Warren had summoned his buff-tails into battle when Blaiz tried to take the nest and they were formidable. The honeybees might be smaller, but they're swift and clever.

And there's a lot more of them.

Solma scans the forest, hugging herself as a breeze whips the tough grasses and sends small stones skittering over the ledge. She watches for signs of movement. Olive or Cobra's bees must have found the way by now. Someone should be coming.

Solma curses herself. She'd been so clear with everyone in the glade: if anyone found anything, they were to wait for others to arrive. If they're to survive this, they need each other.

No one is an island.

Except right now, Solma *is* an island. She and Habu stand alone on this little shelf of rock and no-one's coming. Why is no-one coming?

Habu kicks a stone over the ledge and watches it tumble through the grass.

"Where is everyone?" he asks.

"Dunno," Solma admits and just saying it out loud triggers a sickening cold in her gut. Something's wrong. Habu grew his sunflower ages ago. Back in the glade, Taipan's listening through the mycelia. She'll have detected Habu's flower by now and triggered the other sunflowers to open, alerting the Whisperers to follow the trail.

Olive won't have abandoned her. Nor Cobra.

Something's wrong.

Solma turns towards the cave, knife in one hand as she draws her pistol with the other.

"Let's go, Habu," she says.

"But—"

"Don't argue," Solma snaps. "There's no time. Stay close."

Habu glances back down the hill, then hurries to Solma's side. Solma hands him the torch from her belt.

"Wind the handle and then hit it with your hand a few times."

Habu does and a weak, reluctant beam flickers from the torch.

"Hold it steady," Solma tells him. And with that, she raises her pistol and they head into the darkness.

Forty-Two

Water trickles from the ceiling and the rock is wet underfoot. The air tastes dank and stale. Habu splutters and Solma hushes him.

The tunnel narrows and, soon, they have to walk single file, the ceiling lowering enough that Solma has to duck her head to avoid cracking it open. As the cave tunnel draws them round a corner, Solma glances back towards the entrance. The seam of light that marks their escape is small now and, as they turn the corner, it disappears completely. Habu whimpers and Solma feels his little fingers tighten around her belt. She curses, holsters her pistol and reaches down to offer him her hand. His fingers are clammy in hers.

Solma's pulse roars so loudly in her ears, she's afraid someone will hear it. She takes a deep breath to calm herself, but her heart only hammers more wildly. Habu taps her hip and she glances down at him. He makes a creeping motion with his hands and Solma nods. He's right. They need to move as swiftly and quietly as possible.

Wildwalking. Solma remembers Taipan and Warren's lessons. She softens her knees, tests the ground before she puts her weight on it, careful to keep her movements smooth. She and Habu move along the passage in near silence.

Finally, the tunnel widens again. Habu keeps the torch beam trained on the floor and Solma picks her way over loose stones. The tunnel zig-zags until Solma's lost all sense of direction. Eventually the ceiling lifts a little and she rolls her neck to release the tension in it.

"See anything?" Habu asks, carefully moving the torch beam over the walls. Solma shakes her head.

"Nothing."

A shuffle and whisper up ahead brings them to an abrupt halt and they flatten themselves against the cave wall. Solma's heart hammers as she strains to listen. For a moment, she wonders if she'd imagined the sound entirely, but then it comes again. A movement of loose stones. A groan. A whisper.

Habu lifts frightened eyes to Solma and she beckons him to get behind her. They shuffle along the wall until the tunnel opens out into a small chamber with other tunnels leading off it. Habu slowly scans the torch beam around the chamber and Solma claps a hand to her mouth to avoid crying out.

Shoved against the wall of the cave are a stack of steel cages, just large enough for a redbear cub. Or a human child. Solma reckons, at a glance, that she counts nine or ten, but only the three at the bottom are occupied. Kneeling in muck, clothes coated with grime, are three children. They squeeze their eyes closed against the light as Habu shines the torch on them, but one keeps them open long enough to cry out.

"Sol!" Warren shouts, gripping the bars. He's covered in gunk, his hair grey with dust and plastered to his face. His shirt is torn, feet criss-crossed with cuts and there's a nasty bump on his head. His nose has been running and no-one has bothered to clean him up, so now the skin around his nostrils is red and raw. He's rubbed his eyes, too, and grit and dirt has made them bloodshot.

Solma hurries to him, drops to her knees and reaches through the bars to hold him. She can barely breathe with relief and tears spill down her face.

"You're ok," she says, dropping her hunting knife so she can wrap both arms around him. "You're ok.

I'm sorry, Warren. I'm sorry I weren't there when you needed me, I—"

Warren makes a muffled noise and Solma realizes she's squashing him. She lets go and Warren takes a big, gasping breath.

He gives a weak smile.

"But you're here," he says. "I knew you'd come. I was telling the others."

Solma glances at the cages on either side of Warren's and Habu dutifully turns the torch beam so she can see. To Warren's left, blinking against the light, is Tobias. He rubs his eyes as if he's just woken from a deep sleep and waves.

"Hey, Solma," he says. His voice is croaky, his lips dry and chapped. Solma wonders how often Vulkan thinks of feeding these kids. Or giving them water. She unclips the waterskin from her belt and hands it through the bars.

"Drink," she says as Tobias unstoppers the skin. "But slowly. If you gulp, you'll be sick."

Tobias does as he's told, though he's clearly so thirsty that restraint is an effort. He passes the waterskin back and Solma hands it to Warren, but he shakes his head.

"Addie first," he insists. "She's been here longest."

Finally, Solma looks to Warren's right where the third occupied cage sits at a slight angle. In it, huddled in one corner with her knees under her chin, is a ragged, skinny girl with bright, brutal eyes that glitter in the torchlight. There's a greyish tinge to her brown skin. Her black curls are thick with grime and her robes are dirty and tattered. Tear tracks have dried on her cheeks, leaving crusts of salt. But there's a fierceness to her stare that Solma finds unsettling. She shuffles forward and clutches the bars of her cage. Solma smiles. Addie doesn't smile back.

"You come to rescue us?" she asks, her voice hoarse. Solma's heart clenches.

"Yeah," she says. "We have."

Addie grunts and sits back on her heels. "Took your time," she says. Solma opens her mouth to apologize, then closes it again. Addie's been here for months, shut away from the sun, cut off from her insects and with no certainty of escape. No apology is going to make up for that.

"How are my butterflies?" Addie asks. Solma bites her lip.

"Can't you feel them?"

Addie, Warren and Tobias all shake their heads. Tobias' face crumples. "Not in here," he whimpers. "To deep and dark."

Addie presses her face to the bars. "So?" she insists. "My butterflies?"

Habu shuffles forward. "They're ... um ..." he says. Addie cocks her head at him.

"That good, huh?" she says. "Tobias said they're dying."

Solma watches Addie and wonders how old she is. She's small. Her grimy robes hang off her and Solma sees her collarbone jutting far more than is healthy. She doesn't look much older than Warren.

Her eyes don't look that young, though. They look as if she's watched lifetimes rush past. There's a hardness to them, like she knows to expect the worst in every situation.

Solma decides it's pointless to lie.

"They're not doing great," she says. "They're struggling without you. But they ain't dead yet. Let's get you out of here and then you can go help them."

Addie stares, a frown creasing her forehead. She grunts agreement and sits back as Solma fumbles in her belt for her multi-knife.

She flicks it open and slots it into the rusty lock of Warren's cage, but he bats her away.

"No," he says. "Addie first, remember? She's been here longest."

Solma scowls. "But Warren—"

He folds his arms and glares. "I ain't coming out 'til you open Addie's cage," he says. Solma rolls her eyes but struggles to suppress a smile. He's right. As usual.

"Fine," she says, and moves to Addie's cage, setting to work on the lock. It's not been opened in so long that Solma's worried it's stuck shut. She twists the blade, the knife slipping, and slices the top of her finger. She curses but keeps working.

Addie raises an eyebrow at her.

"Dunno if they even still have the key," she admits. "Haven't been outta here in ... forever."

Anger and sympathy churn in Solma's heart and she works faster. She jabs and chisels at the lock, ignoring the blood dripping from her fingertip.

Finally, there's a dull clunk and the door drops open. Tobias and Warren cheer as Solma helps Addie out.

Poor kid. She's so weak she can barely crawl. When she tries to stand, her legs buckle and Solma only just catches her in time. She scoops her up and the child is so light, it's like carrying nothing more than dried autumn leaves. Solma carries her to Habu and leans her against the wall.

"Wait here," she says, and sets about opening the other two cages. Neither of them are quite as rusted as Addie's, though Tobias' takes some persuading. Solma stands and examines her cut finger as Warren and Tobias crawl to freedom. It's not too deep. She sucks on the cut to stop the bleeding.

Habu fidgets and the torch beam jiggles.

"Solma," he says. "I don't like it here."

No-one answers him. As soon as Warren is out of the cage Solma scoops him into a tight hug and holds him close. For once, he doesn't fight her. His little arms meet around her neck and he squeezes her back.

"Thanks, Sol," he murmurs. "I knew you'd come."

Solma kisses the top of his head. "I wouldn't nev-er've stopped looking," she tells him. "Ever."

Warren's eyes shine. "I know," he says.

"So-ol," Habu says again. "I want to go."

Solma stands and takes Warren's hand. "Me too," she says. "Habu, you lead the way. I'll carry Addie. Let's—"

She stops, her hand snapping to her hunting knife. Habu whimpers and smothers the torch beam. Nobody moves. They all hear the sound of boots ringing on rock. They all see the glow of torchlight approaching down the tunnel.

Solma glances wildly around her, but it's too dark and she doesn't know these caves. The footsteps are almost on them and Addie can't run. She can't even walk.

Then torchlight flares in the chamber, blinding them. Solma squints against the glare. Warren hides behind her hip. Tobias and Habu scurry to her side as three bulky silhouettes appear behind the torch glow.

Three?

Habu uncovers his torch beam, illuminating faces Solma recognizes. They're soldiers in Reya's Guard. Some of the older ones. The middle one—clearly in charge—has a thick shadow of stubble covering his chin. He sneers.

Solma scowls. "What took you so long?" she demands. "Habu sent that signal ages ago. Where's—"

The stubble-chinned Guard raises his pistol, aiming it between Solma's eyes.

"Shut up," he says. Solma shuts up, too stunned to disobey. She searches his face. Is he joking? But he doesn't look like he's joking. He looks like he's waiting for her to give him a reason to shoot.

Solma clenches her jaw, glaring. Norsen was right. She hates that Norsen was right. There were traitors in the Gatra. It's just that Reya wasn't one of them. It makes sense now. The injuries everyone sustained in the forest, as if enemies were everywhere.

Enemies *were* everywhere. Enemies were among them.

And now they're here, with a pistol pointed at Solma's face.

Forty-Three

WHEN WARREN WAS STILL learning to walk, not long after Solma's parents had died and Kobi had been exiled into the wilderness, a yawning emptiness opened inside Solma that sucked the light from her. She remembers little from back then. But there's one thing she can recall with terrifying clarity.

With her best friend gone, and her parents no longer around, some of the village kids started being unkind. The unkindness became cruelty and the cruelty became violence. No one stopped them—no one had time for parenting—so it persisted. One day, four village boys chased her out of the planting fields, towards the managed forest. They laughed when she fell, grazing her knees and cutting her hands. They hurled stones at her, screaming with delight when one struck her in the shoulder and sent her sprawling. They chased her to the tree-line and that's when Solma turned to face them. She remembers staring up at those huge trees, seeing the shadows of vast creatures moving beyond, and thinking she had more chance at survival if she turned and faced the beasts chasing her.

She snatched a branch from the ground, turned and roared, swinging the branch like an axe. The boys skidded to a halt, just out of reach. They laughed, still, but the glee had gone from their eyes. They watched Solma like she wasn't human, but something far more dangerous. Solma, for her part, doesn't remember much of what happened next. She knows she sent one boy home bleeding and, at some point, the others fled. She remembers going home with blood in her mouth and wondering if it was hers. She remembers Bell quietly cleaning her up while Warren tottered in the corner. She doesn't think she was told off, which is a small mercy.

But what she remembers most is the moment she decided to turn and fight. She remembers feeling that the jaws of the world were closing around her and there was no way she was just going to lay down and die. In that moment, it felt like that great emptiness inside her turned inside out and all the truths and fears and angers it had pulled into itself were suddenly catapulted back out, flooding through her like a winter storm. Every nerve ending screamed and she was nothing but rage. A tiny part of her mind, the part that was still Solma, recognized that she would do anything—*anything*—to get out of this alive.

She feels that survival-self clawing its way to the surface now, as she glares at the three traitors, as she shields the children, staring down the barrel of a gun. She waits, willing that fury to rise and take hold.

And it does. Oh, Earth, it does! Every muscle floods with strength, every nerve on fire. She straightens, steps forward, gesturing for Warren and the others to stay put. Warren squeaks in protest.

"Sol?"

Solma doesn't answer. This is for him. It's always for him.

The stubble-chinned Guard sneers. "Drop your knife and your pistol on the floor," he says. He grins. He's enjoying this. "And then you'll help us put them kids back in the cages."

Solma holds out her knife. She reaches for her gun at the same time. Slowly, feigning compliance. She meets his gaze, glaring. She imagines what it'll be like to drive her knife into his heart. She'll take grim pleasure in doing that. It's obvious now why Olive and the others haven't responded to Habu's signal.

They *can't*. This soldier and his treacherous followers stopped them.

Are they dead? Solma pushes that thought aside before it can take hold. They can't be dead. *They can't be.*

Carefully, she pretends to lower her weapons to the floor. She keeps her gaze fixed on the stubble-chinned Guard, watching him. He's an arrogant moron. She can tell that immediately. He leans a little on one hip, pride lifting his shoulders back. There's a wicked smirk on his face. He's enjoying himself.

But it means he's not paying attention. Solma has one chance.

"Vulkan was right," the stubble-chinned Guard says. "He said you was a daft little thing. All fight and no brains. Well he—"

Solma flicks her knife into her hand and launches it straight at the Guard's face. At the same time, she draws her pistol and fires three sharp shots. One ricochets off the cave wall and there's a cry as it strikes a soldier. The stubble-chinned Guard staggers, glancing behind as his fellow goes down. There's a bloody gash across his cheek where Solma's hunting knife struck him. The moment of distraction is all Solma needs. She charges at him, whirls as he raises his gun and slams her blade-foot into his knee. There's a sickening crack and his legs buckle. The gun goes off, firing into the cave ceiling.

Solma grabs his wrist and knees him hard in the elbow. His arm snaps and he grunts with pain. She snatches the pistol from his grip and shoots the third soldier in the thigh just as he's aiming his own weapon at her. She fires a round into his shoulder, too, disarming him, and hands Warren the gun. He takes it tentatively.

Solma stands over the incapacitated Guards, chest heaving, blood roaring in her ears. She watches them sprawled on the floor, grunting with pain. The soldier who took the ricocheted bullet is unconscious. Solma sees blood pooling beneath his shoulder.

She should kill them. Put a bullet in their heads and be done with it. Leaving them alive only means she'll have to face them again later. She lifts one of her pistols and aims it at the stubble-chinned Guard's head. His eyes widen, reflecting the torchlight.

Movement behind her and Warren slips his hand into hers. "Don't, Sol," he says. She looks down, sees the plea in his eyes. "They're not worth it."

He's right. She lowers her pistol. The stubble-chinned guard moans with relief.

"Warren, you and Tobias stay close. We got to get back to the glade. Something's … something's wrong."

She thinks of Olive. Of Cobra. Of Reya and Norsen and the Whisperers. Bell. Roseann. Her friends. Her *family*.

They need her.

Wordlessly, Warren takes Tobias' hand and leads him past the downed Guards. Solma smiles as she sees Warren kick one on the way by. Emboldened, Tobias does the same. The Guard groans with pain. Tobias sticks his tongue out with intense feeling. Pride blooms in Solma's chest. Good kid.

Solma watches Habu scurry after the Keeper boys, then turns and scoops Addie up. "I'm sorry, kid," she says. "This ain't gonna be comfy, but we gotta get you safe."

Addie glares but doesn't complain as Solma hefts her over one shoulder. She instructs the boys to take the soldiers' torches and finds her hunting knife a little way down the tunnel. She gives it to Tobias.

"Anyone comes at you," she tells him, "shove that hard into any bit of flesh you can find. Got it?"

Tobias stares at the blade which is almost as long as he is. He looks up at her, face ashen, and nods once. "Okay."

"Good boy," Solma says. "Stay close. Stay quiet. We dunno how many of Reya's Gatra defected. Trust no-one."

The boys stare at her in silence. Warren squeezes Tobias' hand. They creep up the tunnel the way they came, keeping their backs to the wall.

Outside, it's too quiet. Even the occasional rustle of rodents in the undergrowth has fallen silent. Solma scans the tree-line at the bottom of the hill, ushering the children behind her. They're too exposed out here and getting to the forest means a straight charge down the slope across open ground. There's nothing for it. Somewhere in that forest, her friends are in trouble.

Addie wriggles on Solma's shoulder.

"I don't get it," she says. "The village is well off with the insects. Why'd they turn against us?"

Solma feels her face darken. "Maxen," she growls. "He'll have promised them something better."

Addie grumbles but says nothing more. Solma's eyes dart down the slope, calculating the swiftest path, wondering if the kids can keep up. They need to get to cover. She needs to hide them somewhere safe. But where's safe?

She doesn't know how many of Norsen's Gatra defected, or where Vulkan and Ignis are. How can she protect these kids?

Solma hitches Addie higher onto her shoulder. "We run for the forest," she says. "You stay close behind me, you step where I step. Don't fall. Got it?"

The boys nod solemnly. Solma takes her hunting knife back from Tobias, envisioning disaster should he fall on it. She turns to Warren and hesitates. He's holding the pistol like he's been wielding one all his life. She'd so wanted to keep him away from guns. But she has to trust him.

Warren sees her staring and raises the pistol to the light. He unclips the magazine to check it, thrusts it back in place and flicks the safety on before he tucks the weapon in his belt. He smirks as Solma's jaw falls open.

"I been watching you do it long enough," he says. "I'll be ok, Sol. Let's go."

Addie chuckles. Tobias gazes admiringly at Warren and Habu gapes. Solma turns back to face the forest.

"Ok," she says. "Now."

They keep low, hugging the shadows. Climbing back over the lip of the ledge takes longer than Solma would like, but the kids hunker down in the grass while they wait for Solma to help them down. Then they're running again, zig-zagging down the hillside, stumbling in the grass and only just keeping their balance. Something screeches in the forest and Solma feels ice in her gut. She keeps running until the trees are thick and tangled around them, the ferns plentiful enough to cover their footprints. The sun disappears behind a film of green leaves.

Solma ducks among the ferns and beckons the boys to do the same. Gently, she places Addie against a tree, pushing the ferns around her to keep her hidden.

"I need to find Olive," she says. "And Cobra. Stay here. Stay quiet. I—"

She stops at the look on Addie's face. The girl is staring over Solma's shoulder, her eyes widen, clouding with fear.

Solma's up in an instance, whirling around to face whatever has terrified Addie. And there, standing menacingly among the ferns, is Ig. No, *Ignis*. There's no sign of the bumbling, squinting kid she'd met in the spring. This boy is all casual arrogance and meanness. There's no trace of a squint now, and sunlight reflects in his violet eyes. His fringe is pushed back from his forehead so the inked flame above his eyebrow is visible. She pushes the boys behind her, knife in one hand and pistol raised in the other as he stalks towards them, smirking.

"Been looking for you," he says.

He lifts one hand, palm upwards, and fire bursts across his skin.

Forty-Four

THE FOREST ECHOES WITH Ignis' laughter and Solma tenses, her gun trained on him. She could shoot him now, put an end to this sorry mess.

But ...

Ignis sneers and launches the flame in his hand. It flies in a fist-sized, sizzling ball and Solma ducks as the burning mass rockets past her head. She feels its heat as it slams into the tree above Addie. Flames dance up the trunk.

Habu drops to his knees and drives his hands into earth, Whispering furiously. Water bubbles around him as the plants he's connected with send their moisture towards the tree, helping to absorb the fire.

Solma leaps to her feet as Ignis' laughter echoes through the forest again. But he's gone, disappeared amongst the foliage.

Amongst all this fire food.

A chuckle from her left and Solma snaps to face it, gun in one hand, knife in the other. No one's there. A rustle from the right and she whirls round again. Nothing. Warren clings to her leg, his little face drawn into a frown.

"He's taunting us."

"I know," Solma growls. What she doesn't know is why. *Why* toy with them? Her pulse beats in her ears. She can barely hear anything, but every movement of the forest draws her eye.

He's here somewhere, ready to set their world on fire. Why's he waiting? What does he want?

A noise from the tree draws Solma's attention and she glances behind her to see Addie has managed to stand. She's leaning on Habu and her face is grim with pain, but she's up.

"Gimme a gun," she says. "A knife. Anything."

Solma's heart breaks, but she doesn't argue. She hands her multi-knife to Addie. "You and the boys find somewhere to hide," she says. "Green things'll be harder to set alight, so find fresh ferns. Stay low and stay quiet.

"What're you going to do?" Warren asks. Solma sets her jaw.

"I'm going to make him sorry," she says.

Warren stares, fear and love in his eyes. Solma pulls him into a fierce hug, then shoos him after the others. They drop among the ferns and crawl to safety. The boys keep Addie between them, steadying her. Her face is

drenched in sweat, limbs shaking with effort. Then the ferns close around them and they're gone, hunkering down somewhere they can't be seen.

Solma turns back to the forest. She lifts her pistol and creeps forward. Earth, she wishes Olive was here.

The leaf litter crackles beneath her feet and Solma's aware of how dry it is, how quickly the ground beneath her could burn. She swears she smells smoke. The trees rustle and the sound is like the hiss of newborn flame.

"Ignis!" Solma yells when she's moved far enough away from where the kids are hiding. Her voice sounds strong, brave. She's glad about that. "Come out, you little—"

Fire streaks past her right ear and she sidesteps just in time. Swinging her pistol towards the attack. The fire dissipates mid-air, leaving a stream of smoke in its wake. Laughter echoes from beyond the trees.

"You're an *idiot,* Solma!" Ignis' voice says, ringing through the forest. Solma snarls. To her left, the ground smolders. She leaps aside just as it bursts into flame and Ignis flies out of the undergrowth, a knife glinting in one hand and fire glowing in the other. His face is twisted and furious and the sight almost makes Solma freeze.

He's so ... Inhuman.

And then he's on her and she hasn't got time to shoot. He knocks her pistol hand aside but she catches his wrist before he can jab the knife in her eye. His flaming hand comes round towards her cheekbone and she ducks, swinging her blade-foot into his gut. His eyes widen and he stumbles backwards, the flames in his hands sputtering out. Solma raises her pistol.

"I'll kill you!" She growls.

Ignis just laughs. He clicks his fingers and smoke pours from them, wreathing him in a thick, cloying mist that stings Solma's eyes. She fires off two shots, hears a grunt as one hits its mark, but Ignis is no longer there. Masked by smoke, he's disappeared into the forest again. His laughter sounding pained, now. She wafts smoke out of her face, turning towards the sound.

Where is he?

"What d'you do to Olive and Cobra?" she demands, eyes darting for signs of movement. There's a rustle in the branches to her left. She whirls. A short silhouette slips away. She fires. Misses. Laughter, again.

"What d'you do with my friends?" Solma hates how panic creeps into her voice.

"Ah, you don't need to worry about them," Ignis says. "They're being dealt with."

Dealt with. Solma's got no doubt what that means. Raging, she fires another three shots into the gloom. She hears one hit a tree. The other two streak away into nothing. Solma clenches her jaw. Gets a handle on herself. Warren and the other kids are in this forest. Hunkered down and keeping quiet. She needs to be calm. She needs to be smart.

She forces her breathing to slow, concentrates on her senses. The smoke is acrid, clawing at her nostrils and throat. She breathes slowly. She can't smell, and sight is out. Her eyes sting and the smoke makes the shadows writhe.

But she can still hear as well as she ever could. She cocks her head, listens.

Ignis is a show off. He'll want to taunt her. She just has to wait.

"Want to know what Olive said when she realized half Norsen's Gatra weren't working for Norsen no more?"

Solma suppresses a grin. She can imagine exactly what Olive said, down to the last vivid expletive.

"And your Cobra," Ignis goads. "Cried her little heart out, din't she? Stupid Whisperer."

He's lying. Solma pushes any doubt she has to the furthest corner of her mind and listens for Ignis, for the angle of his voice.

"Ah, and them kids all wailed their heads off," Ignis goes on. "And you're Aunt! Weren't my Dja chuffed to get her? She gave him a good smack round the head back in the village. He returned the favor, y'know."

He's not lying anymore. Solma hears the truth in his voice and panic screams in her ears. She roars, firing two shots before she can stop herself, hearing how the bullets splinter bark.

She's wasting ammo. She needs to be calm. To be smart. But she can't.

Ignis laughs. His laughter burns like fire. It leaves blisters on her heart and sends her muscles into spasm. Her pulse jumps. She can't hear for the shriek of blood in her ears.

"We'll kill you all, Solma!" he yells, cackling. "Every last one'a you!"

Solma spins on the spot, aiming her pistol wildly. She sees Ignis' wiry shadow darting through the smoke. She fires. Misses. Curses. The smoke distorts everything.

"But we'll kill you first!" Ignis cries, and suddenly he's there, flying at her out of the gloom, blood staining the sleeve of his shirt where her bullet clipped him. Solma turns to find his face inches from hers, twisted and snarling. Full of hate.

Like Maxen.

She swings her pistol round but Ignis grabs the barrel and suddenly the gun is so hot that Solma yells in pain, fighting her fingers to release it. Ignis wrenches it from her grip and throws it away. He's grinning. Snarling. Laughing. There's fire in his palms. His hands are on her skin. She's burning. Burning. There's fire on her arms, her shoulders, in her mouth. Her skin pops and smokes.

She screams. Screams like she's trying to climb out of herself, like the pain will kill her if she doesn't let it out.

Suddenly the burning heat is gone and Solma's legs buckle. She's on all fours, gasping for breath, sobbing. A meter from her is the pistol Ignis ripped from her grasp, reduced to a smoking, twisted heap. Somehow, her knife is still in her hand but she doesn't have the strength to use it. The skin on her upper arms is red and blistered, still smoking.

Someone's screaming. Quite close. Solma wishes they would stop. It's loud and it hurts her head. It—

Buzzing.

A deep vibrato cuts through the fog in her mind. She knows that noise. It sounds like spring flowers and crisp morning sun. Like hope.

Bee song.

Solma glances up. Tears blur her vision but she makes out the plump shape of a bumblebee near her face. The little creature hangs in front of her, wings a-blur. Her antennae stretch forward anxiously. Her fur is lustrous black and gold. Shining. Healthy.

Apparently satisfied she's still alive, the bee powers towards the sound of the never-ending scream. Solma follows its path, sees more bees. Hundreds of them. A swarm.

It takes her a while to understand what she's looking at. When she does, she snaps to attention, scrambling to her feet. She's still got the knife, though there's little strength in her arm to lift it.

Ignis stands over her, arms flailing, clawing at his face, where bees form a thick, black hood. He spasms and screams, grabbing handfuls of little bodies and throwing them to the floor. The bees dart and dodge, landing on his skin, stinging and powering off again. Unlike the honeybees, the buff-tails' dagger like stings mean they can attack again and again. Ignis thrashes and grabs at them, but they land on his hands, stinging there, too.

Solma frowns as she watches, wondering how the bees knew. Wondering what made them attack. There's something important about this. Something that ought to make her terrified. But her head feels dim. She can't remember—

Warren appears through the smoke, arms spread wide, eyes glowing with a kind of green Solma didn't think was possible. Bees orbit him like little planets, basking in his light before zooming off to join the attack on Ignis.

Solma staggers as Ignis' hand, still grasping his knife, flails, slashing the air. Smoke pours from his fingertips but it seems, in his pain and panic, he's forgotten how to make fire. Warren grabs Solma's hand.

"Run!" he tells her. "Run now! Get Addie! Go to the glade!"

Solma stares. This is the wrong way round. It shouldn't be *him* saving *her*. He grabs her sleeve.

"Go, Solma!" he yells, turning those glowing eyes on her. His irises look fragmented. Like a bee's. "Ain't you listening? Ain't you seen?"

He points to the sky. Solma squints through the canopy of leaves, scanning the cloudless blue. What's he pointing at. Solma doesn't—

Then she sees it. Smoke. Thick and black, churning into the air from a greedy, voracious fire, pouring into the sky from the direction of the glade.

Olive. Cobra. Bell.

Everyone.

That's where Vulkan is. That's why Ignis was here, taunting them. That's why they waited around, risking discovery for ages even after they had Warren. To destroy the glade. Maxen won't want anyone else having the riches the insects could provide. He'll want control. Just like his father.

"Warren, I—"

"*Go!*" Warren insists. "We'll hold him back. Me and my bees."

She stares at him, indecision holding her fast. She needs to do as he says. Now. The others will die if she does nothing. She imagines Olive and Cobra bathed in flame. Imagines Bell spluttering on smoke, unable to find a way out.

But Warren—

"I'll follow," Warren tells her, sending waves of bees back at Ignis as the Fire Maker falls to his knees. "I promise!"

He meets her gaze. He looks ferocious.

"I *promise!*"

There's no time to argue. The column of smoke above them darkens the sun. Solma cups her brother's chin. "You better keep that promise," she tells him. "You *better.*"

She takes off, haring through the ferns, yelling for Habu and Tobias and Addie.

The glade's burning and her brother's alone out here and there's no *time.*

Forty-Five

Ignis' screams echoes through the forest. Warren winces, but he keeps Whispering his bees towards the attack. His sister needs him.

His friends need him. He's here, alone, fighting a boy he thought was his friend. He can feel himself crying and hates it. He smears angry tears from his face and pushes his bees on. They answer him gladly. Their nest is nearby and they sense the danger Ignis poses, sense the fire at his fingertips and the destruction in his heart. They sting and sting.

And still, for some reason, Ignis can produce only smoke. It pours from his fingers, forming a thick mist around him. Warren feels how it makes his bees drowsy. He sends a heady, warning scent towards them.

Attack! Attack!

They do. But Ignis grabs handfuls of them, crushing their little bodies, flinging them aside as if they're nothing. Warren feels his heart break.

"Stop it!" he yells, calling the last of the bees away. "Stop killing them! Why d'you do it? I *hate* you!"

Ignis stops screaming as the bees draw away, orbiting Warren. Half his face is a livid red and Warren thinks of Maxen, scarred by the attack last year. Ignis looks at him, fury burning in those violet eyes.

"Yeah?" he rasps, throat raw from screaming. "Well, I hate you, too!"

He stands, lifts his hands. And now he's found his fire. It burns, bright and terrible, in his palm, and Warren knows his time is up.

Forty-Six

Solma finds Habu and the others hidden among a thick cluster of ferns. They've chosen a good spot. The only reason she finds them is that they're all shrieking their heads off, hands clamped over their ears. Tears spill down their cheeks and their faces are scarlet.

Habu stands when he sees Solma.

"I don't—" he says, gesturing at Addie and Tobias. "What's happening?"

It takes Solma a moment to realize she's seen this before. Last summer, when Blume's nest was attacked by a moonbadger, Warren had felt something similar. A terrible connection that meant he felt the fear and pain of his bees. What had Cobra called it? Forceful Projection. Right now, neither Tobias nor Addie knows where they end and their insects begin.

"The insects are dying," Solma says, pulling Tobias to his feet and throwing Addie over one shoulder. "The glade's burning. C'mon."

Habu stares at her. "Where's Warren?"

Solma hates the catch in her throat. Her hands tremble at the thought of her brother alone, fighting Ignis with nothing but his bees to protect him.

"Saving us," she says, voice cracking.

Tobias is inconsolable and Habu has to drag him. Addie screams as they crash through the forest, dodging trees and leaping over roots. The column of smoke above is so vast, now, it casts everything in an unnatural dusk. The air smells acrid. Heat whips through the canopy and the trees writhe, as if in fear and pain. Solma keeps expecting Guards to leap out of the shadows and attack them, but it doesn't happen.

Half the Guard, Ignis said. That's at least fifteen soldiers, so where are they? She clenches her jaw and presses on, expecting danger. It's not long before she hears the tell-tale hiss-and-crackle of fire devouring everything it touches.

She stops to deposit Addie at the base of an oak, ordering Tobias to huddle beside her.

"Stay put," Solma tells them. "And for the love of Earth, stop screaming!"

They don't. Or can't. Solma turns to Habu. His face is flushed, ash and dirt smeared across his cheeks.

"I need you to find water," she says. "Can you do that?"

Habu's eyes widen. He shakes his head, then pauses and nods slowly. "I'll try," he says, his voice small and uncertain.

Solma cups his chin. "Try," she tells him fiercely. "Our friends depend on it."

She turns towards the glade, taking off before Habu has time to object, hunting knife in her hand. As she draws closer to the glade, the burns Ignis gave her prickle and sting. She sees the flames, now, wreathing the trees, whipping the ferns and sending dead leaves into tumbling spirals. It drives a cruel wind and Solma raises a hand to shield her face.

Someone's yelling from within the flames. A voice she recognizes.

Olive. They're still alive in that furnace.

How is she going to get through this firestorm? And even if she could breach the wall of flame, how can she get them out?

Laughter behind her. A deep, rumbling cackle that sends a wicked chill shooting down her spine. Solma whips round, knife raised. And there's Vulkan, his arms spread to either side, flames dancing on his fingertips, his palms, all up his arms. He grins and Solma knows he's come to bring the end of the world.

"Your friends'll burn, soldier-girl," he says, and his voice roars like the fire. "Ain't nothing you can do."

Solma lets out a scream of unassailable rage. There are no words for her fury. Only noise. Only violence. She launches herself at him, aiming her knife at his gut.

Vulkan sneers and hurls a ball of flame. It sears through the scorched air towards Solma's head. She ducks and rolls, feeling it scream overhead. Vulkan laughs and throws another fireball, and another. Sparks dance on the burning air and Solma feels them against her skin. Burning. She's on her feet again, charging at him, her free hand curled in a fist. She throws a punch aimed at his head. He raises a burning arm to block her and Solma feints away in time to avoid being set on fire. She jabs her knife at his waist but he dodges aside, throwing out a flaming hand. He catches her across the face and her cheekbone sears with pain. She grunts and jerks away, landing with bent knees and knife raised.

Vulkan isn't laughing now. His face is twisted with anger and he holds one arm awkwardly. Solma sees she's left a deep cut across his bicep, though his flames have already cauterized the wound.

The heat from the glade's fire licks at Solma's back. Someone's yelling from within. She needs to get to them. But Vulkan's conjuring another fireball and there's no time.

There's never any time.

Solma opens her lungs and lets out a deep, animal scream, as she throws herself at him, knife-point glinting in the firelight. Vulkan grins, pulls back his arm to hurl the next fireball at her. He won't miss this time.

He's laughing again, and Solma lengthens her stride, pulse drumming in her ears.

The air beside her hisses and suddenly there's an arrow sprouting from Vulkan's arm. He roars and the fireball dissipates. Solma reaches him just as the pain buckles his knees. She snatches the wrist of his uninjured arm as he falls and twists it behind his back. He struggles, but pain and shock have sapped his strength and Solma holds him firm. She drives her knee into his back, pressing him against the ground, then grabs his hair, wrenches back his head and her knife is at his throat. She snarls.

"Been here before, ain't we?"

Vulkan bares his teeth, eyes aflame with loathing. "Yeah."

Twice before, she'd overcome him, held him at knife point. Both times she'd let him go. She won't make that mistake again.

There's a soft thump from behind but Solma doesn't have to look round to know it's Ana. She shoulders her bow and hurries to Solma's side.

"Nice shot," Solma tells her. "Thanks."

Ana grabs her arm. "We have to get to the others," she says. "Vulkan made a ring of fire around the glade. They're inside, but the fire's closing in. He's burning everything."

Solma presses the blade of her knife harder against Vulkan's throat. "Not if I can help it," she says. Vulkan winces as the blade bites into skin. Blood blooms, bright against the steel.

"Put it out," Solma growls. "And I might just let you live."

"Ha!" Vulkan struggles again but Solma leans her full weight on him, driving the air from his lungs. Flames dance across his fingers and Ana stamps hard on his hand. He shouts in pain.

"Put it out!" Solma yells. Vulkan swears at her. There's a long, low creak from behind and then the crash of a tree falling. Fire surges greedily across the fallen trunk, spitting sparks high into the air. Smoke burns the back of Solma's throat. She can barely see. The calls from within the fire sound more desperate now. Someone's screaming in pain or fear.

"Put it out, Vulkan!"

She hates how frantic she sounds, how her hand trembles. But she can tell from the hardness of his gaze, he has no intention of putting it out. He knows she'll kill him either way.

Fine. She might as well get it over with. She turns her knife in her hand, ready to slash his throat. Warren would hate her for this. But he's not here. He's on his own, fighting Ignis so she can save their friends. He's—

Another cry cuts the heat-stricken air. This time, not from the direction of the glade, but from within the forest. A voice Solma knows like the depths of her own heart. A voice whose fear cuts right to her quick.

Warren. Ignis has him. Ignis is hurting him.

Solma's hold on Vulkan slackens, and that second is all he needs. He bucks beneath her, throwing her sideways. Ana reaches for her bow but Vulkan's on his feet now. He backhands her across the face, leaving a smoking burn where his knuckles connected. Then he's off, charging into the smoke, towards the sound of Warren crying.

Solma hurls her knife after him but it vanishes harmlessly into the gloom. She screams.

"Warren! *Warren!*"

His voice drifts back to her on the smoky air, only just audible above the flames. He's yelling for help. She limps after Vulkan, ignoring Ana's cries of dismay, spluttering on the harsh air.

Nothing else matters. Her little brother is yelling for help. He's—

No. She listens. He's fighting to make himself heard. He's close but she can't see him and Vulkan and Ignis are struggling to keep him quiet.

"Help them, Sol!" he cries. "Go help them!"

Solma freezes. He's not yelling for help. He knows he's caught. He knows if Solma comes for him, it'll doom the others. And they need the others. Bell and Cobra. And Olive.

No-one is an island.

Solma and Warren aren't an island, either. They're part of something bigger. A colony. A *hive*.

The hive needs all its members if it's going to survive.

"I love you, Warren," Solma murmurs. Then she turns her back on him and charges back towards the glade.

Forty-Seven

Solma skids to a halt beside Ana, shielding her face from the searing fire. Its heat is unbearable and the screams from within grow more frantic and terrified. Ana's face is streaked with tears.

"I couldn't—" Ana says, shaking her head. "There were too many of them. They turned on us all at once. I only just managed to get away but they got the others, bundled them into the middle of the glade, and—"

She closes her eyes. Solma clenches her fist, scanning the flames for a way through. There *must* be a way through.

Habu appears from the smoke, spluttering and sobbing.

"I can't find water!" he cries. "I searched the plants. There's not enough!"

Ana falls to her knees and drives her hands into the earth, Whispering frantically. She's trying to connect with the mycelia like Taipan did, but she hasn't had enough time to practice. The fire-wind buffets them and Ana winces as it sears her, blistering her skin.

There's no time for this. Somewhere out there are twelve defected Guards and their friends are burning. Solma glances around. There must be something, anything she can use to batter a path through the fire. Something that she can use to get her friends out—

There's a scream from her left. Not a human scream, an animal one. A scream of rage, fear, indignation. Solma peers into the gloom. She could swear she sees ... shadows moving in the smoke. Rearing and bucking.

Burdock and Poppy!

Solma takes off, charging through the smoke towards the panicking ponies. There's a creak above her and she dives out of the way just as a tree, wreathed in flames, crashes to the ground where she'd been standing. She barely registers the lucky escape, and keeps charging towards the sound of the ponies.

How they got out, Solma doesn't know, but the fire is driving them wild.

No, that's not true. It's driving *Poppy* wild. The poor mare has kicked herself free of the cart but her harness and reins are tangled in some low hanging branches. She bucks, rearing and slamming her hooves into the tree. Her eyes roll, ears pressed back against her head. Her mouth foams and her flanks are drenched in sweat. Solma dashes towards her to untangle the reins, but Poppy's so frightened she doesn't recognize her. She rears, lashing out, and Solma reels back just in time to avoid a hoof in the face. She swears, dodges around the tree and slashes at the reins with her knife. It takes several hacks before the rein splits and falls away but, before Solma can catch it, Poppy shrieks and charges off among the trees.

Solma watches her disappear. The fire creeps closer, catching at the leaves overhead, snaking across the leaf litter and fallen twigs. She splutters on the smoke, and turns towards the cart, which Burdock is still harnessed to.

He's not happy. He prances sideways, ears flattened and eyes wide and staring. But he's not panicking. He paws the ground, skipping away from the fire and then towards it again. He keeps staring into the flames and Solma realizes that he's responding whenever he hears a cry for help. He wants to help his people. His family.

No-one is an island.

Solma lunges for his reins. "Easy, boy," she says, kissing his nose. "Easy. This way."

She coaxes him forward, testing the wheels of the cart. One of them is warped a little but the cart rolls, bouncing over roots. Solma races round behind it and tears everything off it, leaving tent packs and supplies strewn across the ground. She grabs Burdock's reins and pulls him towards Ana and Habu. He doesn't resist. In fact, he's eager, falling into a canter beside her.

Ana's eyes widen as Solma and Burdock emerge from the smoke.

"Where did you find him? I thought—"

"He and Poppy must've bolted when they set the glade on fire," Solma says, leaping up into the driver's seat of the cart. Habu's jaw drops.

"He'll never—"

"He will," Solma says. "He wants to help."

"But he won't make it through the flames!" Ana protests. Solma fixes her with a fierce glare.

"We work together," she says. "I need you two to make me a path through the fire. Anything will do.

Send a tree crashing down, find some water, grow something to smother it. Anything."

Habu starts to cry. Ana shakes her head.

"But—"

"Our friends are dying!" Solma yells. Panic stings her throat. She knows there's only so long she can hold on to this determination. She needs to get through these flames. "My aunt! Olive! *Cobra and Mamba! Taipan and the boys!*"

Habu chokes back his sobs and falls to his knees, his face grim with determination. He shoves his little hands into the soil, grits his teeth and Whispers.

"C'mon, Ana!" he says. "Help me!"

Ana's face is ashen. She kneels beside Habu and pushes her hands into the earth. She stares at Solma, eyes wide and terrified. Solma holds Burdock steady, knuckles white from gripping the reins so tight. Ana closes her eyes and Whispers.

The fire rages on, flames leaping in wild shapes, belching thick, black smoke. The cries from within fade and Solma feels her throat close up in fear. They've stopped yelling for help. They've stopped yelling at all.

"Ana!" Habu says suddenly. "Feel that?"

"I—" Ana frowns, eyes still closed. "I'm not—"

Her eyes fly open and Solma stares.

"Oh," Ana breathes. "Wow."

She's got that faraway look that Taipan had when she found the mycelia, that strange-colored ring around her irises, that otherworldly wisdom from connecting with the fungal network of the forest. She winces.

"It's—it's in pain. The forest is screaming."

Her face twists in agony and Habu grabs her arm. His own eyes open with the same strange colors in them. "Hold on to it!" he says. Sweat pours down his face. "I can feel it, there's—"

"Yes," Ana shouts. "Found it."

Solma has no idea what's going on but both the Whisperers push their hands deeper into the soil, almost up to their elbows. They lean into the earth, faces strained, Whispering under their breath.

The ground rumbles. Burdock's ears flatten against his head.

And then the forest floor erupts. Vines as thick as Solma's torso burst from beneath the ground, snaking over the flames. They catch fire quickly but there are more in their place, rearing from the ground like great serpents, weaving a thick, green mat over the charred ferns and blackened soil. Where they settle over the ground, the flames are briefly smothered.

"Go!" Ana yells. "We'll hold it as long as we can!"

Solma doesn't need telling again. She lashes the reins against Burdock's flanks and he lurches forward, charging over the carpet of vines. The fire roars to life again behind them but they're through! The cart bounces against the damaged ground and Solma's jolted sideways, only just holding on.

The glade is full of smoke, so thick and dark Solma can barely see. But the actual clearing isn't on fire yet. Though it won't be long.

"Olive!" Solma screams, choking as the smoke sears her throat. "*Bell!* Anyone!"

A shape appears in the gloom, a hand grabbing Burdock's rein. "This way!"

The voice is husky but unmistakable. "Olive!"

"They're over here!"

Burdock skids to a halt and Solma leaps from the seat. She grabs Olive's face in both hands and kisses her fiercely. "I love you!" she says.

Olive shoves her off. "Tell me later! After we ain't burned alive!"

Through the smoke, more figures appear. The children splutter and cough. Krait's been sick down his robes but Olive's tied clothes over their mouths and noses to keep out the worst of the smoke. Their faces are blackened with soot and the skin beneath is red with the heat. Olive has a fierce burn across her collarbone. Solma sees there are red welts around their wrists and ankles where they'd obviously been restrained and have, somehow, struggled free. Freed each other. Fought to stay alive. They limp forward with Dyl and he and Olive lift the kids onto the back of the cart. Burdock tosses his head and paws the ground, impatient to be gone.

"Bell?" Solma yells. More people emerge. Bell and Roseann, leaning on each other. Bell has a nasty bump on the side of her head and Roseann's face is covered in blood.

"Kids first!" Bell insists.

"What about the Gatra?" Solma asks as she sees Reya, steering the remaining Guards in front of them. Solma's heart lurches.

"Where are the rest?"

There's only five of them. One clearly has a broken leg and is being half-dragged, half-carried by two of his fellows. They load him into the cart and hop in after him.

"Dead," Reya says. Her face is grim, her eyes haunted, her cheeks streaked with ash and soot. "Addie?"

"Safe," Solma says. She leaps into the seat of the cart. "I'll come back." She glances behind her, scanning her precious cargo. Krait, King and Taipan are safely aboard, as are Jonah, Nessa and Leiff, but—

"Where's Yenn?"

Dyl swears and limps into the gloom. "That damn girl!"

"Go!" Olive yells, whacking Burdock's flanks. The horse doesn't need encouragement. At the sound of Olive's voice he charges towards the vine-carpet, which barely holds open a path. Ana and Habu grow the vines only a little faster than the fire can consume them but there's enough of a gap through the flames that Burdock can push through, galloping at full pelt until they're clear.

The able Guards leap to the ground and help down the young and injured. Solma ushers the children to Ana and Habu. Without needing to be asked, the three young Whisperers drop to their knees and add their Whispering, reaching into the Earth to find growth. Vines sprout from the ground with greater intensity, curling over the flames and smothering them. Solma jumps back into the driver's seat and

Burdock's already heading back into the flames before she's found her balance.

The cart skids, but Solma barely needs to steer. Burdock knows where he's going and there's no way he's letting his friends die.

They burst into the burning glade to find Reya waiting for them, huddled low to the ground to avoid the worst of the smoke.

"Yenn!" she says, and points to where Solma thinks the honeybee hives might have been. Of course. Solma swears.

"Get on the cart!" she yells, leaping down and charging in the direction Reya pointed. The smoke is so thick that her eyes stream. Every breath leaves her throat raw and she feels faintness creeping in at the sides of her consciousness.

Up ahead, she sees the honeybee hives silhouetted in the smoke and in front of them are figures she recognizes.

Cobra and Mamba huddle together, spluttering. Norsen on his knees, trying to scoop Yenn into his arms, but some inhuman force keeps her rooted. Norsen can't seem to move her. Dyl yells his head off, trying to reason with Yenn, who's hugging one of the hives and wailing.

"Sol!" Cobra says, eyes full of relief. "Thank Earth—"

"What's happening?" Solma demands. "We need to go or you'll all—"

"Ridiculous girl won't leave her hives!" Dyl roars, grabbing hold of Yenn's arm and trying to pull her away. Yenn screams louder, shaking her head, tears pouring down her face. Her eyes are distant and un-focused and Solma realizes what's going on. Forceful Projection. Yenn won't leave her bees. She can't. Their pain and fear has rooted her and nothing can move her.

Solma pulls Mamba and Cobra away, shoving them back in the direction of the cart. "Find the others," she tells them. "Get in the back of the cart. Hurry!"

Cobra hesitates, wanting to help, but Mamba pulls her away. They vanish into the smoke. Solma turns back to the hives. One of them is black with char. Dead. With a pang, Solma thinks it might be Fox-glove's hive. The oldest and calmest of the three queens. The far hive is also damaged, a great crack down its side. Primrose's.

Which means the hive that Yenn clings to is the only one that survives. Orchid's hive. The hive they fought so hard to save. The hive that led them to Warren.

That decides it.

"Yenn!" Solma yells, tugging the younger girl's arm. Yenn doesn't move and even using all her strength, Solma can't budge her. Swearing, she turns her attention to the hive. Yenn will follow her bees. Solma bends down, gripping the hive at its base and heaving it into her arms. Realising the plan, Norsen rushes to help, steadying the hive so it doesn't fall.

"Dyl, take Yenn!"

Solma feels a hot sting swell on one hand, another on her arm and pain sears across her elbow too. She grits her teeth. "Dammit, bees!" she growls. "I'm trying to help!"

But they're panicking. Alarmed by the flames, afraid for their lives, the creatures just seem grateful for an enemy they can attack. The little points of pain start to merge together, until Solma's arms feel as if they're aflame. Norsen winces and Solma realizes the bees are stinging him, too. She roars with the effort of holding onto the hive, staggering towards where Burdock waits.

Yenn comes to her senses suddenly, realizing what's happening and begins Whispering. The pain in Solma's arms subsides and a few lethargic bees appear by her head, hovering anxiously around their hive.

Yenn clings to Dyl and he limps behind. His eyes stream and stare wildly. There's a terrible rattle in his lungs and he stumbles often.

The silhouette of the cart appears out of the gloom and Burdock senses Solma nearby. He throws his head back and whinnies, a high-pitched, desperate sound that pulls Solma towards him. She hurries round the cart and she and Norsen heave Orchid's hive into it. Already aboard, Mamba and Cobra reach down to help her.

Solma turns to see Dyl and Yenn a few meters behind. Yenn doubles over, the smoke making her splutter terribly. Dyl grabs her shoulders, coaxing her on.

"Come on!" Solma yells.

Above them, the overhanging trees are wreathed in flame, burning furiously. Fire creeps along a low hanging branch.

"Dyl!" Solma screams. Dyl glances up and sees Solma gesturing frantically. From the cart, Norsen looks up and sees what Solma has seen. He lets out a terrible cry, leaps from the cart and charges towards his daughter.

But he's not quick enough. And all the others can do is watch.

Above Yenn and Dyl, there's an almighty crack and the branch, still burning, falls. Norsen yells. Solma's screaming, too.

And Dyl's tawny eyes meet hers.

They gleam in the firelight. Fierce. Full of love. Solma remembers what he'd said to her that night as he'd talked her into staying.

I'd die for these kids.

I'd die …

He grabs Yenn round the waist and, with monumental effort, hurls her out of the path of the falling branch. She cries out in surprise as she sprawls in the ash-covered grass just in front of Norsen. The branch crashes down, smoke bursting from it as it falls. There's a flash of fire as the grass catches and the roar of the fire grows louder. Solma shields her eyes as Norsen helps Yenn to her feet and the pair run towards the cart.

Yenn scrambles aboard and Norsen leaps up behind. They turn back, yelling for Dyl. Yenn sobs bitterly.

Solma peers through the roaring fire.

"Dyl!" she screams. "Dyl! Come on!"

She searches for any sign of him, but there's none. He hadn't had time to get himself free.

"Sol!" Cobra yells. "We have to go!"

Solma leaps onto Burdock's back. Tears stream her face. She glances back to where the burning branch has collapsed into splinters and ashes.

"I'll come back," Solma promises. "I'll come back for you."

She kicks Burdock on. He rears and charges. In the back of the cart, Yenn screams. The hive jolts and many hands reach out to steady it, holding it firm while Burdock bursts through the flames, his ears flattened, fire reflected in his eyes.

They clear the flames with a jolt and Burdock pulls them to safety. Solma throws all her weight into pulling him to a halt and they slow just as they reach the Whisperers.

"Quickly!" Solma yells, leaping down to help the others. Dyl's still in there somewhere, trapped in the fire, fighting to live. She needs to get to him. She needs to—

There's a great roar of flames and the Whisperers are thrown backwards, their hold on the Earth wrenches loose. The fire engulfs the carpet of vines, crawling up the trees and devouring them so quickly that three or four fall in quick succession. Nessa and Leiff shriek.

Jonah drops to the ground and begins to fit. Roseann kneels beside him.

Solma stares. Smoke pours into the air. Flames paint the horizon orange and there's no way through. There's no way back. Everything is gone.

Someone touches Solma's shoulder and she jumps. It's Olive.

Olive who pulls her into a tight hug as Solma gives in and sobs bitterly. Olive who strokes Solma's ash-clogged hair back from her face and kisses her neck, her cheek, her forehead, her mouth. Olive who tells her it's ok. It's ok. Even though it's *not* ok. The glade is burning and Dyl is dead and Warren—

Warren is gone.

~ Orchid ~

THE STINK OF WOODSMOKE still wafts through the hive, though it's been days since our glade burned. My daughters tell me the flowers are fading. We've struggled to find food even after we were carried to safety, but we're alive. We survived.

And I have many daughters now. Healthy, with powerful wings and shining fur and bright antennae. We aren't quite up to full strength, yet, but the comb thrums with dancing and the cells glisten with honey. Who knows if it will be enough to last the winter?

I wander along the empty cells and lay and lay. There is no end to my laying and I must not stop until the cold and the dark send us into winter slumber. We must catch up.

When the glade burned, the flowers burned with it. The smoke has left us fatigued and confused. We danced about swarming, searching for a new nest, but we weren't strong enough and the flames died out in the end.

The glade is burned. When we return from visiting it, we smell of smoke and death. We bring back memories of destruction, a profound sadness. It's not long before the dance changes and we agree never to go back there. There's nothing left for us now. Instead, we stay among the towering nests of the humans, where there are still flowers for us to forage from. We danced with concern when we were first brought here, worried the humans would harm our hive. But they don't. The not-bee-girl keeps them away, keeps us well protected.

She is subdued after the fire. Her fragrance is sad. She tends us as she always did but we smell the sorrow on her. My daughters say they haven't seen the not-bee-boy in a long time.

The days shorten and dawn takes longer to warm the air. The chill stings our wings and my daughters fan the hive, pushing out stale air and warming the young. We are slowing down, our bodies need warmth and the warmth is fading. We must sleep. But we hold out for a while longer. We want to know the not-bee-boy is alright. We want to know he's coming back.

But there's no scent of him in the air anymore.

Days pass, the autumn chill closes in, the leaves turn and start falling. I don't see this, of course, but I know of it from my daughters' dances. I know the world grows cold. And still, the not-bee-boy doesn't return.

Soon, the chill will grow too much. We will amass in the center of the hive, wings vibrating to keep warm. Soon, we will form the sleeping ball

around our eggs and larvae. I'll be ushered into the center where it's warmest. It'll get so warm in the middle of all those bodies that I will, through winter, fight my way to the outskirts to avoid overheating.

For now, we keep searching, keep filling the comb with sweet nectar. Our not-bee-girl is here for us, tending us, leading us to the flowers that remain. I hope the flowers are there to greet us when we wake. I hope the not-bee-boy returns.

Forty-Eight

A HAND BRUSHES SOLMA'S shoulder. She whirls round but it's only Norsen. Solma sighs and turns back to face the village square, pressing her shoulder blades against the mud wall of a house. She watches her friends pack their belongings.

Norsen doesn't take the hint. Typical. He settles beside her, hands in his pockets. Solma notices he's not in his usual clothes, but in blue, Fei-issue overalls. He's been working the fields with his villagers today. Solma's seen him out there with a sickle and barrow, harvesting. Solma admits a grudging respect for that. Blaiz never stooped to manual labor.

There's been a change in the village since the fire. Once Solma and Olive had everyone out, Reya and the Guard headed to the village. Within minutes, the forest was flooded with Fei, Oritch and a few Yuen. Some carried buckets, others were lugging the huge hoses used to pump water from the river. Solma and the Whisperers filled Burdock's cart with sand and dust to pour on the fire. It took days to put the blaze out. By the time they'd finally defeated it, the glade was ash. Every blade of grass, every flower, every tree. A significant portion of the forest went with it and now there's more work for the Fei and the Oritch to do.

The Keeper kids are beside themselves. Wilted with grief. Nessa and Jonah can't stop crying and Leiff had to be sedated for three days before she could cope with being awake. All agree that some of their insects escaped, but the survivors are pitiful in number and the kids can't hear them, don't know where they are. Their disconnection is painful to watch and it makes Solma think of Warren.

Warren, being dragged through the Earthroot mountain pass, cut off from his bees and his family.

Norsen stands beside her in silence, gazing over the scene in the square, where villagers help Olive, Bell and Roseann load supplies onto the cart. Burdock tosses his head, eager to be off. Poppy stands sedately beside him. After Solma cut her tangled rein, she'd fled to the village where she'd felt safe, but her fear had alerted the villagers. They'd been ready as soon as Reya and her Guard returned.

Norsen's eyes keep flicking towards Solma until she can't stand it anymore.

"How's Yenn?" she asks.

"She's ok," Norsen says. "Better than the other Keeper children."

That makes sense. Solma scans her arm where the faint marks of old bee stings show on her skin. Yenn still has one hive to tend, and Orchid's bees are doing well. Taipan and the other Whisperers managed to grow the parasite-killing mycelia in the village and the bees are thriving. Still, Solma sees the haunted, guilty look in Yenn's eyes. It's hard surviving when others don't. It's hard being ok when everyone around you isn't. She hasn't spoken to anyone except Norsen since the fire.

Norsen clears his throat. "She keeps asking after ... you know."

Solma's heart contracts painfully. She nods. "Yeah."

They'd searched the forest frantically after Vulkan and Ignis disappeared with Warren. For days, they plunged through the smoke, putting out smaller fires and gathering the wounded. A few loyal Guard had managed to crawl away. Some were alive, but barely. Most were no longer recognizable. Their bodies were returned to the village for burial. Among them was

Dyl. Brave old man. Solma misses him. She hopes he knew, at the end, that he didn't have to atone for Norsen's brother.

The Keeper children still wake at night, shouting his name.

Even through the funerals, Solma couldn't concentrate on anything except finding Warren. She and Olive somehow found their way through the smog to the cave entrance in the foothills. But it wasn't an entrance anymore. The rock had caved in, as if blown to pieces. Solma doubts she'll ever know how Vulkan and Ignis managed that. All she knows is that Warren is gone and she has no way of getting to him before he's delivered to Maxen.

She failed, and her brother is suffering.

She turns her face away from Norsen so he can't see the swell of tears in her eyes. A commotion outside a house draws her attention and she looks up to see the three Whisperer boys gather around the entrance as Taipan emerges, holding Yenn's hand and glaring fiercely at anyone who tries to get too close. Taipan's leg is heavily wrapped where she sustained some serious burns, and she limps deeply, but she holds herself tall as she guides Yenn through the babbling boys. With one look from Tai, though, they fall quiet. There's no doubt who's in charge. The boys all have those dark rings round their irises now. Tai taught them to connect with the mycelia. The Whisperers no longer need words and gestures to communicate. As if there's something deeper holding them together. Mushrooms bloom in their footsteps.

Even Mamba conceded a day or so ago. And Solma thinks back to the story he told, the *weirdness* he described.

It is weird. They've got this faraway look to them. But it's also amazing.

Taipan's orange eyes meet Solma's. Her smile falters, and she bites her lip. Solma knows Tai's just as worried about Warren.

His absence has hit them all hard. Bell cries quietly over her cooking when she thinks no-one's looking. Roseann's even more gruff than usual. Ana spends more time with the ponies than is reasonable and Cobra—typical Cobra—rushes around trying to make sure everyone else is ok.

Mamba took it hard, too, and Solma's realized that she wasn't the only one crippled by the weight of responsibility. Solma's barely seen him the last few days. He spends a lot of time walking in the burned-out forest.

"What'll you do now?" Solma asks, more to break the silence than because she cares about the answer.

Norsen shrugs.

"The children are keen to go searching for their insects," he says. "But ... they'll stay in the village for now. They need time to be children, rather than instruments and saviors. We've been lucky those families agreed to take in the orphaned ones. Reya's posted Guards outside the houses but I've given her some time away to help Addie recover. The Aldren are teaching Jonah to read." He pauses, frowning. "I made a huge mistake," he says.

Solma looks at him. The quiet, confident man he'd been nearly six months ago is gone. His shoulders slump, his eyes are sunken into dark craters and his face is drawn with worry lines. Solma thinks she might be looking at another version of herself. She grips his shoulder.

"We all made mistakes," she tells him. "You and I both went after the wrong person when we should've been working together. And now ..."

Her throat closes around the words and she trails off into silence. Missing Warren feels like a bruise in her gut. It hurts so much she can barely breathe.

Norsen clears his throat. "When are you heading out?" he asks. Solma chews her lip.

"As soon as we can," she says. They've spent too long here already. Five days it's taken them to put out the fire and tend the wounded. That's five days' head start for Ignis and Vulkan. Solma clenches her fist.

The Whisperer boys have abandoned Taipan and Yenn to run off some energy. They squeal as they chase each other, getting in everyone's way. Bell shoos the giggling children away from the pony cart, where Burdock is getting excited by their antics. He paws the ground as the kids are led away, and turns to stare at Solma. His long, shaggy mane drifts in the breeze and Solma watches him. She wonders if he knows what's going on, if he's got some inkling of the tinderbox-tension that hangs over Alphor right now.

Something tells Solma he does. He knows far more than anyone gives him credit for. He saved them all, that plucky little pony. And now he stands quietly while a load is strapped to his back so he can guide them, uncomplaining, back across the continent.

As Solma watches, a honeybee lands between Burdock's eyes and he tosses his head with a snort. Disturbed, the bee fires her engine and zooms off back towards her hive. Burdock turns his head, ears forward, to watch her go.

It won't be long, Solma knows, until the bees disappear to sleep through winter, until whatever butterflies and beetles are left slip into stasis to see them through the cold and the dark. Alphor's smallest, most precious life will slumber through the quiet months.

Now, even though the leaves are only just turning, Solma feels their impending absence like a needle in the heart. Whenever the skies fall silent, she fears she might never hear insect song again. It had been gone for so long, after all.

She looks away from Norsen and he, tactfully, says nothing, though she knows he can see.

Olive trudges over to Solma. She smiles, lacing her fingers through Solma's and drawing her into a hug. Solma leans in, breathing the gunpowder-pine-musk of the girl she now knows with absolute certainty that she loves. She nestles into Olive's neck and Olive kisses her shoulder, holding her close.

"It's ok, Sol," she says. "You ready to go?"

Solma leans back and nods.

"Yeah," she says, squeezing Olive's hand. "I am."

She's been ready since her brother was spirited away. Every day they stick around is another day of distance between her and Warren. Leaving is exactly what she wants to do.

Olive kisses her shoulder and wanders over to where Bell's arguing with Roseann about which books it's appropriate to take. They lost many in the fire and Bell is fierce about those that remain.

Norsen turns to Solma and offers his hand.

"Good luck, Sergeant," he says. "If you need us, send a message. Anything we can do ... anything *I* can do ..."

Solma shakes her head. "You've done plenty," she says, shaking his hand. "You got a future here to protect. If you can spread the insects through Alphor, if you can persuade the other Stewards to *share*, then Maxen won't get the power he's after."

Norsen stares at her for a moment, then nods. "Agreed," he says. "I'll do my best."

Solma tries to smile, though smiles are hard to summon these days. She releases his hand, leans down to adjust her prosthesis, then heads over to where the cart is almost packed. Cobra has wrangled the boys into a line. Taipan hugs Yenn goodbye. Roseann and Bell are finally in grudging agreement about the books and

Olive is helping Ana secure her bow and quiver across her back. They all turn, watching as Solma approaches.

And there's no blame in their eyes. Only love. There's only ever been love.

Gold flashes at the corner of Solma's vision and she turns, eyes widening as she sees the huge, healthy bumblebee hovering beside her. She lifts a hand and the bumblebee settles on her knuckle. The sun glints off her gossamer wings and Solma can't suppress the sob that bursts from her.

The bee fires her engine. Her song sounds deep and strong as she lifts into the air. She powers off towards where the forest is still green. Towards the mountains. In the direction Vulkan and Ignis took Warren.

"We're right behind you," Solma whispers. She watches the bee disappear among the trees.

She takes her pack from Olive and falls into step beside Burdock, one hand on the pony's neck. The Gatra open the gate and the village gathers to see them off. Norsen and Yenn stand watching for a long time.

Solma rolls her shoulders and feels Olive's hand in hers. She closes her eyes.

Blink. Warren's face, covered in soot, eyes streaming, but a determined frown hardening his features as he tells her to go save their friends. He must know she'll come for him. He knows she'd go to the end of the world for him. And she will. She *is*.

It's going to be a long winter.

Do you Want to Read More?

Did you love meeting the new Keeper children? Did you enjoy getting to know the honeybee queen, Orchid? You can discover the next book in this series, check out extra content about the world of Silent Skies, and sign up to my readers' club, where you'll receive newsletter updates once per month and get a gift ebook. You can also help other readers discover this story by leaving a review online.

You can do all this by scanning the QR code below. Or visit:

https://subscribepage.io/rlfssseriespage

See you there!

Also By Rebecca L. Fearnley

The *Silent Skies* Trilogy **(Complete)**
The Last Beekeeper
The Hive Child
War Song of the Wild
The Snake's Nest
The Nowhere Chronicles (**(In Progress)**
Doorway to Nowhere
The Darkling Thief
The Howling Mare
A Song of Forgetting
The Shadow and the Scream
Flight of the Bone Crow
A Fearsome, Lonely Heart
Under a Tortured Mountain
The Girl in the Nightmare Tree
A Soul for a Secret
The Rage-Scaled Serpent

Thanks To ...

Any writer will tell you that a book doesn't get written without the support, faith and guidance of many, many people. I'll start with those who've made this book the physical thing that it is. To my editor, Lara, thank you for your brilliant and thorough feedback and for showing such faith in the story and for staying with me through this series. Thank you to my wonderful cover designer, Stefanie, at Seventh Star Designs, for your beautiful artwork in which this story lives.

Thank you also to my wonderful writing group, Lou, Georgia and Daisy, who've beta read this book and continued to push me to be the very best writer I can be, cajoling me through my fear and celebrating my successes. Thank you to my dear friend, Tess, who read this book in its early form, offering her thoughts and being constant with her support. Thank you again to Lucy, Carly from Limb Power and Dave

Goulson, whose sensitivity and accuracy readings for *The Last Beekeeper* informed my writing for *The Hive Child*. Thank you to the wonderful Sue, librarian at one of my residency schools, who has championed and supported me for years now, and whose endless support with The Last Beekeeper has helped it find many new readers!

Thank you to my family. To both my parents, who've remained stalwartly certain that I will succeed in my lifelong writing dream and have supported me in every way possible. Thank you to my brilliant siblings for listening to me cry, panic or celebrate down the phone and talk round in circles when I was feeling particularly overwhelmed. Thank you to my partner and life teammate, David, for your constant patience, faith and reassurance. I know you've had to tell me it will be fine a million times. I almost believe you now.

And lastly, but by no means least, thank you to you, my readers. The people who breathe life into this story. I hope it touched your heart. I hope it made you dream. My story continues to live on through you, and for that I am truly, deeply grateful.

About Rebecca L. Fearnley

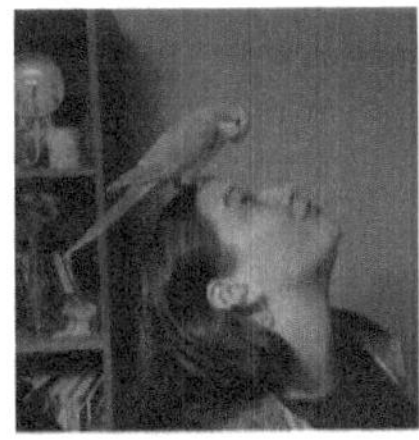

Rebecca has been obsessed with two things since she learned to walk and talk: stories and animals. Luckily, the two seem to be very compatible. In addition to writing, Rebecca is also a teacher and, in 2018, decided that she wanted to write quality books for the young people she works with. Her books tend towards themes of respect for the environment, protecting the planet and the new generation challenging the old to face up to their mistakes.

She lives in Reading with her unusual little family, which includes herself and her partner, a friendly little mini-lop rabbit (called Cleo) and a gregarious and feisty quaker parrot (called Maya).

9 781915 124043